LADY MAGDALEN

ROBIN JENKINS has been hailed as 'the greatest living fiction-writer in Scotland' (*The Scotsman*, 2000). Born in 1912, his first novel was published in 1951; more than thirty works of fiction have followed, many of which have been graced with literary awards and remained in print for decades. Several of his novels have been published in North America and Europe, including *Childish Things* (2001) and the classics, *Fergus Lamont* (1979) and *The Cone-Gatherers* (1955) which are both currently optioned for feature films. He lives in the west of Scotland and is working on a new novel. In 2002 he received the Andrew Fletcher of Saltoun Award for making an outstanding contribution to Scottish life.

By the Same Author

So Gaily Sings the Lark (Glasgow, Maclellan, 1951)
Happy for the Child (London, Lehmann, 1953)
The Thistle and the Grail (London, Macdonald, 1954; Polygon, 1994)
The Cone-Gatherers
(London, Macdonald, 1955; New York, Taplinger, 1981)
Guests of War (London, Macdonald, 1956)
The Missionaries (London, Macdonald, 1957)
The Changeling
(London, Macdonald, 1958; Edinburgh, Canongate Classic, 1989)
Love is a Fervent Fire (London, Macdonald, 1959)
Some Kind of Grace (London, Macdonald, 1960)
Dust on the Paw
(London, Macdonald, and New York, Putnam, 1961)
The Tiger of Gold (London, Macdonald, 1962)
A Love of Innocence (London, Cape, 1963)
The Sardana Dancers (London, Cape, 1964)
A Very Scotch Affair (London, Gollancz, 1968)
The Holy Tree (London, Gollancz, 1969)
The Expatriates (London, Gollancz, 1971)
A Toast to the Lord (London, Gollancz, 1972)
A Far Cry from Bowmore and Other Stories (London, Gollancz, 1973)
A Figure of Fun (London, Gollancz, 1974)
A Would-Be Saint
(London, Gollancz, 1978; New York, Taplinger, 1980)
Fergus Lamont
(Edinburgh, Canongate, and New York, Taplinger, 1979;
Canongate Classic, 1990)
The Awakening of George Darroch (Edinburgh, Harris, 1985)
Just Duffy (Edinburgh, Canongate, 1988; Canongate Classic, 1995)
Poverty Castle (Nairn, Balnain, 1991)
Willie Hogg (Edinburgh, Polygon, 1993)
Leila (Edinburgh, Polygon, 1995)
Lunderston Tales (Edinburgh, Polygon, 1996)
Matthew and Sheila (Edinburgh, Polygon, 1998)
Poor Things (Canongate, 1999)
Childish Things (Canongate, 2001)

LADY MAGDALEN

Robin Jenkins

CANONGATE

First published in Great Britain in 2003
by Canongate Books Ltd,
14 High Street, Edinburgh EH1 ITE

This edition published in 2004

10 9 8 7 6 5 4 3 2 1

The publisher acknowledges subsidy from the Scottish Arts
Council towards the publication of this volume.

British Library Cataloguing-in-Publication Data
A catalogue record for this book is
available on request from the British Library

ISBN 1 84195 492 6

Typeset by Hewer Text Ltd, Edinburgh
Printed and bound in Great Britain by
Clays Ltd, St Ives plc

www.canongate.net

To Helen and Ann

In the opinion of many Scots the most charismatic character in their history was James Graham, Marquess of Montrose. Lady Magdalen Carnegie was his wife.

PART ONE

1

ONE COLD JANUARY morning in the year 1627 the congregation of Kinnaird Parish Church was startled when young Francis Gowrie of Mintlaw stood up in their midst just as the minister, having announced the text, taken from Jeremiah, was about to launch into his two-hour-long sermon. Surprise slowly turned to puzzlement and then to horror and then to anger when Mintlaw began to speak, not with the frenzy of one possessed by the Lord – that was excusable if not always opportune – but in a determined voice, though what he was saying was abominable heresy. The collies tethered at the back of the kirk growled uneasily. Mintlaw was gentry and so could not be promptly seized and thrown out, as idiots and drunks were.

'I would like here, in God's house, to protest against the burning alive of old Jessie Gilmour of Allander, which is to take place next Saturday in Dundee. She is simply an old woman whose wits have gone awry owing to age, illness, and pain. I ask you to consider this: if she were a witch, with powers given her by Satan, would she not have used them against her accusers? She deserves pity, not this terrible death. A just God will never forgive us if we allow this to happen.'

His voice had grown more hesitant, as if he had become aware of the enormity of what he was saying. He stopped abruptly and hurried out of the church, barked at by the dogs.

Though their mood was perforce godly, the members of the congregation were nonetheless not inclined to be tolerant. They were suffering from sore noses, icy feet, frozen ears, itchy

3

chilblains, and their eyes watered from the smoke from the two braziers that vainly attempted to heat the kirk. Therefore they were not only scandalised by Mintlaw, they felt revengeful towards him too. There were mutterings. He should be burned along with old Jessie. Wasn't his family suspected of still favouring the old religion? Hadn't his father, Sir Robert, spent years in the Pope's Italy, collecting books and pictures, it was said, but also no doubt Papist notions?

They all looked towards the minister Mr Henderson, petrified with outrage in his pulpit. He had been a member of the Kirk Commission that had sat in judgment on Jessie and pronounced her guilty.

Then they looked towards the laird, Lord Carnegie, Privy Councillor, Lord Lieutenant of the County, and principal landowner, whose tenants they all were. Though often in Edinburgh on government business, he happened to be present that Sabbath, in his private enclosure with members of his family, among them his youngest daughter, 14-year-old Lady Magdalen.

Carnegie remained calm and dignified. Having endured the screams of men being judicially tortured to make them confess to treason, he was hardly going to let himself be upset by the bleatings of a young fool who hadn't the gumption to keep his opinions to himself. With an impatient gesture he bade the preacher proceed.

No one noticed that Lady Magdalen had gazed at Mintlaw not with horror but with admiration and anxiety.

That evening, in Kinnaird Castle, after family prayers in her father's study, Magdalen asked shyly if she could stay for a little while as she had something to say to him. Always indulgent to her because she was his favourite, reminding him daily of his wife, who had died 14 years ago soon after Magdalen's birth, he smiled and replied that she was very welcome for he had something to say to her too.

Though there was a big coal fire, the air in the room was so chilly that they could see their breath. Carnegie's nose was red and sore with much dighting and Magdalen's hands were numb inside her sheepskin gloves. Happed in thick woollen coats, they sat on either side of the fire, their eyes smarting from the smoke. The candles kept flickering because of the many draughts.

'Well, my pet, what was it you wanted to say to me?' asked Carnegie, smiling.

'Even if old Jessie is a witch, Father, is it *right* that she should be burned to death?'

A frown replaced his smile. Nervously he plucked at his beard. With her meek emphasis she had called into question, unwittingly no doubt, not only the justice of Gilmour's sentence but also the whole authority of the Kirk. That was dangerous.

Among his fellow Privy Councillors Carnegie was reputed to be shrewd and cautious, not easily taken in with false protestations. He got more out of suspects with patient interrogation than others did with thumbscrews. Yet, despite all his experience, he had never been able to fathom this young girl, his daughter. It wasn't that she set out to be deep, sly, or mysterious; on the contrary, she had a sweet open nature and had never been heard to utter a doubting or rebellious word. Yet her father, and others less percipient, were often left with the feeling that there was a part of Magdalen difficult to convince. Only the absolute truth could do it, and that was as rare as swallows in winter. From infancy she had tried to speak it herself, often amusing her brothers and sisters with her muddles and frustrations but at the same time making them ashamed of not being truthful to her.

Small wonder then that her father felt ill-at-ease as he considered how to answer her. He glanced at the books on his shelves, mostly Latin and Greek, but among them was one, signed by the author, which was in English: the late King James's treatise on witchcraft. In that very room the King, in his eager stumbling voice, had spoken about witches, how pernicious they were and how they had to be purged by fire. Carnegie had

5

listened respectfully, taking care not to show by so much as a wrinkle on his brow that, like his friend and colleague Lord Napier, he had doubts as to whether doited old hen-wives could possibly be in league with so mighty a potentate as the Prince of Darkness, who certainly existed, not perhaps as a slippery black creature with long tail and pointed ears, but as an evil influence in men's minds.

It had been easier to temporise with the credulous King, who after all had been an author seeking praise for his book, than with this earnest trustful child. Speaking to the King was an art in which Carnegie had become expert but speaking to Magdalen was somehow like speaking to himself or, put more pretentiously, to God.

'She was properly examined,' he said, curtly, 'and found guilty. Burning is the punishment for crimes like hers.'

'It must be very painful.'

'It is soon over.'

Ten minutes or so of hellish agony, if the strangling beforehand was negligently done. As a man with varied responsibilities he had had to attend burnings, with a handkerchief soaked in scent at his nose to keep out the stench of roasting flesh.

'When I burned my fingers with the handle of the kettle they were sore for weeks.'

Was it possible that she was being ironical? No, that pale anxious face under the white cap and those eyes of speedwell blue were child-like in their candour and simplicity.

'I assure you in her case it will soon be over.'

Shock rendered the victim immune to pain. Or so physicians claimed. But Carnegie had heard screams that had echoed in his mind for days afterwards.

'She gave me flowers once. I was passing her cottage.'

'She should not have done. What kind of flowers?'

'Dandelions.'

Piss-a-beds. Used by apothecaries to promote the flow of

urine. But were not their golden heads infested with tiny black insects, said to be the familiars of Satan? Did they not say, the learned ministers of the Kirk, that it was by seemingly benign acts like the giving of flowers that witches diseased your body or, worse still, corrupted your soul?

Was that mere superstitious nonsense, as scholars in other countries were now boldly saying, and as Carnegie himself was tempted to believe? Though he should have kept his mouth shut, it was possible that young Mintlaw represented the future which would look back on those burnings as acts not of Christian justice but of barbarous cruelty.

Carnegie shrugged and turned to a matter much more important than the incineration of a crazy old woman.

While canny James had been on the throne of Scotland there had been peace in the country. As long as the English gave him his Divine Right and acknowledged him as Head of their Church, he had been content not to stir up what he himself had called the wasps' byke of Scottish Kirk affairs. It might be very different now that his son Charles had succeeded him. Scottish by birth, it was true, but not Scottish in temperament, Charles, by all accounts, was a cold aloof stiff-necked young man, married to a scheming Catholic princess, to whose bad advice he listened too uxoriously. It was rumoured he intended to bring the Kirk to heel by imposing bishops on it. The country would then be split up into factions, those who were for the King and bishops, those who were for the King but not for bishops, those who were for the King and Presbyterianism (an untenable position but the one that Carnegie himself would wish to adopt), and those who were simply against the King's autocracy. It could come to civil war. Prudent men were building up family alliances. Carnegie had already married his eldest daughter Margaret to Lord Dalhousie, his second daughter Agnes to Lord Abercrombie, and his third Katherine to the Earl of Traquair. Now had come the chance to marry Magdalen to young James

Graham, Earl of Montrose. Lord Napier, James's mentor, was all for it; indeed, he had suggested it.

At present James was a student at St Salvator's College in St Andrews. He had written letters to Magdalen. Dutifully she had let her father read them.

They could hardly be called love letters, but then James, like most youths of 16, was still in love with himself. When he had described, wittily, an illness he had had – all his hair had to be shaved off! – it had been evident to the Privy Councillor, though not perhaps to the writer himself, that there was hidden in it a plea for reassurance. In spite of his juvenile bravado, young Graham had seen in Magdalen qualities of steadfastness, loyalty, and devotion that any sensible man would want in his wife.

What she had written in reply her father did not know. He could have seen it, with or without her consent and knowledge, but he had chosen not to. In the interests of the State, he often had to intercept and read other men's correspondence, but always with a sense of shame. Perhaps he had felt too soiled by that practice to want to read his innocent daughter's. In any case, he could easily guess their contents.

'James Graham is looking for a wife,' he said.

It would have been more accurate to say that Lord Napier had decided that young Montrose should have heirs as soon as possible. He was an only son. There was danger of the earldom being lost.

Magdalen smiled. 'Jamie's always looking for something. A golf stick that will hit the ball straighter. A falcon that will fly higher than any other. A subject for a poem.'

'That's James Graham, true enough.'

Lord Carnegie had reservations about young Montrose. James was a little too vain and a great deal too ambitious: the sort of young man who would relish troubled times as giving him greater scope. He ought perhaps to marry some strong-minded woman who would nip in the bud his wildest ventures. From that point of view Magdalen was hardly suitable and might suffer because of it but the marriage would be useful for her family, which mattered more than her personal happiness.

'Will anything happen to Francis for what he said in church?' she asked.

Her father was disconcerted and not pleased. She should have been thinking of young Montrose and here she was talking about young Mintlaw. He had once considered a match between her and the latter for the Mintlaw estate was large and bordered on his own, but Francis's father, Sir Robert, was a feeble aesthete, who would have been of little use as a political ally.

'They were saying that he should be burned too.'

'If he does not keep his mouth shut it could well happen.'

'He's going away to Italy soon.'

'The sooner the better.'

'He says we're all uncivilised and backward in Scotland.'

'Then he had better stay away for a long time. He is the kind of young man who could get himself into serious trouble and also anyone else foolish enough to associate with him.'

She shivered. Her father thought it was the cold but it was really foreboding. She was remembering how Francis mocked the new religion, because of its superstitious fear of beautiful objects.

'James is fond of you, Magdalen. I believe you're fond of him too.'

'I like Jamie fine. When he writes poetry; not when he kills deer.'

'He wants you to be his wife.'

She looked dismayed, not delighted. 'I don't want to get married, Father, not for a long time.'

Carnegie smiled. Here was a virginal dread that did her credit; after all she was just 14; her breasts were scarcely formed. 'It would not take place for another year or so.'

She was shaking her head now in agitation.

He had to speak sternly. 'Most young women would feel greatly honoured by such an offer. The Montrose clan is one of the most distinguished in Scotland.'

'I do feel honoured, Father, but I don't want to get married till I'm twenty at least.'

'He cannot wait that long. It is necessary that he should have heirs as soon as possible.'

'But if I am married, Father, I can never be alone again.'

Her father scowled. Was this immaturity talking or something more sinister? Not all that long ago there had been nuns in Scotland who had taken vows of silence and had lived in solitude. Her sisters had often, in jest, taunted Magdalen with having such an ambition.

'You need have little worry on that score,' he said. 'Your mother used to complain that I was never at home. It will be the same with you and James. He will certainly wish to take part in public affairs. You will therefore be alone oftener than you would wish, except of course for your children. I hope you will not find their company irksome.'

He regretted the sarcasm but she did deserve some rebuke.

'Yes, Father.'

Thus was her consent given, her surrender meekly made. She did not blame her father or James Graham. They took for granted that, being a woman and therefore weaker-minded than a man, she would be content with a big house, many servants, silks and satins, and jewels. How could they know what she really wanted when she wasn't sure herself?

In the old days there had been hospices attached to churches and dedicated to the care of the old and sick. They had been managed by women of rank who in the service of Jesus Christ had given up their lives to that compassionate work. She often imagined herself as one of them.

2

HER BROTHERS AND sisters were astonished when they heard that little Magdalen was betrothed to James Graham, Earl of Montrose. Dutifully they congratulated their father, who had arranged it, and her too of course, but they were not altogether pleased. Jealousy was inevitably part of their feelings for it would mean her, the youngest, being raised in rank above them, but there was also genuine concern. They did not think that she would ever be happy married to a man like Montrose.

They had known James since his infancy and had seen how self-assertive he was, unable to bear not being foremost in everything. At St Andrews University he had won the silver medal for archery twice, because, according to their eldest brother, also called James, he had outranked all the other competitors. Had not Argyll won it too a year or so earlier, though no one could be less martial than squint-eyed Campbell?

It had been assumed by everyone, and particularly by himself, that so handsome a youth, only too conscious of his abilities and deservings, would marry a woman as ambitious as himself, who would help him in his career, for he made it clear, indeed often boasted, that he intended to play a prominent part – he meant glorious – in the affairs of his country. He wrote poetry full of splendid aspirations. His favourite character in history was Alexander the Great and his favourite book Raleigh's *History of the World*. At the time of the betrothal he was 16, with his dreams of glory at their brightest.

Why then, they wondered, had this would-be conqueror of

11

the world agreed to take as his wife their Magdalen who was comely enough but scarcely beautiful, who dressed drably, often in black, read books of sermons, prayed as if she believed in it, loved solitude and sad music, spoke to servants with more fondness than command, and still, though she had never known her, mourned her mother? Had not her sisters jested among themselves, cautiously, for theirs was a strict Presbyterian household, that she had all the makings of a nun? How in heaven's name could she, who loved to stay at home in obscurity, find happiness with a husband on fire to go out into the world and be famous? How could she, so gentle, love a man who yearned for bloody battles? It was true that most marriages among the nobility were arranged for political or dynastic reasons but surely there had to be some points of contact between bride and groom? A shared passion for hunting, perhaps, or for religious observances. In Magdalen's case those were points of difference, since James loved hunting and was at best lukewarm towards religion, whereas she abhorred the killing of animals for sport and was very devout.

As an obedient daughter, she had obviously consented to the marriage to please her father, but it was hardly likely that James had done it to please Lord Napier. James always pleased himself. Since he was in a hurry to beget heirs, he might have been expected to choose a woman built for child-bearing, buxom and broad-hipped, but Magdalen was delicately made and had never enjoyed robust health. Could it be that he loved her? No, James was in love with ideals and poor Magdalen fell far short of those. So what qualities in her could have appealed to him? Her loyalty? No wife would keep her vows more resolutely. Her chastity? She had reached the age of child-bearing without knowing how children were begot. Her sweetness of nature? A man would have to be haughtier even than James Graham not to approve of that. Her docility? She would be as obedient as a wife as she was as a daughter. But what of that quirk of character which

12

prevented her from acceding to anything she thought untrue, unjust, or unkind? She might not voice her dissent but it would be present in her silences. Fortunately James would not notice or, if he did, would be more amused than angry. In any case, the older she got the more resigned she would become.

All the same it would have been better for her if she were to marry Francis Gowrie instead. It was obvious to her sisters, though not yet to herself, that she was in love with him. Whenever he paid a visit to Kinnaird, look how delighted she was. He would bring his lute and they would sing songs together, or his paints and brushes and she would sit beside him in the orchard watching him paint. He never wore sword or dagger and, like her, dressed plainly. Unlike her, though, he did not keep quiet when confronted with what he considered wrong; on the contrary, he was passionately and indiscreetly outspoken: his outburst in the kirk was an example. Since his father was reputed to hanker after the old religion and his mother, long since dead, had been a member of a wealthy English Catholic family, he himself was suspected of papistical leanings, especially as he was never done upbraiding Presbyterians for having removed all beauty from their kirks.

3

IN HIS ROOM in Kincardine Castle James Graham was getting ready to ride over to Kinnaird to pay one of his infrequent visits to his betrothed. It was a warm sunny morning in August, so that windows could be opened and no fires were needed. In the courtyard below, his escort of kinsmen and friends waited for him. Their laughter and the stamping of their horses' hooves on the flagstones could be plainly heard. Mr John Lambie of St Andrews assisted his young master, making sure there were no wrinkles in the lilac-coloured stockings, that the doublet of red velvet edged with white silk was not too bulky at the shoulders, and that the red velvet hat with the white feather sat at the jauntiest angle with just enough chestnut hair showing. Like a good servant he attended to his duties and pretended not to hear the taunts with which Lady Katherine, the earl's younger sister, kept teasing him. If any of his own sisters had talked to him like that, he would have clouted her. The earl, though, did not seem to mind, indeed he seemed to be enjoying her bitter comments. As he preened himself in front of the looking-glass, he hummed a song of romantic love.

Katherine had come home unexpectedly from Loch Lomond-side, where she lived with her sister Lilias who was married to Sir John Colquhoun of Luss.

'All that finery, Jamie,' she said. 'What a pity it won't be admired. Doesn't Magdalen herself always wear sombre hues?'

'Well, Kate, in nature isn't it only the males who are re-splendent? Consider the proud peacock. Consider even the humble chaffinch.'

Katherine herself was wearing the blue dress in which she had ridden from Luss. It was bedraggled and crumpled. Her brother had been surprised to find her so pale, thin, and resentful. He had asked if she hadn't been getting her share of the juicy red venison so plentiful on the hills above the loch and of the fat salmon in it.

'Seriously, Jamie, is she suitable?'

'Suitable for what?'

'You know fine what I mean. Suitable to be your countess. She's a mouse. You intend to be a lion.' She let out a sarcastic roar.

He squealed. 'Whereas you, Kate, are being a shrew.'

There was a burst of loud laughter from below.

'They'll be drunk before they set out,' she said.

'It's a beautiful day, Kate, and they're young and happy. Like me.' He was especially happy then, as he buckled on his new rapier with the golden hilt. 'But not like you it would seem. What's amiss, Kate? Come on, tell me truly. Did you and Lilias have a cast-out? Or was it Sir John's foolish cackling you couldn't stand? I wouldn't blame you.'

He didn't notice how her hands trembled as she picked up the book on his bedside table. Her voice trembled too. '*The Life and Death of Mary, Queen of Scots*. Now if it had been her you were going to visit, Jamie, I could understand all that peacockry.'

From the flash of his eyes and the tightening of his grip on the hilt of his sword, she saw that he was imagining himself as the rescuer of that beautiful and unlucky queen.

Their great grandfather on their mother's side had been the first to strike Rizzio, Mary's Italian secretary, in the Palace of Holyrood 60 years ago.

She could not resist saying, sullenly, 'John doesn't cackle.'

Jamie laughed. 'Oh, Kate, he does. Like a hen that's just laid an egg. It's good for a man to be amiable but not foolishly so.'

He was too intent on admiring himself to notice her angry scowl. 'You make him out to be a weak-minded fool,' she said.

'Well, isn't he? Luckily Lilias seems to be fond of him.'

'Why do you say "luckily"?'

'Because a strong-minded woman such as yourself, Kate, might become very impatient with him. When I was last at Luss, I caught him with his hands up the clothes of one of the maidservants. She was enjoying it, as if she was used to it. I got the impression that Lilias knew about it and didn't mind. A red-cheeked Highland wench, with short skirts: most convenient. Well, Kate, I'll be off. See you in a day or two.'

He blew her a kiss and then hurried out, followed by his servant.

Sobbing, from a mixture of anger, sorrow, and frustration, she went over to the window and looked down.

There were ten of them, riding in high spirits through the gate. They turned and waved their hats at her. They were young, healthy, splendidly dressed, and a little drunk. She could hear them singing as they trotted past the barley field. If they were going off to war, they would be just as joyful.

She did not wish them well.

Yes, John Colquhoun was too amiable for his own good. Yes, he fondled maidservants. Yes, he went from their beds to his wife's and pleasured her too, not out of love but because he was so good-natured. In spite of all that, Katherine loved him and had enticed him into her bed also. He had gone willingly enough and they had done, not once but several times, what was permissible only between a man and his wife. She had got him to promise to forsake Lilias and his children and flee with her to London and thence to Europe. When she went back to Luss in a week or two, she was determined to keep him to that promise, though it could well mean ruin for them both. She loved him, but it was more than that: he would be the means by which she would escape from marriage to some oaf chosen by her family. Just because he had been born a male, Jamie was free to roam the world and marry whom he pleased whereas she, because she was a woman, was expected to stay at home, marry that oaf, and produce a brat every year or so until at 30 she was worn out physically and mentally. That might be good enough for Magdalen Carnegie, but never for Katherine Graham.

4

THE WEDDING TOOK place in November. During the festivities Kinnaird Castle was crowded with representatives of the Graham and Carnegie clans. Among the young ones there was much jollification. Excited by wine, they chased one another all over the big house, letting themselves be caught in dark corners, where kissing and fondling took place, for a marriage seemed always to arouse erotic feelings. What prevented bolder mis-demeanours like fornication and adultery wasn't so much the presence of several dour-faced ministers as the several layers of clothing worn by both sexes, for the castle, despite coal fires, candles, and torches, was cold and draughty.

Similarly happed up, the older men sat in front of the fires and discussed politics, while their wives played cards and gossiped, mainly about their children.

Later in the evenings there were games and dancing. Expert fiddlers had been brought from Dundee.

It was noticed that the bride was often left on her own. No one was surprised and no one made any great effort to coax her into sharing in the merriment. It was her nature, they knew, to wait in the background. Other brides of 15 would have been hysterical with joy and conceit: she sat pale and calm. They would have been wearing the most splendid dress there: hers was the drabbest. If her bridegroom ignored her or, putting it more charitably, left her in peace, why should anyone else disturb her?

The groom, flushed and eager, was at the centre of everything, which of course he considered his rightful place. He did his share of chasing, of illicit kissing, of dancing, and of conversing with the greybeards about politics and religion. He did not need anyone to tell him, though many of the ladies did, that he was the handsomest young man there; his legs in the red stockings were especially admired. None dared say it in her father's house, and indeed none wished to say it for little Magdalen was well liked for her modesty and shyness, but many did think that, though Jamie was bound to soar like one of his falcons, he might have risen higher still if he had been marrying a woman as keen and ambitious as himself.

They would have been astounded, those ladies and gentlemen in their silks and satins, if they had known that, to the silent young girl in the dark blue dress, they looked like savages, especially when they were at table, guzzling. In those terrible visions the meat that they stuffed into their mouths and the bones that they picked up and gnawed were not those of cattle, sheep, or pigs, but of old Jessie Gilmour, cooked at the stake. In the midst of their guffaws and giggles, she heard the old woman's screams and herself screamed, inwardly. It was remarked that she ate very little but it was put down to nervousness having taken her appetite away.

She slipped off once, unheeded, to rest for a while in the quiet and solitude of her own room.

On her way she passed the chamber known as the King's, for it was in there that James VI had slept on the three occasions when he had visited Kinnaird. The last time had been twelve years ago, when she was three. The King had held her on his knee. Since then her father had kept the room like a shrine. It contained relics of the old King, such as his chamber pot adorned with the royal coat of arms. The door was kept locked but the key was available to anyone who knew the ways of the house: it was in the drawer of a small cabinet outside. Every other room in the castle was in use to accommodate the many guests; this one, by her father's order, had been left empty.

She wasn't greatly surprised when she heard voices within. Visitors often asked to be shown where the King had slept. She herself had acted as guide.

As she stole past, she heard the door open behind her with its familiar loud creak. She turned, ready to call a greeting but, when she saw who they were, she was so amazed that she kept silent and drew back into deeper shadow. From other parts of the house came shouts and laughter.

It was a couple who had come out. While the man locked the door and returned the key to the drawer, the woman hung on to him not so much lovingly, it seemed to Magdalen, as possessively. He was willing enough to be possessed but was also anxious to get away before they were seen.

Magdalen knew them. They were Katherine, Jamie's younger sister, and Sir John Colquhoun, husband of Jamie's older sister Lilias.

A few weeks ago Magdalen would have been puzzled as to why they were embracing and kissing so passionately. Since then she had had her innocence and ignorance removed. Her married sisters and her Aunt Euphemia had ruthlessly instructed her on the physical requirements of marriage.

Could Sir John and Katherine have been doing *that* in the King's room, on the King's bed? It would explain their furtiveness, for in their case it would be a great sin. Not only were they not man and wife, they were related to each other, in that he was Katherine's good-brother.

Aunt Euphemia had stressed that, though it was an act permitted by law and sanctioned by God and the Kirk in the case of a man and his wife, nevertheless it was not to be thought about or sought after, for it was in its nature inevitably disgusting, more suitable for animals and peasants than gentlefolk.

Why, then, had Sir John and Katherine done it? Surely they knew that its purpose was to beget a child? What would they do with their child if one resulted? No one would want it, no one would love it. Hadn't Katherine told Magdalen once that she hated children and never wanted any? And Sir John already had two, his wife Lilias being their mother.

Magdalen sighed. She couldn't help it. It was an expression of her bewilderment.

Sir John heard. 'There's someone there,' he muttered. 'For Christ's sake, Kate, give up.'

She held on to him. 'It's always the same, Johnny. As soon as you've had what you want, you want rid of me.'

'No, Kate. There's someone there, watching us. I heard them.'

They both stared in Magdalen's direction.

Ashamed of being a spy, though unintentionally, and also terrified of this secret she had unwittingly found out, Magdalen sighed again.

'There *is* someone,' said Katherine, fiercely. Letting go of him, she rushed towards Magdalen while he, with a groan, hurried off in the opposite direction.

Katherine grabbed hold of Magdalen. 'Oh, it's you, you little sneak,' she said.

She sounded relieved. She was confident she could intimidate Magdalen into not clyping; or, better still, since Magdalen was such a ninny, she could be made to believe that all that Katherine and Sir John had been doing in the King's room was admiring it.

'I want to talk to you,' she said. 'Let's go to your room.' She pushed Magdalen towards it.

It was cold, the fire having died down. It was dark too, for all the candles except one had been blown out.

'I expect you saw who I was with,' said Katherine, having decided what story to tell to this credulous simpleton. 'Sir John Birse, a relation of yours. He wanted to see the King's chamber, so I offered to show it to him. Poor old man, he was telling me about his wife. As you know, Magdalen, she died three months

21

ago. He still misses her very much. Did you see how he clung to me? He was crying.'

She told these lies with bold assurance. 'Didn't I see him once taking *your* hand?'

'Yes.' Sir John, an old man of 60, had held Magdalen's hand timidly and said, with tears in his eyes, that she reminded him of his Mirren. Small and stout, he could never have been mistaken for Sir John Colquhoun, not even in an ill-lit passage-way. No one ever called him Johnny.

'We young women have got to be kind to these old men who have lost their wives. Don't you agree, Magdalen?'

Yes, but Katherine was noted for her repulsing of elderly widowers. Because she was single and beautiful, they came courting. They were lucky not to have their faces scarted.

'They take advantage of it,' said Katherine, with an evil smile, 'as you saw.'

Magdalen still said nothing. She felt sorry for Katherine but she was also afraid. Katherine was like a cat in pain, not to be trusted and dangerous. One would have to be a cunning theologian like Mr Henderson to be able to tell if failing to reject lies or accepting them as if they were true was as great a sin as telling them. But one person Magdalen would never consult was Mr Henderson. He would have no mercy on Katherine. There was really no one. If it had been Francis Gowrie she was going to marry tomorrow, she could have confided in him. She saw then more clearly than ever before that marrying Jamie was a terrible mistake. This was not the only secret she would keep from him.

'Well, we'd better go and join the others,' said Katherine. Her voice was more friendly now. The mouse was either deceived or intimidated: it didn't matter which, so long as it kept her quiet. 'No need to tell them about old Sir John and me.'

Magdalen said: 'I'll pray for you, Katherine.'

Katherine had been going towards the door. She turned, in

22

fury. Her hands with the long nails went rigid: they were indeed like claws. She came closer. 'What do you mean? Why do you think you have to pray for me?' She seized Magdalen by the breasts. Her face was as fierce as murder. 'Don't dare pray for me. Pray for yourself, you silly little cunt.'

Magdalen had heard that ugly word before. Boys, peasants, and female servants used it, but never a lady of quality.

'Whose God do you pray to, Magdalen? Mr Henderson's? Do you think I could ever believe in the same God as that stinking hypocrite? And what other God is there?'

Those were even more terrible impieties than the obscene word. And surely there was another God, He who had sent His son Jesus Christ to teach people to love one another?

Katherine was now weeping, in anger mainly but also in distress. She said no more but rushed out of the room.

After some hesitation, and trembling all over, Magdalen went down on her knees, by the side of the bed, where she prayed every night, and humbly asked forgiveness for Katherine, who was only 16 and whose soul was in danger of hell-fire. For even gentle Jesus had flyted the unrighteous and threatened them with hell.

5

THE WEDDING WAS held in Kinnaird Parish Church, with Mr Alexander Henderson, Lord Carnegie's personal chaplain, officiating. As was not unusual for a day in November, it was cold and wet and the road from the castle to the church had become a quagmire in places. Someone sensibly suggested that the ceremony might be carried out in the castle itself for the convenience of the guests. Neither the bridegroom nor the bride's father was prepared to object but Mr Henderson was affronted: it must be done in God's house, otherwise it would not have His blessing. Faces were made behind the minister's back at his ridiculous and inconsiderate zealotry but none dared protest to his face. Consequently they all had to be conveyed in a relay of coaches, which took some time for they kept getting stuck in the mud. Unfortunately, too, in spite of the minister's prayers for sunshine, the rain came down heavier than ever.

The long delays vexed everyone but they were particularly hard on the common folk whose attendance at the kirk was obligatory for they were Lord Carnegie's tenants or servants and could not afford to displease him, but they would have wanted to be present in any case, in honour of Lady Magdalen. They could not, of course, be admitted to the kirk for it was too small and it wouldn't have been seemly for them to sit in the same congregation as all those gentry. Therefore they stood outside in the pouring rain, doffing their hats as the coaches arrived.

The bridegroom's red-and-black carriage was given a rather

lame cheer for the general opinion among the commoners was that he was too haughty and conceited for his own good.

The bride on the other hand was heartily welcomed. Anyone who went to the castle with a request or complaint was well advised to try and see Lady Magdalen first. Young though she was, she was sympathetic and fair-minded. She would go out of her way to remedy an injustice. Young Montrose, they thought, was getting the better of the bargain, even if his family was of higher rank than hers.

It didn't go unnoticed that while none of the other ladies and gentlemen, including the laird himself, seemed troubled that the villagers were getting soaked, Lady Magdalen, as soon as she stepped from her coach, called to Martha Baird, who was 73, to go home at once before she caught her death of cold. Martha thanked her, hoarsely, but stayed. She wanted to hear the proceedings in the kirk. Though somewhat deaf, she would have no difficulty. As befitted a man high up in the Kirk's councils, Mr Henderson had a voice that would scare a bull.

Magdalen wore the same white silk dress that her mother had been married in. It had lain in a kist for many years and had turned yellowish and musty; it had had to be repaired too where moths or mice had nibbled at it. She had insisted on wearing it, against her sisters' advice. In the kirk she looked so young and virginal that most of the women present shed tears as they remembered their own wedding day. Katherine Graham was not among them. She had complained of a headache. Sir John Colquhoun was there, very pleased with himself, it seemed, seated beside his wife Lilias. Was it, Magdalen wondered, the misfortune of women to love more whole-heartedly and less guardedly than men, so that they suffered more if things went wrong? In Jamie's love poems the feelings of women were never taken into account: women were merely objects to be admired or discarded.

As she stood by Jamie's side in front of the minister, though she smiled shyly as a bride should, she was thinking: why was the kirk so bleak? Why was it not bedecked, if not with flowers at this time of year, then with green leaves and berries? And should there not have been solemn but inspiring music, instead of the shuffling of frozen feet, the sniffing and the coughing? Would not Mr Henderson have looked more impressive and priest-like in scarlet-and-gold robes? As it was, clad in black, he looked as forbidding as he sounded, with grey hairs sprouting from his ears and nostrils, and his breath smelling of greasy mutton. Why did he think it necessary and appropriate to portray God as grim, unforgiving, and revengeful? No wonder Katherine Graham had renounced such a God.

Magdalen found herself thinking affectionately, not of Jamie glowering beside her, but of Francis Gowrie. This was a sin as heinous as Katherine's last night.

When she turned to look at her father behind her she saw anxiety and remorse on his face. Now that the irrevocable words were about to be spoken, he was acknowledging that, out of obedience to him, she had agreed to this marriage which she did not want and which therefore might bring her much unhappiness. Because she loved him, she smiled to reassure and absolve him.

In that glance behind she had seen old Sir John Birse's woebegone face. He was still mourning his wife. The people about him, she saw with gratitude, were being kind to him.

In the congregation were several of Jamie's kinsmen and hunting cronies, as young as himself, whose thoughts, she had discovered, did not dwell on the spiritual aspects of marriage, at that moment being so tediously and lengthily expounded by Mr Henderson, but on the carnal. She had overheard them gleefully jesting among themselves. Jamie had not been present. They would not have dared tease him about his forthcoming role as virginity-taker. They would have been too afraid of his quick temper and fierce pride. Now in the church, seeing their lewd

26

and genial grins, she felt more grateful to them than she did to the minister who was making marriage sound full of duties and empty of joys.

One surly face stood out: her brother James's. He did not like Jamie Graham and resented this marriage. Yet in one respect they were very much alike: they both lacked humour. In James's case it was because he had been born without it, and in Jamie's because his pride inhibited it. Fools, he had once told her, laughed too readily. Perhaps when he was older and wiser and expected less of humanity, he might himself laugh more often.

At present, beside her he was looking glum and disdainful. He thought that his wedding ought to have been taking place in St Giles's in Edinburgh, in the presence of all the nobles of Scotland; the King himself ought to have come up from London for the occasion. Also the minister was being too long-winded and presumptuous. The pride of place at this ceremony ought to have been his, yet here was this dreary-voiced fellow in the black clothes usurping it. He wasn't pleased either that on his green shoes were blobs of mud.

Mr Henderson, ignoring the bridegroom's scowls, did not hesitate to introduce politics into his address. Not only was he binding this young couple in holy wedlock, he was also uniting, so he said, their families, the Grahams and the Carnegies, in friendship and loyalty, so that in the troubled times ahead they would be stalwart champions of Christ's Reformed Kirk.

6

AS A CHILD Magdalen had often exasperated her sisters by seeming to have difficulty in understanding what to normal people was clear as daylight. For instance, she could never be made to see that it was fit and proper, in accordance with God's will, that she should live in a castle with many hearths and chimneys while the children in the village lived in hovels with no chimneys at all; or that they should be dirty, lice-ridden, and sickly, while she was able to change her clothing every week or so and, if ill, have Dr Allen come from Dundee at a gallop to cure her. There had been one girl in particular, Chrissie Alexander, a gardener's daughter, with whom Magdalen had played in the orchard and of whom she had become injudiciously fond. When Chrissie had died suddenly of a fever, Magdalen had wept for days, which was natural enough in a child of eight, but she had also asked questions which were not natural. Did poor girls like Chrissie go to heaven too? And why did some people have so little while others had so much? She had had to be told, rather impatiently, that things on earth, and of course in heaven too, were as God had arranged them. If the peasants were content in their smoky huts, why should she be sorry for them? As for heaven, was it not absurd, not to say sinful, to suppose that peasants with their coarse faces and vulgar souls would be put on the same level as people of quality?

So, after the ceremony in the kirk, here was meek dim-witted little Magdalen become a countess and likely, considering how able and ambitious her husband was, to end up as one of the grandest ladies in the land, at least as far as rank was concerned. How, they wondered, could she possibly do justice to her exalted position?

With that query in their minds, her two older married sisters Margaret and Agnes, and her Aunt Euphemia, went to the nuptial chamber in the evening. They had informed Magdalen that they would be coming. It was the custom, they had explained, for the bride to be made ready for the marriage bed by senior ladies of her family. They would bathe her in perfumed water, comb her hair, and dress her in a new white nightgown.

She received them with one of her sweetest daftest smiles, and then, still smiling, said that if they did not mind she would prefer to make the preparations herself. If she needed help she would get it from her maid Janet.

At first disconcerted, they soon decided that she was being shy and modest, for after all she was just 15. They pitied her, for she had in front of her an ordeal a great deal more embarrassing than their laving of her body. They hinted that she was in need of the kind of intimate advice that only mature women of her own class could give her, not a 40-year-old spinster whose father had been a stonemason. They even made insinuations about Janet's ignorance not only of men's propensities but also of their anatomy.

Into Magdalen's pale face, with the blueness of the eyes accentuated by the shadows under them, there entered an expression with which they were only too familiar: her nun's look, they had called it, sarcastically, for they had always seen it as a sign that her wits had wandered off to God knew where. But there was a startling difference this time. In her voice there was, or so it absurdly seemed, a note of authority, even of haughtiness, as if her husband was already influencing her.

They stared at one another and shook their heads. So this was how her marriage was going to affect her. The silly girl thought it had transformed her into a person of great consequence, like a queen, and therefore all other persons, including her sisters and aunt, were to do her bidding. They had often wondered if one day she would go off her head altogether and had conjectured what form her insanity would take, but they had never dreamt that she would imagine herself to be raised above them all, as if she was the bride not merely of an earl but of Jesus Christ Himself. Was not that how nuns regarded themselves?

They had to humour her for the time being and so they withdrew, protesting. Her father would have to be told, and Mr Henderson. The latter would soon put an end to her peculiar arrogance, which, when they came to think about it, was quite papistical. One thing Presbyterian ladies never did was to think of themselves as brides of Christ.

They were not so far from the truth. It seemed to Magdalen that the mystery of marriage, when she would be made a woman and a child might be conceived, ought to be very private, between her and her husband only, except, of course, for God, not Mr Henderson's angry Jehovah, but gentle Christ, source of all love.

Her maid Janet had listened to the conversation with mixed loyalties. She was a fanatical Presbyterian but she loved her young mistress, though it was a word she usually distrusted. In her experience, people loved only themselves. But she would have given her life for Lady Magdalen. She had once slapped the face of a scullery maid who had had the impertinence to remark that Lady Magdalen 'wad never scart a grey heid', meaning that she would die young. What had made Janet so angry was that she believed it too. Those shadows under the eyes betokened some fatal weakness, as did also the fits of paleness and the bouts of coughing.

Janet disapproved of the marriage, not because she had anything against young Montrose, who, on the contrary, seemed to her a brave handsome youth with a bright future, but simply because in her opinion Lady Magdalen was too young to start child-bearing. It amazed her that Lord Carnegie who loved his daughter was willing to put her life to such risk.

When the three ladies had departed in dudgeon, Janet helped her mistress get ready. She was thinking that if they had lived in Biblical times, she could have offered herself as a sacrifice in her mistress's place. Had not Jacob taken his wife's handmaiden Bilhah to bed? Aye, but Bilhah would have been young and bonny.

'You're very quiet, Janet,' said her mistress, as Janet was brushing her hair.

'Whit is there to say, my lady?'

'Why did you never get married yourself? You must have been bonny when you were my age. You're still a fine-looking woman.'

So she was, with breasts like ripe fruit. There had been men enough eager to suck them.

'You must have had many sweethearts, Janet?'

'I had my share.'

'Were you so particular that you refused them all?'

'I had my brithers and sisters to look efter. My mither dee'd when I was ten. I had to tak her place.'

Magdalen shivered. Her mother had died when she was a baby. 'Do you ever feel sorry never having had any children?'

Janet did not say, could not say, that she often regarded Lady Magdalen as her daughter. 'Whit's the use o' being sorry, my lady? It's too late noo.'

'Of course it isn't. You're not all that old. Look what lovely hair you have.'

Strong, shiny, and black as midnight. When loosened, it fell below her waist.

'Mine's so thin compared with yours.'

'Yours is fine as silk, my lady.'

The silver clock on the mantelshelf gave the time as quarter to eight. Montrose was expected at eight. It was time for Janet to

31

go. That night, and every night afterwards, she was to sleep in a room with four other women servants.

'I'll hae to leave you, my lady,' she said.

'Yes. Thank you, Janet.'

'Will you be a' right?'

'Yes, I'll be all right.'

As she went out Janet couldn't have felt more concerned if she had been Lady Magdalen's mother. Still, young Montrose thought so highly of himself that he would never mistreat his wife. Because it belonged to him, a horse, a falcon, a gun, or a sword was deserving of special honour; so he thought; and so it would be with his wife. For his pride's sake he would be kind to her.

7

AS SOON AS Magdalen was alone, she went down on her knees and prayed, asking God to bless her marriage and any child that she might have.

At last, her legs stiff, she climbed into the big curtained bed and lay waiting. Her heart beat fast. She was afraid that she did not love Jamie as much as she should, nor he her, but surely God would make allowances since they were both so young.

To her dismay and against her will, she thought of Francis Gowrie. With prayer and resolution she had built up a barrier to keep him out of her mind, as a farmer might a fence to keep cattle out of a field of crops; but, it seemed, in spite of constant repairing, there always remained gaps. She drove it out, that wicked thought, as the farmer did trespassing cattle, but not before the damage was done. Yes, she would have been happier if it had been Francis she was waiting for now in her marriage-bed. Yes, she would have looked forward more confidently to life with him at Mintlaw. Tears came into her eyes. To hide them, she covered her face with her hands. But they could not be hidden from God. Would He understand and forgive her? Or would He despise and condemn her?

The celebrations were still going on, inside and out. She heard laughter and singing. She had been told that the rain had stopped and the moon was shining.

It was now half-past eight. Was Jamie putting it off for as long as he could because he was as shy as she? Had he drunk lots of wine to give him courage? Aunt Euphemia had said that some bridegrooms got so drunk that they could not carry out their marital duties. It did not matter, she had added grimly, there were plenty of other nights.

Magdalen had been warned that Jamie would probably be escorted to the door and even into the chamber itself by friends made boisterous by drink and excitement. She was not to be alarmed: it was the custom. It happened to kings and queens.

But Jamie was prouder than any king. Would he put up with such indignity? She did not think so and, sure enough, when at last he came to the door, he was unaccompanied and, after knocking quietly, crept in, carrying his boots, as she saw through the opening in the curtains.

'Are you asleep?' he whispered.

'No.'

'It's damnably cold in here.' He went over to the fire and poked it, but it was almost out. She heard him grumbling. Then he was silent.

She could not see him now for the curtains. Was he praying, as she had done? No. Jamie believed in Fate, more than in God. Indeed, she was not sure that he did believe in God, at any rate not without reservations. 'Is God Mr Henderson's lackey?' he had once asked, indignantly. Then again: 'I find it very hard to tolerate a God that tolerates the presumptions of Henderson and his colleagues.' Since it would have been presumptuous on his own part to believe God had marked him out to have a glorious future, he gave the credit to Fate. 'What I mean is, Magdalen, opportunities will be presented to me. It will be up to me to make use of them.'

He was taking a long time to get undressed, perhaps because he was deliberately putting off getting into bed with her, but it could have been simply that he was not used to doing it himself. All those layers and laces, not to mention the silk stockings uncomfortably tight to show off the shapeliness of his legs, would not be easy to peel off or unfasten, especially by hands made clumsy with wine, cold, and nervousness.

Should she speak to him, offering help? After all she was now his wife.

Suddenly he appeared, wearing only a white sark which scarcely reached his middle. With one hand he covered his male parts; in the other he clutched a sheet of paper.

As he slipped under the clothes his feet touched hers: they were icy-cold. Feeling tender towards him, she put her warm feet against his. Instantly his were withdrawn, and then slowly returned.

Neither spoke for almost a minute.

'This is a poem I wrote yesterday,' he said.

She could not help smiling.

'Would you like to hear it?'

'Is it a love poem?'

'It's more philosophical, I would say.'

At least it wasn't about war. 'I'd like very much to hear it.'

He leant away from her towards the candle and began to read in a sombre tone of voice that, as it turned out, suited the subject matter of the poem:

> I would be high; but that the cedar tree
> Is blasted down while smaller shrubs go free.
> I would be low; but that the lowly grass
> Is trampled down by each unworthy ass,
> For to be high my means they will not do;
> And to be low my mind it will not bow.
> Oh heavens! Oh Fate! When will you once agree
> To reconcile my means, my mind, and me?

He waited for her verdict, with an author's, not a husband's, anxiety.

'It *is* very philosophical,' she said, 'but does it say what you really feel?'

'No one knows, Magdalen, the depths of gloom to which I sometimes sink.'

'But aren't there more times when you feel you are standing on a mountain peak?'

That was his own expression.

'Didn't the astrologer in St Andrews prophesy a wonderful career for you?'

'He said I would become a famous general and win many battles. And the one in Edinburgh said much the same thing.'

But what fortune-teller looking for a fat fee would not foretell a glorious military future for a young earl with eager eyes and a sword with a golden hilt?

'I am to perform great deeds for my country, Magdalen.'

'And what shall I be doing, Jamie, when you are performing your great deeds? Staying at home and praying that you are not killed?'

'There was one fellow,' he said, indignantly, 'who had the impudence to foretell that I would be hanged. I learned afterwards he wasn't right in the head.'

But someone, very sane, had said the same thing to her, humorously it was true, but not altogether. 'In dangerous times like the present,' Francis Gowrie had said, 'ambitious fellows like Jamie Graham could easily end up on the gallows.'

'But if you are to win battles, Jamie, it means there will be war.'

'So there must be, if the King lets himself be ill advised.'

'My father says there would never be war if men acted sensibly.'

'Men must act honourably, Magdalen, whatever the circumstances.'

'Could it ever be honourable, Jamie, to plunge the country into civil war?'

He carefully folded up the sheet of paper on which his poem

was written and tucked it into a pocket in his shirt. Then he blew out the candle, with a long sigh.

They lay in silence. Their feet still touched. Magdalen heard her heart beating. She wondered if Jamie had fallen asleep.

'Magdalen.'

'Yes, Jamie.'

'I expect they've told you what the purpose of marriage is?' He spoke apologetically.

'Yes, Jamie.'

'People ought to mind their own business.'

'Yes, Jamie.'

'So you know what has to be done?'

'Yes, Jamie.'

'One might have thought that God in His omnipotence might have devised some other way, not so repugnant. Less like animals, I mean.'

She had seen a bull in the field affectionately licking a cow before mounting it.

'It's not a thing that can be done with much dignity, is it?' he asked.

As long as it is done with affection, she thought.

'As intelligent beings we must make allowances.'

'Yes, Jamie.'

'I'll be as gentle as I can.'

But because of nervousness it was more of an attack than an act of love. He was inexpert and, of course, so was she, though she tried to help him. There was considerable pain and she gave a great gasp once. He instantly apologised and desisted.

At last it was over. His seed was within her. According to the advice she had been given, she must now behave as if nothing had happened. She must not say anything. For a woman there was nothing to say after, or before, or during; and not much either, it seemed, for a man.

But surely there should have been things, fond things, to say to each other. They were going to spend their lives together and, if God so willed, have several children.

'I hope they explained the situation to you,' he said. 'When I was ill in St Andrews I thought, what if I died and left no heir? The earldom would have been lost. As you know, I have no brothers. Well, there's Harry, but he's only a half-brother and is illegitimate, so he can't inherit. So I realised I must have heirs as soon as possible. One son wouldn't be enough, so many children die in infancy. Daughters, of course, will not do. Unfortunately there's no way of ensuring that children are males. My father had five daughters and only one son: that's not counting Harry. Your father had four sons but also six daughters. So, you see, we really have no time to lose. I'd be grateful, Magdalen, if you prayed for sons.'

But Jamie, she might have said, if we have sons you might want to take them away and make soldiers of them. I want girls to stay at home and keep me company. So in my prayers I shall ask for a daughter also, no, for two, because as you said, Jamie, so many children die in infancy.

8

ACCORDING TO THE terms of the marriage contract, the young couple were to live at Kinnaird until Jamie came of age, after which they could make their permanent home in his family seat, Kincardine Castle in Perthshire. Though he resented at times not being head of the household since he was, after all, above his father-in-law in rank, Jamie was happy enough hunting, practising archery and swordplay, reading books on military campaigns, writing poetry, and discussing politics with the many visitors. To his great satisfaction, both as an earl anxious for an heir and a young man eager to prove his virility, Magdalen was soon pregnant. She suffered badly from morning sickness and persistent backache but was glad that she was doing her duty as a wife. Like everyone else, she hoped for Jamie's sake that the child would be a boy. She even drank various potions brought to her by Janet, which, according to the old women who had supplied them, would ensure that the child in her womb would be a perfectly formed male. There was no harm in this, she thought, so long as the mixture did not have a vile taste, but she objected to Mr Henderson's hectoring prayers in her presence, in which he reminded the Lord that a female child would not do. To Janet she remarked that it would be Mr Henderson's fault if the Lord gave her twin girls. She often made fun of people who, like Mr Henderson, were pompous and self-righteous. Janet was inclined to be shocked by her gentle irreverence.

It took Jamie some time to discover that his wife had a talent for humour which now and then was used to make fun of his pretensions. He took himself so seriously that it was very hard for him to realise that he, so clever and knowledgeable, might be having his leg pulled by a mere woman, who like most women of her age was ignorant of everything except domestic matters. Yet he let himself drift into a habit of talking to her about matters that he didn't think she had any right to be interested in, such as politics and, particularly, the proper place of the Kirk in the country's constitution. He would never have admitted that he was asking her advice; he would have said that he was simply using her as an attentive audience, but all the same he waited anxiously for her verdict and was often taken aback by the percipience she showed, even if it took the form of disagreeing with him.

He wrote a treatise, with many illustrations from history, on the principle, advocated by the late King James and now being applied by his son Charles, that since the King owed his eminence to God he had a right to do as he thought fit, even if a majority of his subjects, or rather of his nobles, disapproved.

He read his treatise to Magdalen. It took half an hour. She listened with satisfactory patience and did not once interrupt.

'Well?' he said, when he was finished. 'What do you think?'

'Do you really believe the King owes his position to God?'

He was reluctant to commit himself. 'There are good arguments in favour.'

'But haven't lots of kings gained their thrones through winning wars?'

'Yes. But they could have argued that it was God who enabled them to win.'

'But, Jamie, isn't everything that happens in the world according to God's will? Doesn't Mr Henderson tell us so?'

'Interminably.' Jamie was thinking that when he won his battles he was going to take the credit, not Mr Henderson's God.

'Doesn't every nobleman have to swear an oath of allegiance to the King? Won't you do it yourself when you come of age?'

'Yes.'

'Doesn't that mean they have to obey him whatever he does?'

'I have made it clear, Magdalen, that there could be crises of conscience. Circumstances could arise when honourable men would feel justified in setting aside their oath of allegiance.'

'But would they be justified in taking up arms against the King? Isn't that treason?'

He frowned. More by luck than by logic she had hit upon the crux of the matter. He had not yet been able to make up his mind whether a subject, even for the most patriotic of reasons, was justified in opposing a tyrannical king by force. Being a woman, she had, of course, no conception of honour. It must have been listening to him that had given her this insight.

9

ONE DAY THERE came appalling news from Luss. Katherine had run off with her good-brother, Sir John Colquhoun, to the Continent, it was thought. Colquhoun and his German servant had been accused of seducing her with love philtres. They had been proclaimed outlaws and excommunicated.

Jamie went almost frantic with anger, frustration, and, above all, shame. He was for rushing off to find Colquhoun and kill him. Poor Kate, he wailed, with his fist tight on the hilt of his sword.

Magdalen remembered the incident outside the King's room. She had given a promise then and kept it even now. 'Poor Lilias,' she said.

'Yes, of course, we're all sorry for Lilias, but think of little Kate, at that villain's mercy, far from her friends. I tell you, Magdalen, it will be my chief purpose in life to seek him out and plunge my sword into his evil heart.'

Don't do it in Katherine's presence, thought Magdalen. She would not take your side, Jamie. If you harmed him she would hate you for the rest of her life.

He was convinced the love philtres had done it. 'They must have poisoned her mind.'

Magdalen could not help shaking her head.

'Well, for Christ's sake, if it wasn't that, what was it?'

Magdalen remembered how Katherine's passion for Colquhoun had been so much more ardent than his for her. 'Perhaps she loves him.'

42

'Love! God Almighty, Magdalen, do not pollute the word. I thought he was my friend too. Who can one trust in this vile and treacherous world? I owe it to my honour and to my family's honour to kill that adulterous beast. Is that not so, Magdalen? Is that not what you would expect your husband to do?'

But, Jamie, if you killed Colquhoun somewhere in France, would you bring Katherine home and cherish her? Would you proudly ignore all the sneers and sniggers? Would you protect her from the vengeance of the Kirk? No, Jamie, you would not. You would give her money and leave her where she was.

So what was likely to happen to Katherine? Sir John, that amiable fool, would soon rue having abandoned his family, his friends, and his comfortable life at Luss for her sake. He would blame her for his predicament. Sooner or later he would forsake her. Influential friends would obtain a pardon for him so that he could come home again. Katherine would be left on her own in a strange land, a young girl with no one to protect her. She was only 18 now. She might have to take up with some other man. He, in his turn, would pass her on.

'Should I go and look for her, Magdalen?'

She knew him well enough now to tell that he wanted her to dissuade him. No one was braver than he in facing a wounded stag. In battle he would suffer a dozen wounds rather than yield. But this, enduring humiliation for the sake of someone he loved, called for a kind of courage he did not have, at any rate not yet. Few men had it. She could think of only one: Francis Gowrie. Yes, Francis would have gone searching for his sister and would have brought her home, in defiance of the world.

Tears came into her eyes. 'Shouldn't you wait, Jamie, till our child's born?'

He misunderstood her tears. It was no wonder. She could not have explained them herself, their source was too deep.

She had offered him an excuse that he could honourably accept. 'You are right, Magdalen, as always. I must wait for that.

43

In any case, alas, my ambitions have been stripped from me. How can I ever hold up my head? How can I take part in public affairs? I must put away my sword and put a straw in my mouth. My fate is not to lead armies but to become a bumpkin. Yet, you know, Magdalen, I loved her most of all my sisters.'

'I shall pray for her, Jamie.'

'Yes, please, pray for her. I want you to pray for her, but if that bigot Henderson or any of his dreary-faced colleagues have the temerity to pray for my sister, I shall tell them to shut their mouths.'

So he would too, recklessly, but it was hardly likely that Mr Henderson or any other minister of the Kirk would pray for a woman whom they would think deserved not pity and forgiveness, but bitter condemnation and, in the end, the fires of hell.

'Pray for her to die and find peace in death. Better dead than living in dishonour.'

'I shall pray for Christ to forgive her, as I am sure He will, and to protect her from further harm.'

He turned away then so that she would not see the tears running down his cheeks. 'You are a good soul, Magdalen. You shame us all.'

10

IT WAS A prolonged, difficult, and painful birth, with the lives of both mother and child in great danger. In the midst of it Dr Allen was taken aside by Mr Henderson, who in a hoarse pious whisper instructed him that, if it came to a choice, he was to concentrate all his efforts on saving the child, even though its sex was not yet known. A compassionate man as well as a conscientious doctor, Allen said nothing but looked dour; whereupon he was bombarded with quotations from Scriptures, the purport of which seemed to be that if the young woman was not going to be able to provide her husband with a plethora of heirs, which was her chief function in God's eyes, then it would be better to let her pass to glory, so that the young earl could marry again, this time a stronger woman to whom child-bearing came easy. The doctor, who secretly doubted the existence of a beneficent God – the likes of Mr Henderson increased his doubts – still said nothing. He knew that blind chance rather than his skill would decide the matter, but he made up his mind to do all he could to save the young mother, even if the child had to be sacrificed.

In the end, after 20 hours of travail, both were saved. The child was a boy too, apparently healthy and likely to survive. On his knees Mr Henderson loudly gave thanks to God. 'Braying ass,' thought the doctor, with a bloody clout in his hand, but he prudently said it to himself.

To Lady Magdalen's father he was more outspoken.

In his study Lord Carnegie poured each of them a glass of claret to toast his new grandson. 'Thanks be to God,' he said.

God or Fate or Chance, thought the doctor, what difference did a name make?

'The outcome might not be so fortunate next time, my lord,' he said.

'What do you mean?' But Carnegie knew very well. From afar he had heard his daughter's screams.

'If next time is too soon,' added the doctor.

Carnegie stared at him gloomily. How could it be delayed, that next time? Was not procreation the purpose of marriage? His own wife had had ten children. He had not spared her. Why should he expect young Montrose to spare Magdalen? For another purpose was the sating of lust, rampant in most men.

'May I speak frankly, my lord?'

Carnegie's nod was curt: not too frankly, it meant.

'Lady Magdalen must be given time to recover her strength.'

'She is in God's hands, like the rest of us.'

'Yes, but more immediately in her husband's hands. He must be persuaded to keep out of his wife's bed for at least a twelve-month.'

Carnegie scowled. The doctor was forgetting to whom and about whom he was speaking.

'If she is not given time to recuperate, another pregnancy would kill her, my lord, and it would not be an easy death. That is my professional opinion.'

'You exaggerate, doctor.'

'I think not, my lord.'

'Certainly you presume.'

'Lady Magdalen is my patient. I have a sacred duty to her.'

'Sacred, doctor?' Carnegie sneered. The doctor was reputed to be an unbeliever.

'We doctors swear a solemn oath, my lord.' In his case, not to God or at any rate to Mr Henderson's God or Lord Carnegie's either, for that matter. It had been to the doctor's own gods: reason, intelligence, and human affection. He had thought then, at 22, and still thought at 62, that they were more worthy of worship than revengeful Jehovah.

'You should know, doctor, that no one has a right to interfere between a man and his wife.'

The doctor was tired. He had had no sleep for almost 30 hours. He had watched a beautiful good-hearted young woman suffering abominably, without being able to help her much. He was dispirited by his own lack of skill and resources. Also his own wife had died just two years ago and he still missed her. They had had three children, all of whom had died in infancy. She had cast up that he saved other women's children, why hadn't he saved hers? He had taken the blame, rather than have her blame God, in whom she fervently believed.

Therefore he was not as guarded and humble as he should have been when speaking to a Privy Councillor about a belted earl. 'If he has to ease his loins, let him use whores. It's often done by young men in his position.'

Carnegie curbed his anger. The doctor was too old. He would have to be replaced by a younger, more respectful man with a knowledge of more up-to-date methods. Not very long ago he had been summoned before the Presbytery to be warned: he had rashly, in the presence of witnesses, called the burning of a witch murder. Now here he was accusing noblemen of resorting to whores. That it was true in many cases did not excuse it. If commoners were allowed to criticise their superiors, chaos would fall upon the country.

'You go too far, doctor.'

Allen bowed his head. He had cringed many times before in the presence of the mighty. 'I beg your pardon, my lord. Old men's tongues sometimes run away with them.'

Older men than you have had their tongues cut out for their impudence, thought Carnegie, bleakly. He hated cruelty but there were times when it was necessary.

'You may go, doctor. You have a long ride ahead of you.'

47

At the door Allen turned. The doctor in him overcame the cautious underling. 'Will not the earl be setting forth on a Continental tour?'

'When he comes of age.'

That would be in about three years. A pity, thought the doctor, but he did not say it.

He was in the courtyard trying to mount his horse – a stiff and clumsy manoeuvre nowadays – when a servant approached and said that Lady Magdalen wished to see him before he left.

He found her pale and weak but eager to thank him again. The baby had been taken away by the wet-nurse. That was a pleasure she would never have, he thought. Gentlewomen did not suckle their young: it was considered vulgar and demeaning. He had often wondered what effect it had on their offspring. Did it explain the violent and callous behaviour of so many Scottish noblemen? Would James VI have sat in Holyrood, counting his fingers, while his mother was being beheaded at Fotheringay, if he had been suckled at her breast when a baby?

Lady Magdalen put out her hand to take his. 'Must you go back today?' she whispered. 'Should you not rest first?'

'I have other patients waiting, my lady.'

Then into the room, dressed for hunting, swaggered her husband, in very good humour. He had just been to see his son. 'A fine boy,' he said, 'with an excellent appetite. Is that not a good sign, doctor?'

'A very good sign, my lord.' But not such good news for the wet-nurse's own child, which would have to do with tainted cow's milk.

'I'm glad I've caught you before you left, doctor. There's something I'd like to discuss with you.'

'Yes, my lord.' Could it possibly be, wondered the doctor, that it had occurred to the young man that another pregnancy too soon would endanger his wife's life? Montrose might not love his wife more than he did the perpetuation of his earldom but only an hour or so ago he had heard her crying out in pain.

Allen took leave of the countess, assuring her that he would be back soon to see how she and the baby were progressing.

Montrose waited impatiently.

Going down the big staircase, he stopped, under a portrait of one of Lord Carnegie's ancestors in a helmet, and stared at the doctor eagerly. Allen was sure he was going to talk about his wife's condition; after all, she had been close to death and was still poorly.

'I have been thinking, doctor, that if it came to war it might be a good idea to have some kind of hospital prepared, to receive and treat soldiers who were wounded. I believe they have such places in France.'

The doctor hid his astonishment. 'Will there be war, my lord?' It was like asking: will winter come?

'Such a place would need an experienced man to superintend it. Someone like yourself, doctor.'

They continued down the stairs, past more of Carnegie's ancestors, most of them in war garb.

This time the doctor did not have to hide his astonishment. 'I, my lord?'

'You are skilled in surgery, are you not?'

Hardly skilled, thought the doctor. He could saw off gangrened limbs and howk out bullets. But then, not even the King's own surgeons could do more. One day perhaps the medical profession would know more and have better resources; but no doubt the military profession then would have deadlier and more destructive weapons.

'I'm happier delivering babies, my lord.'

They were crossing the great stone-flagged hall. More portraits adorned the walls. One was of Montrose, painted by the celebrated Mr Jameson of Aberdeen. It had been a wedding present from that city. With his long hair and olive-coloured doublet, he could have been taken for a girl.

49

'Think about it, doctor. Look about for some suitable place. Discuss it with those of your colleagues you can trust. Funds will be provided. It seems to me that the first thing a commander must do is to win the confidence of his men. If they feel he has their interests at heart they will fight for him all the more zealously.'

And die all the more plentifully, thought the doctor, but he kept it to himself. The war the earl had spoken of would be fought, so the contestants would say, over the question of whether or not bishops should be appointed to govern the Kirk. Surely the most absurd of reasons for men to kill their fellow men. If there was a God would He not tear His beard at such murderous folly? But if it was not about bishops, some other pretext would be found. Was not the Bible full of wars? Men enjoyed the excitement and danger and their commanders loved the glory. Here was young Montrose yearning to be such a commander.

These thoughts passed through the doctor's head as, in a very unmilitary fashion, he mounted his horse. Luckily, between him and old grizzled Nellie there was an understanding: they were to be tolerant of each other's frailties and foibles.

11

THE BABY, CALLED John after Jamie's father, was six months old and Magdalen was pregnant again, when Francis Gowrie came home from Italy, much earlier than he had intended, for who would want to leave the sunshine of Rome for the sleet and snow of Scotland in January? Word had been sent him that his father was dying. He had returned as quickly as he could, only to find his father dead and buried. He was now Sir Francis and master of a large estate. It seemed that he had grown a black beard, arranged in Italian style, giving him a Papist look. While in Rome, he had kissed the Pope's ring. He was so used to speaking Italian that he used it to people who couldn't understand a word. Other young noblemen's souvenirs of their travels abroad were guns, daggers, and swords; his were paintings, sculptures, glass-ware, musical instruments, and other fancy objects more suitable for a Papist chapel than a Presbyterian home.

These reports came from servants at Mintlaw Castle. Janet knew one of the housekeepers there.

'If he's no' carefu',' she said, 'he'll find himself before the Presbytery. Some of the paintings he's brought back are an affront to decency.'

Magdalen smiled. 'In what way?'

'Women wi' naething on except for a bit leaf here and there. Shameless fat hurdies, according to Bella Morton.'

Then she casually added something that stopped Magdalen's heart.

'It seems he's thinking o' getting mairried.'

Magdalen could hardly speak. Who was this lucky woman? 'To some Italian lady?'

'Na, na. Somebody frae Edinbroo. She's no' a lady either. Her faither's a merchant, the richest in the haill country, Bella says. Miss Nancy Dick; that's her name. Mintlaw met her through her brither. He and Mintlaw travelled hame thegether.'

But how could Francis marry a commoner, however rich her father? It was not done. Nobles were not just a superior kind of humanity, they were a different species altogether. Francis would have to get permission from the King or the Privy Council. They might not be willing to give it.

'She must be beautiful,' she said.

'You'd think sae, my lady, but it seems it's no' the case. He's got a picture o' her. Bella got a peek at it. Big and sonsie. A mooth frae ear to ear. Unco fond o' horses, they're saying.'

'Horses?'

'In the picture she's sitting on one. A big black brute o' a stallion that wad frichten maist ordinary women.'

Not to mention Francis, who had always been wary of powerful horses.

'What age is she?'

'Aboot a year or twa aulder than yoursel', my lady. There's talk the wedding will tak place in St Giles's in Edinbroo. Bella says a' the servants at Mintlaw are threatening to leave raither than serve somebody that's common clay like themselves, even if her faither's got bags o' money. If you ask me, my lady, Mintlaw will end up on the end o' a rope. First he insults the Kirk and noo he's insulting the gentry.'

Even so, his wife would be the most fortunate of women.

'They're saying he's going to use her money to turn Mintlaw intae a palace like the kind he saw in Rome, wi' painted ceilings and pictures everywhere.'

Later, when she was alone, Magdalen found herself in tears. It was not in her nature to be envious and she wished Francis and his Nancy well, but she knew now that she still loved him more than she would ever be able to love Jamie. It was a dreadful sin that could never be confessed, but she could not bring herself to pray for forgiveness.

Jamie, much amused, brought up the subject of Francis Gowrie and his bride-to-be. A friend had brought the news from Edinburgh, where it was the talk of the town.

'Daughter of a shopkeeper, would you believe it?'

'An ordinary shopkeeper?'

'Maybe not all that ordinary. Richest in Edinburgh, they say. But a shopkeeper just the same. She's no beauty either. Long-faced, like a horse. Which is appropriate for it appears she's an intrepid horsewoman. Her father's bought an estate just outside Edinburgh – he'd like to be taken for a gentleman. There she spends most of her time on horseback jumping over hedges and walls. Odd, wouldn't you say, considering what a feartie Mint-law himself is.'

'He wasn't a feartie when he spoke up for Jessie Gilmour.'

'Jessie Gilmour?'

'An old woman who was burnt as a witch.'

'Oh. I meant a feartie in relation to horses. As a boy he was scared of them. We used to laugh at him. Now he's going to marry a female Cossack. That's very funny, don't you think?'

'Did your friend say when the wedding is to take place?'

'Soon, I believe. And do you know where it's going to take place? St Giles's. No doubt her father's promised the Dean a handsome donation.'

'Who will attend it?'

'Oh, it will be well enough attended. Half the noblemen of Scotland owe Mr Dick, her father, money. He's a moneylender too, as well as a shopkeeper.'

'Does he charge interest?'

'I haven't heard of him doing that.'

'So he lends as an obligement?' She had been told once by her father that most Scottish noblemen were indigent.

'Expecting obligements in return. They'll turn up at the wedding but that'll be the end of it. No one will ever visit Mintlaw when she's the châtelaine.'

'Except for artists and musicians.'

Jamie laughed. 'Yes, and ostlers too. His own kind will shun him. You see, Magdalen, what a fate you escaped.'

'What do you mean?' she whispered. She could not help blushing.

'Wasn't there talk at one time of your becoming betrothed to him? Well, I'll tell you this, if you had, no one would ever have heard of you; but as my wife you're going to take your place among the great ladies of the land.'

He was only half-joking.

'In this conflict that lies ahead, Magdalen, between those who are for the King and bishops and those who are for the Kirk and the Constitution, Mintlaw and those like him who stay aloof will be despised by both sides and they will deserve it. Men who leave the fighting to others are contemptible.'

12

THERE WERE STILL patches of snow in ditches and on the tops of mountains, and daffodils were beginning to bloom in the Kinnaird policies, when Francis Gowrie paid his first visit after his return from abroad. Magdalen had heard that he had been spending most of his time in Edinburgh with his bride-to-be. Alerted that he was approaching, she was at her window watching him ride into the courtyard. His horse was no prancing stallion but a sedate gelding.

She pressed her hands against her belly, swollen by her second pregnancy. For a moment she let herself wish that Francis was the father. It was a great sin that would take an hour's praying to expiate.

His cautious dismounting was comic, to anyone knowing that he was going to marry a 'female Cossack', but also moving, to anyone who loved him. So Magdalen smiled, with tears in her eyes.

Janet came hurrying in. 'Mintlaw's here, my lady. I'd better tak the bairn awa'.'

'Why? Do you think he'll do the child harm?'

'Maybe no' intentionally, but he could hae brought back some foreign disease.'

'He's been home now for nearly six months.' And yet this was the first time he had come to see her.

'These foreign diseases, they lie in the bluid for years. For safety's sake let me tak wee Lord John to Annie Brodie. In ony case it'll soon be time for his next feed.'

Magdalen hesitated. Did she want Francis to see the living proof that she was well and truly married to another man? But, of course, he would notice her big belly. 'No. Leave the child. I want Sir Francis to see him.'

She deliberately gave him his title. Janet must be made to understand that he was a nobleman, not to be criticised by a servant. Perhaps it was also an unworthy jeer at the absent Nancy, daughter of a shopkeeper.

Minutes later, he was knocking at the door. Her face grim and unwelcoming, Janet opened it.

He was splendidly dressed, in what Magdalen supposed was Italian style. His beard too had a foreign look about it, as indeed did his whole manner as he came over to where she sat, took her hand, and kissed it.

But the greatest difference in him was his air of selfish assurance. He had seen the world and made up his mind how to deal with it to his own advantage. He would not now stand up in church and condemn the burning of a witch. He would still despise those eager to burn her but he would keep it to himself. He was not the generous idealistic young man she had loved, but she still loved him.

'What have they been doing to you, Magdalen?' he asked. 'Have you let them defeat you?'

She smiled, almost in despair. 'As you see I'm with child again.'

'Another heir for Jamie?'

'I hear you're getting married yourself, Francis.'

He had been carrying under his oxter a small square package. Now he unwrapped the brown cloth. 'I've brought you a present, all the way from Rome.' Revealed was a painting, with a gilt frame.

Janet's grandmother, to avert evil, would have crossed herself, but that Papist trick was now forbidden. Unfortunately, none had been put in its place, so Janet had just to gape in horror at the picture, though she could not yet see what its subject was. That it had come from Rome, home of the anti-Christ, was enough.

'Painted by one of the finest artists in the world,' said Mintlaw. 'I bought it for you, Magdalen, because she reminded me of you.'

So, thought Janet, it must be of a woman: with her clothes on, she hoped.

'It's very beautiful, Francis,' said Magdalen. Her voice trembled.

Unable to subdue her curiosity, Janet went over, ostensibly to rearrange the cushions behind her mistress but really to steal a look at the picture.

It was even more shocking than she had feared, though only the child was naked, not counting, of course, the lamb and the deer. The woman wore a blue-and-white robe. This was how Papists portrayed the infant Jesus and His mother. It should have been, therefore, in Janet's eyes, the vilest of blasphemies, and she tried hard to be properly offended; but she could not help seeing a resemblance to Lady Magdalen: goodness shone from her face too, as it did from the woman's in the painting.

'Thank you very much, Francis,' said Magdalen, 'but you know I may not be able to accept it.'

'You mean, Jamie will object?'

She shook her head. 'My father,' she murmured.

'Surely Lord Carnegie will not think that having such a painting in his house will compromise his Presbyterian principles?'

She did not like him sneering at her father.

Little Lord John then woke up and began to cry.

'Take him to Annie now, Janet,' said Magdalen.

Janet picked up the child and tried to soothe him but she did not leave the room. She was not going to leave her young mistress alone with this dangerous heretic.

'Do what I told you, Janet,' said Magdalen.

She spoke quietly but Janet had learned to recognise the note of authority in her voice. It was not simply that of an earl's wife but also that of a young woman whose character was forming and who was determined to say what she felt to be right and true.

In a huff Janet left, carrying the baby.

'You should be careful what you say in front of people like Janet,' said Magdalen.

'Is she one of Mr Henderson's spies?'

'They all are.' Then, with a shiver, she returned to the subject of his marriage. 'Tell me about your bride-to-be.'

'The shopkeeper's daughter, with a face like a horse?'

'Be serious, Francis. Does she like paintings?'

There was, alas, intended malice in the question. It was not likely that a woman inordinately fond of horses also liked painting and music.

'I saw, and heard, Jamie and his troop in the distance. They seemed to be in pursuit of some wretched animal. Practice, I suppose, for the day when he goes to war.'

'He will only go to war if his honour requires it.'

'Ah yes, I forgot. Jamie always was such an honourable fellow.'

She knew what was happening. They were saying goodbye to each other. This was probably the last time they would be alone together. She did not want to be bitter, and neither, she was sure, did he, but neither of them could help it.

'When we are settled in at Mintlaw we would like you to come and visit us. If they allow you, that is to say.'

Like Jamie, and her father, he too misjudged her. The time was coming soon when she would do whatever she considered right, no matter who opposed it. She would not be contumacious, she would be true to her nature and remain gentle, but she would not easily yield.

'I would be very pleased to visit you at Mintlaw. I hear you are making great improvements.'

'An oasis of beauty, in the midst of a desert of bigotry and spiritual blight.'

Soon afterwards he took his leave, but not before hanging the painting on the wall where the light from the window fell on it.

13

USUALLY WHEN JAMIE returned from hunting he went straight to her room, eager to see his son and heir, and though John was still not two to bring him some trophy of the hunt. Today it was a wood pigeon, its feathers soiled with blood. Instead of crowing with delight the infant was frightened and began to cry.

'Are you making him a milksop, Magdalen?' asked Jamie, not altogether in jest. 'Like Mintlaw. We saw him coming here. What did he want?' Then he caught sight of the painting. 'Did he bring this?'

'As a present for me.'

He swaggered over to it, his hand on his dagger.

If he slashes it, she thought, I shall never forgive him.

'He's got a damned impudence, bringing my wife a present without asking my permission.'

She let that pass.

'Has your father seen it?'

'Not yet.'

'I hope you realise that if he and Mr Henderson get together they'll order it to be destroyed.'

She shook her head, meaning that her father wouldn't; but she wasn't sure.

'Do you like it?' he asked.

'Yes. I think it's very beautiful.'

'A piece of idolatry, they'll call it. But as your husband I'm the one to say what you may hang on your wall and what you may not.'

'Yes, Jamie.'

'I don't see what harm it's doing. So you may keep it.'

'Thank you, Jamie.'

'Mind you, it would be different if Lord John was older. I don't think I'd want him exposed to such feminine stuff. That's all right for a little girl, not a boy who might have to be a soldier one day.'

She would pray all the more that the child in her womb would be that little girl.

Next day her father came to her room. He brought a bunch of daffodils but his purpose was to inspect the painting.

'How are you keeping, my pet?' he asked. 'You do not look well.'

'Sometimes I do not feel well, Father.'

'You do not eat enough.'

'I don't have an appetite.'

'Well, the better weather will soon be here, and you will be able to get out more.'

'I would like Dr Allen to come and see me.'

He frowned. Dr Allen was no longer the family physician. He had been replaced by Dr Muirkirk, a younger man whose methods were more modern and whose patients were all men and women of noble birth. Magdalen much preferred the frank and kindly old man.

'I understand he finds travelling difficult these days, because of his rheumatism,' said her father.

'I would like him to be present when my baby's born.'

'Well, we shall see. Is that the painting young Mintlaw brought you?'

'Yes, Father. Isn't it beautiful?'

He gazed at it.

What thoughts, she wondered, were going on in that calm, austere, intelligent head, with the beard turning white? He had read many books and debated with the wisest men in the kingdom. Was it possible that he could see in this small innocent painting a danger not only to his soul and to hers but to the whole country's? She knew that in his heart he did not approve of the burning of witches but put up with it so as not to offend the ministers of the Kirk. Whatever would keep the peace he espoused, even though he might think it ignoble. He did not let himself be bound too tightly by honour, like Jamie.

'Should it be on public display?' he asked, reasonably.

'This is my private room, Father.'

'Still, anyone might see it. Why not keep it hidden and take it out and look at it as often as you wish, when you are alone? In that way it would be safe from any crazy fool with a knife.'

'Yes, Father.'

He smiled. 'I wonder at your preferring Dr Allen. He is rumoured to be an unbeliever. He has been before the Presbytery. Moreover, James is not pleased with him.'

Dr Allen had done nothing about setting up a hospital for Jamie's wounded soldiers.

When her father was gone she sat staring at the painting. How was it possible for anyone not to believe in God? There were so many proofs of His existence. How would the doctor explain his disbelief? Was it some malignant pride that prevented him from acknowledging his Creator? Yet he was one of the kindest and most honest persons she had ever known; whereas Mr Henderson, who believed in God fiercely, was implacable and devious.

14

THE SECOND BIRTH, though not as long-drawn-out as the first was painful and difficult enough. Again the outcome was a male child. Rejoicings and congratulations quite drowned out the moans of the exhausted mother. Dr Muirkirk took the credit but it was Dr Allen who did most of the work and it was his hand that Magdalen held on to tightly. Mr Henderson was, of course, present, praying and exhorting. No one noticed, least of all himself, that Lady Magdalen, in much need of comfort and support, not only did not look to him for it but turned her head away whenever he approached. Perhaps Dr Allen noticed but then he made little attempt to hide his own opinion, which was that the minister was an intolerable nuisance. Once he pushed him out of the way,

When the child was safely delivered and the mother was resting after her ordeal, Dr Allen scandalised the ladies present, Lady Magdalen's sisters and aunts, by advising her, if she felt able, that was to say if she had a good supply of milk and her breasts were not too tender, to suckle the child herself and not hand it over to a wet-nurse, as had been done with his brother Lord John. Not only would it be good for him to be held close to his mother, it might also prevent her from becoming pregnant again too soon, to the detriment of her health.

Liking the idea, Magdalen smiled and nodded but her sisters, Margaret and Agnes, were so outraged that they rushed off to complain to their father. That inveterate compromiser shrugged his shoulders and muttered what was the harm in it if it was done in private and Magdalen herself wished it. Besides, if it did have the effect of delaying a third pregnancy, would that not be desirable? Magdalen had now provided her husband with two heirs and deserved a rest, did she not? Let them remember that she was not yet 19 and had a delicate constitution.

Thus had the Privy Councillor helped to keep the kingdom at peace, and the King when he came north for his coronation would reward him for it, but his daughters had always found his shilly-shally, as they called it, exasperating. Never more so than now. They decided to rebuke the insolent doctor themselves, with Mr Henderson as their ally. *He* was still indignant at being pushed out of the way.

They summoned the doctor to appear before them. He came hirpling, with the aid of a stick. There were specks of blood on his cuffs and he was unshaven. How dared he, they cried, both speaking at once, treat their sister as if she was the wife of a cowherd and not of an earl.

He listened in silence and then had the impudence to defend himself. Had not Nature, or if they preferred it God, made the wives of cowherds and earls, not to mention kings, alike in the matter of motherhood by giving them breasts full of milk for the benefit of their offspring? For his part there was no sight more beautiful than that of a mother suckling her child.

He then hobbled off without waiting for permission. They could hardly have given it, for he had left them speechless.

They looked to the minister, who so far had contented himself with portentous glowers and grunts. Now he cried: 'Such is the arrogance of infidels!'

They frowned, not quite seeing the relevance.

'When he arrived, did you not see him dismounting from his horse?'

They had not. They had better things to do than watch an old doctor getting off his horse.

'He had to be lifted off. Otherwise he would have fallen on his face.' Mr Henderson laughed triumphantly.

They did not see what there was to laugh at.

'So let the servants be instructed not to assist him. Thus shall he be taught proper respect for his superiors.'

The minister thought so highly of his idea that he hurried off to have it carried out.

The ladies were not so sure. They would have been satisfied with a display of abjectness on the doctor's part, they did not want to see him put in danger of physical injury. Besides, if Magdalen heard about it, she would be very angry. So too might their father. Also, if the truth could have been told, they regarded the minister's own arrogance as more offensive than the doctor's.

Servants kept hidden and watched in silence and shame as the old doctor tried to climb up on to his horse. They liked him but they feared the minister more. The wise old beast did its best to help by standing very still.

It so happened that Montrose came into the courtyard and saw the old man in difficulty. Roaring with anger at the servants, he rushed forward to help.

'Thank you, my lord,' said Allen calmly, lifting his hat and ambling off.

Montrose turned to the servants who now crept out. They hung their heads as he upbraided them. One muttered that they had been obeying orders.

'Whose orders, for God's sake?' he cried, but he had already guessed.

He did not wait for an answer. It would not have been fair to them. With furious face he repaired to his own quarters where he sat fuming: he couldn't bear to live much longer in that house, where he had less authority than an upstart priest.

15

ONE MORNING MAGDALEN was in her room suckling her baby, with only Janet and Annie, John's wet-nurse, present, when she was summoned to her father's study. She let the child finish its feed. She could not help it but he was her favourite. He was a Carnegie, whereas John was a Graham. She was resolved to bring him up herself. Jamie could have John to make a soldier of, she would teach James to abhor bloodshed and love the arts of peace.

Always, with her child at her breast, she felt content and absolved. She was also, as Janet often told her, at her bonniest. 'Like the woman in the picture,' Janet had once admitted, grudgingly. Yet today, as on other days too, she noticed Annie staring at her with what looked like pity.

Surely if ever there was a woman who did not need pity from the likes of Annie Brodie it was she. Her husband owned two large houses and estates, whereas Annie's had only a rented one-roomed hovel that had to be shared with pigs. She ate venison and grapes while Annie had to be content with oatmeal and brambles. She dressed in silks and taffetas, Annie in rough hodden grey. She slept on a feather bed, Annie on sacks stuffed with straw. Magdalen's relatives and friends were gentry, Annie's peasants. Not only was it a great impertinence of Annie to pity her, it was a great stupidity too.

Yet, in the great hall, on her way to her father's study, as she looked up at the portrait of Jamie painted by Mr Jameson of Aberdeen, she had an inkling of what Annie meant. Annie's husband wanted only to stay at home and look after his family.

There was Jamie, in his splendid olive-coloured doublet, gazing not at her, nor at anyone, but at some exciting perilous future in which she would have no part. Was he not now planning a tour of the Continent?

Her father got up from his desk to take her hand and bring her over to the fire. All her life he had been anxious about her health. Now, seeing her so pale and thin, and so like her mother in the latter's last days, he felt guilty and gloomy. He had sacrificed her for the sake of his political plans, as like as not fruitlessly, for it was beginning to look as if young Montrose would be a liability, not an asset, as a son-in-law.

'As soon as the weather's kinder,' he said, 'you must get out of doors more often. I would like to see roses in your cheeks again.'

She smiled. She had never been rosy-cheeked. 'What did you want to see me about, Father?'

'This Continental tour of James's, has he discussed it with you?'

'He has just told me that he is going.'

Her father could not help feeling let down by her. She had made little effort to acquire influence over her husband. A cleverer woman would have used cunning, a more sensual one her body, a stronger-minded one her will. But then she was still very young.

'There can be no objection to his going. He is now of age and can please himself. What alarms me, and Lord Napier too, is that he insists on going before the King's coronation in June. Every nobleman in Scotland will be present, except, it seems, James. His absence will be noted. Frankly, I find it incredible that so ambitious and self-regarding a young man as he is should deliberately choose to miss so important an occasion and run a very serious risk of antagonising the King, from whom all honours flow. In God's name, why the urgency? What is driving him away? Why cannot he wait another month or two?'

'He says he has to look for his sister Katherine.'

'To what purpose?'

'To bring her home perhaps.'

'More likely to assault Colquhoun. I would have thought him only too glad to let that vicious dog lie.'

Yes, for if Katherine was brought home, all the shame and misery of her elopement would be revived.

'Perhaps he thinks that if he were to attend the coronation people would laugh at him behind his back.'

'As no doubt they would. He will have to learn that inordinate pride like his attracts such reactions. No one blames him for what his sister did. If he knew how to be humble he would be given sympathy, not ridicule.'

That was true. Jamie just could not bring himself to be humble. That was a lesson life had not yet taught him.

'Perhaps I am to blame,' she said.

'In what way?'

'He finds me dull.'

'Dull?' Her father would have said quiet or reserved or meditative but, yes, to a young man who saw himself as a second Alexander, dull might be the word.

'He thinks I've got no imagination.'

But what woman had? Their minds seldom rose above everyday trivialities. That was how God had meant them to be.

'Many would say he has too much himself.' Carnegie then sighed and gave way to pessimism. He was tired too, having ridden yesterday from Edinburgh in pouring rain. 'I'm afraid the world that James is bent on conquering is not as glorious a place as he appears to imagine. I would be happier myself staying at home with my books and family.'

'Why don't you, Father?'

'The State must be governed. Order has to be kept. What little of civilisation we have achieved we must hold on to. If I gave up, worse men might take my place. Better men too, no doubt, but in the end it is the best who are corrupted most.'

At the risk of showing how dull she was she spoke what was in her mind. 'You think then, Father, that women who wait at home and look after their children are the happiest?'

'Indeed they are.'

'But what if there is war and their husbands are killed or wounded?'

He had no answer ready and doubted if there was one in all his books that would have satisfied her simple soul.

'Will there be war, Father?'

Yes, there would be, and the worst kind, Scotsmen killing Scotsmen for dubious principles. It had happened many times before. He could foresee a time when he and James Graham would be on opposite sides. That would make poor Magdalen's waiting all the harder.

'Not if we are sensible, my pet.'

Which was the most futile of hopes. Small wonder she shook her head, representing not only the women of Scotland but of all the world, throughout history. He was struck by her expression of intense anguish. He had not realised she was capable of such deep feeling. If she was spared, if disease or accident or childbirth did not cause her to die early, she might well grow into a wife that even James Graham would be proud of.

16

IT WAS A sunny day in May when James set out. White doves fluttered about his head. He would be pleased, Magdalen knew, for he would see them as a good omen. If they had been black crows, he might have put off his departure to another day. Fate's warnings must be heeded by Fate's favourites.

Gathered in the courtyard to cheer him and his companions off was the whole household, from Lord Carnegie to the small ragged boy whose task it was to dart out and scoop up the horse dung. A stranger would never have taken Montrose for a man about to leave his wife and infant sons for a year or so. In a long red cloak and with red feathers in his hat, he managed his big horse expertly as it curvetted and struck sparks from the cobbles, frightening Lord John, now aged three, into hiding behind his mother's skirts. She held baby James in her arms.

Lilias, James's sister, now living in seclusion in the ancestral home, Kincardine Castle, had come with her two children to Kinnaird to see him off. At the last minute she ran forward and seized his leg, crying something that could not be made out because of the clattering of hooves and fluttering of wings, but that it was a final appeal her attitude of desperation and his of embarrassed concern made evident. Was the poor lady, they wondered, begging him not to kill her husband as he had publicly vowed to do but instead to bring him safely home to her despite his sentence of excommunication? And was she also asking him to tell their sister Katherine that she too was forgiven and would be welcomed home? Did she think, in her despair, that her brother, so young and so confident in his powers, could produce those miracles of reconciliation?

Knowing him so well now, Magdalen saw that Jamie, though he loved and pitied Lilias, was displeased with her for spoiling his departure and indeed threatening his whole venture. A distraught hysterical woman was not auspicious.

Suddenly, as she let go and sank to her knees, he turned his horse towards the gateway, followed by his kinsman Graham of Morphy, his personal attendant Mr John Lambie, and his clerk Mr Thomas Saintserf. With a last wave of their hats they cantered through the gateway and, within seconds, were out of sight.

The boy dashed out with his bucket. He used his hands as a scoop.

On her knees Lilias picked up handfuls of dung and spread it over her yellow hair.

Handing Baby James to Janet, Magdalen went to console her sister-in-law. She helped her to her feet, removed the dung from her head, and embraced her.

The women servants whispered what a shame it was that the two beautiful young ladies were separated from their husbands. Nothing in the world, they thought, neither beauty nor riches, could compensate for not having your man safe and loving by your side every night.

Lord Carnegie came over, trying to look and sound cheerful. 'Well, let us hope God looks after him and sends him back to us wiser and more content.'

Then, mumbling some words of consolation to Lilias, he hurried with obvious relief back to his study, where he would resume his deep consideration of what was for the good of the country. Yet, thought Magdalen, in the people who made up the country he had little interest. Governing was like playing chess: the pieces were of flesh and blood but they were to be moved about as if made of wood or ivory, without emotions, hopes, joys, and sorrows of their own. She loved her father but, like all

71

statesmen, he was not to be trusted. Had he not admitted himself that the best were corrupted most?

She thought of Jamie, who had gone off so joyfully, having left behind the burdens and boredoms of home. When she had timidly told him that she too would like one day to visit far-off lands, he had laughed. Would she ever find the courage to tell him that it was she and all the women like her who brought up their children and took on the responsibilities of home-making, who were the true sustainers of their country, and that men like Jamie, who squabbled in Assemblies and Parliaments or killed each other in battles did not matter in the end?

17

WHEN JAMIE WAS having his portrait painted in Aberdeen as a wedding gift from the city which had just made him a freeman, he had commissioned the same artist, Mr Jameson, to come to Kinnaird and do a companion portrait of his countess. He had stipulated that it should not be done soon but in two or three years' time, when, though he did not say so, she would no longer be a child and might have some character in her face worth painting.

About two years after Jamie's departure for the Continent, the artist, accompanied by two assistants, on a journey to Edinburgh, stopped off at Kinnaird to carry out his commission. He made it plain, being a brusque little man, that he regarded it as a duty from which he expected little satisfaction. He had heard that Lady Magdalen was a dull girl who would make a dull subject and the result would inevitably be a dull picture, however conscientiously executed. His attitude swiftly changed, for, being a shrewd judge of character, he saw at once that here was a young woman whose beauty was not so much physical as spiritual, a much rarer kind and well-nigh impossible to portray in paint, but a great challenge nonetheless. Often, when painting a portrait of a lady, or indeed of a gentleman, of distressing plainness or downright ugliness, he had had to depend on ostentatious dress or striking backgrounds. The opposite would be required here, where nothing else should matter except the subject's face, into which would have to be put sweetness, intelligence, deep feeling, sadness, and by no means least a sense of fun. For Mr

Jameson, after only one or two conversations with her, discovered that the young Countess of Montrose was the gentlest of ironists who saw through pretensions, his own included. With other aristocratic ladies he had had to use flattery and obsequiousness but with her he could be as free and natural as with his own daughters. The result was he had never painted a portrait with more zest and excitement, even though he knew from the start that it could not be as good as it should: her smile, humorous and yet tragic, was beyond his powers to delineate. He did not think there was a painter alive who could have done it, not even the great Sir Anthony Van Dyck. But he did his best, worked very hard, and was inspired more than usual. During the three weeks that it took, he often went to the hall to study the portrait of her husband, the earl, for he well knew the folly of making the wife outshine the husband – this had got him into trouble before – but he was determined to capture what the young lady had in abundance but what her husband hadn't a trace of, that was to say, true humility, in Mr Jameson's experience, the rarest of qualities, especially among aristocrats.

Her father came to look at the portrait when it was finished. After gazing at it for quite a while he shook his head and murmured 'Poor Magdalen.' He then went off without explaining what he had meant, but Mr Jameson, on reflection, decided that it had nothing to do with the quality of the painting, indeed it could be taken as a compliment, for surely it had to do with the capacity for suffering which gave the young lady her sad distinction and which had been so fortunately – in an artistic sense – caught by the painter.

The whole household, in twos and threes, crept into the great hall to look at it. Some were moved to tears. Afterwards in the kitchen it was agreed that the picture had reminded them of old Jessie Gilmour's prophecy – it had been one of the counts against her – that Lady Magdalen would never 'scart a grey heid'. How would that early and lamentable death come about? Would she just fall sick and die? Would it be the result of too difficult a birth? Would it be an accident, like an overturned coach or a fall downstairs? They foresaw a time when the young earl would greatly regret having gone off to foreign parts instead of staying at home and enjoying his wife's company while she was still young and well. No one he met on his travels, whether princess or queen, would, they felt sure, be as worth getting to know as his own Lady Magdalen.

18

ONE SUNNY AFTERNOON Francis Gowrie rode over to Kinnaird to give his verdict on Mr Jameson's portrait of Magdalen. He had another purpose: to invite her to Mintlaw Castle, where the embellishments were at last completed. His wife Nancy did not accompany him. Not even that intrepid horsewoman dared risk the journey, for she was eight months pregnant.

He still had his black beard and, what suited him less, his cynical smile. Though, from all reports, his Nancy was a jolly young woman – out of the corner of her mouth Janet had whispered 'common' – she had not so far, it seemed, cured him of his disgust with humanity. Perhaps, thought Magdalen, his child would.

He stood beside her in the great hall, looking up at the portrait and sneering.

She wondered what was disgusting him this time: was it the painter's lack of skill or the dolefulness of the subject?

'Well, well,' he said at last, 'who would have thought a Scotsman of our day and age could have done it?'

'Done what, Francis?'

'Recognised true spirituality and put it on canvas. Da Vinci could not have done it better. A wee loon frae Aiberdeen tae. Maybe there's hope for us yet.'

'You like it, then?'

'It's magnificent. He has given you immortality. In a hundred years, in three hundred, when the rest of us are all forgotten, people will look at it and wonder who that ethereal creature was.'

76

'That doleful creature, you mean.'

'Only the obtuse will think that.'

'Will there be obtuse people in three hundred years, Francis?'

'In three thousand. They will be in command then too. Choice spirits then as now will have to seek refuge in beautiful artefacts. You must come and see Mintlaw. Nancy is eager to meet you.'

'I would like to meet her.'

'Will your father allow it?'

But did she need her father's permission? She was no longer his responsibility, being a married woman. Did she need her husband's? But Jamie was far away and, judging by his rare letters, not thinking of her very much.

'The day after tomorrow,' she said.

He was delighted. 'I'll send a carriage.'

'My father has three carriages.'

'Stay for a few days.'

She shook her head. 'For one night only. You see, I am feeding Baby James myself.'

It was he who blushed, not she. 'You really are a choice spirit, Magdalen. You shame us all.'

Her father did object to the visit, not on his own account, he assured her, but on her husband's. James, he reminded her, did not approve of Gowrie or of Gowrie's choice of a wife. In James's eyes, Gowrie was a traitor to his country, in that he would refuse to fight for it, and to his class, in that he had married a shopkeeper's daughter for the sake of her large dowry.

'Francis is my friend,' she said. 'I knew him before I knew Jamie.'

Her father could have pointed out the ingenuousness of her remark. In the war that loomed on the horizon friendship would not deter men from killing one another. What would count most was self-interest. Poor Magdalen seemed unable to see that: she was still too child-like. He did not want to be the one to disillusion her. Let events do it. It was to be hoped, though, that she had hardened her heart by then, otherwise it would surely be broken. Perhaps visiting Mintlaw would be a step towards that necessary obduracy.

19

AFTER THE SPELL of dry weather the roads were firm but still rough and stony. Janet was fearful. She did not trust coaches, which were always breaking down or overturning. Before getting in beside her mistress, she ordered Harry Meldrum to drive slowly and carefully.

Not for crabbed Janet's sake but for his young mistress's, Harry was as careful as he could but, even so, the ten-mile journey was exhausting and bruising. At one point, a steep brae, Janet had to get out and push, with black cattle gazing at her over a drystone dyke. She was confirmed in her opinion that contraptions like coaches were against the Lord's will. He had given us legs and, if we didn't use them as He had intended, then we were showing disobedience and disrespect. It would serve us right if we lost the power of them altogether and were reduced to crawling on hands and knees like monkeys. Laughing, Harry shouted down that in England there were roads so smooth and coaches so well sprung that their occupants could drink wine without spilling a drop, while travelling at ten miles an hour.

'I always kent the English were an ungodly lot,' she shrieked. 'Dae they no' ken the Lord meant us to stay in the place where we were born and no' to go gallivanting aboot?'

Magdalen thought of someone who during the past three years had been doing a great deal of gallivanting about. Would his travels have changed Jamie much? Now that he had had experience of the world and had met many important and interesting people, would he find her even duller than before?

They passed through the gateway in the high thick wall that enclosed the Mintlaw policies and began to catch glimpses through the trees of the tall massive house with its five storeys, small windows, and several turrets. It had been built as a keep by Francis's ancestors in turbulent times and had withstood many sieges. Safe in it, Francis himself hoped to keep at bay the forces of bigotry and barbarism.

Janet had become uneasy. 'They say he got a chapel built for the workmen. Maist o' them were Papists.'

'So were our forebears, Janet.'

'But thanks to the Lord *they* saw the light in time.'

'Were there no good things at all in the old religion?'

'Whit a thing to ask, my lady! It was a' idolatry.'

Francis came running out to greet them and hand them down from the coach. He helped Janet down too, to her great embarrassment. Behind him, more slowly but just as eagerly hospitable, came his wife, hugely pregnant, though cheerful and red-cheeked.

They would have struck Magdalen a pair as ill-suited as herself and Jamie if it hadn't been so obvious that Nancy was very much in love with her husband. Do I, she wondered, give the same impression to visitors? She did not think so and felt a shiver of foreboding.

Nancy showed her goodness of heart, and perhaps her commonness by the enthusiasm of her welcome. She hugged and kissed Magdalen and gave Janet the friendliest of greetings.

Janet was not pleased. She knew her place and would have been more at ease if she had been treated like the servant she was. She did not like, either, the way Mintlaw kept looking at the mistress as if *she* was his wife and not this blatherskite with the loud laughter.

She had been prepared to some degree by Bella Morton's descriptions of the house but her imagination had not been able to cope with the glories she had been told about and, in any case,

Bella was known to be a great exaggerator. 'You ken, Janet, it's jist whit you micht picture heaven to be, except maybe for ane or twa things.' Two of those things stood right there in the entrance hall, a life-sized white marble figure of a man whose hair was curly and not just on his head either, and also the statue of a woman holding a harp in her hands and therefore making no effort to hide her bosom or private parts. Thank God *there* she was as bald as a new-born babe.

Janet's mind fell into confusion. She did not want to be fascinated by these figures, especially the one so majestically male, but she was: she could not keep her eyes off it. Bella had not exaggerated. This was what heaven must be like: black-and-white marble on the floor (instead of grimy stone and sawdust as in Kinnaird), pink-and-white plaster on the walls (instead of bare stone or scuffed wood panelling), and ceilings splendid with paintings of angels with wings blowing trumpets. And in heaven there could be no shame since everyone was sinless.

All the same, remembering her duty as chaperone, she wanted to run forward and turn Lady Magdalen's eyes away from these un-Presbyterian sights, but Lady Magdalen was looking not at all shocked, on the contrary she was delighted and entranced. What was the world coming to, when a young married noblewoman found pleasure in looking at statues and pictures of naked men and women? Mr Henderson would have been running about with a torch in one hand and a hammer in the other, burning and smashing. As a good Presbyterian, Janet would have had to urge him on, she would have had to help him burn and smash, and yet would she not have felt a twinge or two of regret and even of guilt? Could it really be true that all these beautiful things were the Devil's, as Mr Henderson would claim?

Suddenly she noticed another wonder: absent was the faint stink of human waste that pervaded Kinnaird (and other big houses) in spite of all the emptying and scrubbing. In its place was a pleasant perfume. It seemed that Mintlaw had transformed the privies too.

She kept half-expecting to find, in the next room, God Himself seated on a throne of red and gold.

As a small child she had been taught by her mother never to ask the price of things: it was rude, and all the more so if they were gifts, and somehow she realised that young Mintlaw had not collected all these grand and beautiful objects for his own selfish enjoyment but also for that of everyone who came to see them, not just now but for many years afterwards.

She was relieved when Lady Magdalen suggested that she might like to go and have a chat with her friends in the kitchen. She needed to be with her own kind, in surroundings fit for them and herself. This splendour was too much for her. At any moment she might burst into tears.

20

WHAT CONTINUED TO impress Magdalen more than all the works of art, the sculptures, paintings, cabinets, chandeliers, and carpets, was Nancy's artless love for her husband. It was almost worship and yet it had humour in it too. She saw his faults and boldly teased him about them. For instance, she accused him of preferring people in paintings to 'real people'. He did not deny it. In front of a large painting of a Christian saint being burned at the stake, with a crowd watching, he turned to Magdalen. 'Did I ever tell you I went to Dundee to see them burning Jessie Gilmour? You remember old Jessie?'

'Yes, I remember her.' She still saw Jessie in dreams.

'I wanted to see for myself if it was possible that people – Nancy's "real people" – could find entertainment in watching an old woman being roasted alive. Well, I found that they could. There they were, in holiday mood, holding up their children for a better view.'

'Was this Jessie a witch?' asked Nancy.

'She was an old woman whose wits wandered. There are no witches. There never have been.'

'When I was a wee lassie, there was an auld wife that frightened horses. They got nervous whenever she went near them. Everybody said she was a witch. But I don't think she was burned.'

'I came to the conclusion,' said Francis, ignoring her, 'that human beings are incurably depraved, some of course worse than others. Those people boasted of all the burnings they had seen. They had walked as much as twenty miles to see them.'

Magdalen remembered her father's pessimism about human destiny. 'The artists who made all these beautiful things, were they incurably depraved?'

'Bloody-minded tyrants have commissioned magnificent works of art.'

'So there are no exceptions?'

He smiled at her. 'I can think only of one.' He meant her.

She shook her head. She had her faults too: one of them was still loving him though she was married to another man.

Nancy was laughing. She touched her swollen stomach. 'Here's someone who's going to make you change your tune, my love. *He's* not going to be incurably depraved, whatever "depraved" may mean.'

Francis sneered. Anyone who did not like him, thought Magdalen, would have called it an evil sneer. His own son or daughter, it indicated, would, simply because he or she was human, be depraved, in some degree. But then did not Mr Henderson and all the ministers of the Kirk believe that too? Was not one of their favourite sermons about Eve bringing evil into the Garden of Eden or rather into Adam's heart?

She was glad now that she had not married Francis, though she still loved him. Jamie might become a soldier and take part in battles but he would never belittle or hate the men he fought against and perhaps killed.

In one of the paintings there was a nun in a black robe, on her knees praying. That, thought Magdalen, is the kind of life I would have chosen if it had been possible. Then it occurred to her that by that wish she was betraying her children. In a way the nun was like Francis: he confronted humanity with a contemptuous face, she turned her back on it.

In the kitchen the Mintlaw servants were praising their young mistress. They had long ago got over their scruples about serving someone no more blue-blooded than themselves and not much more refined in speech or appearance. They had decided that a shopkeeper's daughter with a kind heart and a lot of money was a more rewarding person to work for than a lord's daughter with hardly any money and too high an opinion of herself. There were none of the penny-pinching economies that went on in many big houses and hurt servants most. Wages were above average and were paid regularly. Mr Dick of Edinburgh must be a staunch Presbyterian: his having amassed so great a fortune was proof of that; and he had brought up his daughter to be one too; she went about the house, singing psalms lustily.

As for Mintlaw, well, maybe it was true that there was a small room which he reserved for himself and kept locked, but many noblemen had similar dens where they liked to get away from the family hubbub. In any case – here their voices dropped – even if it was fitted out as a Papist chapel, it didn't follow that Mintlaw himself was a Papist: he had had it done for the sake of those French and Italian craftsmen. If Janet was going to cast up what he had shouted out in Kinnaird kirk five years ago in defence of old Jessie Gilmour, well, they, for their part, weren't sure any longer that he hadn't been right. Even at the time they hadn't been convinced that Jessie was a witch and, even if she had been, burning her alive had been too cruel.

Janet was dumbfounded. She had known some of those men and women for many years. They had had no education. They couldn't read or write. Yet here they were, just because they had been given soft beds to lie on and coal fires to heat them, daring to criticise the wise men of the Kirk. She saw in their faces something she had never seen before, a pride in themselves, which ought to have been ridiculous in cooks, scullery maids, laundry girls, coal-boys, ostlers, and gardeners, but somehow was not.

Later in Lady Magdalen's bedroom she was dour and sulky.

'I never thought a house could be made so beautiful,' said Lady Magdalen.

85

'A' it taks is money.'

'No. It takes good taste too. Kinnaird will seem very gloomy after this.'

'No' for me. Kinnaird's for living in, this is jist for show.'

'Those wonderful chandeliers!'

'I wadna like the cleaning o' them.'

'The servants all look very content.'

'No' only that, they're sae prood o' themsel's, like a bunch o' bairns.'

'Why shouldn't they be proud to work in so beautiful a house?'

'It's naething to smile at, my lady. Your ain faither willna smile nor ony gentleman that employs servants. *They'll* a' want whit Mintlaw's gi'en his.'

'Don't you think servants' lives should be made more comfortable?'

'Their lives were never meant to be comfortable, my lady. Ask Mr Henderson. He'll tell you. If they're too comfortable, they'll get lazy, baith in body and soul. The Children of Israel in the wilderness werena comfortable. You'll see, my lady, retribution will fa' on this hoose and its maister. The Lord will see to that.'

'I prefer to think that He will give it His blessing and protection.'

21

TO MAGDALEN'S distress, John, and little James too, as soon as they could walk, showed a liking for military games, as if it was inborn in them; which, her father drily assured her, it certainly had been: many of their ancestors on both sides had been redoubtable warriors. Aged six and three respectively, the boys marched about the house wearing wooden swords and banging drums. In vain their mother tried to entice them with picture-books of animals and flowers. Janet tartly reminded her that it was the nature of boys to play with swords and bows and arrows. One day they might have to fight to prevent the Papists from taking over Scotland again. Their mother would be proud of them then.

Magdalen was not all that sure that she would. Killing other men who disagreed with you seemed to her a strange way of proving your love of God.

She still longed for that little girl.

In fairness to their father, she often praised him to them and took them to the great hall to study his portrait. They asked many eager questions. Where was Papa now? Was he fighting for the King? When was he coming back? Why was he staying away so long? Would he bring them presents?

Though James had now been away for three years, far longer than most young husbands and fathers, she never let bitterness or disappointment show. Their father, she told them, was not fighting anyone, for there was no war. He was visiting foreign lands and meeting important people. They would do the same themselves when they were older: it was part of a nobleman's education. He would tell them all about it when he came home. It wouldn't be long now. Yes, of course he would bring them presents.

Then one day a letter arrived from London, addressed to her father. It was curt and almost surly. James expected to be home in two or three weeks: there was nothing in London to keep him there. He asked for preparations to be set in foot so that he could remove from Kinnaird to his own castle at Kincardine as soon as possible. He intended from now on to stay at home and look after his estates. He had had enough of great men and their caprices.

'I fear his meeting with the King did not go well,' said her father.

'Surely the King has forgotten about the coronation?'

'Kings do not forget insults.'

'But Jamie did not intend to insult him.'

'God knows what James intended. The King certainly took it as an insult.'

'But he was very gracious to you, Father.'

At his coronation in Edinburgh Charles had been complimentary about Carnegie's work on behalf of the Crown, and his father's before him. He had made him an earl and had promised him further favours.

'When I spoke to him about James he cut me off.'

'Did he not take into account that Jamie was only twenty-one then?'

'Men have been hanged who were younger. I hope James has now learned that this is an age of intrigues and conspiracies, with every man looking to his own advantage. Even honourable men are compromised. The King, alas, has surrounded himself with time-servers and sycophants. Chief among these is Hamilton, who for some reason is not well disposed towards James. It could be that he is jealous. Everyone knows that James is much more able. But he must learn to curb his tongue and subdue his pride.'

'Do you think he is in earnest when he says he intends to stay at home in future?'

'He was in earnest when he wrote it. I have no doubt, but I cannot see a restless spirit like his content to nibble straws and watch neeps grow.'

'He will seem like a stranger. He will have met so many people that he will have forgotten me.'

'It will take time, my pet. You will have to be patient.'

'I have been very patient, Father.'

'So you have, and I commend you for it. At Kincardine you can both make a fresh start.'

'We had so little in common before, it will be worse now.'

'You have your children in common.'

'Yes.' But she wondered if in a few years' time that would still be true.

She did not want to leave Kinnaird where she had been born and lived most of her life. There were many places, in and out of the house, which she would touch in passing, to reassure herself, as cats did. It would be a long time before there were any such places in Kincardine. She had heard it was a damp gloomy house.

She could not help remembering the beauty and brightness of Mintlaw.

PART TWO

PART TWO

1

ON SPECIAL ALERT, the watchmen on the ramparts were quick to espy and report the approach of Montrose and his two companions, on a dry clear afternoon in May. With one exception, the whole household flocked noisily into the courtyard to greet the returning earl. Southesk held back, though the news had been shouted to him by several. Himself an earl now and, as a Privy Councillor, superior to James in official position, he had decided that not only would it be beneath his dignity, it would also be an unwise policy, for him to make too public a fuss of his son-in-law's return. Until he knew how things stood between Montrose and the King, he had to be discreet. Montrose might well be in mutinous mood. As the King's officer, Southesk must be careful not to appear to be encouraging him.

Magdalen did not at first notice her father's absence. She was too agitated and anxious, indeed almost in tears, and she had her two little sons to hold by the hand. They had gone from being very excited to being very shy and might have run back into the house if she had let go.

It was hard to recognise her husband in this grim-faced, bearded, dusty horseman, who gave her and the two boys brief glances before dismounting and calling for an ostler to take care of his horse. Then he stood staring at the doorway of the house, where her father ought to have been, welcoming him. Whatever rebuff he had suffered at the Court in London, his pride had not been lowered by it; on the contrary, she had never seen him so proud and haughty. Somehow it made him look vulnerable, so that she felt she ought to run forward to comfort and, what was even more absurd, protect him. The doves which had so pleased him at his setting forth were now unheeded. He muttered his displeasure to his two companions who had also dismounted. They looked uncomfortable, as if they had been hearing many grumbles from him recently. They were his servant, Mr Lambie, and his clerk, Mr Saintserf. Young Graham of Morphy had come home by himself more than a year ago.

At last Magdalen found the courage to go towards her husband, pulling the two boys. They were afraid of this scowling stranger, so unlike the portrait in the great hall. James indeed was whimpering.

'Welcome home, Jamie,' she said. She could not stop her voice from trembling.

He gave her a glance calculated and callous in its casualness and then gazed longer but in hardly more kindly a fashion at the two timid little boys.

'What's the matter with them?' he asked roughly. 'God's blood, woman, you have made milksops of them.'

She turned pale. 'They're excited, James. They've been looking forward to your return for weeks.'

She had called him James. Never again would she call him Jamie. That part of their marriage was over.

'Is your father at home?'

'Yes.'

'Where is he then? Is he deliberately avoiding me? Am I in future to be treated like a leper?'

Just then, her father appeared in the doorway, in no hurry, clad in his usual black, and with his gold chain of office round his neck.

'Welcome back, James,' he said, coming forward and holding out his hand.

Montrose took it briefly. 'Did you receive my letter, sir? Have preparations been made for my removal to Kincardine?'

Southesk remained calm, though he resented being addressed as if he was the steward of the household and not its master.

'Yes, James, preparations have been made. Magdalen has been very busy but, no doubt, you will oversee them yourself. In the meantime you will want to refresh yourself. Later we shall talk.'

It was as if they were meeting after only a week or two's separation; so quickly had the old animosity revived.

Magdalen could see that James was wound up, on edge. As his wife, it was her duty to help him relax and feel at home, but he looked ready to repulse her if she tried. Perhaps he was used to being soothed by ladies grander and more practised than she.

He made for his own quarters in the house. She followed, leaving the two boys in Janet's charge.

In the hall he noticed her portrait and went over to stand in front of it.

'Good God, is that supposed to be you?' he asked.

'Yes, James. Mr Jameson came to Kinnaird and painted it.'

'You never were very blithe, but he has made you positively mournful.'

'It is considered a true likeness.'

'Well, I suppose we can always get rid of it and find a more cheerful artist.'

Francis Gowrie had offered to buy it if James didn't like it.

While he was having a bath and changing his clothes she went to the kitchen and arranged a meal for him. She was as courteous as always to the servants, though they had all seen her being slighted. They were careful not to show their sympathy but she was aware of it.

So that they could talk in private, she served him herself.

He ate angrily. 'Why is your father treating me in such an off-hand manner?'

'He is not sure how to treat you, James. None of us is. You have been away so long.'

'I did not know I had to ask anyone's permission as to how long I stayed away.'

He was being petty and knew it and hated himself for it.

'Did you look for Katherine?' she asked.

She knew the question might anger him but not as much as it did. He banged the table with his fist, making the dishes rattle. 'Do you think that because this is not my house but your father's that I can be badgered in it?'

She faced up to him. 'I am not badgering you, James. I would like to know if you have any news of Katherine.'

He was the one who lowered his eyes. 'Well, I have none.'

'Did you not meet anyone who could tell you anything about her?'

'No.'

'Or about him?'

'No. As you can see, this is a topic I find very painful.'

Because, she thought, you did not make much of an effort to find and rescue your sister.

He looked up then and grinned. 'So your old sweetheart Gowrie married his horse-faced shopkeeper's daughter after all. It's the talk of Edinburgh how he's squandered her fortune on turning Mintlaw into an Italian palace.'

'She is not horse-faced and Mintlaw is beautiful.'

He was interested in spite of himself. 'Have you met her? Have you seen it?'

'Yes, I have visited Mintlaw.'

'Did your father allow it?'

'He would have preferred me not to go. He thought you might have objected.'

'I certainly would have. You know my opinion of Gowrie.'

She did not let herself be provoked. She had not yet worked out what her rights were, as a woman and as a wife. They had never been defined. Many would say she had none but this she resolutely rejected.

'If you had brought a great fortune with you, Magdalen, do you know how I would have spent it? On fitting out a regiment.'

And she could have done nothing to prevent it.

'You're never going to forgive me, are you, for staying away so long?'

'I have not said so.'

'No, but it is in your face now and it is in your face in that painting.'

'Why did you stay away so long?'

'What a rash question! Do you really want me to compare the glories of Europe with the dreariness of Kinnaird?'

'Your two sons are here in Kinnaird.'

He winced and closed his eyes. She recognised in him then the youth who had written romantic poetry and dreamed of overcoming all the evil in the world.

'So they are. Fine little fellows. I was too rough with them.'

'So you were.'

He opened his eyes. 'And with you too. I'm sorry. My mind is, I confess, in a state of disorder. I have been ill used by despicable men. Bear with me.'

After he had eaten, he was to go to her father's study and give an account of his travels. She had not been invited.

'I too would like to hear about your travels, James.'

'So you will, more times than you might wish. We travellers are all compulsive braggarts.'

'How did the King receive you, James?'

He shook his head crossly, as if shaking off that impertinent question like a fly. 'That is no concern of yours. I mean, politics is a grimy business. I would not want you besmirched by it.'

He was not being honest. In his present mood, yes, he did believe politics dirtied the soul; but that was not the reason why he wanted her kept out of it. She was not intelligent enough; that was why.

Would he, she wondered, in some agitation, want to sleep

with her that night? Would he assert his right? If so, had she a right as his wife to ask him if he had slept with other women while he was away and, if he admitted it, had she still another right to refuse to let him sleep with her, at any rate that very first night of his home-coming? But what if he took his revenge by spurning her on all other nights? What, then, would happen to their marriage and her hope of that little girl who was to be her companion when James and his sons went off to war?

For the rest of that day Montrose kept aloof from his wife and sons. He sent a written message, short and rather stiff, that he was tired; tomorrow, after a night's rest, he would be better able to comport himself as devoted husband and father.

When she explained to the boys, they were relieved. They needed time to prepare themselves. Today's reunion had been too sudden and overwhelming. They asked many questions.

'Is Father angry with us?'

'Why should he be angry with you? You have done nothing wrong.'

'He said we were milksops. What is a milksop?'

'He just meant that you were very young.'

'I'm nearly seven and James is five.'

'Well, that's very young.'

'Is he a soldier?'

'No, he isn't. There would have to be a war and no one wants that.'

'James and me want it. Don't we, James?'

But James's nod was hesitant.

'Then you're both very foolish. In a war people get killed.'

'Only bad people,' said John.

'Who told you that?'

'Mr Henderson.'

Sometimes the chaplain gave them private religious lessons.

'He said that God wanted good people to win, so He has bad people killed.'

'I'm afraid He has good people killed too.'

They looked at her at first with horrified incredulity and then, as they remembered she was only a woman, who knew nothing about war, with pity and tolerance.

'If he's brought me a sword,' said John, 'for a present, I hope it's a real one that I could kill rabbits with.'

'You're too young to have a real sword.'

'No, I'm not. Maybe James is.'

'No, I'm not,' said James, 'but I wouldn't kill rabbits, I would cut off the heads of thistles.'

'What do you hope he's brought you, Mama?' asked John.

'I haven't thought about it.'

'Would you like a silk dress? A blue one, like the lady in the painting.'

'Yes, I would like that.'

But next morning, when Montrose brought out the presents, there were no real swords and no blue silk dress. The boys, however, were delighted with their suits of armour, made of silver inlaid with enamelled red roses. They had been made for the sons of an Italian duke, said Montrose, and were considered works of art: the silversmith had a famous name. Even Francis Gowrie would approve of them.

'But I see you don't, Magdalen.'

'Mama doesn't like things that have to do with war,' said John.

'They're beautifully made,' said Magdalen.

Montrose helped his sons to put them on. They fitted well enough. In great excitement the boys stalked about, glittering in the sunshine. The roses looked like blobs of blood.

'This, my dear, is for you.'

It was a small book.

'A Bible. In French. As you can see, it has been much used.'

But by whom? There was a fragrance off it. Men as well as women used perfumes but this surely was feminine. Had some woman given it to him, some lover? His signature was scrawled across the frontispiece. The flyleaves were written on too; he did this with all his books. There was a strange drawing of roses with thorns and a cross. There were also, intertwined, the letters J, M, and E. James Montrose, yes, but whom or what did the E represent? That French lady, whoever she was? Had the Bible been hers? If so, was his giving it to Magdalen a gesture of contrition or of contempt? She would not ask now or ever. Perhaps one day he would tell her.

He read aloud one of the sentences he had written. ' "Honor mihi vita potior." "I prefer honour to life." '

'What do you mean by "honour", James?'

He was taken aback. In the early days of their marriage, they had played chess together. Sometimes she had baffled him by some move so shrewd that he had thought it must be accidental. This question was such a move.

'Only a woman would ask that. Every man of breeding knows instinctively what honour is.'

'You should be able to tell me then.'

'It can't easily be put into words.'

'Why not?'

He was still checkmated. 'It is too subtle a concept. I might as well try to explain the beatings of my heart.'

'Women's hearts beat too. Do they have honour?'

'Good God, yes. Everyone knows what a woman's honour is.'

'Does it consist only in her keeping herself pure and so not bringing disgrace on her husband and family?'

He scowled. 'What is all this, Magdalen? You have become quite the little philosopher.'

'I have had a long time to think about these things.'

'What else could a woman's honour consist of? By their very nature, women are not exposed to the strains and temptations of public life.'

Like all men, he thought he knew everything there was to know about women, those simple creatures, but the truth was he, like them, knew very little. She remembered his poems, full of neatly worded compliments but empty of true insights.

'One might say that women are to be envied,' he said. 'At Kincardine your chief concern will be to finish your tapestry.'

Did he mean to insult her? Perhaps he did not realise that he had insulted her.

'And you will have the garden to plant with flowers. It has been badly neglected, I believe. And the household to manage. Useful and honourable tasks.'

This time she was sure that the insult contained in the word *was* intended.

'Shall I not also have my children to look after?'

'Certainly, though I intend to hire a tutor for them. They must be brought up accustomed to manly pursuits.'

'Such as?'

'Riding, hunting, fencing, archery.'

He then turned from her and gave his attention to the boys. They responded gleefully. He was already their favourite. Her they merely loved, him they worshipped.

2

THAT AFTERNOON, WHILE Montrose was at the stables arranging for the removal to Kincardine and watching John and James make good their boasts of being expert and intrepid riders – even if their mounts were small ponies – Magdalen's father came to her room to offer her some advice. He found her working at her tapestry, with Janet's help. He sent Janet away. Magdalen kept on sewing, adding to Christ's foot.

'At Kincardine,' said her father, smiling approvingly, 'you will be kept busy with many similar useful tasks.'

'Yes, Father. So James has already told me.'

Something in her tone made him look sharply at her. There was more than the usual innocence and submissiveness in her face.

He spoke sternly. 'Chief among them will be to take care of your husband.'

'And of my children.'

'Yes, of course.'

'James is going to hire a tutor for them. He says I have turned them into milksops.'

'Be fair. Most fathers want their sons to be trained in martial arts.'

'Most mothers do not.'

'There you show your youth and inexperience.' And also, he could have added, that peculiar singularity – was it retarded development or godliness? – which had so often exasperated her sisters and puzzled him. 'Most mothers, I would say, are proud of

102

their soldier sons. Patriotism is not confined to the male gender, I hope.'

'Like honour?'

'Honour?'

'James and I had a discussion about honour.'

'You know, Magdalen, your mother had opinions too but she wisely kept them to herself. Never once in all the years we were married did she contradict me, though there must have been times when she must have thought I was wrong.'

'But, Father, isn't a wife meant to be a helpmate? Is it not her place, laid on her by God, to advise her husband if she can?'

Was she, this slight girl of 21, making fun of him? And of all men who domineered women? He had met many couples where the woman was by far the more intelligent of the two and yet, because of custom, was expected to say nothing while her husband spouted nonsense.

'In domestic matters only,' he said, rather feebly.

'Should she just stand by in silence even if she is convinced that what he is doing or is about to do will destroy him?'

' "Destroy him"? Upon my soul, you use strong words. Yes, she should, nonetheless. Sitting at home among her children, how can she be in a position to judge her husband's actions? Her first consideration must be the success of her marriage. You will have more children, my pet. There will be girls among them. Let them be your life's work and your abiding delight.'

'Yes, Father.' She added a few more stitches. 'How did the King receive James in London?'

Her father frowned. 'Has he not told you himself?'

'No.'

'Then evidently he does not want you to be told.'

'I jaloused that. Is he going to give up politics, as he said in the letter?'

'That was not to be taken seriously. Do not doubt it, Magdalen, your husband will play a prominent part in his country's affairs. He will not be left alone, even if he should wish it. Those opposed to the King's policies would dearly like to recruit him to their cause.'

'Can it ever be right, Father, for subjects to take up arms against the King, even if they think he is acting like a tyrant?'

She asked so ingenuously and yet it was so very pertinent a question, one that would vex men's minds more and more as the King's encroachments grew.

Ideally, the King should rule for the good of the whole country and, to that end, surround himself with wise and impartial counsellors. Unfortunately, the present King was sly, devious, and autocratic, his advisers venal, sycophantic, and incompetent. Honest men, like Southesk himself, who wished to give him their loyal support, might have to compromise their principles or abandon them altogether, and so be no longer honest. There would be much changing of sides, many charges of apostasy.

He was not prepared to explain all that to a young woman of 21, even if she was his beloved youngest daughter. So he got up, rather abruptly, and left.

3

HER FATHER WAS right. Magdalen did find plenty at Kincardine to keep her usefully occupied. First, though, she had to overcome homesickness. She missed, unbearably, scenes near and far that she had known and loved all her life, from the hills in the distance to the large rowan in the garden on whose trunk were carved the initials of all her brothers and sisters. Kinnaird too had been surrounded with pleasant fields and woods, whereas Kincardine had barren moors all round it while the castle itself was begirt with tall pines that, especially on dull wet days, seemed to harbour malignant spirits, unlike the rowan which had kept them away, or so tradition believed.

She had to get to know and win the trust of servants who, to begin with, were just that, servants, and not old friends like those at Kinnaird.

A deputation from the kirk session of Auchterarder, men twice or three times her age, came, caps in hand, to say slyly that they had heard that at Kinnaird, young though she was, she had dispensed relief to the poor of the parish. Would she be so gracious as to take charge of it here too? She suggested that they should apply to her husband. It was the earl, they said, who had sent them to her.

The village dominie, Mr Blair, a worried-looking young man in threadbare clothes, was also passed on to her by James when he came begging for equipment for his school and, more diffidently, a few extra merks of stipend for himself. He divulged that the minister of the parish, Mr Graham, was opposed to any increase in the dominie's pay. Schoolteachers must be kept in their proper place, which was well beneath that of ministers. Magdalen liked the meek modest young man and promised him what help she could.

She tackled all these tasks bravely, though she was soon pregnant again and suffered badly from morning sickness.

James was now a more considerate, more adept lover. Had she to thank a number of French and Italian ladies for that? She did not mind, nothing would matter if only it was a girl this time. Nightly she prayed for one. She had a selection of names ready. Katherine was not among them but Lilias was.

Her unhappy sister-in-law had at her own request moved out of the castle into a small secluded cottage on the estate. There she lived alone, her two children having gone to stay with their Aunt Margaret in Dalhousie, where it was much more comfortable and they were spared their mother's lamentations. A stream with deep pools flowed past her house and James was afraid that she might drown herself in one of them, but Magdalen felt sure that the hope of Colquhoun's return one day would keep her alive. If she heard that there were guests at the castle, she would walk with bedraggled clothes and unkempt hair to assail them with questions about her husband. This was a painful embarrassment to James.

He too kept himself busy, reading, writing, thinking, hunting (often accompanied by the two boys) and entertaining visitors, mostly from Edinburgh, with some of whom he had long private conversations. One was the famous Earl of Rothes, who arrived one day with a company of gentlemen.

Rothes was then the most popular man in Scotland because of his championing of the Presbyterian cause against the King, but he did not strike Magdalen as being at all devout. It was his other reputation she was reminded of, that of a flirtatious charmer. It was said by his detractors that, when he found the comely rich heiress he was always on the look-out for, he would at once retire from the ecclesiastical fray and settle down to live in sybaritic comfort, probably in England, where such an heiress was more likely to be found than in poverty-stricken Scotland. His appearance was striking, hair black as coal and face white as milk. It was rumoured he had a consumption and, indeed, coughed a great deal: in spite of which he was very good company, with frank and witty comments on the leading men of the day, not excluding those in his own party.

One evening, when the discussion was again about the King's threatened encroachments, with James the most passionate in opposition to them, Rothes, cool as ever, said, with a smile at Magdalen: 'That is all very well, James. But is it worth civil war? Is there anything on God's earth that would justify the killing of Scotsmen by Scotsmen?'

'Surely there is, John. Scotsmen who join in with the English to subvert their country's constitution and rob their Kirk of its rights are traitors and deserve to die.'

Rothes was amused. 'But, James, is not war a gamble, with the winners taking all, including the heads of the losers? Yours is much too handsome to end up on a spike above the Tolbooth in Edinburgh.'

Magdalen remembered how her father had once, in grim jest, prophesied that fate for James.

But James would not have it that war was a gamble. It was a noble crusade, or ought to be, and those in the right would always prevail if they had enough faith in themselves and their cause.

Magdalen noticed Lord Rothes's henchmen exchanging winks. Did they, in his absence, mock James's youthful idealism? Like many others, they would wait to see how the situation developed; if not to their advantage, they would back out. James, though, man of honour, if he gave his word, would keep to it, even if it led to his destruction. If she could, if he would listen, she must find a way to warn him.

'But surely, James,' Rothes was now saying, 'if history teaches us anything, it is that right prevails only when it is supported by superior force?'

'No, sir. There are enough instances in history of right prevailing not because of superior force but because those who fought for it were willing to die to the last man.'

'Willing to kill, do you not mean? Wars are won by killing, not by dying. One of the damnedest things, you know, is that one's opponents, stubborn scoundrels, will never admit that their cause is vile and give it up. Even on the gallows they are prepared to argue that they were in the right. I shouldn't wonder if, when they appear before their Maker, their first words are indignant justifications. A man can always be persuaded of the errors of his ways if he is alive, never if he is dead.'

Those seemed to Magdalen wise and true words, though negligently drawled. Yet, to her amazement, all the time Rothes was carrying on a dalliance with one of the tablemaids, Cissie Baxter, a bonny, buxom, cheerful girl of 17. He kept giving her smiles of intrigue and she, though not so accomplished at the game, kept returning them, with blushes. Once he let his hand alight on her buttock. The gem in his ring glittered; as did her eyes. Her bosom heaved. She became clumsy in handling the dishes. She had the reputation of being too free with her favours, but this was a great gentleman, not a coarse bumpkin. She would be able to boast till she was an old woman that she had been to bed with the famous Presbyterian earl. There might be a bagful of guineas in it for her and, if she had his bastard, more bagfuls.

That was how Cissie saw it. How did Lord Rothes see it? Would he, so intelligent in other matters, risk contumely and ridicule for the sake of a few minutes' pleasure with a maidservant, whose cheeks were red and whose breasts were large? Suppose he got her pregnant. She might be pleased to have an earl's bastard, but what of him? Would it not trouble his conscience that he had a son or daughter being brought up in a mean cottage, with for a stepfather a cowherd or ostler or baker, or whoever Cissie eventually married?

His henchmen were aware of what was going on and found it entertaining. This did not surprise Magdalen, but so too was the Revd. Mr Graham amused, which astonished her. The old minister had been drinking more wine than he should but not even when drunk should he be condoning and even encouraging these preliminaries to fornication, that heinous sin. When he looked up at Cissie, it was not to freeze her with a puritanical scowl but rather to give her a maudlin blessing. Lord Rothes, the Kirk's foremost champion, was the Lord's anointed and could do no wrong, and must be indulged in all things. That was how she interpreted the white-haired minister's crapulous leer.

Meanwhile, James was searching his memory for instances from Greek and Roman history of right triumphing over might. He was quite oblivious to what was going on between Cissie and his chief guest.

Afterwards in their bedroom she decided not to mention it. In any case James had himself drunk too much and besides was hoarse with talking; so he quickly fell asleep. As she lay beside him in the dark she thought she heard coughing; but it could have been the wind.

4

NEXT MORNING, LORD Rothes was as urbane as ever as he sat beside Magdalen in the courtyard in sunshine, watching James and others put on a display of swordplay and archery. A few minutes before, she had had a bad bout of sickness and had come out to recover in the fresh air.

'Are you feeling better now?' he asked, with genuine solicitude.

She could easily understand why women were charmed by him. Was it possible that this elegant gentleman, so civilised and so much in command of himself, had last night lustfully made use of a servant girl's luscious body?

'Yes, thank you, my lord,' she said.

'My friends call me John. I would very much like if you would. I shall take the liberty of calling you Magdalen: such a beautiful name. It is heartless of me to say so, Magdalen, but a little pallor becomes you wonderfully. I don't wonder that Jameson was inspired to paint that marvellous portrait.'

'James doesn't like it.'

'James, if I may say so, is a better judge of a war-horse than of a painting.'

He turned his head away for a bout of coughing, with his handkerchief at his mouth. 'I beg your pardon,' he said, when he had recovered. 'May I confide in you, Magdalen?'

Surely he was not going to confess about him and Cissie?

'Were you present when your good-sister Lady Lilias asked me if I had heard aught of her husband Sir John Colquhoun?'

'Yes, I was present.'

So had James been, squirming and glowering.

'I'm sorry to say that you heard me tell a lie.'

'Do you mean, you have news of him?'

'Yes. A friend of mine, also a friend of Sir John's, I may say, returned from the Continent a week or two ago. He met Sir John in Paris.'

'Was Katherine with him?'

'No. I'm afraid I have no information about the young lady. She was not mentioned. My friend was given the strong impression that Sir John is confident that he will be pardoned in a year or two's time and allowed to return to his estate on Loch Lomond. I understand his wife is willing to have him back.'

'That is all she lives for. She has long since forgiven him. Will he be pardoned?'

'He has influential friends. I have to say he was always a popular fellow.'

'He treated Lilias shamefully.'

'So he did but, as you say, she has forgiven him.'

'What will happen to Katherine if he comes back? What has happened to her? No one seems to know and no one cares.'

'In such cases, Magdalen, a man's friends are not inclined to pass moral judgment on him. They think they do not know all the facts and forby they are too conscious of the motes in their own eyes.'

'Women see it differently.'

'I am sure they do.'

'Poor Katherine.'

'Poor Katherine indeed. I must be frank, though, and say that I have heard she was herself a great deal to blame.'

'She was only seventeen.'

'Ah yes, very young.' Was he reflecting that Cissie Baxter was no older?

'Why didn't you tell Lilias the truth? It would have made her happy.'

'I feared it might do the opposite. But, if you think it would give her any comfort, please tell her yourself. You can assure her that her husband is in good health. His only complaint seems to be lack of money.'

'Have you told James?'

'I would sooner put my head in a lion's mouth.'

Just then James approached them, panting, sword in hand. His white shirt was soaked with sweat.

'Tell me, James,' said Rothes, smiling, 'is the sword really an effective weapon? Is there not nowadays a school of thought in military academies, which believes it is not? When the swordsman's arm is raised to deliver the blow the sturdy pikeman sticks him in the belly. I am referring to a swordsman on horseback, which of course is how gentlemen fight.'

'The pikeman's skull is cleft in twain before he has time to deliver his blow.'

'In which case would he not simply pierce the horse's belly, so that it would rear up and unseat its rider? When he is sprawling on the ground, how easy to despatch him! Or is there an agreement among soldiers that horses, which, after all, have never been asked their opinions, ought as far as possible to be spared?'

'A good war-horse is an active combatant,' said James. 'A cavalry charge, for those making it, is the most exhilarating thing on earth, and for those facing it the most fearsome.'

'Have you ever taken part in a cavalry charge, James?'

'At Artois, at the academy there, they arrange mock charges. I have taken part in those. The foe were dummies stuffed with straw. Nevertheless, it was exhilarating to slash off their heads.'

'James, you are making your lovely young wife feel faint.'

James apologised, somewhat perfunctorily, and then went over to his sons, who, wearing their silver armour, were seated on stools, fascinated by the flashing swords.

'How childish men are,' she murmured.

Rothes chuckled. 'How can I deny that? You should hear the debates in Parliament.'

'Is there going to be war? My father thinks so.'

'There will be, unless one side gives way.'

'Will one side give way?'

'Ah, that is the question, as the fellow says in the play.'

'And what is the answer?'

'Most men think that if their cause is good and that of their opponents bad then it would be immoral and cowardly to give in without a fight. As you know, that is decidedly James's view.'

'Yes.'

'He is not yet quite won over to our way of thinking. He still has some small theological doubts about taking up arms against his monarch. We shall send some divine to persuade him. Someone reasonable. James has a horror of fanatics, though, to be candid, is he not one himself when he has a sword in his hand?'

Cheered on by his sons, James was giving them an exhibition of how to slash off imaginary heads.

5

LORD ROTHES AND his entourage had hardly left the castle, when Magdalen, in the room where she kept the household accounts and interviewed anyone with a request or complaint, had a visit from Mistress Nicholson, the housekeeper, a big dour-faced woman of about fifty, with a mannish voice and mannish hands. According to Janet, she was very pious and spent hours praying. 'No' asking the Lord, mind you, but telling Him.' She was disliked and feared by most of the maidservants. Magdalen herself found her intimidating and would have got rid of her if she hadn't been at Kincardine longer than Magdalen herself.

'I'm sorry tae trouble ye, my lady,' she said.

Magdalen always felt tingles of unease when this woman addressed her. It wasn't that she was rude but, on the contrary, that she was so ingratiating: it did not go well with her harsh voice and coarse face.

'It's no trouble, Mistress Nicholson. Please sit down and tell me what's the matter.'

'If you dinna mind, my lady, I'll staun'. I ken my place, no' like ithers I could name. I wadna be here, my lady, if I didna think I owed it to you, to his lordship the earl, and to oor Saviour Jesus Christ.'

I am pious myself, thought Magdalen, at least I try to be, so why am I so often distrustful of other people's piety? Especially this woman's. She always comes to have some girl punished, never to plead on any girl's behalf.

'What is it you wish to tell me?'

114

'I'm laith tae soil my mooth and your ears, my lady.'

Why, then, speak with such gloating relish?

'It's aboot that shameless young whure, Cissie Baxter.'

Was she deranged? Did not many women at her time of life, especially if they had never been married, suffer changes in their bodies which also affected their minds?

Mistress Nicholson was now panting, as if she had just run up a flight of steps. 'She used her whure's tricks to win her way intae Lord Rothes's bed.'

'Please do not use that word in my presence.'

'There's nae ither word tae describe her, my lady. She took money.'

'Is your complaint against Lord Rothes too, who gave her the money?'

'She did a' the enticing, my lady, wi' thae big white briests that wad entice Christ Jesus Himsel'.'

Magdalen's scalp went cold with disgust. There was spittle on the woman's chin.

'She should be whupped. On her bare erse. Till the bluid rins. Till she screamed for mercy. I'd dae it mysel'.' Her voice rose to a demented shriek.

There is someone else present in this room, thought Magdalen, being defiled by the evil in this woman's mind: my unborn daughter. Was her innocence already destroyed before she was born, as indeed Mr Henderson was fond of saying in his sermons?

Mistress Nicholson, having lost all control of herself, was weeping and mumbling obscenities. She kept raising her right arm as if it was wielding the bloodstained whip.

Magdalen stood up. The woman would have to see a doctor; obviously, she was not well in her mind. She might have to be locked up in the meantime. There was a cell in the basement of the castle where in the old days mad people had been confined.

Magdalen remembered Francis Gowrie's saying that the people watching old Jessie burn had laughed. They must have been ill in their minds too.

Who in the world was sane? In a few years' time there might be war, with Scotsmen killing Scotsmen, in the name of God. Was not that the greatest insanity?

She put her hand on Mistress Nicholson's arm, to restrain it. To her horror, it was seized and covered with wet kisses.

'I'm sorry, my lady, I'm sorry. It comes ower me at times. I canna stop it.'

She let go and rushed out of the room.

Magdalen involuntarily rubbed her hand against her dress but that filthy thing, whatever it was, now stuck to it and nothing would ever get it off again.

Usually so ready with advice and information, Janet this time was sweirt. She stood, tight-lipped, her fingers going as if counting beads. 'Dinna ask me, my lady.'

'Is the poor woman mad?'

'She's first in kirk every Sunday and it's her voice you hear abune a' the ithers singing psalms.'

But was not excessive religiosity a form of madness, causing the destruction of churches, the wrecking of beautiful works of art, and the burning of old women?

'What is the matter with her, Janet? I can see you know. Has it to do with her age?'

'She's the same age as me. And, like her, I was never mairried.'

'What has that to do with it?'

'Mair than you think maybe.'

Magdalen began to understand. She had sometimes wondered if being a spinster, and a virgin, accounted for Janet's own peculiarities. According to Mr Henderson, women were intended by God to get married and have children: that was their chief purpose in life. Therefore, they must have done to them what produced children. If they remained virginal all their lives, did they become unfulfilled and embittered? But, in that case, what of nuns?

It was a most un-nunlike young woman who came flouncing in, with curtsies just too extravagant to be respectful. There was mischief in them or perhaps it was fairer to say they were meant in fun. For Cissie was far from conscience-stricken. She was very pleased with herself and she looked on Magdalen as her mistress, yes, as the earl's wife and therefore a great lady, yes, but also as a young woman like herself.

'You wanted to see me, my lady?'

Magdalen could have called her Baxter and so put her in her place, but she did not have the heart.

'Yes, Cissie, I did want to see you.'

Better to leave Mistress Nicholson out of it. Simply reprimand the girl for having the impudence to sleep with a guest. But how to put it?

'I believe, Cissie, you made a nuisance of yourself last night with one of his lordship's guests.'

Cissie had no inhibitions about sitting down or about crossing her legs either, to reveal shapely ankles. She burst out laughing. 'A nuisance! That's a new name for it. I ken auld Nicholson was here clyping aboot me, but I'll explain aboot her in a meenute. Lord Rothes is the guest you mean, my lady. Weel, he invited me. I wasna sure I should, but Mr Graham the meenister whispered tae me it wad be a' richt, the Lord wad forgie me. So I thocht I should obleege the gentleman. That's a' there was tae it, my lady.'

When Magdalen had got her breath back, she said, in a faint voice: 'Did Mr Graham actually give you permission?'

'That he did, my lady. I could tell you things aboot him that wad amaze you. He wanted me himsel' aince. In the kirk it was. He held me back after the kirk had skailed. He went doon on his knees, begging me, wi' tears in his een. That's the gospel truth. May I roast in hell if it's a lie.'

117

Magdalen indeed was amazed. 'He couldn't have been aware of what he was saying.'

'You mean, because he was drunk? Weel, he wasna drunk in kirk, was he? In ony case, I've heard him and ither meenisters say that there are chosen folk, chosen by the Lord I mean, wha canna dae wrang nae maitter whit they dae. Weel, I thocht Lord Rothes was bound to be ane o' them, so if he was excused sae was I.'

What she was saying, though absurd, was sound Calvinist doctrine.

Magdalen was in danger of appearing the one at fault. How dare she reprove this happy, good-hearted, obliging girl!

'Did he give you money?'

'I hope you'll excuse me saying that's private, my lady.'

'Didn't it occur to you that you could have become pregnant?'

'Sure it did. It occurred to him tae. Maybe I *am* pregnant.' The glance she directed at Magdalen's stomach said: 'Like you, my lady.' She went on: 'I was going tae tell you aboot auld Nicholson.'

Magdalen should have stopped her then but didn't.

'She's got a spite against me. Dae you ken why? You see, she likes tae hae a lassie sleeping wi' her.'

But what was so shocking about that? Beds were scarce and had to be shared. Magdalen herself had often slept with one or other of her sisters.

'The trouble is, she canna keep her haun's tae hersel'. If you see whit I mean, my lady.'

Magdalen saw, and blushed, and felt nausea. She could only too easily imagine those big mannish hands busy all over a young girl's naked body.

'I telt her straight tae her face I wasna haeing ony auld wife pawing me, so she's been waiting for a chance to pey me back. I hope you don't mind me saying this, my lady; there are lots o' things going on in the castle that you nor my lord the earl ken onything aboot.'

Yet, where in all this was his lordship, the earl? Too immersed in national matters to bother about what was going on in the parish or even in his own castle. He would dismiss this affair of Cissie and Lord Rothes or that of Cissie and Mistress Nicholson as parochial clishmaclavers, not worthy of the future general's attention. Yet it was these which would be avidly talked about all over the parish, in every house and croft, not the threatened imposition of bishops or the insolence of Hamilton, the King's favourite, or the sinister ambitions of Argyll, or the suspect loyalty of Gordon.

'Can you keep a secret, my lady?' asked Cissie, now very much the co-conspirator. 'I'm betrothed, or I think I am'. She made a face.

'Betrothed?'

'Weel, we've exchanged vows, ower a stream: according tae an auld custom, he said.'

'Who is he?'

'You'd never guess.'

There were any number of men in the parish who had a fancy for Cissie.

'He's never dirtied his haun's,' said Cissie, giving a hint.

Not an artisan or servant then.

'I'd better tell you, for you'd never guess. The dominie, Mr Blair.'

Magdalen was astonished and not pleased. Mr Blair was a graduate of St Andrews University and his father had been a minister. He was in a class well above Cissie's. Surely he should be aiming higher than an illiterate maidservant however bonny. He was so serious too, while she made fun of everything.

'He wants me tae gang tae Dundee tae meet his mither. If she approves o' me then we'll get mairried. But I don't ken that I want tae mairry him. No' because I think he's too guid for me, even if he can write Greek and I can hardly write my ain name.'

'What are you trying to say, Cissie?'

'When he fin's oot aboot me and the gentleman, for somebody's sure tae tell him, he'll still want tae mairry me. That maks me want tae bre'k his hert.'

'Because he loves you so much you want to break his heart? That's a strange thing to say.'

'It's because I think I love him and I dinna want tae.'

In that case, better for them both if the marriage never took place. All the same, Magdalen would have liked to have the wedding in the castle, with all the village invited: so much more joyous than preparing for war.

Cissie got up. 'Weel, I'd better get back tae the kitchen.'

Back to the dish-washing, the scouring of pots, the scrubbing of tables, the sweeping of floors.

'Mind you,' she said, at the door, 'I'd try tae mak him a guid wife.'

6

LORD ROTHES'S EMISSARY, Mr Robert Murray, minister of Methuen, a quiet scholarly man, came to Kincardine a few days later and lost no time in removing James's last doubts as to the propriety of opposing, by arms if necessary, a king driven to despotic acts through the influence of malignant favourites. The Lord's blessing, if the insurrection was on His behalf, was assured. Mr Murray cited instances from the Scriptures. He urged James to hasten to Edinburgh so that he could play his part in the debates, negotiations, and preparations. If he delayed too long, opportunities, such as political and military appointments, might be missed.

All that was what James wanted to hear.

Soon after the minister's visit he set out for Edinburgh. At that time the capital was indeed a wasps' byke which the clumsy interventions of King Charles had overturned. He just could not understand why he, the King, answerable only to God, should not appoint bishops to oversee the Scottish Church, if that was what he wanted. The Scots might not like it but that was beside the point. Their duty as subjects was to comply even if it meant their having to jettison dogmas and prejudices. For peace and Christian unity to be restored to the country, all that was needed was for the King's edicts to be heeded and obeyed. To him it was incredible, not to say humiliating, that the Scots should keep on sending relays of representatives to London, assuring him of their loyalty and devotion while at the same time in Edinburgh and other towns dissidents gathered round Mercat Crosses vowing defiance and rebellion. If he persevered, surely they must come to their senses and acknowledge how contradictory and contrary their behaviour was.

Instead of coming to their senses, they went, in the King's view, totally mad. On 23 July 1637, in the High Kirk of St Giles, when the dean, Dr Hanna, started to read from the new liturgy, as the King had ordered, the large audience, nobles in the galleries and commoners below, immediately protested, the former with well-bred restraint but the latter with plebeian fury. Bibles, stools, and insults were hurled at the unfortunate dean and a riot ensued. Finally the kirk had to be forcibly emptied and the doors locked. Out on the streets any prelate unlucky enough to be recognised was in danger of being seized and hanged.

Though the mob's violence disgusted Montrose, he did not give up his allegiance to the anti-bishop, and therefore the anti-King, faction. He soon became one of its leaders, buzzing as angrily as any. Once, from the top of a beer barrel, he harangued a large crowd, causing Lord Rothes to jest that one day he might find himself addressing a much larger crowd from a much higher position. He was voted to be one of the five nobles on the Commission to negotiate with the King and, in February 1638, was among the first to sign the National Covenant in Greyfriars Kirkyard. This, though dedicated 'For God and the King', was inevitably seen by the latter as downright defiance; the former's approval was taken for granted. Some senior Presbyterians, among them Magdalen's father, called for caution but their advice was angrily rejected by the majority, among whom Montrose was the most outspoken.

Convinced that only force would subdue the treasonous Scots, the King began to make preparations for war.

The Covenanters were likewise employed. Arms were bought. Envoys were sent to Germany to recruit among the Scots mercenaries there. Noblemen hurried home to fortify their castles and conscript their tenants. None was more energetic than Montrose, now a colonel.

Magdalen's father kept her informed. 'I am afraid,' he wrote, 'that James has become one of the hottest heads among the malcontents. I shall not vex you with an account of what took place between him and me at the recent General Assembly in Glasgow Cathedral. Enough to say that, though manifestly in the wrong, he chose to pick a quarrel with me in that public place and used some intemperate language. I would shrug my shoulders and leave him to his fate if he was not my favourite daughter's husband and the father of my grandsons, and also if I was not convinced that he has perversely chosen the wrong side since he is at heart much more Royalist than Presbyterian and will discover that too late when he has become irretrievably committed. No doubt there will be a great changing of sides and back again in the course of the forthcoming conflict, but James's sense of honour is such that, when at last he realises that he has chosen wrongly, he will still persist and then be in the tragic position of fighting for what he no longer believes in. This would leave him disillusioned, embittered, and vulnerable. I entreat you, therefore, my love, when he returns home to drum up soldiers among his tenantry, to use all your influence to keep him with you for as long as you can. When a man is in doubt as to where his true duty lies – and what honest man is not, in these bewildering times? – surely it is not dishonourable to stay at home with his family, helping his country, not by taking part in sterile debates or a useless and ruinous war, but by putting his estates into good order. I hear rumours that James's are already encumbered with debt and hardly able to afford the expense of fitting out and maintaining any considerable body of militia.'

7

WHILE THOSE TURBULENT events were taking place in Edinburgh with, as the participants thought, the fate of the kingdom at stake, life went on in Kincardine in a quiet uneventful way, or so it would have seemed to a passing stranger, who would not be aware of the various local dramas: such as, for instance, the betrothal of the dominie, Mr Blair, to a maidservant, Cissie Baxter, now the speak of the parish, as indeed was also Cissie's winning her way into the great gentleman's feather bed. It was generally agreed that, if she married the dominie, she would make his life a torment, and it was hoped that his lordship, the earl, or, in his place, her ladyship, would forbid the marriage.

One Saturday afternoon, when the dominie, bespectacled and knock-knee'd, with his pockets stuffed with books, arrived at the castle to see her ladyship, John Galloway, the gatekeeper gave him a lewd but friendly grin. Like every male in the parish over the age of puberty, not excluding, if truth be told, the 70-year-old minister, Galloway often day-dreamed of having Cissie himself in a feather bed, he wearing a white silk nightshirt (such as Lord Rothes had worn, according to report) and Cissie wearing nothing at all.

It so happened that afternoon that Lady Magdalen was not feeling well. There was a sharp pain in her womb. Dr Muirkirk had been sent for. She was terrified of losing her daughter. She found it difficult therefore to be as patient with Mr Blair as she should. She had concluded that he ought not to marry Cissie but instead some older more respectable woman, perhaps the widow of a schoolmaster or minister, who would see to it he was well fed and decently clothed. Besides, his wishing to marry an ignorant, immoral, and sensual girl like Cissie suggested his unfitness to be a teacher of young children, as it seemed some parents were complaining. Some of the jokes being told about him and Cissie had come, in watered-down versions, to Lady Magdalen's ears.

That afternoon she was ready to cut him short. She would not forbid the marriage because she did not think that she, or James, or Mr Graham, or anyone, had a right to do so, but she would let him know that she did not approve of it. Was she to some degree prejudiced by her own not very successful marriage? She asked herself that and shrank from answering it.

She was quite taken aback, and thrown into remorseful confusion, when he began to talk, eagerly, not about Cissie and himself, but about two of his pupils, a boy and a girl, John Reid and Mary Ranald, who were so exceptionally gifted that they deserved, in his opinion, to be sent to University. He knew this was not possible in Mary's case but perhaps a place could be found for her in some nobleman's household as a kind of governess to small girls. As for the boy, if funds could be found to award him a scholarship, the University would be pleased to accept him once they were given evidence of his abilities: already he could tackle mathematical problems beyond the reach of the dominie himself. Mary's father, a tenant farmer with a few stony acres, might be unwilling, for he had an ailing wife and needed Mary at home to look after her brothers and sisters, but perhaps he could be persuaded by her ladyship. John's father, on the other hand, though only a tender of pigs, was proud of his son's talents and would make sacrifices to give him the chance to cultivate them. It was not uncommon for the sons of poor men to attend Scottish universities and rise to eminence. In John's case, unfortunately, there was a difficulty: he was a very diffident boy, too easily discouraged. It was a pity he did not have Mary's spirit.

Magdalen was more interested in the girl. She could well be found a position as child-minder or nursemaid, but she would have to be personable and well-spoken, as well as clever.

'The girl,' she said, 'how old is she?'

'They are both twelve.'

'What is she like in appearance?'

He hesitated. 'She is beautiful.'

That was more than Magdalen had expected or wanted. Not coarse-featured would have been quite enough. Few noble-women were likely to take into their employ a girl of low birth who outshone them in beauty.

'Is she uncouth in her speech?' As so many of the village children were.

'She can speak very well when it is necessary.'

What paragon was this, clever, spirited, beautiful, and well-spoken? Did such flowers sprout on middens?

'Can you bring her to see me, Mr Blair? And her father too.'

'Yes, my lady. Shall I bring John and his father too?'

'In their case, I think we should wait until my husband comes home.'

'When do you expect his lordship?'

'Any day now. As you may know, Mr Blair, there is danger of war. My husband will have more important matters on his mind than a village boy's education.'

'I want myself to ask his permission to marry.'

Suddenly she felt faint. There was a roaring in her head: was it of cannons? She smelled smoke: had the castle been set on fire? She heard screams: men were being butchered, women raped, and children kicked aside. James was in the midst of it all, exulting.

She heard the dominie say, anxiously: 'Are you all right, my lady?'

Then Janet came rushing in and ordered the dominie to leave. The birth, now imminent, might be the death of her young mistress, without fools like the dominie causing her extra stress.

8

TWO DAYS LATER, when James came home, he had little time or inclination to take an interest in parochial affairs; among which he seemed to include her pregnancy, for though, as he hurried to and fro, he did ask her how she felt, he hardly waited for an answer. There was always some messenger to be received, another to be sent out; important visitors to confer with; recruiting forays to be made (taking John with him in spite of the boy's susceptibility to sore throats); recruits to be drilled and instructed; and the forthcoming campaign to be planned. He was realising his boyhood ambitions. Only on the battlefield would he be happier. So Magdalen thought, with some bitterness.

He designed for himself a uniform that would suit the rank of colonel and also of general. The jacket was bright red, so that his men could easily see him on the battlefield and be given heart. It also meant, Magdalen pointed out, that he would just as easily be seen by the enemy and become a target for their cannon and muskets. That was a risk, he said cheerfully, incidental to high command. When she asked him how it was that, though he was only 27, he was about to be made a general, when there must be a number of noblemen among the Covenanters a good deal older, he replied that perhaps he was the only one foolish enough to put up with the expense, vexations, and rivalries, but she knew it was more likely to be because he had, now more than ever, such an uncanny belief in his destiny that even those who did not like him – her own father, alas, was one – could not help being impressed. No one doubted that he would prove to be a bold and resourceful commander. Corpses scattered about battlefields would give him no pleasure but they would give him no pause either.

Magdalen made no attempt to dissuade him but once she said to him, quietly but resolutely, that women like her, who stayed at home and gave birth and looked after their families, contributed more to the country's weal than politicians, soldiers, or ministers. He hardly listened, for he was reading some papers, but he nodded, not because he agreed with her but because he wished she would not bother him with such nonsense, harmless though it was, in the same way that he sometimes did with John and James.

She did not ask him what was to be done about his sister Lilias or Mrs Nicholson or Cissie and the dominie or the dominie's prize pupils. He did not see fit to discuss with her what he would have called the great issues of the day, so perhaps this was her way of retaliating, but she had another worthier reason. She wanted to make those decisions herself. She was a woman now and had learned a lot about people in the past year or two.

Once she asked him if he would stay at home until the child was born. It would depend, he replied, on the political situation at the time.

He asked her to do him a favour. Would she sew a piece of blue ribbon on to his bonnet? He intended to have all his soldiers wear such a ribbon. It would be the badge of the Covenanters' army.

He could have had many others to do it for him. Was asking her his way of saying how sorry he was for having neglected her in the past few weeks?

She felt like refusing. Why should she, even in so small a matter, assist him in his military life? It would be like showing approval or acceptance of something she abhorred. But she subdued her pride and meekly obeyed.

She sewed on the ribbon one evening as they sat by the fire, with the wind roaring in the chimney. James had put away his papers for the time being and was polishing his sword with the gold hilt. It would have made a good painting, she thought wryly: the warrior prepares for battle, with his wife's assistance.

Yet his mind was not on slashed faces or cloven skulls.

'I have left instructions that, if Beatrix marries, 250,000 merks will be paid by me or my heirs as a marriage settlement.'

Beatrix, his youngest sister, was the only one still unmarried; except, of course, for Katherine.

'Do you agree?' he asked.

'Yes, James, I agree.' Though she had been warned by the lawyer that so generous a sum could scarcely be afforded, considering James's military expenses.

He sighed. 'Poor Lilias. I wish I could do more for her.'

'She is becoming reconciled.' Because she was now hopeful that her husband would come back to her one day.

'Reconciled to a lifetime of unhappiness, through no fault of her own.'

Magdalen thought of the women whose husbands would be in his army, thousands of them. Many of those husbands would be killed or wounded and their wives too would have to be reconciled to a lifetime of unhappiness through no fault of their own.

'Poor Katherine,' she said, 'I wonder what has become of her.'

He went on polishing and said nothing.

'If she were to come back, James, would you welcome her? Would you let her come and live with us here in Kincardine, where she was born?'

'It would not be possible.'

It would take a different kind of courage from that needed on the battlefield. He did not have it, not yet anyway.

'Sir John's friends have not cast him out. They are trying to have him pardoned. Why should not Katherine's friends help her?'

'That is how a woman would see it. I understand that. You put humane considerations first. You are free to do so. Men cannot, especially those in responsible positions, who have to set an example. For them honour must come first.'

But surely, James, there is greater dishonour in leaving your sister alone and unhappy far away among strangers?

Two days later her third son Robert was born.

9

THE BABY WAS only three days old and James, with his company of soldiers, was about to march off to join the others who would make up the Covenanters' army when a woman from the village came to the castle, asking to see her ladyship. Janet reluctantly brought the message. 'Of coorse she canna see you, my lady. You've hardly got the strength tae speak, faur less listen tae her grumbles. I ken Agnes Gillies. She's a greeting-faced creature. You've got enough troubles o' your ain.'

The greatest of Magdalen's troubles, though she would never have admitted it to anyone, was the difficulty she was finding in cherishing little Robert as she should. Utterly innocent, he nevertheless represented the greatest disappointment of her life. At first she could not bear to hold him in her arms. James's sympathy was jocose: what warrior strain was in her that caused her to bring forth men children only? But she was not to repine, he added cheerfully, she was young and had plenty of time to have half a dozen daughters. Janet couldn't hold her tongue and reminded him that her ladyship was delicate, just one more pregnancy could kill her, as old Dr Allen had said. Dr Muirkirk, though, rebuked her, saying she was talking nonsense. The Lord had meant women to bring forth children in abundance and had given them bodies able to do it. He had known ladies with narrower pelvises than Lady Magdalen who had had ten of a family. Not all of them had lived but that was part of the Lord's plan too: He took away the weak and left the strong.

Magdalen insisted on seeing Mrs Gillies. How could she turn away a woman three of whose children had died in infancy?

She received her in bed. Janet was present, as restrictive as a jailer. Mrs Gillies was to stay no longer than five minutes. She was to keep a certain distance from the bed. She had to cover her mouth whenever she coughed or sneezed.

Mrs Gillies was a sad watery-eyed woman with a red nose and a bad complexion. She had sackcloth wrapped round her feet to protect them from the frost which had turned the roads hard as iron. She had walked two miles to the castle. She had a hoarse cough and a whining voice. She was very pregnant too, for, as Janet had whispered, the eleventh time.

'I'm sorry tae disturb you at sich a time, my lady,' she whined.

God forgive me, thought Magdalen, I am having to struggle against being disgusted by this unfortunate woman. 'How can I help you, Mrs Gillies?'

'I thocht maybe you could speak tae his lordship. You see my Rab's name's doon on the list o' them that's tae gang to the war. It's no' fair, my lady. Rab's forty-five, which is too auld for fechting, and forby he's needed at hame.'

I feel closer to this poor soul than ever I did to any of my sisters, thought Magdalen, and yet I cannot help her.

'What does your husband do, Mrs Gillies?'

'Rab's a blacksmith. They tell me they need blacksmiths tae mend their swords and shoe their horses, but shairly they can find younger men.'

'Does your husband want to go, Mrs Gillies? Has he volunteered?'

'Aye, the gowk. He thinks it'll be jist a holiday. He's been telt they're going tae Aiberdeen. He's got cousins there he hasna seen for years.'

'The war won't last long, Mrs Gillies. Your husband will soon be back with you again.'

'But he could be killed, couldn't he? He could lose an airm or

133

a leg. Whit wad we dae then if he couldna work? Sterve, that's whit.'

'Did your husband sign the Covenant, Mrs Gillies?'

'He put his mark on a bit o' paper. I don't ken onything aboot a Covenant. They a' say they're for the King but it's the King they're going tae fecht. I dinna understaun'.'

Nor I, thought Magdalen. 'They say the King wishes to impose bishops on us.'

'Bishops!' Mrs Gillies said it as she would have said 'Pigeons!' The one mattered as much to her as the other.

Magdalen felt very tired and depressed. It made her speak curtly. 'There's nothing we women can do but pray that our husbands come back to us safe and well.'

'Can you no' put in a word tae his lordship, my lady?'

'I never interfere in my husband's affairs.'

Was she making Mrs Gillies pay for her own disappointment in not having been given a daughter?

Janet then grabbed hold of Mrs Gillies and pushed her out of the room.

Later that day, when James looked in to ask how she felt, she mentioned Gillies the blacksmith.

'Is it fair to take him? He's forty-five, with seven children and another expected.'

'Oh, he'll be safe enough. Blacksmiths are too useful to be risked. They mend weapons, they don't use them. In any case I believe the fellow's keen to go.'

Yes, because he thought it would be a chance to see his cousins.

10

DISCONSOLATE NOW THAT their father had gone off to the war with his blue-bonneted band of recruits, leaving the castle a much less exciting place, John and James weren't at first interested when their mother told them that she was expecting visitors from the village. People were always coming to ask her for something, mostly women, some with sick babies in their arms; one, a daftie, had brought a dead baby, wanting Mama to bring it back to life. Usually the boys kept well out of the way but this time it was different, for the supplicants were to be Mary Ranald and her father; the dominie was bringing them. John and James had attended the village school a few times and knew of Mary as the dominie's star pupil, who could read Greek. They asked permission to be present and, adding to their mother's amazement, put on their best doublets, red and white in John's case and yellow and black in James's. This, it seemed, was to impress Mary though, when she teased them about it, they indignantly denied it.

They sat on stools on either side of their mother in the great hall, waiting for the visitors to be shown in. Outside it was a sunny afternoon, very suitable for practising archery or galloping on their ponies.

Magdalen's own curiosity to see this remarkable girl was increased. She herself had dressed as if to receive persons of quality. Really she was emulating her husband. In his bright red uniform he was in command of 6000 well-armed soldiers. Her troops consisted mainly of the poor and the sick but she felt the same responsibility for them as he did for his.

The dominie led them in, but it wasn't he or the small stout man in Sunday clothes with him that she gave her attention to: it was the girl with them. Her heart beat faster, she breathed with difficulty, for she had often wondered what her own daughter, if she ever had one, would be like, and here was a girl to compare her with.

Her first reaction, strangely enough, was relief. Her daughter would never have to wear a dress like that, long and shapeless, made of rough hodden grey, or such clumsy clogs. But this girl wore them as if the dress was of taffeta and the shoes of silk. The dominie's praise had not been extravagant after all. Mary Ranald, in spite of a complexion reddened by exposure to wind, rain, and sun, in spite of a slight stoop from bending in the fields, and in spite of hands coarsened by much hard work, was indeed beautiful: long fair hair flowing down her back and bright blue eyes that, without a trace of furtiveness, gazed round at all the splendours, the paintings, the tapestries, the suits of armour, the carved ceiling, and the great armorial shield above the mantel-piece.

Into Magdalen's own eyes came tears. They seemed the only way to salute this girl, so unfortunate in one way, that she had been born into poverty and hardship, and so fortunate in another, in that she had been given beauty, intelligence, and courage. But perhaps those rare gifts would turn out to be misfortunes too.

'This is Mary, my lady,' said the dominie proudly, 'and this is her father, Thomas Ranald.'

'You must be very proud of your daughter, Mr Ranald.'

He crushed his cap in his big hard hands, scowled at his boots, and spoke in a sullen voice that suited his dour face. 'She's needed at hame, my lady. Her mither's a sickly body and there are five ither bairns. That's a' I've come tae say and noo I've said it.'

'I have explained to Mr Ranald,' said the dominie, 'that if

Mary was found work in keeping with her talents she would be paid for it. With the money he could pay for help on his farm.'

'It's no' jist the money, my lady. It's the ideas it micht gie her. She'd come tae think she was better than her ain folk. She's a poor man's dochter, and that's whit she maun remain.'

Of course he was right. Though as a child, Magdalen had been puzzled by it, she had come to accept that it was God's will for some people to be born into privileged noble families, and for others, much more numerous, to be born commoners. Everyone accepted it: here was Mr Ranald proclaiming it now. James, her husband, so courteous to those beneath him in rank, nevertheless took it for granted that their proper place *was* beneath him. Had not Francis Gowrie to apply for special permission to marry his Nancy, though her father was the richest man in the country? Magdalen's father, the wisest man she knew, had said that the arrangement was necessary if civilisation was to be preserved.

Still, if this girl Mary Ranald kept in mind that she was of lowly birth and always would be, surely there could be no harm in finding her a place as minder of small girls in some noble-woman's household. Her charges, however young, would be far above her in rank. She would know that and so would they and so proper order would be maintained.

But was she not now holding her head a little too high and smiling at the boys in a way that annoyed John and embarrassed James? She seemed to be regarding them as her equals.

Meanwhile the dominie was arguing her case but neither her father, who had heard it all before, nor Magdalen, who was too intent on studying the girl, paid any heed.

'What does Mary herself want?' asked Magdalen. She wanted to hear the girl speak; what she said scarcely mattered.

Mary's voice was quiet and pleasant, though she spoke with exaggerated correctness. 'I want to stay and help my mother but I would like it if I could have books to read.'

But would she have the leisure or the energy left after all her tasks, to read them? In any case, what was the use of reading more and learning more if her fate was to become a drudge in the house and in the fields, first for her parents and then for her husband one day?

The dominie looked with appeal at Magdalen. She had to shake her head. There was nothing she could do.

It was a defeat, but then the odds against were too great.

James's battles would be fought against forces not so well armed as his own, not so dedicated, and not so well led, so that his victories, brilliant though they might be, were always achievable. Hers, on the other hand, would have to be won against such invincible foes as mankind's age-old customs and prejudices, and God's ordinance.

She asked the dominie to wait behind. The boys she sent away.

As the girl crossed the hall, she paused to look up at Magdalen's portrait and then turned to look at Magdalen herself. Her father pulled her away.

'Mr Blair,' said Magdalen, 'I have been intending to let you know what my husband said regarding your other pupil, John Reid.'

The dominie waited, pessimistically.

'If the University authorities are prepared to accept the lad as a student, my husband will pay his expenses, provided he makes progress and wins good reports.'

The dominie's gloom lightened. 'That is very kind of his lordship.'

And very typical too. Not many young men, in the throes of preparing to lead an army to war, would have spared the time to help a pigherd's son.

'What of yourself, Mr Blair? Are you and Cissie still betrothed?'

It had not been regularised and given the blessing of the Kirk. It still remained pagan promises exchanged over a running stream: absurd, but somehow romantic. Certainly it had seemed so to James, who had jested that, when he had time, he would write a poem about it.

Magdalen herself still believed that the marriage would be a mistake and bring misery to them both. 'I should tell you my husband would not object to your marrying Cissie.'

The dominie looked grateful.

'Has Cissie been to Dundee to see your mother?'

'Not yet, my lady.'

According to Janet, Cissie had been behaving herself recently: no flirtations, no saucy language, no flaunting of her person. It appeared she was trying to make herself fit to be the dominie's wife. To Magdalen's surprise, Janet, suspicious and jealous old maid, was on the girl's side.

'Would you marry without your mother's blessing, Mr Blair?'

'I would, but Cissie is not sure.'

'Well, that is to her credit. If there is to be a wedding, Mr Blair, we shall celebrate it here in the castle.'

With all the villagers present, sharing in the young couple's happiness, and with Magdalen herself presiding over it, it would represent a victory in her own war.

11

THE BRIGHT DRY days of spring and early summer that year suited alike the release of cattle from their winter prisons, with the big bulls gambolling for joy like lambs, the ploughing of fields, with attendant gulls screaming like men in pain, and the movement of troops. Reports, brought by passing travellers, peddlers, and beggars, came to Kincardine of the fighting in the North. The war was going well for the Covenanters. They had captured Aberdeen from the Royalists. Their commander, the young Earl of Montrose, was proving himself resourceful and resolute.

Then, one wet warm day at the beginning of June, when the countryside was at its most verdant and peaceful, with roe deer, bolder now that their hunters had taken to hunting men, ventured up to the walls of the castle, half a dozen men of the parish came hobbling home from the war, honourably discharged.

One was Gillies, the blacksmith. He lacked his right arm and had a fearsome, still raw, wound from brow to chin, so that it was difficult to make out what he was trying to say. Two had lost legs and were dependent on crude crutches. The remaining three had head wounds not yet healed and covered with grubby bloody bandages. Their clothes were ragged and filthy, as well as soaked. They had walked more than 100 miles. They brought a message from the Earl and delivered it before going on to their own homes.

'Things have gone very well for us and we should all be able to return home soon. Our losses, thank God, have been light and those of our adversaries heavy. This, though regrettable, should be a discouragement to them about stirring up trouble again. These poor fellows bringing this message were unlucky in that a cannon ball fell where they were stationed. Even so, they held their ground heroically against an unexpected cavalry charge, especially Gillies, the blacksmith. I count on you, Magdalen, to comfort their wives and families and give what help you can. They are to be pitied because of their misfortunes and afflictions but do not forget they are also to be commended in that, without flinching, they did their duty to their God and King. My love to you and the boys.'

There was what looked like dried blood on the paper but it wasn't only that which made her shudder. It was James's jubilation. How, she wondered, would he have written if he had been defeated. There was, too, that persistent hypocrisy, or moral blindness, of saying that the wounded men had done their duty to their King when they had been fighting against the King. Surely the King must look on them, and on James also, as traitors.

Sick at heart, but smiling for their sakes, she received the six men in the great hall. Even those with crutches would not sit down in her presence. By their insisting on giving her her place as a great lady, she felt obliged to play the part, though she felt ashamed and wanted to weep for them. She sat on her throne-like chair while they stood bowing their heads before her. It would have made a painting for one of Francis Gowrie's Italian artists: the wife of the commander-in-chief being gracious to common soldiers broken by war. With what loving meticulous skill their soiled bandages and her immaculate collar and cuffs would have been painted. He would have taken special pains with the handkerchief she held in her hand, ready to be put to her nose when the stink off them, of blood and sweat and human waste, got too offensive. He would not have missed the blue ribbons in the bonnets that they clutched in their hands.

Servants, peeping in, thought how grand the young countess

141

looked, and how gracious. They noticed how she had to put her handkerchief to her nose, and who could blame her? They could not help tittering nervously as they watched her listen intently to Rab Gillies, trying to understand what he was saying. A few minutes ago in the kitchen they hadn't been able to make out a single word because of his maimed mouth. The mistress could not, like them, laugh and weep and hug the poor man. She had to remain dignified.

In pain, and still liable to die from their wounds, and with beggary in front of them and their families if they were unable to work, it would have been only natural if they had been loud with complaints and self-pity, but no, on the contrary, they did not speak of themselves but of old Dr Allen who had saved many lives with timely amputations, and especially of James, her husband and their general. It had been a great honour to serve under him. Where the danger had been greatest, there he was, in his red jacket. His words of encouragement during an affray and of praise after it had been from the heart. No man in the army was too lowly to escape his notice and regard. And he had shown himself to be merciful: too much so for many people. Ministers with the army and some officers had not been pleased with him for not allowing the city of Aberdeen to be pillaged.

She felt proud of her husband. If there was no more war and he was able to stay at home with her and the boys, she could learn to love him as Nancy loved Francis.

She asked the men if they had any news of Mintlaw Castle. They had none. So far as they knew no harm had come to it.

She sent them away with gifts of money and promises of help.

As they were going out of the hall, they were confronted by the Earl's two sons, who were fascinated by their wounds and mutilations. Lord John, now aged ten, went forward to look more closely at Gillies's ravaged face, but his brother, Lord James, shrank back.

Bowing and touching their foreheads, the wounded men

142

went on their way, their sticks and crutches tapping on the stone floor.

Lord John drew his toy sword and slashed at imaginary faces but James ran up to his mother and hid his face in her lap.

Alone in her room, with the door snibbed, she wept and then sat staring at the painting of the Madonna and the infant Christ. It had lost its magic: it was no longer a comfort and assurance. This woman with the pale, pretty, characterless face and spotless garments did not, it now seemed to her, represent as truthfully or as movingly the agony and martyrdom of motherhood as the women of the village did, with their careworn faces and shabby clothes. She thought particularly of Mrs Gillies, whose latest child had recently died.

Mr Henderson and his kind would want to destroy the painting, not because it was inadequate but because it was a symbol of Papacy. Her own disappointment with it went much deeper, deeper indeed than she understood.

She took it down, wrapped it in cloth, and put it away in a cupboard. She would give it back to Francis so that he could hang it among his other works of art.

She realised how inadequate Francis himself was. He was not keeping apart from the war because he loved his fellow men too much to want to kill or injure them, for whatever reason; he was doing it because he despised them. He had made his house beautiful to show his contempt.

Was there a way other than James's participation in controversies and wars and Francis's white-handed aloofness among his paintings? Yes, there was. A way where the horrors and miseries of war had to be endured, though no blow was struck, and where, though debating chamber and battlefield were far away, their consequences had to be bravely tholed and patiently remedied. The way of women.

12

JANET GRIMLY ADVISED against holding the wedding in the castle. 'You've nae idea, my lady, whit they can be like, especially at waddings, whaur they lose a' sense o' decency.' Was this, wondered Magdalen, the disgruntled old maid speaking? Poor Janet could hardly be enthusiastic about weddings, since she had never had one herself. It turned out, though, that she was right about the behaviour of the guests.

It began in the kirk itself. Since the local gentry stayed away, the ordinary folk had the place to themselves. They pushed and shoved for seats at the front, where their betters usually sat. They jested lewdly at the expense of the bridegroom, who looked as if he was about to be hanged, not married, and of the bride too, for Cissie, though splendid in a blue dress with hat to match, was uncharacteristically subdued and moody, like, it was gleefully pointed out, a cow in season ready for the bull. It seemed too that the old minister's lust for Cissie had become known, for his pious exhortations to chastity were greeted with chuckles and giggles.

Though secluded in the laird's enclosure, Magdalen heard most of it.

'If you think they're bad noo,' whispered Janet, 'jist wait till they've had lots tae drink.'

In the carriage on the way back to the castle Janet gave more advice. 'As soon as the meal's ower, my lady, slip awa' up tae your room and snib the door. They'll no' mind. If you stay, you'll be a damper on them.'

'Why, what are they likely to do?'

'Things that wad shame the heathen tribes o' Africa.'

'But, Janet, they are respectable men and women, with large families.'

And those most likely to misbehave, the young unmarried men, were away at the war.

'They hae sich little pleasure in their lives, my lady, that when they get the chance they dinna ken when tae stop.'

Did not some of them walk 20 miles to see an old woman burned alive?

Tables were set out in the great hall. The castle servants were not too pleased at having to serve such guests. Magdalen herself sat at the top table, with Janet – her self-appointed protectress –, Mr Graham the minister, the bride and groom, and the bride's parents. The dominie's mother had refused to attend. Magdalen picked out, at other tables, Mr Ranald, that dour man, paying more than neighbourly attention to the big lusty woman beside him who could scarcely be that 'sickly body', his wife; Mr Gillies, being helped to eat and drink by his wife, who did not look well or happy; and three of the other wounded men and their wives. Of the remaining two, one had died and the other was too ill. Mr and Mrs Reid were pointed out to her by Janet, a diffident pair, who tried to join in the jollifications but were not at their ease. Nearly everyone there was above them in station. Their having a son bound for the University did not make up for their not owning a kailyard of their own.

As ale was consumed in large quantities by men and women alike, the jollifications grew noisier and less and less restrained. Some women unbuttoned their dresses, not minding that their bosoms were exposed. These were fondled by illicit hands.

Mr Graham was amused. 'The Children of Israel,' he said, 'were allowed special licence by the Lord at weddings. After all, what is the purpose of matrimony? Is it not the provision of souls for His glorification? For that purpose to be achieved, our priapean instincts must not be submerged.'

145

Poor Mr Graham, thought Magdalen, pitying him when she ought surely to be condemning him. His wife had died some years ago after a long illness. Since then he had employed a succession of maidservants, all chosen for their youth and plumpness. None had stayed long. There was a rumour that one had left with money in her pocket and a child in her womb. Hours of praying on his knees on the stone floor of the kirk had not, alas, submerged his priapean instincts.

Magdalen felt herself blushing but it wasn't noticed among all those flushed and jolly faces.

She remembered Mrs Nicholson, now employed in an inn of ill-repute in Dundee.

The bride's parents were so crushed in spirit by being at her ladyship's table that they were unable to eat or drink. Given permission to join friends at another table, they were instantly as gluttonous as the rest.

The bride herself continued to be quiet and demure, though she had to endure being kissed by tipsy male guests, most with beards. They came swaggering up to claim that right.

It was, Mr Graham explained, a traditional custom. In olden times kisses had not sufficed. Priapus had been given his proper role then.

By this time the minister had emptied a bottle of claret and was well through another. He kept quoting Latin to the dominie, to cheer him up, it seemed, but depressing him still more.

The dominie ate little and drank less. Was it possible, thought Magdalen, that this shy frugal scholar hoped to find, in Cissie's soft body, enough joy to compensate for the lack of intellectual and spiritual companionship? Still, he ought not to be looking so gloomy. Was not his wedding also a communal celebration? The war in the North was over and the men of the parish, including their absent host, would soon be home again.

When the meal was ended and the tables were being cleared away for the dancing to begin, Magdalen slipped away, unnoticed. Janet asked permission to remain, implying that she wanted to see that things did not go too far, but Magdalen saw that Janet, censorious old maid, was more fascinated than disgusted by the display of priapean instincts. Was she hoping that, in some dark corner, some virile ploughman would take from her what she cherished but also hated, her virginity sweet once but now sour?

On her way to her room, Magdalen looked in on the boys. They had been forbidden to go near the festivities. They had not minded much. 'Who wants to see a lot of stupid peasants getting drunk?'

She was awakened by the noise of guests skailing. They seemed greatly excited. Women screamed. She wondered, as she fell asleep again, what had happened to Janet.

Next morning Janet was sourly reluctant to give an account of what had gone on after Magdalen had left. 'I'd raither no' say, my lady. It's no' fit for your ears.'

'Did Mr Blair take part in the dancing?'

'He was gi'en nae option. He and Cissie were dragged to their feet and flung intae the ring.'

'He must have been very embarrassed, poor man.'

'No' hauf as embarrassed as he was later.'

'Oh. And what happened then?'

'Dae you really want tae ken?'

'Yes, of course.'

'According tae custom the bride and groom are hurled in a cairt tae their hoose, wi' flo'ers roon' their necks.'

Magdalen laughed. 'A friendly custom.'

'Freen'ly maybe, but they went too faur. When they got them tae the schoolhoose they stripped them baith bare naked and threw them into bed.'

'Oh.' Making love, or consummating a marriage, was difficult enough in private; with a crowd of drunken peasants looking on, it must have been an ordeal. 'Did you see this yourself, Janet?'

147

'I did not. I was telt aboot it. Some got stripped themsels. I'll say nae mair.'

'Good heavens!'

'You may weel say "guid heavens!", my lady. That's the kind o' folk we are, nae better and nae waur than ither folk.'

Janet had not meant to give herself away. Guilt and remorse had forced it out of her. There was no one she could confess to and the man with whom she had sinned had probably already forgotten it, not just because he had been drunk at the time but also because he had thought it of little account. She had offered herself, body and soul, to the Devil and he had laughed. Worse still, he had dared to console her, saying it wasn't her fault it was such a foolish failure; at her age, with her lack of experience, what else could she expect? He had promised to tell no one and perhaps he would not, for he was a married man with a jealous wife.

If others got to hear about it, they would laugh too. Her life would be ruined. She would have to do away with herself.

Her ladyship was laughing, when she ought to have been looking shocked and disgusted: not at Janet's own transgression, which, if God was pitiful, she would never hear about, but at the shamelessness of people in general.

It was not a contemptuous laughter; indeed, it had Janet in tears, for there was forgiveness in it, for everyone.

She went closer to her mistress, for she had become short-sighted of late. 'Whit has come ower you, my lady?' she asked humbly.

There was a change, but what was it? It could not be maturity, for she was still only 24. Was it understanding, that the Bible spoke of? Aye, that must be it. She understood more deeply and so was able to make allowances. When the Earl came back from his war, he would have a surprise waiting for him. He had left behind a young wife whose opinions, timidly expressed, he had listened to politely but hadn't heeded, and whose silences he had discounted as indicating that she had nothing useful to say. Great general though he now was, he would find in her a quality that transcended all his. He had courage, intelligence, and authority; she had goodness.

13

WHEN JAMES CAME home, he stayed only for a week. Urgent affairs awaited him in Edinburgh, where envious rivals had to be prevented from belittling his recent achievements and from spreading rumours that he was not wholly in agreement with the principles of the Covenant but secretly yearned to join the Royalists. Among these detractors, he told Magdalen, was her brother James. Her father too was still antagonistic but, being an honourable man, would never stoop to clandestine intrigues like the others. Magdalen, he remarked, more and more reminded him of her father.

When he saw in her what Janet had seen, her goodness (though he did not then think of it as that), it was in an unlikely place and at an unlikely time: in bed, just after he had made love to her, not very willingly. He had thought he should not, since Baby Robert was only a few months old and it might be harmful to her to become pregnant again so soon. Had not Dr Allen given that advice? But Magdalen had been eager to take the risk, not really to show her love for him but in the hope that her next child would be a girl.

After it was over, he was struck by the look on her face.

'You know, that's exactly how you are in Jameson's portrait.'

'Am I looking so mournful then?'

'I was wrong when I said that. I looked at it again today and saw what Rothes saw. Whenever I meet him, he asks after you.'

She smiled. 'Has he found his wealthy heiress yet?'

'It seems he has: the Countess of Devonshire. But all his friends fear a grimmer bride awaits him. He coughs up blood. He has not long to live.'

'I'm sorry. I liked him.'

'He will be greatly missed: though, to be truthful, he has always been inclined to put personal considerations before his duty as a patriot.'

'Perhaps he thinks that, if he is true to himself and to his friends, that is the best way of showing himself a patriot.'

James chuckled. 'That is the kind of remark your father often makes. I am never sure whether it is very wise or very dubious.'

James was attending a conference at Berwick with the King when Francis Gowrie and his wife paid an unexpected visit to Kincardine. Their arrival was made remarkable by the magnificent white stallion that Lady Gowrie rode and which she had prancing all over the courtyard, striking sparks from the cobbles. Unlike most other guests, she wasn't content to let her horse be taken to the stables by servants but went with it herself to make sure that it was well looked after.

Magdalen noticed, with surprise, that she looked to the horse for companionship more than to her husband.

Francis himself was more interested in the contents of a leather bag that he took from one of his attendants. From it he produced a beautiful silver chalice.

His eyes grew small, like a miser's, she thought. 'The finest example of its kind in Scotland,' he said. 'Look at that exquisite engraving: Christ raising the dead. By Cellini, a famous Venetian sculptor and silversmith. I bought it from Sir John Rhynie, whose family looted it from a church in Knox's time.' He then took out two gold goblets. 'Made by a Florentine craftsman for James IV. Engraved with hunting scenes. I bought them from Lord Lithgo's widow.'

'Have you been going round buying up people's prized possessions, Francis?'

'Prized, perhaps, but not appreciated. They will be safer at Mintlaw. Otherwise they might have been melted down. On the whole, though, it hasn't been a very successful foray. Scots spend their money on things of use, not on things of beauty.'

Magdalen wanted to ask him about his little daughter, but did not.

Later, while they were dining, Francis made malicious fun of James. 'So James is at Berwick talking to the King. The question all Scotland is whispering is: will he come back?'

'Why should he not come back?' asked Magdalen.

'Back to the Covenant fold, I meant. Are they not expecting him to reveal himself as a ravenous wolf? There's some glory, I suppose, in serving the King, but none in having to heed the wishes of a pack of rabid ministers, and we know, do we not, that James has always had a great thirst for glory?'

'He is trying to serve his country.'

'By waging or stirring up unnecessary wars? By urging Scotsmen to kill Scotsmen? By laying waste the land?'

'By protecting our constitution. By defending the rights of the Kirk.'

Francis sneered. 'They have you well schooled, Magdalen. There was a time when you wouldn't have thought those worth one man's life, let alone the lives of thousands.'

'No one is being killed now. The war is over.'

'But everyone knows it will be resumed soon if the King does not get his way or the Estates theirs. Whatever noble claims they make, they are all serving their own interests, James being no exception. Did you know that he had the impudence to send a gang of armed scoundrels to Mintlaw with a copy of their absurd Covenant? I was to sign it or be arrested. They showed me their warrant, signed, if you please, by James and others, who included, I may say, your own brother, James.'

'Did you sign it, Francis?'

'I did, with swords at my throat and prayers in my ears, but it signified nothing. I do not intend to join their army or contribute one merk to their war fund.'

Nancy intervened. 'Horses don't bother with politics. You can trust a horse. If you treat it well, it will burst its heart for you.'

Her husband ignored her. 'Why have you let them change you, Magdalen? When I was in Italy, I used to tell them about the little Scots girl, Magdalen Carnegie, who, in a land bound with bigotry, kept her soul free.'

'That was foolish of you, Francis. I was only thirteen when you went to Italy.'

'You were seeking the truth then.'

Was the compliment deserved? Had her childish anxieties amounted to that?

'Why do you think I am not seeking it now?'

Nancy again spoke. 'If I was a man, I think I would fight for the King. He likes horses. At the time of the Coronation in Edinburgh, he told me in Holyrood House that he was worried about a favourite horse of his, it had hurt a leg while hunting. He was afraid it might have to be put down.'

'Can you imagine a more bizarre conversation?' asked Francis with another sneer.

Magdalen could easily imagine the King, beset by nobles wishing to get something out of him or scheming to outwit him, finding refuge in this simple girl's enthusiasm for creatures whose loyalty could always be relied on.

She was in bed when there came a knocking on her door. Janet opened it. Outside stood Nancy in a white nightgown, holding a candle. 'The mistress has gone to bed,' said Janet, rudely, 'wi' her prayers said.'

'Who is it, Janet?' called Magdalen.

'It's me, Magdalen,' said Nancy.

'Come in, please.'

Surly Janet stood aside and Nancy strode in. Magdalen had not realised before how big and strong she was. (In the kitchen the

153

joke was that Lady Gowrie could pick up her husband and carry him under her oxter.) She was the kind of woman who could, without risk, bear a dozen children. Yet she had only one, with no sign of another.

'Please leave us, Janet,' said Magdalen. She saw that Nancy wanted the conversation to be private.

Janet went off in a huff.

Nancy sat on a low stool, with her legs, under the nightgown, wide apart. Her hands were on her knees, as if holding reins.

'Francis doesna sleep wi' me,' she said.

Well, not all husbands slept with their wives. It did not necessarily follow that their marriages had failed.

'When I touch him, he grues.'

Magdalen had noticed.

'I'm no' sure if it's just because I'm a woman. He told me once that women's bodies are repulsive. That was the word he used. Yet he looks for hours at paintings wi' naked women in them. Is it because I am plain Nancy Dick, no' a high-born lady like you, Magdalen?'

Francis had always been excessively and curiously fastidious. The bodily contact that was necessary between a married couple might well repel him.

'He says making love reduces us to the level of animals.'

So it did, if love was lacking.

'I hope you don't mind me saying all this, Magdalen. I had to say it to somebody. You ken him better than I do. You were going to marry him yourself once, weren't you?'

'We were never actually betrothed.'

'He still loves you. He thinks how much happier he would have been if he had married you instead of me. But he would never have been able to make Mintlaw so grand and that's all he lives for.'

'Tell me about your little girl, Nancy.'

Nancy's face brightened but, moments later, was glummer than ever. 'I'm hardly allowed to see her. He says I'll make her vulgar like myself.'

Earlier, when talking about her feats as a horsewoman, she had remarked that her 'erse was like leather'.

'I was wondering if you would speak to him, Magdalen. He wants you to think well of him. He doesn't care a button what I or anybody else thinks of him.'

'I would like to help, Nancy, but I don't think I should interfere.'

'Sometimes I think I'll run away. Like your good-sister.'

'It didn't turn out well for poor Katherine. What is your little girl's name?'

'Mary, after his mother.'

'Is he fond of her?'

'In his own way. But, if he doesn't want me, why should I stay with him?'

'You must stay, for little Mary's sake.'

'She wouldn't miss me. He's seen to that.'

Nancy stood up. 'I'm keeping you from sleep. Thanks for letting me talk to you. You're a good person, Magdalen. I'd like very much if you would come and visit me at Mintlaw again.'

'I'd like that too.'

'Francis says you could be in danger here, if your James changes sides and goes over to the King. For revenge they might burn the castle down.'

Magdalen's father in a letter had hinted at that too. 'Be ready at all times to come to Kinnaird, you and your children.'

Before Nancy left, she came over and gave Magdalen a hug.

They stayed three days. When they were leaving, Magdalen had the painting of the Madonna ready, wrapped in cloth. She presented it to Francis in the entrance hall.

She had once loved him, perhaps she still did, but she could not have borne for him to touch her. A man might despise

155

humanity for its many faults, its greed, its callousness, and its cruelty, but surely he should make exceptions of his wife and daughter.

Outside in the courtyard Nancy could be heard talking joyfully to her big white horse. When she was on its back, she did not have to fear her husband. Managing a horse was the one accomplishment in which she outdid him.

'What is this, Magdalen?' he asked, but he had already guessed, wrongly, as it turned out.

He unwrapped the cloth. He frowned, in disappointment, it seemed.

'Don't you want it?' she asked.

'I hoped it was the portrait of another woman.'

She blushed. 'That's not for sale.'

'It will be some day. It will become my proudest possession. But why are you returning this? It is one of the finest works of one of the finest painters in the world.'

'What makes it so, Francis?'

'A hundred things. The delicacy of the colours. Look at that wonderful blue. Its atmosphere of holiness.'

What did he, who scoffed at religion, mean by holiness?

'I used to find it holy,' she said, 'but not so much now.'

'What changed your mind?'

She hesitated. She must be true to herself but not false to her husband. 'A few days ago I visited one of the village women in her hovel. Her face was covered with sores. She had just given birth. The baby was dying.'

'What has all that got to do with this? This is art: beautiful. What you have described is reality: hideous.'

'Poor Mrs Baillie's love for her child seemed to me more beautiful.'

He stared at her with a strange expression. Was he about to laugh with derision or declare his love? 'Life is ugly and hateful. Art is the only protection.'

156

Outside in the sunshine Nancy was letting John and James ride her enormous horse. Magdalen felt anxious.

She shook her head. Love, she thought, was the only protection.

'Art succeeds where everything else fails.'

Could she reply that love never failed? Not truthfully. It had failed in Katherine's case and in Nancy's.

'I've promised Nancy to come and visit her and little Mary.'

'Make it soon. You will be very welcome.'

'It will depend on James.'

'You mean, if he hasn't plunged the country into war again.'

'You have never once spoken to me about your little girl.'

He seized her hand. His voice was suddenly hoarse. 'Take care, Magdalen, lest you be left with no protection at all.'

Then he hurried out and handed the painting to one of his attendants.

As she watched them canter across the courtyard Magdalen stood in the doorway, waving. John and James ran after them, shouting and waving their caps.

'She let us ride the stallion,' cried John.

'We liked her,' said James, 'but we didn't like him.'

'He doesn't like hunting,' said John. 'He said he'd rather listen to music.'

'Or look at paintings,' said James. 'He was always looking at your picture, Mama. Wasn't he, John?'

'Every time we went into the hall, he was looking at it.'

Magdalen turned and went into the house. There were tears in her eyes. She did not think she loved Francis now, though she once had, but the thought that he still loved her and perhaps was unkind to Nancy because of it, gave her joy when it should have given her grief. Whatever happened to her, she would find comfort in thinking of him standing in the hall, looking up at her portrait.

14

THE NEGOTIATIONS WITH the King at Berwick were fruitless, each side continuing to distrust the other. Yet, when James came home to Kincardine for one of his hurried visits, he struck Magdalen as curiously confident, uplifted indeed, with a gleam in his eyes as if he had made a decision that, in the meantime, he intended to keep to himself. She knew what it was: he had finally made up his mind that his true duty lay in serving and not opposing the King. He would wait until the time was right for what the Covenanters would call his treachery and he himself his honourable conversion.

When she asked him about his personal dealings with the King at Berwick he replied brusquely that he would prefer not to talk about it but, later, he was more forthcoming to John and James, who had declared themselves fervent Royalists.

They asked him eager questions. She sat by in silence, sewing, with little Robert in his cradle at her feet.

What was the King like?

Gracious, kind, and majestic, with a beautiful face that was often sad.

Why was it sad?

Because both his kingdoms were unruly.

Why were they unruly?

Because the King's advisers gave him bad advice.

Why did he not get rid of them?

Because he was loyal, too loyal, to servants whom he thought were loyal to him.

How had he received Father?

Most graciously.

Did Father kiss the King's hand?

Yes, with pride and joy.

Did Father have a private audience with the King?

Yes, he was given that honour.

What did the King say to him?

What a King said to a subject in private was confidential but, since they were loyal little fellows, who could keep a secret and one day might fight for the King, he would tell them.

(Here James glanced aside at Magdalen, who kept her eyes on her sewing.)

The King had said that, though Father appeared to be on the side of his present enemies, he knew that it was not really so, he understood very well that Father had to be patient and cautious for the time being, because the King's enemies were in truth his enemies too, and they were ruthless and dangerous men.

But you aren't afraid of them, Father?

No, but it was sometimes prudent to disguise one's real feelings.

Was the Earl of Argyll the leader of Father's enemies?

The Campbell was certainly the most cunning of them.

Was it true that Argyll wanted to get rid of the King and put himself in his place?

Who had told them that?

Mr MacDonald, who used to be their tutor.

Someone ought to warn Mr MacDonald to stick to the history of the past and leave the present alone.

Mr MacDonald had also said that Argyll's Highlanders were savages who couldn't speak English and didn't observe the rules of civilised warfare.

(Here Magdalen's needle paused. She would have liked to ask what those rules were.)

It was true that Argyll's men went in for robbery and needless butchery.

If they ever came to Kincardine, Father would drive them away, wouldn't he?

He would do his best.

Mama had said that their uncles, Lord Carnegie and Lord Dalhousie, were on Argyll's side. Was that true?

Yes, but they should realise that in troubled times like the present, it was sometimes advisable for members of a family to be on opposite sides. In that way, whichever side won, the family would not be ruined.

But was that honourable?

(Here Magdalen paused again, waiting, like the boys, for an answer.)

It was not necessarily dishonourable. A man must, of course, have faith in the cause he espoused, otherwise he would do well just to sit at home.

But only cowards sit at home. Isn't that so, Father?

If a man is able-bodied and his country is in danger, then if he is content to sit at home, he deserves to be called a coward.

Didn't it mean that one member of a family might come face to face with another on the battlefield?

It sometimes happened.

Later, when the boys had gone off to bed, she asked her question meekly: 'Will there be war again, James?'

He frowned. 'It would be better if you did not concern yourself with such matters.'

'If there is war, my husband may be opposed to my brothers. He could be killed. So could they. My home could be destroyed. My children could be at risk. Yet you tell me I should not be concerned about such matters.'

'You have your children to look after and this house to manage. Those are your concerns.'

'Did you not tell me once that honour is more important to you than life?'

'That is what I believe. What are you imputing?'

She trembled but felt she had to say it. 'Is it honourable to let men like Lord Rothes keep on regarding you as their friend and ally when you are all the time waiting for a suitable opportunity to join their enemies?'

He jumped to his feet, with a shout of anger. 'By God, if a man had said that to me, I would have killed him.'

'That is how it appears to me, James.'

'Yes, because you know nothing, you have been nowhere, you lack imagination, you have no idea of the complexities involved. Is it your father who has instigated you to insult me?'

'My father's advice is that I should keep my opinions to myself.'

'Excellent advice. Why not take it? You have complained about my long absences. You are going the right way to make them longer.'

'I would be sorry if I did that, but am I not allowed to say what I think?'

'No, you are not.' He was about to leave the room then but turned at the door, as if repenting of his arrogance. Perhaps, too, he felt pity for her and some respect. His smile seemed to convey all that. He came back in and sat down. 'Well, what else do you think? Let me have it all. I can see it's time I got to know my wife.'

'You think, James, you and the Earl of Argyll and the Earl of Rothes and the King and my father and Mr Henderson and all the rest of you, that you are making the history of our country with your arguments in Parliament and your wars but it is not so. What you are all doing is wasteful. It benefits no one. You do not build up, you break down, you destroy. Scotland is a poor country, but it is you, all of you, with your quarrels and wars, who have made it poor and who keep it poor. Mr Gillies, the blacksmith, was once a happy man, of value to his neighbours; now he sits at home feeling useless and afraid to speak because even his own family makes fun of his painful mumblings. If there are more wars, there will be many more like him.'

He stared at her in astonishment. 'Who have you been talking to? Who has given you these ideas? Not your father, it would seem, since you have included him among the destroyers. Was it Francis Gowrie?'

'Francis cares only for his works of art. No one has given me my ideas. I can think for myself.'

He grinned, deciding to be tolerant. After all, she was young and knew nothing of the world. 'Just so long as you do not pervert my sons.'

'You have already done that, James. They think that war, that killing people, is glorious.'

PART THREE

PART THREE

1

MAGDALEN HERSELF WAS unwell and Janet was dying of a painful disease when Lord Sinclair, sent by the Estates, came to Kincardine with a band of black-clad inquisitors to search the castle for evidence against James, who, with his friends Napier, Keir, and Blackhall, was imprisoned in Edinburgh Castle accused of conspiring with the enemies of the Covenant. Forewarned by her father, she went through James's papers to destroy any that she thought might incriminate him. If the charges against him could be substantiated, the penalty was death and Argyll would not shrink from exacting it.

In the library she looked in the big charter chest, where all the Graham documents were kept, while the boys took down every book from the shelves and vigorously shook it. They resented what they were having to do: it amounted, they said, to an admission that Father might be guilty. They found nothing in the books save a lock of hair: yellow, so not their mother's; probably their Aunt Lilias's. But Magdalen wondered if it could have belonged to one of James's sweethearts before he was married, or perhaps the Frenchwoman who had given him the Bible.

In the chest she came upon a bundle of letters tied with blue ribbon. A faint scent came off them. She wondered at first, with her heart giving a leap of joy, if they were those written by her to James but quickly realised they could not be, she had never written so many. Were they from the same woman whose lock of hair he had treasured? A quick glance showed that they were in English.

There was a copy of the Cumbernauld Bond, an agreement entered into by James and other noblemen to band together to prevent Argyll from seizing power for himself. It was no longer secret: one of the signatories, in a delirium, had given it away. But, just in case, Magdalen threw the copy into the fire.

She found nothing else likely to harm James.

What she also discovered was that there was nothing amongst all those papers that made mention of her. If she were to die tomorrow, she would be remembered only by her portrait in the hall.

Meanwhile, John and James, like conspirators, were talking about riding to England to see the King and urge him to send an army north to rescue their father. There would be a great battle. Argyll and his followers would be defeated and hanged as traitors. Father would rule the country in the King's name. There would be peace and justice.

Magdalen listened sadly. They assumed, like their father, that the King was to be trusted but it seemed to her that Charles would not hesitate to betray or desert even his most faithful allies in order to get his own way and James, after all, in the King's view, had been and indeed still was a Covenanter, who had fought against the King, not as a common soldier either but as a successful general. Surely he must think of James as a traitor.

According to her father, James would be immediately released from prison and given back command of the army if he were to reaffirm his loyalty to the principles of the Covenant in such a way as to make it impossible for him afterwards to repudiate them. 'Though, to speak the truth, what those principles now are is a matter for bitter controversy. I must warn you, my pet, that your husband is embroiled in dangerous ventures and could well forfeit his life. My influence, alas, would not be able to protect him but it should avail to save you and your children. Be ready at all times to flee to Kinnaird.'

On her way to her room to lie down she looked in on Janet

and found her still with her face resolutely to the wall, saying nothing.

'Is she still in pain, do you think?' whispered Magdalen to the nurse.

'Aye, but she never utters a cheep.'

Magdalen sat by the bed. She was in tears. This dour old woman had been like a mother to her for many years. She had been present at the birth of all Magdalen's children.

'It's me, Janet,' she said. 'Is there anything you would like?'

Janet seemed to reply, but neither Magdalen nor the nurse could interpret her faint mumble.

It was just as well, for Janet, her mind having slipped back to her grandmother's days, when ministers were priests, had tried to say that she would like to confess her sins before she died. Such a practice was now condemned as Papist.

She said no more and, after half an hour, Magdalen left to go and rest. 'If there is any change, let me know at once.'

The four inquisitors were dressed in black and as bleak-faced as hangmen. Their other duties were assisting the Kirk's commissioners in investigating cases of witchcraft and afterwards in supervising the burnings. They were under the command of Lord Sinclair, who showed, by his dress, black like theirs but lustrous and expensive, and by his manner – he smiled a lot – that he was not to be regarded as one of them, he was no ferreting clerk, he was a man of rank and breeding, a representative of the Estates. He mentioned that he was acquainted with Magdalen's brother, James, and, like many others, thought highly of her father. He had been authorised to say, and it gave him the greatest pleasure to say it, that she herself was in no way under suspicion. It was known that she favoured her father's views more than her husband's.

She wondered how anyone in Edinburgh could possibly know her views on anything.

Lord Sinclair's smile grew slyer still. 'I am also authorised to tell you, Lady Magdalen, that if your husband, James Graham, were to come back into the fold, he would be warmly received. We of the Covenant need men of his excellent qualities. Command of an army is waiting for him. If you should wish to add your voice to the many exhorting him to return to his former allegiance, I would be pleased to convey to him a letter from you to that effect.'

'Would only my husband read it, my lord?'

'I would deliver it personally into his hand.'

But not before letting his masters see it.

He clapped his hands and his henchmen, up to now as still as statues, began their search.

It was soon obvious they had done it often before, in other tainted houses. They knew where to look: behind pictures and tapestries, inside suits of armour, inside coal scuttles, under floor coverings, in the secret drawers of cabinets (they knew where the springs were and how to release them), and behind panelling: expert fingers tapped and trained ears listened.

Magdalen was present in the library when they went through the contents of the charter chest and riffled through the books. She hated seeing those agile fingers untie and unfold, those cold eyes peruse, documents that contained the history and honour of the Grahams. The scented letters caused no pause, comment, or smirk; nor did the lock of hair. Everything was returned to its place meticulously.

The search lasted for four hours. Articles were unearthed that had long been missing: three marbles, a silver spoon, and a brooch that had belonged to James's mother.

Lord Sinclair came to her with a problem. The old woman who was ill, he was sorry but her bed must be searched. It would not be the first time that such a hiding place had been used.

'The old woman is dying,' she said.

'Papers of importance have been found hidden in coffins.'

'Nothing is hidden in Janet's bed. I give you my word.'

He reflected, looked into her eyes, and smiled. 'Well, that is good enough for me.'

It was after eight in the evening when they were finished, too late for them to find accommodation elsewhere. Nevertheless, she did not offer them hospitality. They had come with ill will towards her husband, whose house this was. Let them sleep under hedges.

But Lord Sinclair, with still another variety of slyness in his smile, produced a second warrant, also signed by members of the Estates. It ordered every householder to provide food and shelter for these servants of the State. It would be paid for.

'We shall leave early tomorrow morning,' said Sinclair. 'We have still your husband's house at Old Montrose to search.'

If he expected an invitation to dine with her, he was disappointed. He had to dine alone.

His clerks ate in the kitchen, at a separate table in a corner. They did not speak to the servants who attended them. They hardly spoke to one another. Their grace before the meal lasted at least five minutes. While eating, they read little black, battered books of devotion.

The servants muttered angrily among themselves. One, an ostler called Simpson, who had drunk too much ale, lost his temper and, in a loud voice, asked the uninvited guests who had given them the right to come and ransack a gentleman's house like thieves. The one who had said the grace, turned round and replied that the Estates in Edinburgh had given them the right and the work they were doing was God's work: the extirpation of apostasy. Simpson, cowed by the big words so quietly spoken, remembered that the crushing of thumbs was God's work too, and said no more.

Though loath to be beholden to him, Magdalen wrote a letter for Lord Sinclair to take to James. In it she said she hoped the conditions of his imprisonment were not too harsh. She was confident that his name would soon be cleared and he would be set free. He was not to worry about her and the boys, they were all fine. They prayed for him every day and looked forward to his safe return to Kincardine.

When she reread it, she was dismayed by its lack of warmth. This could not be explained entirely by her knowing that James's enemies would read it. Surely a letter written in these circumstances, with her husband's life in danger, should be wet with her tears and crumpled by her agitated fingers? Yet here it was, neat and passionless. What was the matter with her? She felt ill, her back ached, she was upset about Janet, but it was more than all that. There was this strange remoteness. Praying did not help. Even God seemed to be growing more and more distant.

2

AFTER FIVE MONTHS of imprisonment James returned to Kincardine, unwell, depressed, and embittered. The King had at last come to Edinburgh, and what had he done? He had, it was true, saved James's life and got him released from prison, but, as against that, he had made Argyll a marquis, thus showing he was going to depend on him and not on Montrose to champion his cause in Scotland. Everyone knew that squint-eyed Campbell was not to be trusted, everyone but the King. What was the use of risking one's life and liberty for the sake of a King who preferred a self-seeking, devious traitor to a patriot? Magdalen, listening to these monologues, suggested meekly that perhaps the King did not know whom to trust. Had not his ancestors died violently at the hands of subjects? Also, could it not be that it was not in his nature to trust anyone, since he himself was untrustworthy?

Peevishly James rebuked her for criticising the King. She did not understand. Like most women she saw things too simply. Let her get on with her tapestry.

She came upon his latest poem on his desk in the library. She did not think he would mind her reading it; after all, in the early days of their marriage he had read all his poetry to her. One verse stood out. She could easily imagine James's vaunting voice reading it aloud:

> Like Alexander I will reign
> And I will reign alone.
> My thoughts shall evermore disdain

A rival on my throne.
He either fears his fate too much
Or his deserts are small
That puts it not unto the touch
To win or lose it all.

She did not understand it. Did she really see things too simply? James seemed to be imagining himself as King, which surely was dangerous as well as treasonous. Was it not that very ambition that he and the other signatories of the Cumbernauld Bond had accused Argyll of? For the first time she took seriously what Lord Rothes had said in jest: that James might end up on the gallows.

What terrified her also was that she had begun to feel that she was two persons, one James's wife and the boys' mother, and the other that strange young woman in the portrait, who looked down on them all, including herself, with sad sympathy and foreboding. Desperately she tried to make the one drive the other away. She responded to James's love-making with an eagerness that surprised him. He thought it was her obsessive desire for a daughter, and so it was, but it was also her way of defying that other self which kept foreseeing the ruin of her family. For the same reason she kissed and hugged the boys often, to their embarrassment. She wore bright clothes, unlike the Magdalen in the portrait, who was dressed in black. She put rouge on her face, to make a contrast with those pallid cheeks. She laughed often, but it was hardly genuine laughter, and caused not only James and the boys to look at her in wonder but the servants too. It was whispered anxiously in the kitchen that the mistress's mind was breaking down under the strain of having a husband with so many powerful enemies. But, when it was learned that she was pregnant again, everyone was able to relax in relief, *that* was the reason for her strange behaviour. It was resolved in the kitchen, and indeed throughout the parish, to pray that this time her wish would be granted. At the back of all their minds, though, was the fear that she might not survive this fourth birth. How pitiful it would be if she were to die having the daughter that they had all prayed for.

James hardly looked up from the letter he was writing when she gave him the news. Did she feel well? Should Dr Muirkirk be sent for? Perhaps she should now employ some companion to fill Janet's place. In any case, she must take plenty of rest.

When drier weather and firmer roads made travel easier, Lord Napier, Sir George Stirling of Keir, and Sir Archibald Stewart of Blackhall, James's friends and co-conspirators, paid visits to Kincardine and talked for hours with him in the library with the door locked.

James began to make preparations for a long journey. When Magdalen asked where he was going, he shook his head. How long would he be away? The same answer. Later he relented and said it was better that she did not know. There might come a time when 'brutal fellows' would put her and the boys to the question and the less they knew, the safer they would be.

She was sure then that he was going south to offer his services to the King. If the Covenanters found out, they would consider their accusations of treachery to be justified. His life would again be in danger. But what of his honour, which he regarded as dearer to him than life?

It was not the worried wife who went to the library to challenge him as to the honourableness of his stealing off to England to plead with the King, it was that other Magdalen Carnegie, who had always wanted to be told the truth and to tell it herself.

It was May. The trees, especially the hawthorns and rowans, were at their most splendid, with masses of fragrant white blossoms. The windows in the library were open, and the air, after the fetid odours of winter, was fresh and sweet. Snow still glittered on the tops of distant hills.

'Are you going to the King, James?'

He paused in his writing, as if listening to the birdsong outside.

'I am not asking as your wife.'

He glanced up at her, puzzled.

'Though, as your wife, I should have a right to know.'

He smiled. Pregnancy, he knew, could affect women's minds. 'Did I not explain that it would be better if you did not know?'

'Do you remember, James, you once tried to explain to me about honour?'

He frowned. 'What are you talking about, Magdalen?'

'You think, do you not, that you have a duty more important than your duty to your family?'

After a pause, he decided to give her an answer, though her question was impertinent. 'Yes, I do have such a duty. Every man of honour has. His duty to his country. They do not necessarily conflict.' He could not resist adding: 'Most wives understand that.'

'Most wives are never asked.'

'Good God, Magdalen, are you suggesting that husbands should ask their wives' permission?'

'No, James, though it would seem only fair for a husband to consult his wife when he is about to set out on a journey from which he might never come back alive. But I am not here as your wife, begging to be consulted. I am here as myself, Magdalen Carnegie, wishing to know the truth.'

He sneered. 'The truth? Is that all? The wisest philosophers have sought it for centuries without ever finding it. Yet you want me to hand it to you as if it was a flower to be plucked off a bush.'

'Only the truth, James, about your journey to see the King.'

In his anger he crumpled the letter he was writing. 'You must be mad,' he muttered.

'I once asked you what you meant by honour. You could not tell me. You said it was something men felt in their hearts. Women, being inferior, could not feel it.'

'I did not say "inferior". I said "different".'

'If you said "different", you meant "inferior". Is it honourable, James, for you to give undertakings to your colleagues, those who signed the Covenant with you, and then go off behind their backs to deal with the King?'

'I gave no undertakings.' He said that between clenched teeth.

'They would say that was why you were released from prison.'

'I was released because the King demanded it. Let them say what they like. They are liars and rogues, most of them. They do not know what honour is. Magdalen, you go too far. Was it your father who put you up to asking these questions?'

'My father has always believed that in your heart you wished to serve the King and not the Covenant. So he will not be surprised if you change sides. He has been a politician too long.'

'He would never have allowed himself to be lectured by your mother.'

'Lord Rothes said there was no right or wrong, no honour or dishonour, only winners and losers. You passionately disagreed.'

'I still disagree. I would not accept him as an authority on honour. He does not care enough.'

'Do you think, James, I care too much?'

'Upon my soul, Magdalen, I do not know what to think. You have always had this morbid streak in you. Your sisters used to tease you, did they not, saying that, in the old days, you would have become a nun?'

She shook her head. He had been amused when she had given back the picture of the Madonna but he had not been interested enough to ask why she had done it.

She left then, leaving him chewing his quill and also, still once again, fingering that tender place in his mind which she had with her foolishness inflamed. *Was* his secret journey to the King dishonourable? Surely not, since his motive was to find a way by which the King and the Covenanters could be reconciled, so that the kingdom could become peaceful and more prosperous.

3

ON HIS ROUNDS of gentlemen's houses, Dr Muirkirk arrived at
Kincardine Castle one afternoon, accompanied by his assistant
and his valet, who did not, however, travel with him in his
comfortable carriage. Over the years he had got into the habit of
regarding himself as a gentleman who obliged other gentlemen
with advice about their health and not as a professional purveyor
of services for which he expected payment. He had another
source of income, which he kept secret. He sent to the Estates in
Edinburgh any information he picked up concerning families
whose loyalty to the Covenant was suspect. Others would have
called him a spy. He thought of himself as a patriot and a good
Presbyterian. Nowhere were his ears more alert than in Kincardine Castle, home of that notorious would-be defector, James
Graham, and nowhere was his manner more ingratiating and sly.

As he chatted to Lady Magdalen about her pregnancy, he put
in amiable enquiries about her husband, hoping to find out if it
was true that Graham was then in York waiting to be received by
the King. The doctor remembered her as a simple, spoiled, rather
perverse girl, who had petulantly preferred that boorish old
sawbones, Allen, to himself. It was her petulance he was
depending on, to make her give her husband away, without
really being aware that that was what she was doing.

To his consternation, however, he found himself confronted
by a young woman who, though clearly unwell, was far from
self-pitying or weak-minded. With those truthful brown eyes
fixed steadily on him, he could hear his voice sounding more and

more false and, to recover some sincerity, he had to talk about other subjects than her husband.

When she asked him to examine Lord John's throat, so frequently painful, she sat by, asking intelligent questions, which revealed to him, as well as to her, how limited his knowledge was, and indeed that of all his profession. Old Dr Allen, she remarked, had told her once that the human body, like Africa, was a vast continent of which so far very little was known. Intrepid explorers would be needed to extend our knowledge. Did Dr Muirkirk agree? Dr Muirkirk, his self-satisfaction dwindling, had to confess that he did. Wistfully he recalled his youthful idealistic days as a student at College, when he had prayed that God would choose him to eradicate disease and so benefit all mankind.

Lady Magdalen was to disconcert him still more. When she was a small girl at Kinnaird, she said, Dr Allen, calling at the castle, had taken the opportunity to treat servants and tenants. Those who could walk had come to the castle, those who were bed-ridden or crippled had been visited in their homes. Would not Dr Muirkirk care to offer his services in the same way?

She asked with apparent ingenuousness but he wondered if she was being ironical. Her smile was charming but ambiguous. What kind of noblewoman was she, showing concern for creatures, who, to tell the truth, were scarcely more intelligent or valuable than beasts?

Dr Muirkirk was dumbfounded. It had been years since he had personally attended a patient of the plebeian sort and even longer since he had stepped inside one of their obnoxious hovels. How could he have kept his clientele of aristocrats and genteel folk if he had come to them with the stink and infections of the lower orders exuding from him? He had left all that to fellows, like Allen, who weren't far removed from peasants themselves. Dr Muirkirk's own father had been a minister.

He could not get out of it. Excuses kept surging forward in his mind but those honest brown eyes kept him from uttering them. Besides, he felt that he wanted her good opinion, not only here on earth but also in the next world, in which, as a staunch Presbyterian, he strongly believed and into which she would surely be welcomed by Christ Himself.

In a room with the windows wide open, he and his assistant, Sneddon, received an assortment of sick and injured plebeians: women with fluxes, men with scythe wounds, and children with pocked faces. He would have dismissed them all very briefly if Lady Magdalen had not been there, not merely watching but lending a hand. It horrified, but at the same time chastened, him to see her lift on to her lap an infant whose face was hideous with scabs and comfort it while Sneddon smeared the pustules with salve. Even the child's mother was aghast. Like a good nurse, Lady Magdalen showed no revulsion and controlled her pity.

With one patient, though, she could not help showing distress. A handsome young girl of about 14, with long yellow hair, came in, accompanied by her tearful mother. She herself was dry-eyed and said nothing while her mother explained how, for the past six months, she had lost weight and coughed up blood. It was an obvious case of consumption. Throughout the country there were thousands. There was no cure. She would be dead within a year. Not even if she was to rest in a silk bed and eat grapes could she be saved. Had not Lord Rothes died recently of the same disease?

Lady Magdalen did something that Dr Muirkirk, as a Presbyterian respecting rank, found shocking. She got up and took the girl, who was taller than she, in her arms. There were tears in her eyes. The doctor heard in the distance a cuckoo calling. For the rest of his life, whenever he heard that elusive bird, he would remember that scene.

A bachelor, he now and then wished he had a wife to talk things over with. Never more so than then, for he would have liked very much to discuss with a helpmate that gesture of Lady

Magdalen's. The young countess's face, he would have said, with its peculiar pellucidity, had shone like an angel's. He had never thought he would envy James Graham, that traitor and anti-Christ, but he did then for, in Lady Magdalen, Graham had as his wife the most sincere woman Muirkirk had ever met.

The consultations went on for hours. Muirkirk himself and Sneddon had never worked harder in their lives. Small wonder they were exhausted. So was Lady Magdalen, which did not prevent her from saying that, if Dr Muirkirk did not mind, tomorrow they would call on some people in the village who were bedridden.

Dr Muirkirk did mind very much but could not say it to her face. He saw Sneddon looking dismayed and did not blame him.

She invited them to dine with her. Muirkirk never dined with his assistant who, in other big houses, ate with the servants but he let it pass that evening. How could he, a minister's son, show more pride than an earl's daughter?

Sometimes, in noblemen's houses, if the wine had been plentiful and the merriment boisterous, the doctor would be offered one of the serving maids to sleep with: not a silly young giggler but a deep-bosomed mature woman who knew what a man needed and how best to give it him. That night there was such a woman among those who brought the hot water for his bath, and she gave him encouraging smiles; but he found, when he retired for the night, that he preferred praying on his knees on the hard floor to lying in the arms of a soft naked woman. He had once heard a minister of the Kirk, who had drunk too much, make a joke to the effect that fornication, if the woman was worth it, was as quick a way to the Lord as any. Dr Muirkirk had laughed with the rest but, that night, as he prayed, he vowed never again to regard women as mere providers of carnal pleasure: even if, as the bibulous minister had claimed, the Scriptures said in several places that that was what Jehovah had intended them to be.

4

ONE WARM AFTERNOON in June 1644, John and James were guddling for trout in the burn close to the castle when they heard the watchman's trumpet. Horsemen were approaching. Perhaps it was Father at the head of an army. Some months ago, two English noblemen had come to Kincardine with a message from the King, asking Father to join him in England. Since then, they had heard that he had been appointed the King's Lieutenant in Scotland. The last news of him was that he had raised the Royal standard in Dumfries, expecting all the border lairds to flock to it. Had he captured Edinburgh on his way north? Such a triumph would surely rouse Mama out of her sad moods.

Racing across the field among the black cattle and clambering over the drystone dyke, the boys stood in the road, with their bonnets in their hands, ready to wave them. But only six horsemen came cantering round the bend where the herons nested and the one in front was their Uncle James, Lord Carnegie. They did not trust him. He was one of Argyll's men and so their father's enemy. He had always been jealous of Father.

Carnegie drew up his horse. He did not greet them cordially. He had never forgiven his father for marrying his sister to Montrose and he found it hard to forgive his nephews for being Montrose's sons.

'How is your mother?' he asked gruffly.

Not long ago, she had had a fourth child, another son. The birth had left her weak and moody and the disappointment had not helped.

'Mama is not very well,' said James.

'If you have brought a message,' said John, haughtily, 'you are to give it to me. I shall take it to Mama.'

Some of the horsemen scowled at what they considered typical Graham arrogance.

'You're just bairns,' said their uncle contemptuously, and spurred on his horse.

His companions followed.

The boys ran towards the castle, by a short cut.

'Do you think,' panted James, 'they have arrested Father again?'

'If they have we shall go to Edinburgh with a hundred Grahams and set him free.'

It would take many more than that, and where were they to be found? Even among the tenantry there were some who did not approve of Father's having gone over to the King.

'Would they really hang him, John?'

'They would never dare,' shouted John.

But both of them knew that even Kings had been put to death.

Asked by the housekeeper not to make so much noise with his high-heeled riding boots, Carnegie was conducted to his sister's room. He found her happed up in a chair. He could have wept. She looked so small. Her face was yellow and there were dark patches under her eyes. Though she was not yet 30, there was grey in her hair. His love for her had always contended with his hatred of Montrose, so he found it easy to blame her husband for her condition.

'She suffers pain, though she never complains,' whispered the woman.

And he had come to add to it, by telling her of her husband's vile treachery and imminent doom.

'Dear Magdalen,' he said, taking her cold dry hand, but not for long. Her illness might be smittal. He had been warned by his wife not to bring it back to her and their children.

'What brings you here, James?' she asked. 'Is Father ill?'

'No, no. Father's fine. He's sent me, Magdalen, to bring you and your children to Kinnaird, where you will be safe.'

'Are we not safe here? Who is going to harm us?'

'No one as yet but, if James Graham perseveres in his efforts to embroil his country in civil war, there could be some who would want to take revenge on his family.'

'Not men of God surely?'

Not for the first time he missed her irony. 'In the meantime, he has been driven back into England, where it seems he is trying to raise an army of English, Irish, and Germans too, with which to invade Scotland. He does not care how many Scotsmen are killed. Really, Magdalen, your husband has become a notorious villain.'

'Only if he loses,' she murmured.

James had always lacked subtlety. 'What do you mean? He is bound to lose. The whole country is united against him. He deserves the fate that is in store for him. He has never been a good husband to you, Magdalen. I warned my father. Other men, when they go off on a Continental tour, are content with a year or less. He stayed away for three years. How much time has he spent with you at home? Very little. He has preferred meddling with plots and intrigues.'

Yes, all that was true, but James, her James, would have simply said that he was following his destiny, which was to save Scotland, even if many Scotsmen had to be killed and many Scotswomen widowed.

She closed her eyes.

'I'll come back later,' said her brother. 'You're tired. You need sleep.'

He was thinking that what was in front of her, not far off, was the long sleep of death. He shuddered as he went out.

Outside the room his two nephews were waiting, bristling like guard dogs.

He felt sympathy for them. If it had been he who was the notorious traitor, he would still have hoped that his sons would not have disowned him.

'Your mother is going to sleep,' he said. 'Better not disturb her.'

'Why have you come, Uncle James?' asked John.

'Your grandfather sent me to bring you all to Kinnaird.'

'Why should we leave Kincardine?'

'Because you are no longer safe here.'

'No one would dare harm us. My father is the greatest general in Scotland.'

'A general without an army.'

'The King will give him an army.'

'The King needs every soldier to quell his English rebels but, if he had any to spare, they would be Englishmen, and perhaps Irishmen too. Any Scotsman leading such an army into his own country would deserve eternal shame.'

Remembering his sister's sick sad face, Carnegie was ashamed of himself for taunting her sons, who after all were just children. 'In Kinnaird your grandfather will explain things to you better than I can.'

'The doctor said Mama is too weak to travel,' said little James.

That was true. Carnegie's pity increased. They were Graham's sons, well indoctrinated by him, but they loved their mother. There was no happy future in store for them, their mother dying young and their father, hardly any older, ending up on the gallows. Their grandfather, Southesk, and Carnegie himself, would do everything they could to save the title and the estates but they might not succeed. Carnegie had once heard Argyll say that Montrose and all his tribe must be extirpated. The boys should not have blue ribbons in their bonnets, but black, as badges of death and dishonour.

183

'Whether you stay or not,' he said, 'troops will be quartered here. Your father has been declared an outlaw. Soon he will be a fugitive. Every place where he might seek shelter will be watched.'

But he had said enough in the meantime. Besides, little James had tears in his eyes and was trying hard not to weep, while John's young face was almost repulsive with useless hatred.

'If you want to help your mother – and your father too – persuade her to come to Kinnaird as soon as she feels able.'

Then he left them.

Later, while their uncle and his companions were dining, John and James crept into their mother's room to consult with her or, rather, to put to her John's plan. This was for her and the two youngest boys to go to Kinnaird, while John and James slipped off to England to join their father; perhaps one or two kinsmen might accompany them. John was enthusiastic, but James could not help looking scared at the prospect of travelling hundreds of miles, through areas occupied by Covenant troops. He was, after all, only nine and still afraid of the dark. Besides, he did not want to leave Mama, who needed them more than Father did.

'If James doesn't think he's strong enough,' said John, scornfully, 'I'll go alone.'

'You're the one that takes sore throats,' retorted James. 'Isn't he, Mama?'

They had never seen her so old and ill. James wondered, in terror, if she was going to die. Her breath sounded like little whistlings. She looked from one of them to the other with haunted eyes.

John did not notice. 'Uncle James said they will send troops to Kincardine to arrest Father if he pays us a visit. But, if he comes, it will be with a great army and he'll drive them away.'

'If your Father invades Scotland with an army,' said his mother, 'he will be wrong, very wrong.'

'Wrong?' cried John, horrified.

Even James was shocked.

They knew that their mother hated war and talk of war but then, did not all females? They hadn't minded when she had rebuked them for pretending to kill each other with swords or arrows but to call Father wrong was shocking.

'What do you mean, Mama?' asked James, taking her hand.

'His army would be made up of Englishmen and perhaps Irishmen too. Many Scotsmen would be killed, many Scots-women made widows. There would be many like Mr Gillies.'

'But he would be fighting for the King,' cried John.

James, though, wasn't quite so sure now. So many times had Father gone to the King, only to be turned away. Also Father had been a general in the Covenanters' army which had fought against the King.

'Father's the King's Lieutenant in Scotland,' said John. 'People should do what he tells them. All Scotsmen should join him. If they don't, they deserve to be killed. Isn't that so, James?'

But James was remembering the scar on Mr Gillies's face.

'Women don't understand,' said John. 'Father said so.'

James, looking at his mother, wondered if she didn't under-stand better than John, better even than Father. It was she and not Father who had been kind to Mr Gillies and the other men who had been wounded. It was she who had wept with the wife of the one who had died. It was she who visited their homes and gave them money.

John went into a sulk. 'I expect you want us to run away to Kinnaird.'

James waited anxiously for her to say that she did. He would rather be at peaceful Kinnaird than at Kincardine, surrounded by hostile soldiers.

She shook her head. 'No, I think we must stay here. That's what your father said we should do: until he sent us other instructions. This is our home. No one has a right to drive us away from it.'

That mollified John a little. Afterwards, he was to say to James that it wouldn't be fair to blame Mama. She was a woman and she wasn't well.

5

IT WAS SOME weeks later before Covenant troops appeared at Kincardine, ten horsemen and 50 infantry. Without asking for permission, they encamped in the fields round the castle. What angered John and James even more was that they wore blue ribbons in their bonnets. That was Father's emblem. How dared these renegades wear it.

John was for sending the fiery cross into the Highlands. He would carry it himself. He wasn't too young. Hadn't Lord Lewis Gordon led a cavalry charge when he was only thirteen?

The boys were proud of Mama. Though unwell, she looked not only beautiful but also very brave as, dressed in black, she confronted the commander and made it clear to him that he and his men were not welcome.

Major Andrew Strang was fat and red-faced, with a loud voice. He wore a blue sash round his belly and walked with a straight-legged strut as if, John whispered to James, he had pissed in his breeks. So he would too, they felt sure, if ever he found himself on a battlefield, with guns roaring and swords flashing. But he did not lack impudence. Rudely he told Mama that he and two of his officers would sleep and eat in the castle. When she asked what authority he had to make such demands, he slapped his sword hilt and shouted that force of arms was his authority but, if she was a stickler for legality, unlike her husband, he could show her his warrant from the Estates. Did she not realise that the country was in a state of war, thanks to the traitor Montrose? This castle and everything in it would soon be declared forfeit. She and her two oldest sons should think themselves lucky that they were not shut up in one of their own dungeons.

Magdalen noticed one of the officers frowning with distaste. Later he introduced himself as Captain Charles Ratho and he apologised for the intrusion upon her. There were, he assured her, gentlemen among the Covenanters. They were not all hectoring boors. He expressed regret that he and her husband were on opposite sides: it was, he said wryly, a thing decided almost by the tossing of a coin. He had always admired James Graham.

He was able to give her reliable news of James: he was now in Scotland, hoping to raise the Highlanders. The Gordons, though, were divided as usual. In Ratho's opinion, James's best plan would be to slip away to France. If he remained in Scotland, he would be seized sooner or later. What would happen to him then? In Ratho's gloomy grimace Magdalen saw the gallows.

John and James boldly ventured among the tents. They were their father's spies. Perhaps they could find out things that would be useful to him.

To their chagrin, they met no hostility. Indeed, when the soldiers learned who they were, they were received with rough but kind jocularity. These men from Fife, they soon discovered, weren't real soldiers: they were wheelwrights, shoemakers, joiners, bakers, and artisans of that sort, all of them Reservists out of practice. They did not handle their weapons with skill or zest; they drilled clumsily. They were hoping they were never called on to fight in earnest, especially against fellow Scots. If it was a case of repelling an invasion by foreigners, that would be different, they would fight then to the death but still without enthusiasm: killing wasn't their trade. They made useful things, like houses and shoes and bread. That was their way of serving their country, and all they wanted was to get back to it and be left in peace.

John and James could not help liking them and being amused by the jokes they played on one another but, at the same time, James was pleased that they were such half-hearted soldiers, it would make Father's task of defeating them so much easier. John had to remind him that the regular Scottish army, now in the north of England under the command of General Leslie, was better trained and equipped. They would not run away. To defeat them Father would need not only Highlanders but Irish too. Would it be right, asked James, to use the Irish who were said to be savages? John replied scornfully that in a war the only thing that mattered was to win.

Magdalen listened to her sons with sadness and foreboding.

One evening all the servants rushed out into the courtyard. Someone had said that he had seen great armies massed in the sky. What they saw were clouds red with sunset but fear and superstition easily turned them into armies. Someone called for silence: he had heard the touking of drums. They were silent and, sure enough, they too heard the drums. These were sure signs of imminent and bloody war.

Magdalen tried to find comfort in acts of benevolence, though these were not so gratefully received as before. The people's attitude seemed to be, it was her husband who was causing the distress, so why should they be thankful to her for trying to relieve it?

Two recipients were unequivocally grateful. These were the dominie and his wife, Cissie. With her father's help, Magdalen had got him the offer of a school in Perth, with more than 50 pupils and five times his Auchterarder stipend. He might have refused it but for Cissie. Already with one child and with another expected, she had surprised everyone, herself most of all perhaps, by being a doting mother and a faithful, but firm, wife. What her husband lacked in ambition and push she supplied. They had gone to Dundee to see the dominie's mother. That lady had seen at once that Cissie, though common as dirt, would do her son more good than some respectable wishy-washy daughter of a minister. She would take care that John got the rewards his qualifications entitled him to. The baby had been called Mary, after the old lady.

Magdalen had asked them to come and say goodbye before they left Auchterarder for good.

The dominie was nervous and deferential, though evidently proud and fond of the child on his lap. Cissie was wearing her best dress, she explained cheerfully, and didn't want it soiled.

Magdalen reflected that she had never seen her James nurse any of their children. There was an enviable intimacy about the family life of the lower orders. She could not help smiling, though, indeed had to repress laughter, as she paid the usual compliments to the baby. Whether it was her imagination or coincidence, she could not help seeing a resemblance between the tiny face with its long chin – the Leslies were famous for their long chins – and Lord Rothes. She was sure that the child was not Rothes's but it certainly looked like him. She was not absolutely sure that it was the dominie's: it certainly didn't look like him.

Cissie pretended to be indignant at the way the soldiers outside had whistled at her but she was obviously pleased and flattered. She liked her husband to know that he hadn't got the worse of the bargain. She was not in the least interested in the soldiers as men about to engage in bloody battles. They were simply admirers of the female form, especially when it was as shapely as hers. The looseness of her red dress concealed the swelling of her stomach.

'Did you hear, my lady,' she whispered, leaning towards Magdalen, 'that Mr Alexander, the new meenister, came upon twa o' them in the kirkyaird, wi' twa lassies o' the neighbourhood. It was bricht moonlicht tae, so he saw clearly whit they were up tae.'

'Now, Cissie,' said her husband, 'her ladyship's not interested in village tittle-tattle of that sort.'

'That's whaur you're wrang, Mr Blair,' she retorted. 'Her ladyship's always been interested in everything that went on. Yin o' them's getting mairried, my lady: her faither and Mr Alexander hae seen to that. The ither yin cannae, though, because the sodger's already got a wife in Pittenweem. Mr Alexander says he and poor Maggie will gang straight tae hell, but isnae the Bible fu' o' fornicators and adulterers, as auld Mr Graham used tae ca' them?'

Old Mr Graham, himself a would-be adulterer, had since died. Was he now in hell offering excuses?

'Is not the soldier more likely to go to hell for killing his fellow men?' Though, as she spoke, Magdalen was remembering that in the Bible there were more deaths in battle than fornications or adulteries. 'What do you say, Mr Blair?'

Cissie was aware of an understanding between her husband and her ladyship that excluded her. Mr Blair was educated, her ladyship was gentry. Cissie herself was common as daisies. She did not mind. She might not yet be able to read and write, though she was learning, but she had confidence in herself. If the whole country fell into ruin because of war or anything else, she and her family would survive and prosper. She would give the Lord His share of the credit but the biggest share would be her own . . .

As they were leaving, with the baby in its father's arms bawling her little head off, Magdalen wished them well. To her husband, the famous earl and now the King's Lieutenant, the dominie was the traditional figure of fun, the godly gumptionless scholar inveigled into marriage by a loose young woman with breasts 'like pomegranates', but it seemed to her that Mr Blair's role, that of teacher, was of greater value to the country than James's. She felt envious of Cissie, not because of her robust health that would enable her to live until she was past 70 or because of her exuberant femininity that caused men to whistle, but because, in her schoolhouse in Perth, she would be free to love her children and cherish her husband without feelings of guilt or shame.

6

MAJOR STRANG TOOK pleasure in informing her from time to time how badly things were going for James. Her father, more sorrowfully, sent similar news and again urged her to come to Kinnaird. He was trying to find out which of her sisters was prepared to go to Kincardine to keep her company, but she should bear in mind that these were perilous times and her sisters might wish to stay at home with their own families: their husbands might well insist on it.

She replied proudly that there was no need for anyone to come and keep her company. She had her sons. Besides, she was James Graham's wife. Let no one forget that.

None of her sisters came.

One day Strang rushed into the castle with a company of soldiers and ordered them to search it from turrets to dungeons. The rest of his men, he told her, were ransacking every hut, shed, byre, and privy in the neighbourhood. Into every pile of straw pikes would be thrust. People would be questioned with swords at their throats. Would she like to know why? Because there were reports that her husband had been seen. Shunned as an upstart by many whom he had arrogantly assumed would rally to his standard, he had left the Borders with one or two companions and come north, stealthy as thieves, hoping to raise an army among the Highlanders; which showed how deluded and desperate he was. The Highlanders might be as thick-headed as stots but they had enough sense not to join in a venture bound to fail, with no lucrative booty. Someone somewhere, he said, taunting her, would betray Montrose, either out of loyalty to the Covenant or for money, what did it matter? He would be hauled off to Edinburgh, on a donkey with his hands tied behind his back so that the populace could show their contempt and anger by pelting him with stones and offal. He would not be so high and mighty then. In Edinburgh he would be hanged forthwith. If she wanted to go and see it, said Strang, whether out of cruelty or crass consideration, it could be arranged.

Though she held her head high, she could not help imagining the scene, the mob yelling and the ministers grinning with hideous satisfaction, as they did at a witch's burning. In private she wept, not only at so ignominious a fate befalling one so proud and brave but also because James would have died without their love for each other having been given a chance to flower. He had put what he saw as his duty to his King and country before his love for her and their children. He had not seen it like that, but it was the only way she could see it. In her heart, therefore, was a small irreducible element of resentment. She could not help it: it was her woman's nature, just as he would have claimed that putting honour first was his nature as a man.

That hunt and others were unsuccessful. James was not found or betrayed. Likely, said Strang sourly, he had managed to slip out of Scotland and was now in France, enjoying the favours of the beautiful ladies there.

Then, one day not long afterwards, Strang came to her with a very different face: terror, not gloating, this time suffused his pudgy cheeks. He could not keep it out of his voice. Did she know what her scoundrel of a husband had done? He had allied himself to the Devil. Thousands of Irish savages had landed in the west and Montrose had gone to join them, intending to lead them against his countrymen and his countrywomen too, for everyone knew what these Irish were like, they raped women, they bit off fingers to get rings, they impaled babies on spears, they cut off prisoners' private parts and fed them to dogs. These were the fiends that her husband was about to turn loose on decent Scots people.

She gave him the answer that James had once given her. 'They are the King's subjects. Why should they not fight for him?'

But she felt sick with shame and foreboding. 'If he uses the Irish,' her father had written, 'he will be execrated for centuries to come.'

She heard Lord Rothes's mocking voice: 'Only, dear lady, if he is defeated. If he is victorious, he will be acclaimed the saviour of Scotland.'

Next day Strang and his soldiers left Kincardine in a panic, leaving equipment scattered over the field.

Charles Ratho came to say goodbye and thank her for her hospitality. He was despondent.

'It seems James and his damned Irish are making for Perth, destroying everyone and everything in their path.'

She shook her head. James would never allow it. Had he not saved Aberdeen from pillage?

'Will there be a battle?' she asked.

'Aye, there will be, and not very far off either. If the wind's in the right direction, you might hear the guns.'

'Who will win, do you think?'

'We should, for we'll have more horsemen and guns, and Lord Elcho is a competent enough commander, I suppose.'

Did he include her in that 'we'? What side did he, or Strang, or her father, or even James, think she was on? None. She was to stay at home and attend to her sewing.

'Why should you not win then?' she asked.

'Our regulars are in England, under Leslie. What we have are mostly the sort you saw here. They're soft. They hate soldiering. For God's sake, who likes it?'

She could have named one.

'All they want is to get back to their wives and bairns.'

'Is that not natural?'

'I suppose it is, but it's not the right attitude to take into battle, especially when they're going to be faced by the Irish. *They* love slaughtering people. They're never happier than when drenched in blood.'

'Have they not got wives and bairns too?'

'I've heard their women are fiercer than the men.'

A trumpet sounded. The trumpeter seemed agitated.

'Well, Lady Magdalen, I must be going. Stay indoors for the next day or two and keep all doors locked.' He tried to smile. 'Pray for me.'

He took his leave then, sadly, as if going to his death; whereas James, she thought, would go off to war like a bridegroom going to his wedding.

7

THE BOYS WERE up on the ramparts early, before the doves who slept there were properly awake. Through an old field glass of their father's, they took turns in scanning the countryside, particularly eastwards, in the direction of Perth. On distant hills they saw wreaths of mist, which they pretended were puffs of smoke from cannons. Once they heard a noise that had them staring at each other, their eyes wide. Was it the scream of a soldier pierced by a bullet or slashed by a sword? They knew what it was, a rabbit in the teeth of a weasel; but they went on pretending. They had no sympathy for the terrified doomed creature: their sympathies were with its killer. For the weasel represented Father's Irish and its victim the Covenanters. They had overheard Captain Ratho telling their mother how timorous the latter were and how fierce and bold the Irish, and they had themselves listened to the men from Fife talking dismally about their prospects. In the battle that might be taking place at that very moment, Father was bound to win. The more of the enemy who were killed the better, because it would mean they would be all the weaker if a second battle was fought, so that Father would win that one too and so be free to march on Edinburgh. Like their mother, they imagined Father in the capital but they saw him on a high throne in Holyrood House, like a king, for he was there in place of the King. He would send for them and they would take part in the triumphal ceremonies. Mama, though, would have to stay at home because she wasn't well; but, even if she had been fit to travel, she wouldn't have gone. Was it because

197

she was a woman that she hated war and talk of war? It couldn't be because she was religious for, in the Bible, weren't there many wars? And Presbyterian ministers had come every week to preach to the Covenant troops, urging them to be ready to smite the foe. It had struck the boys as comic, the ministers so keen for battle, the soldiers so sweirt.

They stayed on the ramparts all day, having food sent up to them. If they did not keep a constant look-out, they would be letting Father down.

They saw eagles, antlered stags, men scything, a woman lifting her skirts to her waist to ford a burn, herons being mobbed by hoodie-crows, and other usual sights. If they had been older, they would have become discouraged but, at gloaming, they were still as expectant as in the morning.

Nonetheless, when what they were on the look-out for did happen, they were taken by surprise, or at least James was. It was his turn with the field glass and, when he saw the three men come running out of the Cushat Wood, he took them to be shepherds or foresters, though they were seldom in such a hurry. Perhaps they were chasing a deer, though he could not see it.

'What is it?' cried John, grabbing the field glass.

He soon picked out the three men running so desperately that they kept falling and jaloused at once who or what they were: soldiers with blue ribbons in their bonnets but with no weapons; these they must have thrown away so that they could run all the faster. Were they, therefore, being pursued? As yet, he could not see any pursuers.

'They seem to be coming here,' said James. 'Who are they? What do they want?'

'Don't you know? They're Covenanters and they've run away from the battle.'

Then he saw who were chasing them. Here were Father's Irish, one, two, three, four of them, all with shaggy hair and beards, bare legs and arms, and brandishing claymores red with sunset or could it be with blood?

'Let me see,' said James, taking the field glass.

Often, when out in the fields or the wood, especially in the gloaming, they frightened each other by imagining that those rocks or those trees were monstrous men. Now here were such men.

'They never take prisoners,' cried John, exultantly. 'They're going to kill them.' And he hoped they would, right there in the field below, where he could see it done.

But James was horrified. 'Shouldn't we tell Mama?'

'What could she do?'

But James was off, down the narrow spiral stone stairway and along the several passage-ways to his mother's room.

She was working at her tapestry, alone. 'What's the matter?' she asked. 'Have you hurt yourself?'

Only then did he realise that he was weeping. 'Soldiers, Mama. Coming here. Running. Chased by Irish. They're going to kill them.'

Many years afterwards, when his mother was long since dead, he still remembered how she had put her needles and thread into their basket, got up, left the room, descended the stairs, and crossed the courtyard to the gate. She did not seem to hurry, yet she must have, for, keeping up with her, he found himself panting.

Half asleep, for it was stuffy in the small gatehouse, John Galloway hurried out to do her bidding: which was to open the gate and be ready to close it again.

The three fugitives appeared, stumbling, gasping, and clutching at air. One's neck was bloody. James recognised their uniform as that of the Fife regiment. Perhaps they had been stationed here and had remembered it as a place where they might find sanctuary. They collapsed at Mama's feet, babbling. So thick their Fife accents and so distorted their voices with terror, James could not make out what they were saying but it was easy to guess. There was a stink of shit off them. He hoped his mother did not notice it.

Should she protect them? They were Father's enemies. On the battlefield they would have killed him if they had got the chance. They would have been given a large reward.

Before the gate could be shut again, in his astonishment, Galloway was slow, three of the Irish appeared. Mama confronted them, heedless of their big swords and savage cries. James had never thought of her as a heroine; now he did and always would.

She had another surprise in store for him. He had not known she could speak Gaelic, well enough at any rate for the Irish to understand her. James himself had not learned it but he knew what she was saying, that this was their commander James Graham's house and she was James Graham's wife. How dared they come to it with blood on their swords.

They stared at one another in bewilderment. One glanced up and saw the Graham crest carved in the stone above the gate. He pointed it out to the others. They mumbled apologies and crept away, like hounds ordered to leave a deer's carcase that they had been about to devour.

John was there now, gazing with disgust at the three soldiers on their knees at his mother's feet and then at her with a strange expression. At 14, he was already taller than she. More than ever he resembled his father, not her. 'Why did you let them in?' he asked.

She turned and looked at him as if she had never seen him before. 'Do you not know why?'

'They are Father's enemies.'

'Would your father have let them in?'

John was not willing to answer that but James cried: 'Yes, he would, John. He said soldiers must be merciful.'

'Not to cowards. They ran away. Cowards don't deserve mercy.'

James shuddered. He had often felt afraid that, on a battlefield, he would not be as brave as he should. Therefore, he felt great sympathy for these soldiers who had run away. At the same time he felt revulsion against the whole world, including John and, yes, Father too. Only his mother was exempt. Her he deeply loved, though he now realised he did not really know her. He had never tried; he had taken her for granted.

Servants had gathered in the courtyard. Some recognised the three soldiers. James noticed one old woman crossing herself.

Mama gave instructions for the soldiers to be taken away and cared for; she would talk to them later. Then, stared at by everyone, in awe, she walked across the courtyard into the house with great dignity. No one would have been surprised if she had suddenly sunk to the cobbles, dead or dying; but no one was surprised when it did not happen. Courage kept her on her feet, with her head held high. Some of the women were in tears.

Somewhere, perhaps in captured Perth, Father was celebrating his victory. Here Mama was breaking her heart. Because of his own doubts and fears, James tasted a little of her despair.

He could never have explained it to John, who saw things so differently. Mama, he thought, had let Father down, not because she was a traitress, but simply because she was a woman. So, at the first sign of violence and blood, she had given way to pity and softness.

James would have said that it was impossible for him ever to hate his brother but he came very close to it then as he listened to John disdainfully finding excuses for Mama.

8

MAGDALEN WOULD NEVER forget that look on her son's face. Anger she would have expected, and disappointment, and even contempt, for he had inherited his father's opinion of women that they were weak creatures with no conception of honour; but not hatred. He had been like a young priest who thought she had defiled his temple and mocked his gods.

Back in her room, busy again with her needles and threads, her hands trembled. Another woman – Katherine Graham, for example – would have had the resolution to keep the gates closed and let the three men be butchered. In Biblical times, such a woman would have gone out afterwards and dipped her hands in the blood. On her knees, she would have thanked God for the death of her husband's enemies. And God would have looked down on her with favour, for she had shown fidelity to her husband, whom in His sight she had solemnly sworn to obey.

That was one way of looking at it. Mr Henderson would have pointed out another. Since all Covenanters were servants of God, by saving three of them she had pleased Him. She might not have her reward on earth but she would certainly have it in heaven.

They all knew what God wanted. Why not, since it was what they themselves wanted. She did not know what she wanted and, therefore, even if she had been so presumptuous could not instruct Him. Instead, she felt herself withdrawing further and further to a place where there could be communication with no one, not even with God. If it was not stopped before too late she would become like a woman of stone. They would all say, with pity but without much surprise, that she had finally gone mad.

There was a knock on the door. She did not have to ask who it was. She recognised, in the timid sound, James's anxiety and love.

He was carrying a sprig of rowan berries. They were reputed to bring good luck or, at any rate, to keep away bad.

'Are you all right, Mama?' he asked.

She smiled and came a great way back into the world. 'Yes, I'm all right.'

'John's sorry. For speaking to you the way he did.'

But not perhaps for looking at her the way he had done.

James pretended to be interested in her sewing: it happened to be the head of Jesus.

'We couldn't really have let them be killed, could we, Mama? They weren't armed. They wanted to surrender. They should have been taken prisoner. That's how civilised soldiers fight.'

Civilised soldiers. He must have got the expression from his father. Soldiers killed men who had done them no harm. How could it be done in a civilised fashion?

'John thinks so too now.'

Poor John, so keen to be a soldier and yet, with his weak constitution, unfit. If a bullet or sword did not kill him, cold and rain would.

'He's going to talk to you about it. Later. One of them's got a big gash in his neck. Mrs Witherspoon couldn't stop the blood. She says he'll die.'

Mrs Witherspoon had some skill as a nurse.

'The other two are all right. They said he was married with three children. He was a locksmith. Will you go to Kinnaird now, Mama? John wants to go to Perth to join Father.'

'Will you come to Kinnaird with me?'

He frowned. 'I'd like to but I think I'll have to go with John. You understand, don't you?'

'Yes, I understand.'

'I'll come and visit you at Kinnaird as often as I can. They said they ran away because the Irish were so ferocious. They saw them cutting off heads and tossing them to one another like footballs, with the blood dripping. They couldn't stand it, they said. It was like fighting devils from hell. Do you know how far they ran, Mama? Twelve miles! There were about twenty of them at first. The rest were caught up and killed. It must have been terrible seeing heads cut off and used as footballs. Do you know, Mama, I think I might have run away too. Don't tell John I said that.'

'I won't tell him.'

'Or Father. Please never tell *him*.'

'I won't.'

'I wonder what's happened to Mr Blair the dominie, and Cissie. They went to Perth; didn't they?'

'Yes.'

'But Father wouldn't allow the Irish to kill the people in the town, would he?'

'No.' But what if it had been a condition of the Irish's allegiance to him that he did not prevent them from killing and plundering?

A few minutes later, James left to go and see what John was doing.

He had no idea that he had, for the time being at least, saved his mother from turning to stone.

9

NEXT DAY, LATE in the evening their kinsman Graham of Braco arrived at the castle with a message from Father: the two boys were to join him in Perth, where they would be safer; and Magdalen was to take Robert and little David to Kinnaird for the same reason. Braco would escort them.

He was a small sulky-looking man with a dour sense of humour that not many appreciated. He was prouder of his prowess as a farmer than of his rank as a gentleman. It was his ambition to breed bigger and fatter cattle.

The journey would have to be carried out as secretly as possible. James Graham, he reminded them, was at that moment the most hated man in Lowland Scotland. Many people wanted to be revenged on him for relatives killed or wounded at Tippermuir. It wouldn't matter to them, any more than it had to Herod, that his children were innocent. Hurting them would be a way of hurting him. Ministers would be the first to point that out.

The boys begged him to give an account of the battle. In a dry flat voice, as if he was describing some mundane matter, like a cow calving, he told of men disembowelled while still alive, heads hacked off with the mouths still open with cries for mercy, and private parts sliced off with claymores swung like golf clubs. Even John began to look green and sick.

As Magdalen listened, she wondered what part James, lover of honour, merciful soldier, fastidious gentleman, and poet, had played in the butchery. Seeing the question in her eyes, Braco remarked that James had chosen to fight on foot, with a half-pike as his weapon. He had not seen him use it but he had heard him shouting encouragement to the disembowellers and beheaders. His boots had been splashed with blood.

But it had been a glorious victory, hadn't it? said John.

By God it had. It was said two thousand Covenanters had been killed. A man could have walked on corpses all the way to Perth. And yet, said John, the Covenanters had had more men, more cavalry, and more guns. Wasn't that so? Aye, it was. Didn't that show that Father was a much better general than Lord Elcho who had commanded the Covenanters?

It did, but another reason could be that the men from Fife had had no stomach for blood-letting, whereas the Irish had enjoyed it like a feast. Also, since both sides had gone down on their knees before the battle to ask God's help, it looked as if the God of the Irish, who were Papists, mind, was better at miracles than the Presbyterians' God.

No, cried John indignantly. God had given Father victory because his cause was just.

Aye, that would be right, said Braco drily. Everyone knew that just causes always won.

To Magdalen, later, when they were alone, Braco gave his opinion that in spite of James's remarkable victory and other victories that might follow, he could not, in the end, win. He had turned most of Lowland Scotland against him by his use of the Irish. Braco himself had had enough of slaughter. After delivering the boys to their father, he was returning to Braco, to look after his cattle and do some thinking. Other members of the Lowland Scotch gentry would be doing the same. They just could not bring themselves to fight alongside Highlanders and Irish on behalf of a King who, though born in Scotland, had chosen to become an Englishman, and who had a Catholic wife, whose advice he foolishly heeded.

But if James's kinsmen and friends would not help him,

thought Magdalen, he really was doomed, in spite of his first victory. She felt great pity for him.

Braco was not much interested in the three soldiers whose lives she had saved. There must be dozens like them, he said, who had managed to escape from their pursuers. James had forbidden such pursuits but the Irish once they had tasted blood, were uncontrollable.

She did not feel well enough to travel. Besides, if she remained in the castle with her two youngest children, it was less likely to be attacked and destroyed.

Braco was doubtful. The Covenant troops who came would have been instructed by Argyll to blow up the castle and leave it uninhabitable. There would be ministers with them who would see to it that they did their duty.

Braco enjoyed talking through his nose, in imitation of fanatical preachers.

They set off soon after dawn. Magdalen was up to see them off, though it was chilly and still dark and she had had a sleepless night with pain and worry. James was proud that he was to ride a horse and not a small pony, but he could not help his voice trembling as he said goodbye. He promised to come back soon.

John had to show that at 14, he was a man, whereas James, at twelve, was still a child. So he did not cling to his mother as James had done or have tears in his eyes. He tried so hard to be manly and looked so like his father that, though she smiled, and, in a calm enough voice gave him sensible advice about looking after his health, she was very close to weeping, for there in the courtyard, under the red sky, with the horses snorting and stamping, and in the distance a curlew calling, she had a premonition that she would never see him again. She did not have the same premonition about James, so it could not be her own death that would prevent their meeting; it must be his own.

After they were gone, she remained in the courtyard for a while, as the sky grew lighter. Outwardly, she looked composed:

so much so that servants watching were divided as to whether to admire her fortitude or condemn her apparent lack of feeling. They themselves would have been lamenting loudly if they had just seen their sons riding off to join their father in a war where they might be killed.

They did not know that she was feeling so trapped in despair that she would not be able to pray. She would not know what to say to God, just as she had not known what to say to James, her husband. She had tried to write a letter to him but could not find words both loving and truthful.

When she was a child, her father had warned her never to put God to shame; never to ask God to do for her what would be unfair not only to others but also to God Himself. Surely He was never more shamed than when men killed one another in His name, with both sides praying.

She shivered, and Mrs Witherspoon hurried forward to place a blanket over her shoulders.

Mrs Witherspoon, a minister's widow, had been engaged as nurse companion after Janet's death. She was a handsome ambitious young woman, with red hair and a fine figure.

10

LATER THAT DAY Magdalen went to the room where the three soldiers were being cared for.

Mrs Witherspoon opened the door but was reluctant to let her in. One of the men was dying, she said: there was a danger of infection. What she really meant was that it was unseemly for a great lady, wife of a marquis, to be seen showing concern for common soldiers. Mrs Witherspoon believed strongly in rank, not only because God had ordained it, as the Kirk taught, but also because she considered herself above all the other servants in the house. Lady Magdalen's disregard of rank was another consequence of her illness, which weakened her mind as well as her body.

'I promised I would speak to them,' said Magdalen.

'One's past speaking, my lady.'

'Then I shall speak to the others.'

'Well, just a minute, my lady.' Mrs Witherspoon went in and reappeared shortly with a peculiar look of satisfaction. She had been proved right.

'He's just passed on, my lady. You don't want to see him, I'm sure.'

But Magdalen did, though it would be the first time she had seen a dead person.

He was lying on a low bed, with his face turned towards her. His eyes were still open and he seemed to be smiling. He looked strangely content and purified.

Mrs Witherspoon went forward and threw a blanket over his face.

The two other men were on their feet, bowing their heads to Magdalen. One, hardly any older than John, was weeping quietly. He tried to hide his face with his hand, which was bandaged. He was blaming no one, not even the Irish soldier who had dealt the vicious fatal blow. His grief was simple and beautiful.

His companion was older. He had large hands, which he kept wringing. Was he the baker and did he imagine he was kneading dough? Was it his way of holding on to sanity? Of reminding himself that one day he would be making bread again?

'I'm very sorry,' said Magdalen.

He looked up at her in surprise. He had not expected to find her concern sincere but he saw that it was. 'Whaur will Willie be buried, my lady?'

'In the kirkyard, surely. I would like to write a letter to his wife. Would you take it to her?'

He nodded, still amazed.

Mrs Witherspoon frowned but said nothing. Such a letter would be a mistake. Whatever the rights and wrongs of the war that the Marquis had started, it was not proper for his wife to be seen giving comfort to his enemies. The poor young lady did not realise that that was what she would be doing. The letter would end up in the hands of people who would use it against her husband. She was kind-hearted but ignorant as a bairn in so many ways. How could she have avoided it, brought up in the lap of luxury and protected from the harshnesses of life? Mrs Witherspoon herself had had a difficult childhood. By the age of ten she had experienced more hardships than her ladyship ever would even if she were to live till she was 70, which, alas, was most unlikely.

After the funeral, which Magdalen attended, she wrote the letter, signed it, and handed it personally to Mr Simmers, the baker, who promised again to deliver it. She never suspected, that behind her back, Mrs Witherspoon would go to him and demand it back: her mistress had changed her mind. He handed it over without saying anything, though he looked confused and disappointed.

As soon as he and his companion had set off on foot for Fife, well supplied with provisions, Mrs Witherspoon hurried to her own room, where there was a fire burning. She intended to burn the letter without even unsealing it but she found herself hesitating. She was still convinced she would be doing her mistress a service but, with the letter in her hand, she began to feel guilty. That feeling increased when she gave in to curiosity and read it. It was short and simple but full of genuine feeling: so much so that Mrs Witherspoon, as dry-eyed as any woman in Scotland, was almost in tears. The woman in Pittenweem would have treasured this letter all her life. She would have passed it on to her children and they to theirs. For Lady Magdalen had written, not as a great lady condescending to an underling, but as one wife to another, as one mother to another.

In the end Mrs Witherspoon hid it at the bottom of the kist where she kept her Sunday clothes.

11

ONE WET OCTOBER afternoon, Covenant troops arrived at the castle: a strong contingent of horsemen and infantry, with, as was soon demonstrated, a piece of artillery. As she lay ill in bed, Magdalen heard the neighing of horses, the rattle of military equipment, and the shouting of orders. Then she, and everyone else in the castle, was startled by the roar of the cannon. Mrs Witherspoon came, white-faced and panting, to report that the cannon ball had knocked down some tall trees nearby.

'Have they come to destroy the castle, for spite? Surely they will allow everyone to leave first. What will you do, my lady, that canna walk?'

Magdalen did not reply. She was thinking that, in spite of pain and weakness, she would refuse to be driven out of her home. She would defy them, not so much for her husband's sake as for the sake of all women victimised by war.

Mrs Witherspoon was not reassured by her mistress's calmness; on the contrary, it alarmed her still more. For some time now, Lady Magdalen had been withdrawn; even her children could not reach her. She was deranged, some thought; and no wonder, now that her husband was the most hated man in the kingdom.

That evening, in the gloaming, there came a hammering on the gate, as if with the hilts of swords.

'Go and tell Mr Galloway to let them in,' said Magdalen.

Mrs Witherspoon was fearful. 'What if they've come to cut our throats?'

'I hardly think so.'

Mrs Witherspoon hurried away, wringing her hands.

Magdalen did not feel calm. She felt frightened and near to despair. She tried to pray but could not. So many prayers were being sent up to God, how could He choose which ones to answer? Those who had come to destroy the castle had no doubt prayed for the success of their mission.

But if I lose faith in God, she thought, how can I live? And if I die, shall I go straight to hell and never, through eternity, meet my mother?

Mrs Witherspoon, in much excitement, brought their message. 'Four of them, my lady: three officers and a minister. They want to speak to you. I told them you were sick in bed but he said, the one in charge, Sir Archibald Hutcheon; he said his name was, said that, if you didna go to them, they wad go to you. That big red-faced man that was here before, he's one of them.'

'Major Strang?'

'Aye, that's him. There's a minister too. He's the fiercest of them all.'

'Please help me up, Mrs Witherspoon. I shall receive them here.'

'But you're not fit, my lady.'

'Just help me, please.'

'It'll be the daith of you.'

Protesting all the time, Mrs Witherspoon helped her young mistress out of bed, noticing again how thin her legs were, mere spurtles: it was just as well her body was so light. How much pain she felt Mrs Witherspoon could never be sure. She gave little sign; only a sudden gasp now and then. Your man, thought the harassed housekeeper, as she helped to put on the black dress, ought to be here, or your father, or one of your brothers. You shouldn't be left by yourself in this cold dreary house. The Marquis, wherever he was, should think shame, leaving his young wife to waste away, with no one to talk to but servants, for recently there had been very few visitors. Little wonder there was so much grey in her hair and so much sadness in her eyes, though she was barely 30.

When dressed, with her hair brushed, she sat in a chair, holding tightly on to its arms. In the candlelight, she looked, thought Mrs Witherspoon, like a young queen, but one close to death.

'Please tell them I am ready to receive them,' she said.

As she went down the dark narrow stone stairs, Mrs Witherspoon wondered what would happen to herself if the castle was destroyed and she lost her employment. She would have to go to her sister in St Andrews, though she did not care for her brother-in-law, a common shopkeeper.

Major Strang marched up to her. 'How much longer are we to be kept waiting?' he bellowed.

She noticed the other officers scowling at him.

She addressed his superior. 'Her ladyship will see you now, sir, in her room.'

'How is she? Is she very ill? Is she able to talk?'

'Yes, sir, but not for long. She's very weak. Please show her consideration.'

'As much consideration as her husband showed the people of Aberdeen,' shouted Strang.

Mrs Witherspoon did not understand. At the castle they had heard nothing about Aberdeen.

As they went up the stairs the minister spoke anxiously: 'This sickness of your mistress, is it smittal?'

'The doctor didna think it was.'

Mrs Witherspoon opened the door. 'Here are the gentlemen to see you, my lady.'

Strang pushed her out of the way and was first into the small room, much to Sir Archibald's annoyance. The minister snorted as if distrusting the air, though it was scented with herbs.

Sir Archibald looked uncomfortable, not because he was afraid of catching a disease but because he felt ashamed. It was one thing blowing up the house of a damned traitor like Montrose, but quite another thing molesting this young woman, who in spite of her illness looked so brave and beautiful.

The minister kept close to the door, which he would not allow to be shut, though the draught caused the candles to flicker.

Sir Archibald introduced himself.

She remembered him. 'Did you not once visit my father's house at Kinnaird?'

'I had that honour, madam. I have always been an admirer of your father.'

'I'm sorry I cannot entertain you as I should have liked. As you can see, I am not well.'

'I'm very sorry indeed.'

'You remember me?' jeered Strang.

'Yes, Major, I remember you. You were offensive to me once and you are being offensive to me again.'

Mrs Witherspoon noticed the third officer, a younger man, smile. Evidently he did not care for Strang.

Strang laughed. 'Did you know, madam, that your husband, James Graham, has been excommunicated, a price has been put on his head, and all his property is confiscated?'

She ignored that, though she would worry about it later. 'Have you news of Captain Ratho, Major?'

That put an end to his bluster.

'Captain Ratho was killed at Tippermuir,' said Sir Archibald.

'He was one of those who did not run away,' said the young officer.

'I am very sorry,' said Magdalen. 'He was kind to me.'

'Thousands were slain at Tippermuir,' said the minister, 'thanks to your husband's devilish treachery and ambition.'

Sir Archibald had his duty to do. Since he did not like it, less now than ever, he spoke more harshly than he wished. 'I have to inform you, Lady Magdalen, that by the order of the Estates, I

215

have come to destroy this house, as being the home of a notorious and proscribed traitor.'

'It is my home too. Am I also branded as a notorious traitor?'

He shook his head. He knew about her saving the lives of the Covenant soldiers. If she was a traitor it was to her husband, not to the Covenant.

He glanced angrily at the Revd John Clarkson, but there was no help on that gaunt fanatical face.

Major Strang was again jeering. 'Have you heard what your husband, the traitor James Graham, did at Aberdeen lately?'

With her head held high, she waited for him to tell her. He did it with gloating.

'He let loose his Irish savages on the people. They killed and raped and plundered.'

Her instant reaction was not disgust or horror but pity: not for the unfortunate citizens of Aberdeen but for James, forced by circumstances into actions utterly repugnant to him.

'He will roast in hell for it,' said the minister.

She tried to keep her voice steady. 'And in revenge you have come to destroy my home, harry me and my children, terrify my servants, and make us all homeless. Is that war, gentlemen?'

Sir Archibald looked baffled and ashamed; so did the other officer; but Strang and the minister were exultant.

'Aye, by God, it's war,' cried Strang.

'War that your husband, the traitor rebel, brought about,' cried the minister. His voice, though, was muffled by the handkerchief he now held to his mouth.

Sir Archibald, a regular soldier, had a high opinion of his profession and its principles. Her apparently guileless question defeated him. All he could say was: 'I have my orders, madam. You have until two o'clock tomorrow to clear the castle of all its inhabitants and of any valuables you wish to preserve. I shall put a company of soldiers at your disposal. I bid you good-night.'

He turned then abruptly and left.

216

Mr Clarkson, still holding the handkerchief to his nose, followed; so did Strang, laughing: but the young officer came over to Magdalen and whispered, in an agitated voice: 'I assure you, Lady Magdalen, some of us do not enjoy this task that has been laid upon us.'

'But you will nonetheless carry it out?'

'We are soldiers. We obey orders.'

He fled then, shame-faced.

There could have been triumph in defying them and in showing up their ultimate cowardice, if it had not been for the picture in her mind of women screaming at the hands of the Irish, and of James, sick at heart, letting it happen because he had a war to win.

12

THERE WAS NOT much sleep for anyone in the castle that night. Most of the servants had already gathered their belongings together and packed them in readiness. There were grumbles that this war had nothing to do with them, it was a quarrel among the gentry; why should porters and parlour maids suffer? Some, in whispers, confided to others whom they trusted, that it was the Marquis's fault, all those secret journeys to England, and his deserting the cause of the Covenant to fight for the King. Perhaps he deserved to have his castle blown to bits, for weren't he and his Irish busy blowing to bits the castles of other noblemen? But surely their mistress was innocent. There were prayers said for her that night.

She herself did not pray. She lay awake for hours, listening to an owl hooting, a mouse scraping, and her own heart pounding. James was now doomed, she was sure of that, in spite of his victories. He would be hanged as a traitor: a cruel and unjust fate. She imagined him in his cell on his last night. What would he be thinking? Of his sons, no doubt; of the King, whom he had not been able to save; and of her? She hoped so but did not believe it. In any case she herself would be dead by then. Tears came into her eyes. She and James and the children could have been happy together if he had been content to stay at home, winning fame as a poet rather than as a soldier. She remembered lines he had written and murmured them aloud in the room that was now dark and cold because candles and fire had gone out:

'But if thou wilt be constant then
And faithful of thy word
I'll make thee glorious by my pen
And famous by my sword.
I'll serve thee in such noble ways
Was never heard before;
I'll crown and deck thee all with bays
And love thee evermore.'

She had pretended that it was addressed to her but of course it wasn't. It was addressed to some more glorious creature, the mythical embodiment of all he believed in; she fell far short of that. Perhaps she had never tried hard enough to measure up to his ideal, but what mortal woman could have?

She hoped it was not true that he had let his savage Irish soldiers plunder Aberdeen. After all it was his enemies who had told her. If it had happened, it could have been without James's sanction, indeed against his will. Those bloodstained savages she had seen at her gate would not be easy to keep under control. But, if he had let it happen, as a deliberate manoeuvre of war, what part had her sons played in it? Her heart broke as she thought of John, secretly sick at heart but pretending to approve, and of poor James, who would have been openly appalled. She had failed, not only as a wife but as a mother too. It was no use her offering excuses, such as her youth, her timidity, and her inevitable submission to her husband's so much stronger will: she could have tried harder.

Early next morning, she had all the servants assembled in the great hall. Dressed in black, she was assisted by Mrs Witherspoon down the stairs. She sat in the high throne-like chair, under the portraits of herself and James. She tried to look more resolute than she felt.

Everyone was present, down to the lad who kept the court-yard clear of dung. They all gazed at her with frightened faces and kept shivering, from fear and cold. Outside it was another dank, damp, dull day.

She spoke slowly, for she was still short of breath. She was afraid that at any moment she might break down and weep. If she were to do that, she would be letting James down. It was his honour she had to uphold.

'You have seen the soldiers. Their commander has told me that, at two o'clock today, they will begin firing their cannon at this house. That is the order they have been sent to carry out. You must therefore take all your possessions and leave, as soon as you can. Soldiers will be sent to help. You may choose not to accept their help.'

She paused then, for those soldiers could be heard entering the courtyard.

'But whaur are we to gang, my lady?' someone called.

'Surely your friends and relatives in the district will give you shelter?'

'Some o' us are no' frae this pairt, my lady. We hae nae freen's or relatives nearby.'

'Still, someone will take you in, until other arrangements can be made.'

Mrs Witherspoon was smiling. She wasn't worried. She would find refuge in the manse, being friendly with the minister's wife. Besides, being a good Presbyterian, she looked for favour from the soldiers, not harm.

'Whit aboot yoursel', my lady?' someone cried. 'And your twa bairns?'

Her children, Robert aged seven, and David still a babe in arms, were there, in the charge of their nurses, on whom, God forgive her, they depended more than they did on her.

'Whit aboot *your* valuables, my lady?'

'They will remain here. I think they will be safe.'

They stared at one another. Safe? Did she say 'safe'? How could they be safe with cannon balls smashing into the walls of

220

the castle? The poor lady was truly out of her mind. What she said next proved it.

'You must all leave but I myself will remain.'

Did she think that, if she was in the castle, it wouldn't be bombarded? She could be right for, after all, her father, the Earl of Southesk, was an important man who knew other important men, and her brother Lord Carnegie was a friend of the Earl of Argyll. But what if she was wrong? Terrible things were done in war. In her place, they wouldn't have taken the risk, but none of them dared try to dissuade her. She was not one of them, in spite of her kindness.

The soldiers, led by a shy lieutenant, came into the hall, wearing capes that glistened with rain. He made his way through the throng of servants to Lady Magdalen. He looked unhappy. He had a wife of his own, and two children. In the officers' mess tent last night he had been on the side of those who had argued that the castle did not have to be destroyed then, it could be done later, after Montrose's army had been smashed once and for all.

'Lieutenant Rutherford, my lady,' he said, nervously. 'I have been instructed to offer you and your children escort to our camp. There you will be hospitably received and afterwards, if you wish, delivered to your father's house at Kinnaird.'

'Thank you, Mr Rutherford, but this is my home and I do not intend to leave it.'

He was taken aback. Obduracy on her part had not been envisaged. A sick young woman of no particular character, that was how she had been described.

He had no authority to use force to make her leave. He doubted if anyone had. The Estates would not wish to offend her father or her brother, Lord Carnegie, who was a valued ally of Argyll's.

Meanwhile, the soldiers were giving assistance. A few of the servants angrily declined it but most were grateful. One or two women wept.

Lieutenant Rutherford went again to speak to Lady Magdalen, though he would rather have faced a charge of Irish.

'I was instructed, Lady Magdalen, to warn you that, if you choose to remain here, the consequences will be on your own head.'

'I am aware of that, Mr Rutherford.'

If she had scowled or looked down on him as if he was rubbish – after all, his father was a tradesman from St Andrews – he could have borne it with head held high, for he was a soldier obeying orders, but she spoke so pleasantly and smiled so serenely that he crept back, confused and ashamed. That the young lady was brave and proud he could have expected, considering her lineage, but she was also kind; not only that, she was also humorous, even in those desperate circumstances.

13

WHEN LIEUTENANT RUTHERFORD reported Lady Magdalen's attitude, Mr Clarkson, with support from Major Strang, was all for having her bodily removed but Sir Archie growled that it wouldn't do. The lady was of higher rank than himself and he knew her father. She was ill and not in her right mind: probably female troubles, he muttered. Rough treatment could kill her. And, though he mentioned this to no one, Sir Archie could not get out of his head that question of hers, which could be regarded as childish or wise, according to how you looked at it. 'Is that war, gentlemen?'

Everyone was aware of another very sound argument against treating the young lady roughly, though none was bold enough to voice it, not even Mr Clarkson. If Montrose had another two or three victories like Tippermuir and Aberdeen, he might well end up justifying his title of King's Lieutenant in Scotland and be in a position to have them all hanged. In spite of what had happened at Aberdeen, he was reputed to be fair-minded and merciful, but he was bound to punish severely any who had ill-treated his wife. It didn't matter that it had never been much of a love match. Hadn't he gone off on a Continental tour that had lasted *three* years, leaving her with two infants? That had hardly indicated passionate attachment. It had been the talk of salons and taverns. Still, whether a man loved his wife or not, his honour resided in her. If she was abused, so was he.

Thus, in their tent, as they drank their claret, the officers chatted, with a forced jest or two. They decided, best leave the lady and her castle alone. Time enough to blow it up later, when Montrose was no longer a threat.

No one asked Major Strang his opinion, but then no one ever did. In any case he was usually too drunk to give it. No one liked him, drunk or sober. He wasn't the only one who had run away at Tippermuir but none had run faster or squealed louder. Demotion or even cashiering was imminent. Sir Archie couldn't stand him and didn't hide it.

At a quarter to two, trumpets were sounded in warning and the gun was trained on the castle.

It was raining heavily. The soldiers took shelter in their tents. Only those in charge of the gun were out in the open, getting soaked. There was a good chance that, if the order to fire was given, nothing would happen because of the wetness. On his knees in the mud, Mr Clarkson prayed. More than one artillery man was tempted to kick his backside.

Then, about two or three minutes to the hour, through the mirk and rain, they saw something appear on the ramparts. Was it a crow or a spectre? The soldiers muttered uneasily; in the old days, they would have crossed themselves. Officers with field glasses soon made out that it was a person dressed in black. Roused from his prayer, Mr Clarkson snatched a field glass. It was the traitor-rebel's woman, he howled. The Jezebel had been lying. How could any woman seriously ill have climbed up there?

They could have told him. By showing great courage and determination.

She was motionless, with no waving of her arms in defiance or entreaty.

Mr Clarkson shrieked the order to fire, like a spoiled child afraid that the treat it had been promised was going to be denied it. Sir Archie muttered an oath of a blasphemous nature, which would have shocked Mr Clarkson had he not been deafened by his own hoarse exhortations.

224

The poor young lady must be getting soaked to the skin, said the soldiers, themselves shivering. If a cannon ball or a fall into the moat didn't finish her off, a chill would.

Mr Clarkson was now giving a ranting account of wilful, wicked, and lewd women in the Bible who had been chastised by the Lord. The soldiers found it entertaining.

Suddenly, Sir Archie, with another oath, ordered everyone to their tents and strode off to his own. Only the minister was left by the gun. Falling on his knees, he hugged the long wet iron snout, like a man embracing his sweetheart, or the other way round. The soldiers' comments were sardonic and obscene. If that was holiness, they could do without it.

Next day the soldiers folded their tents and marched off, gun and all. Most were thankful that they hadn't knocked down the castle, though Sir Archie might be in trouble for not carrying out his orders. Mr Clarkson was sure to clype on him.

The servants returned, at first wary as cats not yet sure there were no dogs about. Then rejoicing broke out. Ale was produced and drunk. They had been spared by the Lord so, to show Him how grateful they were, they danced and sang and cuddled. There was no minister to spoil the fun.

Until word came that Lady Magdalen, whose courage had saved the castle, was seriously ill and might not last out the day. They crept off then to fulfil their various duties.

14

FOUR DAYS AFTER the departure of the Covenant troops from Kincardine, George Graham of Braco came at a gallop to the castle, mud-splattered and exhausted, and was greatly surprised not to find it a smoking ruin. He had supposed that Sir Archie Hutcheon's punitive mission had been carried out. In still greater surprise, he listened as he was told by several excited voices speaking all at once how Lady Magdalen, by her courage and steadfastness, had shamed the Covenanters and sent them away dragging their big silly gun behind them. Unhappily, the effort had been too much for her and she was now very ill. Her man, one woman rashly cried, ought to be there, looking after her, instead of killing and robbing the folk of Aberdeen. For the Covenant soldiers had informed the villagers of that atrocity.

Braco had with him his two nephews, Tom and Gavin Maitland, the sons of his sister, Meg. Tom was 20, Gavin 18. Since Meg was a widow, her man having died ten years ago, her boys were her life. If anything happened to them, she would not want to live. For that reason she had forbidden them to go and fight for Montrose, though he was their chieftain, or for the Covenant, though she was a devout Presbyterian. They had had to beg her to let them accompany Uncle George to find out what had happened to Lady Magdalen, who was a far-out relation by marriage.

Before going to see Lady Magdalen on her sickbed, Braco asked his nephews to remain in the great hall in the meantime. Disease, he reminded them, killed more people than guns or swords. All the bravery in the world was no defence against it.

Mrs Witherspoon remarked drily that what ailed Lady Magdalen could hardly be smittal or *she* would have caught it long ago.

So his nephews were with him when he went quietly into the small room that smelled of fumigatory herbs.

Lady Magdalen recognised him at once and smiled. He was wondering if she was as delirious as he had been led to believe when she asked what, in the circumstances, was hardly a sensible question: 'Have you brought news of James?'

No, he had not, he did not even know in what part of the country James was with his army. He could have lied but it was in his nature to be truthful. 'I'm sorry, Lady Magdalen. I know nothing of James.'

He could not help contrasting her thinness and paleness with his own Jean's rosy-cheeked plumpness. Into his mind then came a memory of Jean feeding her hens by the back door, where the lilacs grew. As always, it gave him courage and hope.

'Somebody will hae to gang and tell the Marquis,' whispered Mrs Witherspoon. 'She'll hae gone before he gets here, but he's got a right to be told.'

Aye, but who was to be the messenger? It would be a dangerous and arduous journey and Braco had promised Jean, and Meg too, to come straight home.

Besides, to be candid, what was the point of risking one's life – the danger wasn't of falling off a cliff or drowning in a torrent, it was of meeting desperate armed men, deserters or stragglers, who would cut a man's throat or a woman's, for that matter, for a handful of merks or a chicken – when the message one brought would hardly be heeded, not because Montrose did not care whether his wife lived or died, but because he would not be able to leave his army lest it disintegrated, as armies composed of Highlanders so frequently did.

Opening her eyes, Lady Magdalen whispered: 'Please bring back my sons to me, George.'

So she remembered that it had been he who had taken them to join their father. He had thought at the time that they were too young to be campaigning in the Highlands, especially when winter was approaching. Braco himself had no children.

He was trying to think of an answer when, thank God, she fell asleep again.

In private, Braco put it to his nephews. He exaggerated the dangers and difficulties of the journey: mountains to cross, burns in spate to ford, moors and bogs to traverse, storms of wind and rain and maybe snow to endure, and, worst of all, renegade soldiers to avoid. He pointed out that, if they did safely deliver their message, Montrose might not be grateful. It would give him still another worry. Perhaps he would rather not know about his wife.

Tom and Gavin were not discouraged. On the contrary, they saw it as a challenge and an adventure. They had often gone hunting over rough country, they had slept out of doors, and they would like very much to visit Montrose's camp. Maybe they would stay and fight for him. No, they would not, replied their uncle, sternly. Had they not promised their mother, on the family Bible?

Braco seldom prayed, but that night he did. Not on his knees, or with his hands clasped or his eyes closed, but lying in bed, in the dark. He did not ask for miracles but simply that Lady Magdalen would recover and he would be able to return Meg's sons safely to her. He thought of Jean but did not include her in his prayer. His love for her was too private for that.

15

BRACO WOULD HAVE liked to by-pass Perth. It was now in the hands of the Covenanters again and there was a risk that he might be recognised, for – God help him! – he had been one of the victors at Tippermuir, who had marched triumphantly into the town, to be stared at with fear and hatred by most of its citizens. Then, when he had brought John and James Graham to join their father, there had been cheers from Montrose's troops but, from many others, sullen, watchful silence. If he was recognised, he would be arrested as a spy, and his nephews with him. They would be lucky not to be hanged forthwith. Like the ladies in the ballad, Jean and Meg would wait a long time before they returned.

Still, they had to venture into the city. They needed to dry their clothes, soaked in a heavy downpour, and dry beds to rest in. They had also to find a doctor willing to travel to Kincardine, and they had to do some speiring as to the Royalist army's present whereabouts.

Tom and Gavin were amused by their uncle's cautiousness. He was getting old, they said. Hadn't he told them the city would be thronged with men on the loose? Why should anyone notice them in particular?

Just in case, they entered the narrow ill-lit streets after dark, and almost at once were challenged by an officer in command of a street patrol. He was suspicious of three armed men who had evidently ridden far and fast. They were ordered to halt. Their horses' bridles were seized. They were asked their names and business.

Among the many smells in the old town, the most prominent was that of fear. No wonder, for the blood of the many wounded at Tippermuir still stained the cobbles and out of the night might rush, at any moment, those Irish fiends.

Braco had his answers ready. He and his sons were visiting their kinsman, Mr Blair, not long ago appointed schoolmaster in the town. After the recent occupation by the Irish savages, they were anxious as to how he and his family had fared.

It was a plausible pretext and the officer seemed satisfied. He could not himself direct them to the schoolhouse but one of his soldiers could. It was by the river, he said. Braco thanked them and then he and his nephews headed their horses in that direction, at a walking pace.

Tom and Gavin weren't quite so defiant now.

Braco had not intended to call on the dominie, whom he had never met, but it occurred to him now that the schoolhouse would be a safer place to spend the night than an inn. The dominie owed his promotion to Lady Magdalen, who had persuaded her father to find him his present post. For his patroness's sake, surely he would give them shelter.

Usually dominies' houses were small in comparison with ministers' manses but this one, built of stone, was of a generous size. Indeed, it was as big as Braco's own, though he was called 'laird'. The school was attached and there was a play area with trees. Not far off, the river could be heard.

It seemed the burghers of Perth considered their children's education worth spending money on.

Tom and Gavin waited with the horses under the trees while Braco found his way up the path to the front door.

There was a knocker in the shape of a man's head. (He learned later it was supposed to be John Knox's.) He banged it but not too loudly. Enemies were all around. He shivered with cold, but also with apprehension. He thought of Montrose's army camped in some remote windswept glen where the sun seldom shone.

Was Montrose at that very moment looking up at those stars and wondering, for he was an imaginative man who wrote poetry, if, against the background of eternity, it really mattered who prevailed, the King or the Covenant?

The door opened but not wide. 'Wha is it?' asked a young girl's voice. 'Whit d'you want?'

'Will you please tell your master that a messenger has come from Lady Magdalen?'

'Leddy wha?' She giggled.

Another young woman's voice was heard. 'Who is it, Maggie?' She was trying to speak in an educated fashion, as a schoolmaster's wife should. Braco grinned. This must be the famous Cissie who had slept with Lord Rothes: he had heard the story from Montrose himself. A humble maidservant, she had enticed the foolish dominie into marriage. But she seemed to be making an effort to be a credit to him.

Maggie replied: 'It's somebody saying he's got a message frae some leddy ca'd Magdalen.'

Mrs Blair then opened the door boldly though, when revealed, she had an infant in her arms. 'Are you from Kincardine, sir?'

A pleasant warmth and smell exuded from the house.

'That's right. My name's George Graham of Braco.'

She was wearing a white apron that did not conceal the swelling of her belly. She and the dominie would have a schoolful of bairns before they were finished. Childless Braco felt envious but wished them well.

'Have you brocht a message frae her ladyship?'

'Not exactly that, Mrs Blair. We are on our way – my two nephews are with me – to find the Marquis and tell him that she is at death's door.'

'Oh, my God!' She burst into tears. 'We always said she'd never scart a grey heid.'

'Is your husband at home?'

'Aye. He'll be very sorry to hear this news. Come awa' in, Mr Graham.'

Braco followed her in.

There was a fire burning in the small pleasant parlour. A kettle sang. A black cat washed its face. Hippings were hung up to dry.

'We werena' expecting company,' said Mrs Blair, removing the hippings with her free hand. 'John!' she shrieked, and then remembered she was the dominie's lady. 'Maggie, would you tell maister there's a visitor frae Kincardine.'

There were still tears in her eyes. 'John and I owe a loat to her ladyship. John says she's the maist genuine person he's ever met.'

Genuine? What did it mean? Braco, a gentleman, called 'laird' in his own small domain, appreciated her and her husband's feelings but he could not help thinking that their speaking so familiarly of Lady Magdalen was an impertinence. The distance in rank between her and them was immense, as far as the earth from the stars.

She proceeded to be more impertinent still. 'We a' thocht the Earl should hae stayed at hame and ta'en care o' her.'

How insolent of servants to think such a thing! But all Braco could find to say was: 'He's a marquis now.'

'He wasna gieing her a single thocht a week or twa back when he cam into the toon after the battle. He sat on his big black horse, looking like a king. They were a' taking aff their caps and bending their knees.'

Braco had seen it himself.

Blair came in as she was speaking. 'Now, Cissie, how could you tell what the great man was thinking?'

'The great man'. Was that sarcastic? thought Braco. If it was, it was worse than impertinent, it was damned impudent.

'Those terrible Irish brutes of his,' cried Cissie.

'They behaved themselves reasonably well.'

'But no' in Aiberdeen.'

'No, not in Aberdeen.'

'That poor young lady, shut up in that dreary cauld castle, in pain maist o' the time, while he that should hae been comforting her was instead letting his savages molest ither women. Nae wonder it's broken her heart.'

'She wouldn't know about Aberdeen, Cissie. Perhaps she still doesn't know.'

'She knows,' said Braco, grimly.

'And it's killed her. John, Mr Graham's on his way to tell the Earl that her ladyship's deeing.'

The dominie was silent. He shut his eyes. Braco did not think, though, that he was praying.

'I am sorry to hear that,' he said. 'Mr Graham, my house is at your disposal while you are in Perth.'

'He's got twa nephews with him,' said Cissie.

'They're outside, with the horses,' said Braco.

'Then we must go and bring them in.'

Blair led Braco outside to where the stars were brighter and the wind colder.

From what Montrose had told him, Braco had expected the dominie to be a thin, weedy, round-shouldered, gullible young man, and indeed he was young and thin and round-shouldered, but he was by no means gullible. He had a confidence in himself that reminded Braco of Montrose himself, though the Marquis, of course, acted in great matters and the dominie in small.

Quietly Blair welcomed Tom and Gavin and showed them where to stable their horses at the back of the house. Braco could tell from their shame-faced silence that they had been amusing themselves with the usual jokes about dominies: how these, spending their lives scolding bairns, became themselves peevish and small-minded. It certainly did not apply to Mr Blair.

In the parlour, Mrs Blair had a meal set out on the table: hot broth and cheese and bread of her own baking. Her hospitality was admirable but it was also part of her ridiculous and repre-

233

hensible assumption of equality. Braco found the food choking him a little, tasty though it was.

Tom and Gavin ate hungrily and did not refuse second helpings.

Braco had decided not to tell about Lady Magdalen's heroism but Tom and Gavin related it eagerly.

'That's war for you,' cried Mrs Blair, 'firing a cannon at a castle fu' o' women and children.'

'Be fair, Cissie,' said her husband. 'They did not fire it after all.'

'Because her ladyship shamed them oot o' it. But they'll fire it next time.'

She was right but Braco wished she would go and attend to her housewifely duties elsewhere. She showed no sign of leaving; indeed, she did most of the talking. Braco noticed that the dominie let her speak on so long as she was talking sense and, to be fair, most of what she said was sensible enough. She reminded Braco of his Jean.

'Dr Muirkirk's her ladyship's usual doctor,' she said, 'but she's never liked him. In ony case, he's gone oot o' toon. They're saying he made himself scarce before the wounded were brought in. Curing a lady's headache's mair in his line than cutting aff a sodger's leg.'

'Who would blame him?' murmured the dominie. 'A lot less messy and a great deal more profitable.'

Braco frowned. There it was again, that peculiar insolence. Dr Muirkirk might well be a mountebank but he was a gentleman, practising a respectable profession. This pair ought not to be mocking him. Braco did not read much but he had listened to clever men in Edinburgh talking about wicked and dangerous ideas spreading up from England. Was Blair one of those madmen who wanted equality for everyone?

'There's Dr Pettigrew,' said Mrs Blair.

'I doubt if he would cross the street to wait on Montrose's

wife,' said her husband. 'He boasts of having signed the Covenant three times.'

'Weel, that leaves Dr Sloan but he's very young.'

'And honest enough to admit that his knowledge is very limited. Nature cures, he says, not his medicines.'

'Old Dr Allen used to say the same,' said Mrs Blair.

So, as a matter of fact, did George Graham, Laird of Braco, who had lost faith in doctors ever since one had so badly set the broken leg of a tenant's son that the lad was left a cripple for the rest of his life.

He changed the subject for one that would, thank God, have no interest for Mrs Blair. 'Tell me, Mr Blair, is there any talk in the town as to the whereabouts of the Royalist army?'

It was Mrs Blair who answered. 'Everybody kens that. I was in the market this morning buying eggs and they were saying that they're at the Blair of Atholl, whit's left o' them.'

'It seems,' said Blair, while Braco gaped, 'that Macdonald has gone with most of his Irish on some expedition of their own into Argyll, while most of the Lowland gentlemen are going home for the winter, to look after their own personal interests.'

Braco was surprised neither at this information being common knowledge, for spies and scouts were busy all the time, nor at the information itself. That was the curse of a crusade like Montrose's: men joined it as it pleased them and left it in the same way. On the other hand, Leslie, the Covenanters' leading general, then in England with the regular Scottish army, commanded men who had sworn their oaths and drawn their pay and therefore could be shot if they deserted.

16

AS THE RAVEN flew, it was less than 30 miles to Blair Atholl and the first half, to Dunkeld, lay through the pleasant fertile vale of Strathmore, along the banks of the Tay. Here horses could be used, for the road was tolerable. Thereafter, it became a steep mountain pass frequently broken by burns: horses would be more of a hindrance than a help.

In the cosy parlour, with the dominie's ink-stained finger tracing the route on the map, it looked straightforward enough, but Braco listened with a gloomy face. It was not the dangers of the journey but the fear that their mission would be regarded by Montrose as unnecessary and even unwelcome. If he had ministers with him, and nothing was more likely for if he prevailed there would be bishoprics to be handed out, he would have them say a prayer for his wife and that would have to be that in the meantime. If Braco's Jean had died, nothing in the world would matter after that. But then, he had not been chosen by the King and by God to save the kingdom. Montrose would think that there would be time, after the final victory, to mourn his wife and re-bury her with appropriate pomp but, until then, she had to be a sad irrelevancy.

They set out soon after dawn, with the sky still red, their saddle-bags stuffed with provisions supplied by Mrs Blair. Their horses had been fed and rested and were in good fettle. At that hour the town was empty and they were soon clear of it, heading for the mountains in the distance, their tops wreathed in pink mist. A cool breeze blew. The dominie had greatly amused Tom and Gavin by staring up at the sky and holding up his hand to feel the wind and then forecasting it was going to be a fine day. He was being so like a schoolmaster, they thought, pretending, as he had to do to impress the bairns, that he knew everything. They found even more amusing and kept making jokes about the fact that he had so bonny and big-breasted a wife with such a flirtatious wink. Sourly, Braco rebuked them. He had been as lustful as they at their age and usually made allowances, but he had a premonition, which often possessed him, that God was waiting for a chance to chastise them, and where better than among these wild regions into which they were venturing? There had never been a minister in the pulpit at Braco who had taught that God was kind.

When they began to sing a ditty with a jaunty tune and many verses, none of them proper, he would have liked to ask them to sing a psalm instead but they would have laughed, knowing how stubbornly silent he was in kirk, or they might have obliged him by singing one through their noses like an old minister they had once known. Braco gave up thinking about God and thought about Jean instead and was comforted.

The closer to the mountains they came, the poorer the houses, the stonier the fields, and the skinnier the cattle. Twice abuse was yelled at them, once by an old woman and the second time by a gang of children as wild-haired, dark-skinned, and unclothed as heathen Hottentots. What harm have we done them? asked Gavin indignantly. Braco replied that if you have had your possessions, miserable though they were, and your cattle, skinny though they were, stolen by men you had never seen before, you weren't likely to feel kindly towards strangers afterwards. Soldiers of any army considered that they had a right to take what they needed. Their cause, whatever it was, and their weapons, gave them that right. Sometimes they paid compensation, but mostly they did not. The Marquis would not allow his soldiers to steal, said Gavin, and was told to remember what had happened at

Aberdeen. Wars, said Braco, were not won by men hampered by scruples. But, said Gavin, hadn't there been a time long ago when knights had fought according to rules of chivalry? He had been told about them in school. What, asked Braco, was chivalrous about smashing men's skulls as if they were eggshells?

Until the day he died, he would remember an incident at Tippermuir. He had seen one of the Irish washing the blood off a young soldier's face by pissing on it. He had told no one, not even Jean, and never would.

Once they passed close to a large house that was now a blackened ruin. It must have been a very pleasant place to live in, with its orchard and its burn with trout in it. On the grass were red stains that looked like blood. God knew what had happened to the inhabitants. There was no safety for anyone in a time of war, with rival armies pursuing each other. If a man was known to favour one side, then the other side would burn down his house. If he favoured neither, his danger was even greater, for it meant that both sides would regard him as fair game.

They met few other travellers. All were silent and suspicious. Trust, like the heather, was withered. Hands went readily to guns or dirks.

At Dunkeld, the inn, like the village itself, was a sordid place that stank of goats and pigs. The innkeeper was small, with a red beard and dishonest eyes; his wife had most of her teeth missing and not enough self-respect left to cover up her bosom. If you wanted proof that Scotland, especially in the Highlands, was poverty-stricken, here it was. Yet Montrose and the Estates could find vast sums of money to wage their futile war.

Braco and his nephews agreed, without having to debate the matter, that they would rather sleep on beds of frosted bracken out of doors than in this rat-hole. Outside, it was very beautiful, with the sky clear and the high peaks glittering in the evening sun.

The landlord had a stable but was unwilling to take charge of their horses. Reivers often came howling out of the hills. They would cut throats for a hen, let alone three good horses. He showed no interest in why they were there or where they were going.

Other men did. They came in, two of them, keen-eyed, active, dressed in leather jackets, and armed with swords and pistols. They sat in a corner, sipping whisky, and saying nothing, but their eyes were quick and questing. They were not ordinary travellers but men on duty. Were they spies? If so, Montrose's or Argyll's? Montrose's surely, for somehow they reminded Braco of Montrose himself. They had the same air of dedication.

At last he got up and went over to them. 'Good evening, friends. I would like to introduce myself. George Graham of Braco.'

'Braco?' said the one with the black moustache. 'And what brings the Laird of Braco to this outlandish place?'

'I have a message for the Marquis.'

'What marquis is that?' asked the other, with the fair hair.

'Montrose. I am a kinsman of his.'

'Those likely-looking lads, are they your sons?' asked Black-moustache.

'My nephews. Grahams too, on their mother's side.'

'Is it your intention to remain with the Marquis after you have delivered your message?'

Braco became alarmed. 'We have come from Kincardine. The message is from Lady Magdalen. We have to report back to her.'

'Those horses outside, are they yours?'

'Yes. We were advised to leave them here as the road is not suitable for horses.'

'It's rough in places but passable enough. We leave in half an hour and would be pleased to have your company. With the horses.'

Braco went back to his nephews. They misread his worried face.

'Are they Argyll's men?' whispered Tom.

'No. Look, lads, there's no need for you to go any further. You promised your mother to go straight back home. She'll be worried to death about you.'

'We'd rather go on with you,' said Tom.

Gavin nodded.

Braco was in a desperate quandary. Should he and his nephews go no further but let the two spies carry the message to Montrose?

He was still trying to decide when half an hour later they set off for the Pass of Killiecrankie and Blair Atholl. He and his nephews were on horseback. The two spies strode alongside.

17

NEXT DAY, AT dusk, they arrived in the glen where Montrose's army was encamped. Braco and his nephews were exhausted from the effort all that day to stay in the saddle as the horses lurched like boats in a storm. Frequently the terrified beasts had to be dragged by the reins across places where the track had been washed away. Yet, as Braco had cursed and complained, Tom and Gavin, pretending they were cavalry-men, had put up with all the difficulties manfully. Showing how young they were and how gullible, they were delighted at the praise given them by their companions, who said they were coping like seasoned dragoons.

If he had to go back without them, if he had to tell Meg that they had joined Montrose's army, it would not merely be a matter of her never forgiving him, it would be more serious than that, she would go out of her mind. But surely when they saw the Irish, those cruel butchers, they would be shocked out of their romantic ideas of heroism and chivalry?

The camp consisted of a great array of tents and other makeshift shelters round a stone house that was Montrose's headquarters. Dozens of camp fires were lit. There was a smell of roasted venison.

They hadn't been there ten minutes before they realised there was an unusual air of excitement. They soon learned the reason. Alistair Macdonald, leader of the Irish, had that very day returned from his foray to the west. It had been feared that he might stay away all winter or indeed might never return at all, which would have meant the end of Montrose's campaign.

It was the first time Tom and Gavin had seen the Irish. Confident that they would be repelled by the shaggy hair, the bare legs, the unwashed smell, and the uncouth manners, Braco was dismayed when instead they were fascinated by the size of the swords and the gallus swagger. Here were warriors who would fearlessly attack and rout an enemy far more numerous and better armed; as, indeed, they had done at Tippermuir.

They said all that to each other but their uncle overheard them. He reminded them how cruel the Irish were but they smiled and, gently mocking him, pointed out that in battle you had to kill your enemies or they would kill you, and it was surely not possible to kill in a kindly fashion. In desperation, he told them what he had vowed to keep a secret to his grave: about that Irish savage who had pissed on the face of the dead soldier. Well, said Tom after a pause, in the heat of battle a man had to piss somewhere. Then he and Gavin, thinking it a joke, laughed.

He had known them all their lives. Now they had become strange and unknowable.

It seemed a conference had been going on for hours between Montrose and Macdonald, as to the army's next move. Montrose was for marching south. From reports he had received he was convinced that, in the Lowlands, many men now hesitating would join his standard when they saw how irresistible his army was. Another victory or two like Tippermuir and the way would be open to Edinburgh. Within a month the whole country would be theirs.

Unfortunately Macdonald was refusing to take his men into the alien south. He wanted the whole army to go west, ravaging Campbell country all the way to Inveraray. It would mean a march over high mountain passes that might be blocked by snow and, if it came off, would do great damage to Argyll's pride but it would hardly advance the King's cause.

It was thought by the Lowlanders round the camp fire where

Braco and his nephews were being entertained that Macdonald would get his way and, sure enough, when the council of war broke up, the Irish coming out of the house were laughing and congratulating one another in their barbarous tongue, while Montrose's Lowland officers were glum.

Braco and his nephews had been in the camp almost three hours before Montrose sent for them. In his place, thought Braco, if I had been told that messengers had come with news of Jean, I would have wanted to hear it immediately. Nothing in the world would have seemed more urgent. But then, that is why, thank God, I am only a minor laird and a breeder of cattle, while Montrose is the King's Lieutenant and a famous general.

At last Montrose's personal servant, a youth no older than Gavin, came to take them to his master.

Montrose received them in what was evidently his private room. There was a camp bed in a corner. On the wall hung a portrait of the King. It seemed to Braco that haughty Charles wasn't at all pleased at his primitive surroundings. On a small table were glasses and a bottle of wine.

Montrose's sons sat by the fire, John with a cloth round his neck and James happed in a blanket.

Montrose came forward cordially, holding out his hand. Tom and Gavin were awed. They had been expecting to see in his face the magic of genius and they did not disappoint themselves. That he was hardly above middle height and was slightly built in comparison with Macdonald did not matter. He wore dark serviceable clothes with only one decoration, a silver star given to him personally by the King.

Braco, on the other hand, saw him, as many Lowland Scots noblemen did, as a young upstart, who had dragged the country into civil war for the sake of an unworthy King but also for his own ambition's sake. Everyone knew that, as a youth, Montrose had dreamed of military glory; now, as a man, though still a young one, he was determined to achieve it, whatever the cost.

To such a man, the illness of his wife, or even her death, was bound to be of small significance.

'Well, George, I believe you have a message from Magdalen.'

No tremor in his voice, no gasp of anxiety, no wetness of eye. But then, how could he plan battles in which thousands would be killed if he showed weakness at the death of one woman, even if she was the mother of his children?

He shook hands with Tom and Gavin. 'I remember you as youngsters. Which one of you was it that shot the eagle?'

It had been Tom, with an arrow. He was not proud of it. The great bird had flown off with the arrow in its breast, proabably to die in its eyrie. But he was proud that Montrose had remembered it.

'Not really a message, James,' said Braco. 'I have brought news of her. She is very ill. She may, at this very moment, be dead.'

'Is that what you have come all this way to tell me?'

The two boys were not so calm or was it so callous? Painfully, the older of the two turned his head to glower at Braco, while the younger let out a sob.

Braco then told how Lady Magdalen had risen from her sickbed to defy the Covenant troops and save the castle.

'Nobody will save Inveraray Castle when we get there,' said John, hoarsely.

'Poor Mama,' wailed James.

'Who did you say was in command?' asked Montrose.

'Sir Archie Hutcheon.'

'I know Sir Archie: a gentleman and a scrupulous soldier. Thank you, George, for taking the trouble to come here and tell me this, but what did you expect me to do? Leave my post? Abandon my men? Give up my cause or, rather, the King's cause?'

'It would be only for a short time. You could be there and back in three days.'

'In those three days I could lose three hundred men. To keep the pot boiling, George, you must not let the fire go out.'

'What good could Father do?' asked John angrily. 'He is not a doctor.'

Braco felt sympathy for the boy. 'Your mother said to me: "Please go and bring back my sons." I promised I would try. So here I am.'

'May I go, Father?' asked James, trying hard not to weep.

'I see no reason why not.'

'Will John come with me?'

'I am going to Inveraray,' said John, 'to burn down Argyll's castle.'

You will never come back alive, thought Braco. Only strong healthy men would survive that lunatic march.

'You have no children of your own, George, as I remember?' said Montrose.

'That is so.' Braco let himself be provoked. 'Doesn't it trouble you, James, that you may never see your wife alive again?'

'Yes, George, it troubles me very much. I hate death. Anyone's death. Does that surprise you? I see it does. You find it incredible, considering my present occupation. But no man would be killed if everyone was loyal to the King, as everyone should be, according to the laws of God and man.'

Braco resented being given a political sermon, especially from a man who had once fought against the King. 'Lady Magdalen is very highly thought of.' He meant, by everyone but you, James.

'She has a pleasing nature.'

'Much more than that. Mr Blair, the dominie, said she was the most genuine person he had ever met.'

Montrose smiled. 'How dare Mr Blair pass judgment on his betters. Genuine? What a curious word to use.'

'I know what he meant.'

'Well, George, I shall give you a letter to take back. That is all I can do in the meantime. James will accompany you. It has been my intention to send him home, not to Kincardine, but to my house at Old Montrose, where he will resume his studies under his tutor, Mr Forret. When do you intend to start back?'

'Tomorrow morning.'

Tom had been itching to speak. 'My lord—.' Shyness overcame him, and perhaps shame too, for he knew that what he was about to say would distress his uncle.

'Yes?' Montrose was smiling.

'Gavin and I would like to stay and join your army, my lord. Isn't that right, Gavin?'

Gavin nodded, keeping his eyes off his uncle.

'We saw some out there not any older than us,' said Tom.

'I'm just fourteen,' said John.

'I believe you brought horses,' said Montrose. 'We are very short of cavalry.'

'Your mother,' said Braco bitterly, to his nephews, 'gave you permission to go with me to Kincardine to find out what had happened to Lady Magdalen, in return for a promise that you would return home as soon as possible. Are you going to break that promise? And your mother's heart?' He turned to Montrose. 'Would you encourage them to break it?'

'Since you ask me, George, I have to say that a man's loyalty to his King supersedes all other loyalties.'

'Even to his mother?'

'Even to his mother.' Montrose's voice was cold. His mother had died when he was a child of six.

'And to his wife?'

'Yes.'

'Do you really in your heart believe that, James?'

'I would not be here, George, if I did not believe it with all my heart.'

'Even if the King has shown he does not deserve loyalty?'

'I shall pretend you did not say that, George.'

246

'Why not have one of your Irish cut out my tongue and then piss on my face to wash away the blood?'

'You are distraught, George. As I told you once before, go back to your black cattle.'

'With a straw hanging from my mouth, you also said.'

'Well, George, you were assuring me you preferred farming to soldiering.'

Montrose turned to Tom and Gavin. 'Don't decide now. Sleep on it. Let your uncle try to dissuade you. In the meantime, Alex will take you to your quarters. I'm afraid it will be a sack stuffed with bracken on the hard ground in a rather leaky tent. Good-night.'

As, led by Alex, they made their way among the tents, they heard, coming out of the darkness, someone singing. The words were unintelligible but the grief they contained chilled Braco's blood.

'Some Irish woman,' said Alex, casually, 'mourning for her man. They're always at it.'

Braco stopped to listen. There were other noises, dogs barking, children crying, men laughing, and wood crackling on fires, but this one, of the woman breaking her heart for her dead husband, dominated them all.

'If you saw her,' said Alex, 'you'd laugh. Face like a witch's and no teeth.'

'We knew a dog once,' said Gavin, 'that sat by its master's grave, howling. Do you remember, Tom?'

Tom did. They laughed at the memory. Alex joined in.

They were too young to recognise in that unknown Irish woman's song a sorrow as old as the hills and as deep as the sea.

18

MAGDALEN DID NOT die. When young Dr Sloan arrived from Perth, he found her sitting up, with, as Mrs Witherspoon gladly pointed out, more colour in her cheeks than there had been for many months. She was able, too, to take gruel and chicken broth without at once vomiting it up. It was a miracle, but there had been so many prayers beseeching God to spare her that it was not so astonishing after all. No, it was not, thought the doctor, for though his patient, the most aristocratic he had ever treated, did have a redness in her cheeks, it was scarcely that of rude health and, though she spoke to him blithely enough, it was her braveness of spirit overcoming her weakness of body. For, as he was to tell his own wife when he got back to Perth, the Marquis might win the war and be hailed the saviour of his country but he would not have Lady Magdalen by his side in Holyrood Palace unless his triumph came very soon.

She knew it herself. As she lay in bed well happed up, for the room was cold – it was now late November – she considered how most usefully to spend the days she had left. She would do more for the sick and the poor. She would write more often to her father and sisters and brothers. She would visit Mintlaw and see again all those beautiful things. She would finish her tapestry. She would practise on the lute and sing the songs she used to when a child. She would take more interest in the welfare of her servants. In the spring she would have the whole house cleaned, for her husband's and her sons' return. She would plant more flowers in the garden. She would make jam out of raspberries and wine out of elderberries. She would read some of James's books and improve her mind. She would be a better mother to poor Robert and little David, who in recent weeks had had to depend on others for care and affection. She would blame no one, least of all James, her husband, for her misfortunes. Above all, she would try to be a loving uncomplaining wife.

Though she smiled during the day, there were times, in the dead of night, when she shed tears, knowing that she would never be able to do all those things she wanted. She had always been an ineffectual person, a failure as a wife and not much of a success as a mother. She did not deserve to be remembered.

One afternoon, Mrs Witherspoon, big-eyed with excitement, came in crying that Master James had just arrived in the court-yard, not very well, poor lad, but safe, thank God.

'John too?' asked Magdalen, her heart racing.

'No, my lady. He's still with his father. But Mr Graham will explain, I'm sure.'

She had planned, when John and James returned, to greet them as boys of 14 and 12, respectively, would wish to be greeted by their mother. How many times had James, under John's influence, reproached her for treating him as if he was a lassie. So she had meant simply to hold out her arms, take their hands, laugh, and say, 'How you've grown' or something like that. But when James came in and ran to her and, bursting into tears, hid his face against her breast, she could not help stroking his fair hair and kissing his soft face, which was wet with tears, his and hers. Neither of them spoke. He wept, more and more sorely, like a girl indeed, and she loved him for it, though his father, and certainly his brother, had they been there, would have been ashamed of him.

At last, remembering his brother's frequent admonitions never to do anything to disgrace their family, he withdrew from his mother's embrace, stood up, dashed away the tears with his hand and, in a voice involuntarily shrill, cried that, though he was

249

pleased to be home, he was not to stay with her at Kincardine, he was to go to Old Montrose, where his tutor, Mr Forret, was waiting for him. That was Father's command, as she would see in the letter that Mr Graham had brought for her.

Just then Graham came in. He bowed as he handed her the letter. Why, he wondered, did she remind him of his Jean? She was so frail and those roses in her cheeks were false. She had escaped death this time but not for long. Beneath that brave smile, she was profoundly unhappy. Yet she did remind him of his stout, cheerful, red-cheeked wife, who would, thank God, live for many years yet.

Like Jean, she was genuine, to use Mr Blair's word so hard to explain. Like Jean she did not have in her a trace of insincerity, pretence, conceit, or self-delusion.

'Where are your nephews, Mr Graham?' she asked.

Braco's bitterness and disappointment were assuaged just by looking at her. 'They chose to remain with your husband.'

'Do you mean they have joined his army?'

'Aye.'

'But they promised their mother they would go straight back home. They told me so themselves.'

'Hearing the war-horses snort, my lady, was too much for them.'

'But they are so young.'

'There were some yonder even younger.' Including your own son, he could have said.

'Their poor mother, she will be desolate.'

'Aye, she will.' It was the right word. Like a woman in the Bible, Meg would put ashes on her head and speak to no one.

'I'm very sorry. It was my fault.'

'No, my lady, it was not your fault. They had their minds made up to try soldiering.'

'Do you know, Mama,' said James, 'they're going to march through the mountains to Inveraray.'

'Who are?'

'Father and his army.'

'In the spring, do you mean?'

'No. Now. In a week or two.'

'But there will be snow on the mountains.'

'They think the Campbells will not be expecting them.'

'But surely your father will not allow John to go with them. He knows how he takes sore throats just by getting his feet wet.'

Up to the oxters in snow and icy water, thought Braco, he'll get more than his feet wet.

'John wanted to go,' said James. 'He said he was going to burn down Argyll's castle. Father said John would be safer with the army than anywhere else. Because he's Father's heir, the Covenanters would like to seize hold of him and keep him as a hostage. It doesn't matter about me. I'm not his heir.'

James then rushed out of the room to go and see how his dog, Prince, was but really it was so that no one would see him weep.

Braco and Lady Magdalen gazed at each other.

He was thinking that James might become his father's heir before very long.

Her mind was in a state of anguished confusion.

'He said he is not to stay with me,' she said at last. 'That he is to go to Old Montrose. At his father's command.'

'So I understand. We were supplied with an escort. They are waiting to take James to Old Montrose.'

'Now? Today?'

'They are impatient to get back to take part in the march into Argyll.'

But, she wondered, would James consent to go with them? If she begged him to stay with her? Would he disobey his father for her sake? Had she the right to ask him? By law and by custom a father had complete authority over his sons, a mother had none. The ministers of the Kirk said it. So did the Bible. She had promised God that she would be an uncomplaining wife, which

251

also meant an obedient wife. But did a mother's love for her children count for nothing? Or her children's love for her? James would rather stay with her. His father must have known that. All her married life, her opinions, wishes, and hopes had been disregarded or dismissed, courteously, sometimes even affectionately, but always with a finality, as if her having a personal point of view on any subject was an impertinence, to be indulged so far but no further. Her father, who loved her dearly, had treated her like that too.

She read the letter. It was short. Had James thought that he might be writing to a dead woman and, therefore, there was no point in writing at length?

'Dear Love,
I write this in a great hurry, after a long and exhausting day. George Graham has brought me the dismal news that you are again ailing. God grant that you will recover soon. If I could, I would come but duties prevent me. I send James in my stead. However, in the present circumstances, I do not wish him to remain at Kincardine and have, accordingly, instructed him to hasten from there to Old Montrose, where he will be able to resume his studies under his old tutor, Mr Forret. I advise that you yourself, as soon as you are well enough to travel, with the two youngest boys, go to Kinnaird to be under the protection of your father. John sends his love. God keep you.'

If she had wished to weep, she could not. Her tears, like her heart, were frozen. Surely he had not intended to write so coldly. Here was her mountain pass, blocked with snow.

Braco watched her dourly. He would not tell her what her husband had said to him as he had handed over the letter. 'My two youngest boys, George, if it is necessary, could you personally see that they are delivered into the safe keeping of their Grandfather Southesk?' He had meant, if their mother is dead.

'They will wait, my lady, for a day or two,' he said. 'I shall see that they do.'

But how? There were six of them, all hardy fellows, skilled with weapons. Any one of them singly could overcome him. They had their orders and would carry them out ruthlessly.

Once, as a child, Magdalen had seen a rat caught in a small iron bucket. She had not seen it really, she had heard its screams, for those who had caught it, some farm lads, had poured boiling water through a hole in the lid. She had protested but too faintly for any to hear. Besides, who cared about a rat? Now she too felt trapped in a narrow space, unable to see her tormentors. No more than the rat could she look for help. There was her husband, far away, too busy with military duties to give any thought to her. There was her father in Kinnaird, who would tell her to obey her husband and leave the rest to God. There were her brothers and sisters, who would say that she ought to have known this would happen if she married James Graham. And there was God, most aloof of all, despite her prayers. What had she done, or not done, to offend Him?

I am going to die soon, she thought, and the prospect of death should be, if I am a true Christian, joyful, not terrifying, but I am so terrified that I can hardly breathe. God and His angels may welcome me but what will happen to my children when I am gone? In heaven, shall I be aware of their unhappiness but not be able to comfort them? In that case, heaven would be hell. Will my husband, if he wins his war, put up a large headstone over my grave, not because he loved me but because I was the wife of the King's Lieutenant? If he loses, will he, in his cell, before they take him out to be hanged, think of me or will he, in the midst of his woes, have forgotten me?

George Graham was saying that he would have to leave. He would speak to the men below and try to persuade them to wait for a day or two before taking James away. They ought to be glad of the rest. He himself was anxious to get home. His wife would be worried. He had to tell his sister that her sons were now soldiers.

'Will there ever be a time when there are no wars?' she asked, when he was at the door.

'When pigs can fly, my lady.'

19

LATER, JAMES CAME back, when she was alone. It was cold in the room, in spite of the coal fire. Candles flickered and tapestries covering the stone walls stirred in the many draughts. He crouched on a stool by the fire, she lay in bed. They could not see each other's faces.

'They're going to let me stay till the day after tomorrow,' he said.

'Yes. Mr Graham said he would ask them.'

'It wasn't Mr Graham. They wouldn't listen to him. Father told them they could wait. They would do anything for *him*.'

Yes, they would not only die for him, they would kill for him too. She remembered Rothes's ironic remark that wars were won by killing, not by dying. Rothes was dead himself, killed by consumption. In heaven, was he amused at having met such an unheroic end? Or was he in hell, paying for all those ironies?

'I don't want to go, Mama.'

She could not tell him to disobey his father. Her own vow of obedience was more sacred than any soldier's.

'Why can't I stay here and then go with you to Kinnaird? I'd rather be at Kinnaird than at Old Montrose with Mr Forret. Why can't Mr Forret come to Kinnaird to teach me?'

Because your father does not want you to come under the influence of your grandfather. 'Didn't you say that to your father?'

'I couldn't.'

'Why not?'

'Because John would have made fun of me, wanting to be with my mother.' He mimicked his brother's sarcastic voice. 'He says I should have been a girl.'

You would have been, she thought, if I had had my wish.

'It was horrible in the camp, Mama. Once, some men came back. They had been in a skirmish with some enemy troops. One had a great gash on his face, like Gillies, the blacksmith. His face was bright red with blood. He was screaming with pain. He died afterwards. I didn't really faint, though John said I did. He laughed at me. Some soldier you'll make, he said.'

She remembered James's rebuking of her for turning his sons into milksops. Yes, she had favoured James in the very hope that he would grow up hating violence.

'Sometimes I hated him.'

'Who?'

'John. He said crueller things to me than anyone else did.'

'Because he loved you more than anyone else.'

'Not more than you, Mama.'

'I love you both.'

'If I loved somebody, I wouldn't say cruel things to him.'

Perhaps you would if that somebody brought you bitter disappointment.

'There aren't many people I do love. You, Mama. Grandfather Carnegie, sometimes. My dog Prince. John, but only when he's kind to me. That's all.'

'Don't you love your little brothers Robert and David?'

'Yes, but I don't know them really. They're too young.'

But did any of them in her family know one another as they should? If James had been content to stay at home, it would have been different. How could a man who had dreamt of disrupting the whole country, for whatever reason, noble or otherwise, and was at present disrupting it, how could he have kept his family close together?

'Surely you have left someone out?' she said.

256

'Who?'

'Your father.'

He gazed into the fire. He was in tears. 'I'm not sure, Mama. I used to, when I was small. I still do, sometimes. He never speaks about you, Mama. When I spoke about you, he pretended to listen, but he was really thinking about other things, like how many Highlanders had gone off or how many bullets were left or what was happening to the King in England.'

'Well, those would be important matters to him.'

'Did you know, Mama, the Irish have their women and children with them? Horrible women. They sing by the fire and sing sad songs. They clean the blood off the swords.'

She shivered as she imagined herself confronted with James's sword sticky with blood.

20

AT THE BEGINNING of March, there was a spell of cold dry sunny weather. The roads were rutted but hard. Her brother James, Lord Carnegie, came again, sent by their father, to take her and her two young sons to Kinnaird. He was not this time, he said, to accept a refusal, whatever the state of her health. If necessary, a bed could be made up for her in the carriage.

He had a dozen armed horsemen with him. There were people, he said, who, if they knew she was Montrose's wife, would try to do her harm: people who had had relatives and friends killed at Tippermuir and Aberdeen.

She was willing to go. She had her husband's permission.

Her brother was huffishly reluctant to give her news of her husband. From this she jaloused that the reckless raid into Campbell country must have succeeded. If it had been a disaster, James would have gloated over the telling of it. Bit by bit, using the wiles of childhood, she got out of him the information that Montrose and his army had reached Inveraray and burned it down. Argyll had fled by sea. Worse than that, admitted James sourly, was what had happened afterwards at Inverlochy, where a strong force of Campbells had been decimated. Argyll again had escaped by sea. He had appeared before Parliament in Edinburgh, with his arm tied up in a scarf, as if he had been a combatant. He had reported that fewer than 30 of his followers had been killed but no one had believed him and soon it had emerged that the true number was 1500.

'Your husband's hands, Magdalen, are now so deeply stained

with Scottish blood that all the water of the Tay could not cleanse them.'

She asked if there was news of her son, John. No, but, if he had been killed or badly hurt, it would have been joyously proclaimed.

As her oldest brother, James felt it his duty to speak to her severely. 'You don't seem to realise, Magdalen, that your husband and your son are going to end up on the gallows. You must prepare your mind for that.'

'Would they hang a boy of fourteen?'

'He's a rebel in arms, and the son of the most notorious rebel in the land.'

'But what if James, my husband, wins? Who will be hanged then?'

He felt cross. She had always asked silly questions like that. In a child, they had been annoying, though forgivable, in a woman with four children they were intolerable. 'Do you want him to win, Magdalen? In your prayers, do you ask for his victory?'

'In my prayers, I ask for the fighting to end.'

'Aye, but how do you want it to end? With his victory, so that he will occupy Holyrood and lord it over us all, with you by his side? Is that what you want, Magdalen?'

She shook her head.

'No one can prevail in Scotland if he has the Kirk against him. Your James has been excommunicated. He is doomed, therefore. You are still a young woman. You can marry again, this time a man of your own choice. Father has already agreed to it. He is sorry now that he married you off to Montrose. I said at the time it was a mistake but no one listened to me.'

James had brought with him Mr Stevenson, the Dundee lawyer, who was to make arrangements for the management of the Kincardine estate while she was away. He had done it before while she and James were living at Kinnaird in the early days of their marriage but this time there were additional matters for him to attend to. Lady Magdalen set out certain conditions which he had to agree to but, inwardly, he thought that, since her illness was responsible, it would be easy for him to obtain a dispensation to break any promise he had to make. She did not seem to understand that the estate and various other Graham properties were heavily mortgaged, to help pay for her husband's expensive war. Otherwise, surely she would not have insisted that all servants paid off should be given generous compensation or that pensions paid to various tenants must be honourably maintained. When he said he did not know where the money would come from, she said that she had put together a number of her belongings which she wanted him to sell on her behalf. Among them was the painting of herself by Mr Jameson of Aberdeen. Sir Francis Gowrie of Mintlaw had once offered to buy it. He would give a good price. The transaction, though, must be kept confidential.

Mr Stevenson felt obliged to ask if her husband would sanction such a sale. Her husband, she replied, had never liked the painting: he thought she looked much too doleful in it. So she did, thought the lawyer but, as he was to tell his wife when he got back to Dundee, not half as doleful as she looked now, when the ravages of disease were turning her skin yellow and causing dark shadows under her eyes. He could not help being amazed that this small fragile young woman, if her husband took over the country on the King's behalf, as he seemed very capable of doing, could become the foremost lady in the land, after the Queen.

21

ANXIOUS TO TAKE advantage of the dry weather and firm roads, James lost no time in organising the journey to Kinnaird. There were three carriages, one for Magdalen and Mrs Witherspoon, one for Robert and little David and their two nurses, and the third for valuables, including paintings of past Grahams and a kist containing documents relating to the Graham family. James merely shrugged his shoulders when told that Magdalen's own portrait was not included among the other paintings. Mr Stevenson was taking this to Dundee to be sold: she needed the money. It seemed a sensible idea to James. The money would come in useful and he had never cared for the painting anyway. Mr Jameson had been a bit too clever and given little Magdalen qualities she had never really possessed.

The cavalcade set out early, in sunshine, though the air was icy. Everyone's breath was visible. It might have been a funeral, so quiet and tearful were all those, servants and tenants, gathered in the courtyard. They knew they would never see Lady Magdalen again. She had to be cleeked to her carriage and helped up into it but, even so, she paused to look round at them all and wave. They saw that she was in tears and they marvelled, as they had often done before, how, though so young, she could have the dignity of a great lady and at the same time a shared humanity. If she had also at times a peculiar remoteness, it could have been caused by pain or by the strain of having for her husband the most hated man in Scotland. The story was that she had been strange when a little girl, so much so that her family had been afraid for some time that she wasn't quite right in the head. But, if she was abnormal, then it would be a better world if everyone was abnormal like her.

She kept the window open, in spite of the cold. These fields and trees, she would never see them again, and these people beside their miserable dwellings.

So am I seeing them for the last time, thought Mrs Witherspoon, and thank God for it. It was no grief to her, she had no tears in her eyes, she did not let herself suffer for the sake of clowns hardly any more intelligent than their own pigs. Though as staunch a Presbyterian as any woman, Mrs Witherspoon, in her mistress's place, would have been wearing crimson satin instead of plain grey cloth, and her fingers would have sparkled with rings, and her neck with necklaces, unlike Lady Magdalen's, which were unadorned. As she gazed at her mistress, Mrs Witherspoon felt comfortable and safe. In every respect, from plump fingers to plump neck to plump bosom, she was much more womanly. Any stranger glancing in would have taken her for the marquis's wife and Lady Magdalen for the parson's widow. But really Mrs Witherspoon did not envy her mistress her high station. It was safer and more comfortable to be one of the people: not a peasant like those grinning dolts, but a citizen of good standing, with money saved up and the freedom to spend it as she pleased.

In Kinnaird, and even in Holyrood if her husband was victorious, Lady Magdalen would be like a prisoner, partly because of her poor health but also because she would be allowed to meet only persons of equal rank to her own; and, from what little Mrs Witherspoon had seen of those grand personages, they were not worth meeting. And if the Marquis was defeated and hanged, Lady Magdalen would be despised and disgraced. So Mrs Witherspoon, wearing her most solicitous expression, hugged herself in self-congratulation. She smiled as she reflected that, at a large and busy house like Kinnaird, there would be on the staff gentlemen of substance, who would look with admiration on so handsome a woman as herself. If she found the right man and he made the right offer, she would marry again: not that she pined for a marriage bed – look what it had done to the poor soul opposite her – but she did feel that she had missed something, poor Mr Witherspoon never having been able, owing to too much piety and too little pith, as her mother, now deceased, had once described him.

In Perth, an incident confirmed Mrs Witherspoon in her belief that she was more fortunate than her mistrsss. It was necessary to stop in the town at an inn so that the ladies, and the two nurses, could use the privies. They could hardly, like men, relieve themselves behind dykes or in woods. At any rate, Mrs Witherspoon could not or rather would not. Lady Magdalen said she wouldn't mind, thus showing an indelicacy that Mrs Witherspoon had noticed before in high-born ladies.

Three coaches, attended by a dozen horsemen, attracted attention. A crowd gathered outside the inn. The Graham crest was noticed. Rumours were tossed about. Montrose had been seized and was being taken to Edinburgh. Then, when Lady Magdalen and Mrs Witherspoon came out and climbed into the carriage, someone hit on the truth. 'It's Montrose's wife!'

Other cries were heard, angry and threatening. 'What's the bitch daeing here?' 'Drag her oot and dae tae her whit her man did to mine at Tippermuir!' Faces, twisted with anger, appeared at the window. Mrs Witherspoon was terrified that they would think she was Lady Magdalen. She got ready to scream that she was Mrs Witherspoon, a supporter of the Covenant.

The danger lasted less than a minute. The mob was swept out of the way by Lord Carnegie and his horsemen, who used as little force as they could, for, after all, the crowd was made up of loyal Presbyterians; most of the men there had signed the Covenant.

Mrs Witherspoon had noticed that the women were more vicious than the men. She wasn't surprised. She had once got her hand badly scarted trying to separate two drunken trollops fighting over a worthless man.

Lord Carnegie bent down and looked into the carriage. 'Sorry about that, Magdalen,' he said, with a chuckle. 'No harm done?'

'Are the children all right?'

He laughed. He was remarkably jolly, considering that his sister had almost been mobbed. 'I don't think they noticed the children. It's your husband they'd like to get their hands on.'

Lady Magdalen lay back on the cushions with her eyes shut. She looked calm but surely did not feel calm.

Mrs Witherspoon herself was still shaking. She deserved, she thought, extra payment. Having to act as nurse as well as companion was onerous enough, without running the risk of being assaulted.

'Poor creatures,' whispered Lady Magdalen.

Mrs Witherspoon had to ask who.

'Those unhappy women.'

'Those wild beasts, if you ask me.'

'No.'

Mrs Witherspoon waited for more but that one word was all Lady Magdalen said until they reached Kinnaird about two hours later. Night was falling, but Mrs Witherspoon could see that it was indeed a more pleasant place than Kincardine, with spacious grounds, and the house itself, as they approached it up a drive half a mile long, looked really like a house and not a grim fortress like Kincardine. Yes, she could be content here for a year or two. Eligible gentlemen would pay visits, on business and for pleasure. As Lady Magdalen's companion, she would be able to meet them, she would dine at the same table and sit in the same drawing room. At 35, she was in her prime, still able to bear children, with a body that would entice any virile man. Every night for years she had admired it in its nudity.

She could not help feeling pity, with a touch of contempt, for the small, emaciated, yellow-faced, worn-out woman opposite her.

22

IN SOME OBSCURE way, her father seemed to blame her for all her husband's misdeeds. He never said so but it was in his face and voice as he told her how many men were killed at Tippermuir, Aberdeen, and Inverlochy, and how many houses of Covenanters had been wantonly burned to the ground, for Montrose, 'that chivalrous cavalier', was now waging war as his Irish did, ferociously and without mercy. He took particular pleasure in telling her that one of the houses destroyed had been Mintlaw, Francis Gowrie's shrine to beauty. A band of Irish, inflamed with bloodlust and *usquebaugh*, had made no distinction between paintings of the Madonna and Child and paintings of classical gods and goddesses like Apollo and Diana. He did not try to conceal his exultation. Mintlaw, the sceptic, worshipper of beautiful objects, had got what he deserved. Did he think he could stand up in the kirk and accuse godly men of cruelty, and get away with it? Did he think he could fill his house with paintings and sculptures by Papist and atheistic artists and not be punished? The Irish were savages, though, in their own way, Christians. Was it not clever of the Lord to use them to chastise the arrogant unbeliever?

She asked what had happened to Francis himself and his wife and child.

Expert in speaking in Parliament and General Assembly, in such a way as to hide his true feelings, her father could not keep from showing a triumphant glee that, in spite of his white beard and senatorial gravity, was childish. 'I believe Lady Gowrie and

266

the child were safe in Edinburgh when it happened. They had not been living at Mintlaw for some time. Mintlaw himself, I understand, perished in trying to save his toys.'

The word revealed the poverty of her father's mind. Yet he was reputed to be one of the wisest men of his generation.

'He was right then,' she said, 'in calling us all barbarians.'

Though possessed of one of the readiest tongues in Scotland, her father could not, in the few seconds before she turned away to weep, find an answer.

23

AT KINNAIRD, SOUTHESK was king. Every messenger was brought before him even if the message was not for him personally. So the lone horseman who arrived in March, with a provocative blue ribbon in his cap, was hauled forcibly to the Earl, though he cried that it was the Earl's daughter, Lady Magdalen, he had come to see. His reward for that was to have the bonnet struck off his head with force enough to make his nose bleed. Unsubdued, he said that he came from the Marquis and earned a few more buffets for his impudence.

Southesk sat at his desk, stroking his beard and staring at the bloody-nosed envoy from his son-in-law. Though Kinnaird was a house famed for its hospitality, there was a dungeon where thumbscrews were ready if necessary. This insolent rebel looked as if he would benefit from their acquaintance.

'What is your name?' he asked.

'Thomas Kinkell of Kinkell House.'

A man of quality therefore. Southesk knew Kinkell: a small but prosperous property on the shores of the Forth. Here was no common agent. It must be an important message.

Southesk instructed one of the guards to give a cloth to the prisoner – for such he was – to wipe the blood off his face.

'And what has brought you to Kinnaird, Mr Kinkell?'

'I have a message for Lady Magdalen.'

'From whom?'

'From the Marquis.'

'The Marquis?'

'The lady's husband, my lord.'

'Ah, you mean my daughter.'

'Yes, my lord.'

'Well, what is your message?'

'I have to give it to her personally.'

Was it worth crushing the fellow's thumbs to teach him humility? Hardly. 'My daughter is not well. She is confined to her chamber.'

'I am very sorry to hear that.'

'So, if you tell me what your message is, I shall see that she receives it.'

Kinkell hesitated. 'I was charged to give it to her in person.'

'But she is not well, Mr Kinkell.'

Kinkell shook his head. He was more angry than afraid when one of the guards struck him in the back.

'Well, Mr Kinkell, since that is your attitude, I shall send to find out if my daughter is able to come and hear your message from your own lips.'

'Thank you, my lord.'

At a signal from Southesk, one of the guards went out.

As they waited, Southesk made conversation. 'Have you come far, Mr Kinkell?'

'Far enough.'

'How is my son-in-law?'

'The Marquis is very well.'

'Why do you keep on? You will all hang in the end, you know.'

'In the end the King's standard will fly from every castle in Scotland, including Kinnaird.'

Well, thought Southesk, it wouldn't take much effort, physical or moral, to put up a flag if that was all that was needed. He had taken care not to be too dogmatic. His attitude had been that it would hardly be the end of the world if bishops were

269

appointed. He could disguise his boredom listening to a bishop just as well as when listening to a moderator.

He went back to studying the State papers in front of him or, rather, made a pretence of doing so. He was really preparing himself for when Magdalen came in, if indeed she was able to come down the stairs. She did not say much these days but her eyes still looked for the truth as they had done when she was a child; not so guilelessly as then perhaps, but still with the power to make him feel dishonest and guilty.

She came in, dressed, as always, in black, though it accentuated her pallor. He had suggested brighter clothes and had got out of the kist dresses of her mother's, brilliant reds and greens and yellows. Unfortunately they had disintegrated on being handled: mould and moths had done for them.

Mrs Witherspoon was with her, holding her by the arm.

Southesk frowned. He had not taken to Mrs Witherspoon. She presumed too much. He had been warned that she was having an intrigue with his nephew Malcolm Carnegie, at present a guest in the house.

'What is it, Father?' asked Magdalen.

She turned and looked at Kinkell. The guards, her father noticed, at once relaxed their grip.

'Who is this gentleman?' she asked.

'Thomas Kinkell, my pet. He has brought a message for you.'

'For me? Who is it from?'

Southesk felt great unease. He loved her and did not want her hurt. 'From your husband.'

She breathed then with difficulty. A chair was brought forward for her. 'What is it?' she whispered.

'He has not said. His orders were to give it to you personally.'

She looked at Kinkell. 'What is your message, Mr Kinkell?'

He had come prejudiced against her. Now he was looking at her with pity and respect. 'I think, my lady, we should be alone when I tell you.'

'No. Please tell me now.'

He had turned as pale as she; his voice faltered. 'I regret, my lady, to have to inform you that your son, Lord John, died two days ago of a fever. He was buried in Bellie graveyard.'

Bellie, thought Southesk. Near Gordon Castle. So Montrose was still trying to gain the support of the fickle Gordons. If he ever succeeded in that, his campaign would be greatly strengthened. But had not the boy been subject to sore throats and fevers? If he had taken part in the mad expedition into Argyll, no wonder he had caught a fatal cold. Convenient for Montrose, who had as good as killed his son, to be able to blame a fever.

Magdalen was still dry-eyed. She sat very straight. Her hands were motionless on the arms of her chair. It was as if she was showing how a soldier's wife should receive dreadful news.

'Did he suffer?' she asked.

Kinkell hesitated. The boy had said strange wild things in his delirium. 'Not very long, my lady.'

'Was his father with him?'

'Yes, my lady. The chaplain too. The whole camp mourned. He was a splendid lad.'

'Thank you, Mr Kinkell. Please tell my husband—'

But what could she say to James? That she had warned him about their son's proneness to colds? That it was his fault, therefore, that John was dead at fourteen? No. Better to say nothing. She thought of her other son, James, and was afraid for him.

'Tell my husband I am very sorry for him.'

'Yes, my lady, I'll tell him.' Kinkell knew what she was suffering. She was, he thought, a fit wife for his general.

Magdalen rose. 'Mr Kinkell, do you have any news of two young kinsmen of my husband's who joined him recently? Gavin and Tom Maitland.'

'They are both well, my lady.'

'Thank God for that. Father, I would like Mr Kinkell to be treated well.'

So she had noticed the swollen nose. Southesk could not very well rebuke her for hinting that the messenger might be ill treated, for he had been thinking of applying some forcible persuasion to find out something of Montrose's present whereabouts and future intentions.

'Mr Kinkell is free to go as soon as he pleases.'

'Should he not be given some refreshment?'

'If he wishes.'

But Kinkell did not wish. 'Thank you, my lady, but I would prefer to leave at once.'

'Very well. I wish you safe journey and godspeed.'

With a bow to her and then to her father, Kinkell hurried from the room.

She saw the guards look at her father who gave a slight shake of his head.

She went over to the window, where she would be able to see Kinkell ride down the driveway. She felt like crawling into a corner to weep but she resisted it, she would weep, but later, when she was alone.

At last there he was, mounted on a grey horse, cantering down the driveway. He might be arrested when out of her sight, but surely her father would not be so dishonourable.

In a few hours he would be reporting to James, her husband. Surely she should have gone with him. But she was not able, through illness and, in any case, her father, anxious not to offend the Estates, would have prevented her. Worst of all, James would not have been pleased to see her. He thought that she had been disloyal to him and so, perhaps, she had been. But to whom or to what should she have been loyal? She had not known before the war began and she still did not know now that it was being fought. She should remember that she was not alone, many mothers were mourning their sons. When she wept, she would be weeping for them all.

24

AFTER JOHN'S DEATH, Magdalen withdrew into herself. She had been hurt too much, poor lady, they whispered. Her infant son, David, was put into her arms in the hope that his happy gurglings would at least make her smile, but she stared at him as if he was a corpse too. When seven-year-old Robert asked her tearfully if he would ever see John again, she just stared at him. When her father asked if she would like James to be brought from Old Montrose, she shook her head and seemed on the point of speaking. Trying to encourage her, her father was far from guessing that, if she had spoken, it would have been to say that she no longer trusted him. He had gloated at Francis's death and the destruction of Mintlaw, and, if she had not shamed him, would have ill-treated Mr Kinkell.

Mr Henderson was sent for. Though sorry for her, he felt obliged to scold her for not seeking consolation in the Lord. He did it as gently as he could, which wasn't really gently at all, for he was too accustomed to castigating backsliders. He conceded that it was natural to mourn, especially for a mother. God was not heartless. But grief should be expressed in words, not in obdurate silence, like animals; and after it should come Christian gratitude and joy. Lord John's body was rotting in the graveyard at Bellie, beside the Spey, but his soul was singing with angels on the banks of a far grander river, in heaven. It had to be remembered, though, that he had died while in the service of the anti-Christ: it would be entered against him in the celestial ledger, for the Lord demanded His due. However, since he had been only fourteen and was under the malign influence of his father, the traitor-rebel, God would make allowances.

He said all that on his knees on the hard floor, with a few involuntary sighs.

He would have been greatly discomfited if he had known that Lady Magdalen was noticing how grubby were the white sleeves of his sark, how the knees of his breeks had been patched more than once, how the hairs in his nostrils and ears were whiter now than they had been at her wedding, and how his performance had become mechanical, having been done too often to have any genuine feeling left in it.

She broke her silence then. 'Where *is* heaven?' she asked.

He paused in his prayer to glower at her. He wasn't sure whether the question was stupid or mischievous.

It was really one of the guileless questions she had asked as a child and to which she had never got answers.

In one of Francis's paintings there had been a picture of heaven, as the artist had conceived it. White buildings with shining towers. Flowers. Butterflies. Winged angels. Pink clouds. Musicians with happy faces.

She had thought it beautiful but there were no mysteries explained, no revelations, no marvellous fulfilments.

Meanwhile, Mr Henderson was gnashing his gums in vexation. 'In a bairn,' he said, portentously, as if in a pulpit, 'such a question might be pardonable, though not permissible. In an adult, it is blasphemy. For implicit in it is the implication that heaven does not exist and, therefore, that God does not exist. Men, and women too, have been justly burned at the stake for such blasphemies. Your mind, Lady Magdalen, is disturbed by grief and, therefore, I make allowances, as God does to unhappy sinners who have temporarily lost their way.'

'Yes, but where is it?'

Minutes later he was solemnly telling her father that her

condition was very serious, grief and sundry disappointments had made her a child again, with the typical childish characteristic of not listening to answers but simply repeating questions.

25

THE EARL WAS unfair in suspecting Mrs Witherspoon of having an intrigue with his nephew, Malcolm. It would have been more accurate to say that Malcolm was laying siege to her virtue and she was not repelling him as wholeheartedly as she might: tepid water instead of boiling oil. In spite of certain drawbacks, he would do admirably as a husband, being heir to an ample estate. At 22, he was at least ten years her junior. He frequently laughed: a sign either of perennial good humour or weak-wittedness; not that it mattered. He was very amorous: lecherous would have been a truer word, for he had already, so rumour said, bairned two maidservants. One afternoon, this lively young gentleman, finding her alone in the music room, had fondled her bosom from behind and thrust himself against her. She had repulsed him but not instantly, and reproached him but not very angrily. He had gone off humming.

That night, while she was getting ready for bed, indeed while she was once more admiring her soft white rounded body and seeing it through his eyes, the door opened and in he crept. There was no lock, only a defective sneck. In a trice, he had her tumbled on to the bed, with himself on top of her. He said nothing, nor did she. What could she have said? That she hoped he understood this was more binding than a formal betrothal? She had heard before of a ravisher, a nobleman too, having to marry the woman he ravished. So, in the next two or three minutes, she suffered him to do what the late asthmatic Mr Witherspoon had never managed in five years of marriage; that was, inject his seed into her. If he got her with child, he would certainly have to marry her. Thus reassured, she found it quite pleasurable.

The moment he was spent, he leapt up, turned his back, pulled up his breeks, and rushed off, pausing at the door to blow her a kiss . . .

She went to sleep with a satisfied smile. The deed of marriage had been signed, not with a pen, but with a more authoritative instrument.

Next day, she sought him eagerly but he was not to be found. He had gone hunting, she was told.

That night, he came again to her room. She had omitted to have the sneck repaired or the bolt oiled. Intentionally? She smiled at herself in the mirror. She put on perfume, lingered over her undressing and spent more time than usual in brushing her hair, which came below her navel and was the same alluring hue as that on her body. She kept expecting him to enter.

An hour later, she was in bed, alone, seething with annoyance, when the door flew open and in he sprang, dressed in white sark and pink hose. Before she could protest at his recent tardiness and present impetuosity, he was in bed beside her, making love, not at all like a lover, more like a woodman axing a tree. He wasted neither breath in speaking nor energy in fondling. It was like an urgent visit to the privy. Before she could have counted to 30, he was done and gone.

She felt insulted and degraded. She had been used like a whore – no, worse than that, for with a whore he would have taken longer, getting his money's worth.

Next day, she was told he had left Kinnaird and returned home, to prepare for his marriage to the youngest daughter of Lord Linton.

There was no one she could complain to or vent her anger on. She was more deserving of pity than Lady Magdalen, yet everyone went out of their way to be considerate to her ladyship, while all that Mrs Witherspoon got were malicious smiles, as if those visits to her room, and their purpose, were not as secret as she had hoped.

She did have one offer of help. After praying with Lady Magdalen, Mr Henderson came sneaking into Mrs Witherspoon's room and offered to pray with her. At first, she thought he must have found out about her fornication. He had prayed with her once before, at Kincardine, both on their knees facing each other. His breath had stunk. To her astonishment, for he was old as well as reverend, he had paused in his rantings to liken her breasts to 'two young twin roes which fed among the lilies'; a quotation, he had informed her, from the Song of Solomon.

This time she declined and he went off in a sanctimonious huff.

26

SOME THREE WEEKS later, Lady Magdalen was in her room sewing, attended by Mrs Witherspoon who was supposed to be sewing too, but whose fingers frequently turned into claws, and on whose face appeared now and then grimaces of fury.

Lady Magdalen noticed. Since her recovery from the shock of John's death, she had been more solicitous than ever about other people, too much so, thought Mrs Witherspoon, ungraciously.

'Is your toothache bad again, Margaret?' she asked.

Mrs Witherspoon had given toothache as the explanation. The truth was she had already missed her monthly and feared that she was pregnant. Also, she was suffering from an intolerable itch in her tenderest part, so that she could scarcely sit still. Therefore to be asked in that meek martyr's voice if her toothache was bad was most exasperating, especially as her teeth were better than her mistress's. Moreover, two days ago, the Earl had summoned her to his office. Anticipating a proposal of marriage to his nephew – her state of mind causing her to indulge in wild expectations – she was shocked to be told curtly that she must look for another situation. Lady Magdalen's companion should be a lady of rank, not a promoted housekeeper. She would, of course, be compensated. He would be obliged if she gave Lady Magdalen to understand that she was leaving of her own accord.

She had almost blurted out that she was carrying his nephew's child but it would have been inopportune, considering that she was not yet sure. She had instead given a display of good breeding and dignity, which had noticeably impressed him, particularly as she was wearing a red velvet dress that showed off to their best advantage her 'two young twin roes which fed among the lilies'.

Inwardly, she had been screaming with pique.

These painful reflections were interrupted by the pounding of horses' hooves outside, many horses, many hooves. There was jingling of harness.

Mrs Witherspoon's first thought was that soldiers had been sent to arrest her. She would be dragged off and publicly whipped, as was often done to fornicators. It would be held against her that her partner was ten years younger. They would say that she had led him into sin. Mr Henderson would say it loudest of all. She had made a mistake in rebuffing him. She should have let him make pets of the twin roes.

Crying out at the injustice of it all, she had to pretend that she had pierced her finger with the needle.

Lady Magdalen, that withered leaf, looked up sympathetically. 'What is the matter?'

Mrs Witherspoon rushed to the window. Yes, they were dragoons, but far too many surely for the arrest of one woman. More likely, they had come to arrest Lady Magdalen or the Earl. She knew they were Covenant troops, for the Royalists had few cavalry.

Look at them, conceited brutes, in their fine uniforms. Their horses looked nobler. All men wanted from a woman was one thing and, when they had got it, they threw her away like an apple core.

'They look very pleased with themselves,' she said. 'They must have come from a victory.'

It occurred to her that they might have the Marquis with them as a prisoner. She would enjoy seeing him in chains.

But she needed to hurt someone, to ease her own torments, of body and soul. She went back to her sewing and imagined that

280

she was pushing not one needle but a hundred into that part of young Carnegie's anatomy, so soft and yet so rampant.

'Dragoons, my lady,' she said. 'Dozens of them, a whole army. Do you think they can have the Marquis with them, as a prisoner?'

Lady Magdalen shuddered. 'I hope not.'

'They could be taking him to Edinburgh.'

'But why would they bring him here?'

'Perhaps he wanted to see you.' Before they hang him, she added, but to herself. There would be many hangings. With luck, young Carnegie's would be one.

What was making Mrs Witherspoon more and more vindictive was the need to scratch. Twice already she had had to leave the room to do it and put on more salve. If she had caught the pox or was pregnant, it would vex her a great deal more than if a thousand Royalists were hanged.

Heavy footsteps were heard outside the room. Spurs clanked.

'My God,' cried Mrs Witherspoon,' they've come to arrest me.'

'Why? What have you done?' asked Lady Magdalen.

There was a knock on the door. It opened and in strode the Earl, looking very grave in his black clothes. His beard was white. It looked as if it had been newly washed.

'I wasn't to blame,' cried Mrs Witherspoon, hysterically. 'He forced me.'

Southesk gave her a frown of disapproval and surprise. Evidently, he did not know what she was talking about. The great man, who knew all the secrets of the State, did not know what went on in his own house.

'Magdalen, my pet,' he said,' you have a visitor.'

She gazed bravely at him. 'Did it need all those soldiers to bring him?'

'It is not your husband.'

They did not know but she thought for a moment that it

281

might be Francis Gowrie, who had not after all perished with his paintings.

'It is James, your son. They are taking him to Edinburgh as a hostage. Do not be alarmed. He will come to no harm.'

'But why are they taking him? What harm has he done? He is only a child.'

'He is now his father's heir.'

There was then a hearty bang on the door and in swaggered an officer in a red tunic and blue breeches. His sword and spurs threatened to trip him up in the small room. He had a swarthy spotted face, with a black moustache and long black hair.

He gave Mrs Witherspoon a boldly lustful grin.

He bowed to Lady Magdalen. 'Major-General Sir John Hurry at your service, my lady.'

Everyone had heard of Sir John Hurry. He had once fought on the Continent as a mercenary, then for the army of the Parliament in England, then for the King, who had knighted him, and now he had changed sides again and was fighting for the Estates.

He was looking at Mrs Witherspoon as if she had no clothes. She returned the compliment. His legs were bandy and hairy, his thighs muscular from gripping a horse's flanks. He would make love at a gallop. Would he take time to remove his spurs?

Lady Magdalen was staring at him in horror. It grieved her that this brash and unprincipled adventurer who loved war for its own sake should be persecuting her sensitive son.

'Why have you arrested my boy, Sir John? He is only a child.'

'Orders, my lady. Nothing personal. He is to be taken to Edinburgh where he will be lodged in the Castle with some kinsmen and friends. I give my word no harm will come to him. He asked to see his mother and damned if I saw any reason why not. Two hours, my lady. Then we must push on. May I say, though I am in the opposite camp, that I have enormous respect for your husband. Damned if I don't regard him as the finest soldier in all Europe, with only one exception.' He roared with laughter. 'Mind you, he can't win. Odds against too great. If I have the honour of grabbing him, I assure you I shall see that he is treated like the gallant gentleman he is.'

Then Sir John clattered out, with a last urgent glance at Mrs Witherspoon. He was inviting her to spend the two hours with him.

She smiled as if tempted but she was thinking that what he deserved was a bullet between those insolent eyes or better still a dose of the pox. He wouldn't sit so proudly on his horse then.

On her way to her room to put on more salve she passed soldiers. Young James was among them, pale and frightened, but she was in too great a hurry to greet him.

Magdalen waited for her son to come in. 'Will he be in chains?' she asked.

Her father smiled. 'No, no. He is not that kind of prisoner.'

James then entered, looking very like John, thought his mother, though she had never noticed any resemblance before. He was trying to be brave and grown-up. He smiled at his mother but kept his distance. He was waiting till they were alone.

Southesk prepared to withdraw. 'I shall come back later,' he said, 'and hear your story.'

'I have nothing to tell Grandfather. They just came and took me and Mr Forret.'

'Have they treated you well?' asked his mother.

'Yes. When they are not killing one another, soldiers are very kind.'

Southesk smiled at that and left.

Immediately James rushed to his mother and knelt by her chair. He burst into tears. She knew they were not for himself. She stroked his fair hair, remembering that other beloved head with the dark hair. James had accused John of saying cruel things to him; for that reason, he had loved him only sometimes. But now he wept sorely for his dead brother and she wept with him.

27

MAGDALEN HAD NEVER been taken in by Margaret Witherspoon. She knew her to be vain, ambitious, and selfish but, against that, she was very fond of little Robert, whom she made a fuss of and who liked and trusted her. When he hurt himself, it was Mrs Witherspoon he would run to to have the place kissed better, and she would clasp him to her ample breasts, of which she was so proud and which she boldly displayed, wearing dresses more suitable for dissolute ladies of the court than a Presbyterian minister's widow. Magdalen did not love her as she had loved Janet but she was sorry for her and admired her. She carried herself so well, whereas Magdalen stooped; was red-cheeked, so that she didn't need rouge, though she used it, while Magdalen was irremediably sallow; and she had a mass of auburn hair, so much more beautiful than Magdalen's own, which was thin and grey.

When Mrs Witherspoon came one day, pale and tearful, and said that she had just been told by the Earl that she was to be dismissed, Magdalen's first reaction was indignation. How dare her father and her brother, James, who she was sure had a hand in it, do such a thing without consulting her. Sympathy soon followed. She asked Mrs Witherspoon to sit down and tell her about it.

Mrs Witherspoon sat down and dabbed her eyes with her handkerchief. Her tears were genuine, though there was more anger in them than hurt. They did not prevent her from gazing at her mistress with calculation. If she told the truth, with only minor departures from it, would this simple-minded good-hearted ninny forgive her and take her part? It never ceased to amaze Mrs Witherspoon that Lady Magdalen was the daughter of an earl and the wife of the most notorious man in Scotland. The trouble was how to explain to this well-meaning ignoramus those visits of her randy cousin to Mrs Witherspoon's room. For Mrs Witherspoon was sure that Lady Magdalen, though she had borne four children, knew nothing of the sexual appetites of men. As a young girl, she had been teased by her sisters for her nun-like innocence, and she had never really got rid of it. So, as Mrs Witherspoon sat there, peeping through her handkerchief and ready to drop on to her knees in supplication, she could not help thinking how absurd it was that she, so much handsomer and so better adapted to the ways of the world, should have to beg this grey-haired, flat-chested, sickly little creature to save her.

'What reason did my father give?' asked Lady Magdalen, though she had guessed.

Her brother, James, Lord Carnegie, had grumbled to her that Mrs Witherspoon ought not to be her companion: it was a position for a lady of quality. He must have grumbled to their father too.

'He said your companion should be a lady of quality.'

Yes, but Magdalen could tell from Mrs Witherspoon's eyes that there was another reason. She knew Mrs Witherspoon far better than Mrs Witherspoon ever suspected. 'Did he say anything else?'

'He didn't say it, my lady, but I think he thought your cousin Malcolm was too attracted to me. As if that was my fault! I'm sure I gave him no encouragement.'

'Malcolm does not need much encouragement, I'm afraid. He has been in disgrace before.'

So the little ignoramus knew about the two maidservants. Yet she did not look scandalised or disgusted. Like most people of high rank, did she believe that a gentleman was entitled to use women of the lower classes in any way he wished?

Mrs Witherspoon felt revengeful. Yes, she would tell the truth, leaving nothing out. She would make Lady Magdalen squirm. Mrs Witherspoon was squirming herself, because of the itch.

'He came to my room at night,' she said.

'Without an invitation?'

'I certainly did not invite him. He just opened the door and walked in.'

'Wasn't your door bolted?'

'The bolt is stiff with rust.'

'Didn't you once tell me that you slept without nightgown or drawers?'

'Except when it is very cold.'

'It has been quite cold these past few days.'

'I always have a good fire in my room.'

'When he saw that you were undressed why did he not withdraw?'

God save me from the obtuseness of the ignorant, thought Mrs Witherspoon. Moments later, she was wondering if there hadn't been a little irony in that question. Far from being obtuse, had Lady Magdalen jaloused what she had been up to, but was more amused and sympathetic than prudish and censorious?

'Because he had come with evil intentions, my lady.'

'How did he reveal those intentions?'

'He proceeded to undress himself with great rapidity.'

'Why did you not cry out? Someone would have heard.'

'I did not want to get the young man into trouble.'

'Yes, he is very young; only twenty-two, I believe.'

'It is a very lusty age for a man.'

Mrs Witherspoon remembered that the Marquis had been only 17 when he had got married. Mr Witherspoon had been 45: a flaccid age.

Lady Magdalen was waiting like a child for the rest of the story. 'What happened then? What did he do?'

'He pushed me on to the bed, my lady, and ravished me.'

'I believe lawyers do not consider it ravishment if the woman gives even the merest encouragement.'

Now, where in God's name had this cloistered creature heard that? But was patting his buttock encouragement? Lawyers would say so.

Lady Magdalen spoke like a lawyer. 'You are a robust woman, Margaret. Could you not have resisted?'

'I was petrified with shock, my lady.'

'Yes, of course, so you would be.'

It was time, thought Mrs Witherspoon, to throw her first bombshell. 'I think I am with child, my lady.'

It failed to explode. 'After only once?' murmured Lady Magdalen.

'Twice. He came the next night too.'

'Did you forget to have the bolt oiled?'

'Yes, I forgot.'

Mrs Witherspoon was now sure that Lady Magdalen was having fun, though not maliciously. Whatever support Mrs Witherspoon would need she would get. Not for the first time she was being given an insight into the depth and strength of Lady Magdalen's character.

'My monthly is already two weeks overdue, my lady.'

'Mine is often overdue.'

Yes, my lady, but you are an unwell woman, whereas I am strong and healthy.

'This child, my lady, it would be a Carnegie, wouldn't it?'

But the bastards of the two maidservants had been Carnegies too. What had happened to them? Up and down Scotland there were earls' sons working as ushers and earls' daughters working as sempstresses. My child, Mrs Witherspoon vowed, will not be disowned so easily. I will not be frightened off by a sermon from Mr Henderson.

It was time for the second bombshell.

'Your cousin has given me an infection.'

'What sort of infection? You look well.'

'A venereal ailment. It does not show on the face. It is called the pox, my lady.'

'I have heard the name. Is one of the symptoms toothache?'

'No, my lady. The ache, or itch, is elsewhere.'

Talking about it made the itch worse. Mrs Witherspoon, by this time, was almost screaming with the torment of it.

'Poor Margaret, is there nothing you can do to alleviate it?'

'I have a salve that gives temporary relief. Your cousin must have picked it up from some loose woman. He should go and see a doctor.' Before half the women in Angus were infected.

'So should you go and see a doctor, Margaret.'

'I would have to go to Dundee.'

'Then you must go to Dundee. We shall say that you wish to visit your aunt.'

'I have no aunt in Dundee.'

'We shall invent one.'

'Suppose, my lady, the doctor tells me that I am with child. Do I get rid of it? There are women in Dundee who do such things for money.'

'Sometimes the woman dies, I believe.'

'Often she dies, my lady.'

'And the poor child lives, with no one to love it?'

'Or hate it, my lady.'

They gazed at each other, with profound understanding.

'What if your father tells me not to come back?'

'I shall tell him I want you to come back.'

Mrs Witherspoon then knelt and embraced her mistress at that moment, her confidante and friend. Her embrace was returned. Both women wept and laughed together.

28

WITH THE AID of a stick, Magdalen went to her father's study. She had asked Mrs Witherspoon not to accompany her.

Busy at his desk, he jumped up and assisted her to a chair. Any time she wished to speak to him, he said, she should send for him.

'It's about Mrs Witherspoon, Father,' she said.

'Ah yes. That troublesome woman. I have been considering a replacement for her. There's Sir Thomas Sinclair's daughter, a widow of forty or so; by all accounts, a godly woman.'

'I want to keep Mrs Witherspoon. I do not want her sent away.'

'Your brother, James, is of the opinion that your companion should be a lady of breeding and, as you must have noticed, he now regards himself as head of the family.'

That was said sarcastically. As a friend of Argyll's, James was always boasting that the family was now under his protection.

'It is no business of James's. Mrs Witherspoon is *my* companion, not his. I like her. I want her to stay.'

'Mr Henderson says she is a Jezebel.'

'Mr Henderson said that Jessie Gilmour was a witch.'

Southesk was startled. He had forgotten all about Jessie Gilmour. That had been 15 years ago. God knew how many more old women had been declared witches since then. Southesk could see little connection between Mr Henderson's calling Mrs Witherspoon a Jezebel and his condemning an old woman as a witch. But then, poor soft-hearted Magdalen had always been a poor logician.

'I was informed that she was making a nuisance of herself to your cousin Malcolm.'

'Who told you that, Father? Was it Malcolm himself? My understanding is that he was making a nuisance of himself to every woman in the house under thirty.'

Southesk was taken aback. It was true, but how had she, shut up in her cell like a nun, known it? Did she also know that he had been caught in bed with not one naked scullery maid but two?

'Mrs Witherspoon wishes to visit her aunt in Dundee. She will be away for two weeks. When she comes back, she will be my companion again.'

'James won't be pleased.' But that might not be a bad thing. James needed his wings clipped.

'Do I have your promise, Father?'

There was no impertinence in her voice, but a quality that commanded respect. She suffered continual pain, she grieved over the death of one son and the imprisonment of another, and, the heaviest cross of all to bear, her husband was the infamous 'traitor-rebel', Montrose. Yet here she was exhausting herself on behalf of a vulgar self-seeking woman who would show her little gratitude.

'Very well, my pet, I promise. Now tell me, how are you feeling?'

'I'm quite well, thank you.'

There were tears in his eyes but none in hers as he cleeked her to the door. 'Shall I call for someone to help you?'

'No, I can manage. I have to exercise my legs, you see.'

Yes, he saw, as he watched her creep shakily and bravely along the corridor, like a woman three times her age. God help you, James Graham, he thought, even if you win a kingdom, you will have been the loser.

29

AFTER MONTROSE'S NEXT victory, at Auldearn, the Estates, in rage and panic, summoned Magdalen and her father to Edinburgh, to be interrogated as to their relations with the 'traitor-rebel'. They were ordered to bring with them Montrose's third son, Robert. If Magdalen could satisfy them that she was 'a loyal and reliable person', she might be allowed to keep the boy; otherwise, he would be taken from her.

She was not well enough to make the journey, though she very much wished to, in the hope that she would be allowed to visit James in the Castle.

Before setting out for the capital, her father had a long talk with her in her sickroom. He found it bright with daffodils, arranged in silver bowls by Mrs Witherspoon, herself a bright presence with her red-and-white velvet dress and auburn hair. He and James, it seemed, had misjudged the woman. She and Magdalen were more like friends than servant and mistress. They were often heard laughing together.

Finished at last, Magdalen's tapestry depicting Christ in a field of lilies covered one of the walls. It struck Southesk that Christ had a resemblance to James Graham in his portrait on another wall but it could have been an illusion. Surely Magdalen did not have the skill, let alone the wish. What was not an illusion, alas, was that her face was as yellow as the flowers. Like them, she had not long to live.

Montrose's portrait would have to be taken down and hidden. She had always been his favourite child and yet he did not know her as well as he should. He had been too busy with other matters, which, God help him, he had thought more important. Indeed, it was those matters, more than fatherly affection, which brought him to her room that fine fresh April morning.

When he appeared without her before the Estates, they would accept the excuse that she was not well, for they were, some of them at any rate, compassionate men with daughters of their own – besides, they would have the reports of their spies – but they might propose sending agents with a list of questions for her to answer. She must, therefore, be prepared.

Not only her own freedom, possibly her life, might be at stake, so also were the safety and well-being of her sons. Southesk was still convinced that, in spite of his latest victory, Montrose would be overcome in the end. Revenge would be exacted. There would be hangings, banishments, incarcerations, and expropriations. Southesk himself had shown in public that he was opposed to his son-in-law. Had they not exchanged angry words at the General Assembly in Glasgow? Moreover, his heir, Lord Carnegie, was a staunch Covenanter. Still, Southesk, for Magdalen's sake, had voted against the confiscation of Montrose's properties and Argyll had not been pleased. His own position, therefore, in these shifty times, was not absolutely secure. It could depend on his youngest daughter, Montrose's wife.

She had always loved truth and he had honoured her for it, but, in the present circumstances, it could be disastrous. She would have to be coached in the art of giving a misleading impression without actually lying. What better teacher than her father, who had held his place as a Privy Councillor for more than 20 years?

Mrs Witherspoon, having made Lady Magdalen comfortable, withdrew. He ought to be grateful to her. Perhaps he could repay her by finding her a suitable husband: some gentleman of not too high a rank but of ample fortune.

Magdalen's voice was so weak and hoarse he had to lean

towards her. 'Is it true, Father, what James has told me, that George Graham of Braco has been arrested and is a prisoner in Edinburgh Castle?'

'If James told you, it is no doubt true. He knows better than I do what goes on.' Southesk spoke bitterly. He had once been in the know himself.

'But George is on no one's side, Father. He hates war.'

'What sensible man does not? Triumphant generals are few. I expect Graham was arrested because he fought at Tippermuir and, more recently, took his nephews to join the Royalists.'

'But he did not. He went to tell James I was ill. I asked him to go. His nephews went with him. They stayed of their own accord. He didn't want them to become soldiers. He said their mother, his sister, would never forgive him.'

'Well, he will have plenty of time in the Castle to brood on the undeserved blows that fate heaps on our hapless heads. But I have not come to talk about George Graham. I want to talk about you, my pet. Since you are not able to go to Edinburgh, inquisitors might be sent to question you.'

'What about? I don't know anything.'

'They will want to find out if your loyalty is to the Covenant or to your husband.'

'But I must be loyal to my husband. I gave that promise when I got married. God was my witness.'

Such an answer would flummox the greybeards, with the ministers of the Kirk at their backs. They had always to be careful to keep a place for God.

'I have to speak seriously, Magdalen. You must understand that your husband, when he is caught, will be treated as a felon. He will not be given a trial. He will be hanged forthwith. The mob will be encouraged to pelt him with stones and abuse.'

She turned her head away, to hide tears. She was remembering the young man who had read the gloomy poem to her in their marriage-bed. He had never really believed that he would be a failure. He had always been confident that one day he would be famous. So he was now. All Europe had heard of him.

'Why are you saying this to me, Father?'

'Because we must not give his enemies the opportunity to drag us all down with him.'

'They would not harm my boys, would they?'

'They are his boys too. The viper's offspring, I have heard them called. They will be seen as the possible focus of future rebellions.'

She shook her head. She would not allow it. But she would be dead.

'Will not the Estates listen to you, Father?'

'I am seen as a man with a foot in either camp: an ignoble and ludicrous posture.'

'Not ignoble and not ludicrous either. Isn't there right on both sides?'

'Usually there is, but those who acknowledge it, in public at any rate, do not win battles or gain power. Men who hope to succeed must proclaim themselves wholly right and their opponents wholly wrong.'

'But what if James, my husband James, wins?'

Southesk frowned. This was dangerous ground. 'He cannot win.'

'But he won at Tippermuir and Aberdeen and Inverlochy and now he's won at Auldearn.'

'Astonishing victories, no doubt, but useless. He has not yet been confronted by the main Scots army, under General Leslie. They are still in England. They will outnumber him greatly in men, guns, and cavalry. His Highlanders desert him by the hundreds. Better for him, Magdalen, if he is killed on the battlefield.'

So he would be, she thought, looking up at his portrait. He would never let himself be taken prisoner and humiliated.

Her father thought that it would be better for her too if she died at the same time as her husband. She would not then have to endure the anguish and shame of knowing that his head was stuck on a spike outside the Tolbooth in Edinburgh and she would not have to dread every day some messenger coming to tell her her sons had been found dead in their prison cells. Poor Magdalen, she had played no part in the great dramas of the age. History would not remember her or hear of her. Yet she had suffered as much as anyone.

She was weeping now. She could not help it. There were times when the weakness of her body took over and courage failed.

What could he say to comfort her? That he would look after her boys when she was gone? So he would if he could, but he was an old man without authority. That her mother was waiting for her in heaven? He was supposed, as a good Presbyterian, to believe that, but he found it hard; all the harder because of the ministers' rantings on the subject.

He got up, saying he would come back later.

30

IN AUGUST, WHEN the rowans were in flourish, Montrose came
to Kinnaird to visit his wife and sons. He did not come slinking
on foot at night, a fugitive, fearful of pursuit, but rode on a big
black horse in sunlight. In his hat was a blue feather and on his
breast the silver star given him by the King. He wore no breast
plates. He did not look grim as Mars, but happy, like a man
looking forward to seeing his wife and children after an absence
of more than a year. His companions, for there was a troop of
horsemen with him, heard him humming and winked at one
another. The general was happy, as he deserved to be. Only one
small shadow fell over his happiness: Lady Magdalen's illness.
But he was young, like them, and would marry again, this time
not an ailing obscure woman who had been a hindrance to him
but someone more worthy, a royal princess perhaps. For after
his last two victories, at Alford, and then, only two days ago, at
Kilsyth, he was now master of Scotland, on the King's behalf.
After this visit to Kinnaird, which would necessarily be brief, he
would return to the army at Kilsyth and tomorrow they would
all march, banners waving and pipes playing, to Glasgow and
thence to Edinburgh, where he would proclaim the supremacy
of the King. The Covenant lords like Argyll would scurry off to
their holes, like rats. Not that they needed to fear for their
miserable lives. The general was merciful: too much so at times.
Covenanters had hanged patriots faithful to the King; he had
forbidden retaliations. The people of Scotland would soon
discover that the long dreary Presbyterian winter was over

and royal summer was come at last. There would be nationwide celebrations.

As the man in command, with all the responsibility, Montrose could not afford to be so carefree. He had to worry about the haemorrhage in his army. At that very moment many of his Highlanders were on their way home to their glens. They did not trust the people in the Lowlands and their loyalties were to their own clans rather than to the King in far-off England. Some of his older, more cautious officers, were also urging him to retreat northwards to build up his army again. It was sensible advice, but how could he, given this opportunity to re-establish the King's dominion, turn his back on it, whatever the risks?

These apprehensions were banished from his mind as he rode down the avenue of magnificent beeches towards the house. So many sights here were familiar to him. There, for instance, was the tree on which he had carved his and Magdalen's initials after their marriage, on a wet dull cold December afternoon.

He held his breath as he remembered how eager she had been, in her own quiet shy way, and how he, so stupidly, had laughed at her — no, worse than that — had sneered at her as a mere child. Who was it had called her genuine? Mr Blair, the dominie. A peculiar word, Montrose had thought, but now it struck him as very appropriate. With shame he recalled how he had once lectured her on honour, foolishly assuming that, as a woman, she could have no conception of it. Now, all these years later, he realised that he had never met anyone more honourable.

All the reports he had got concerning her health had been to the effect that she was poorly and could not have long to live. So, God forgive him, he had got into the habit of discounting her. She would die soon, he would mourn her, sincerely enough, for she was the mother of his children, but not too long or too woefully, for he had a kingdom to win.

She should have married a stay-at-home like Francis Gowrie. But he did not like to think of Gowrie. The burning of Mintlaw and Gowrie's death were among the misdeeds that kept him awake at nights.

He would not blame her if she refused to see him.

As he cantered into the courtyard he remembered how angry he had been to see old Dr Allen trying vainly to mount his horse, orders having been given to the servants not to assist him. He had been attending Magdalen at John's birth. Later, though condemning war, he had worked 20 hours at a stretch trying to save the lives of soldiers or lessen their pain.

All that, thought Montrose, as he dismounted at the door of the castle, had been in another dispensation.

Wearing a black cap and a long black gown, with a gold chain round his neck, his father-in-law, Southesk, appeared in the doorway. He was carrying a black, battered book. Was it so that he could not be expected to shake hands with the 'traitor-rebel', or was it a Bible, symbol of high-minded neutrality?

Into the courtyard crept servants, keen to see the famous general, whom they remembered as a young bridegroom, who had spent more time hunting deer than accompanying his wife.

He looked about him. 'It brings back memories, my lord,' he said.

They were not all happy, though. He had found it irksome living in another man's house, especially this man's. 'I see few changes. *He*, though, as I recall, is different.' He was referring to the small boy scooping up the dung. 'In my day he had fair hair.'

'Even dung-gatherers grow up, my lord.'

An odd remark to be greeted with, thought Montrose, amused, as he followed his father-in-law into the house. Some of his officers had wanted it to be searched first, in case assassins lurked, but he had rather angrily turned it down. He had often felt uncomfortable in Magdalen's house but never unsafe.

'How is Magdalen, my lord?' he asked.

'Not well.'

'I am very sorry to hear that.'

'You should have come oftener, James.'

'Yes. But circumstances prevented. And my two boys?'

'Both well. Magdalen will see you in her room. She seldom leaves it.'

'Does the doctor visit her regularly?'

'He does, to little avail. Mrs Witherspoon will come and let you know when Magdalen is ready to receive you.'

Famed for his quick daring decisions, Montrose was hesitant then. He had looked on many dead men with pity, but also with resolution. He was not sure how brave and resourceful he would be when he looked at his dying wife. He had not been fair to her. He had not thought then and he still did not think now that she had had any right to have a say when he had left her to go and fulfil his destiny, but he had vaguely seen her point of view, the woman's point of view, and he saw it much more clearly now, after the deaths of so many sons and husbands.

Southesk spoke. 'Is it the case that Lord Gordon was killed at Alford?'

'Aye.' Montrose could not help giving a gasp of pain and sorrow. Gordon had been one of his closest friends. Moreover, his death, by a musket ball, had made it all too likely that the fickle Gordons would again desert the cause.

'May I speak frankly, my lord?'

Montrose smiled scornfully. When had this old fox ever spoken frankly? 'Who in these treacherous times can afford to be frank, my lord? But what is it you would like to tell me?'

They were interrupted then by Mrs Witherspoon's appearance, with little Robert by the hand. She had prepared not only her mistress for this important visit, she had prepared herself too. She wore a fresh dress of green-and-white taffeta and, in her splendid hair, combs sparkled.

Montrose was struck by her beauty, particularly as it was accentuated by a frown of disapproval. She was letting him know she was on her mistress's side.

He lifted up his son. 'Whom does he favour, my lord?' he asked.

'They say he has a likeness to me.'

'And therefore to his mother.' Montrose smiled but he had begun to tremble.

He could have had love but he had chosen danger and adventure. He had never before doubted his choice but now, for a few moments, he did. He would need more courage to face Magdalen than to confront General Leslie's army. In a way that he would have found it hard to describe, he had betrayed her and, by so doing, had turned his back on something more valuable than high honours. She could have brought him incomparable happiness. Under her influence, he could have written poetry that would have earned him more lasting fame than military victories.

But these were unpropitious thoughts for a general with a campaign to bring to a victorious conclusion. He had betrayed his wife, he must not now betray his comrades and his King.

Briskly he put the boy down and turned to Mrs Witherspoon. 'If you would be so kind, madam.'

'Yes, my lord.' Taking Robert's hand, she led the way.

Passing the King's Chamber, he stopped, tried the door, and found it locked. Robert took the key out of the drawer for him. He opened the door and went in. He bowed his head. Here the King's father had slept. Here, though he did not know it, his sister Katherine and Sir John Colquhoun had committed adultery.

He was really putting off time before he faced Magdalen.

'Do you know who once slept here, my lad?' he asked.

'The King, sir.'

'Not the present king but his father. One day I shall take you to see the King.'

'Yes, sir.'

They went out again and locked the door. Robert put the key back in the drawer.

Outside Magdalen's room, Mrs Witherspoon took Robert's hand again. 'Come with me, Robert. You will see your father again before he leaves.' To Montrose she said: 'Please go in, my lord. Lady Magdalen is expecting you.'

He was left at the door alone.

Down in the courtyard, his officers were laughing. They must have been supplied with ale and wine. It was strange – inside the room was a woman who would not harm a fly and who loved him, at least as a woman must love the father of her children, and yet he, who could control the fierce Irish and, without hesitation, launched attacks on forces twice as strong as his own, felt afraid.

At last, he knocked softly and went in.

Thanks, no doubt, to Mrs Witherspoon, the room was cheerful and sweet-smelling, with bowls and vases of roses. On a wall was the tapestry Magdalen had worked at for years. Was he being fanciful in thinking that Christ bore a resemblance to Francis Gowrie? His own portrait was on another wall. Where, though, was hers? He had never liked it but he missed it now.

'You look well, James,' she said, from the bed.

It was the same bed they had occupied after their marriage. In it she looked as small as a child. Her illness, whatever it was, had her by the throat so that breathing and speaking were difficult. It had caused hollows in her cheeks and dark bruises under her eyes, but it had not taken away the eagerness.

He felt tears in his own eyes.

'I am sorry to see you so ill,' he said.

She held out her hand. It was thin and cold. There was sweat on her face.

'Do you have pain?'

He didn't have to ask. He had seen enough pain to read the signs.

'A little.'

302

He had knelt before the King. He had knelt to God, two days ago, before the battle. Now he knelt by her bedside.

'Have you seen Robert and wee David?' she asked.

'Robert, but not David yet. I shall see him before I leave.'

'They say David is very like you.'

He remembered how she had longed for a little girl.

'What a pity, Magdalen, all your children are boys.'

She smiled. 'I would have liked a little girl. But which of my boys would she have displaced? Tell me about John.'

He had wondered what he would say when she asked that. Should he be the penitent husband or the sorrowful father or the stoical soldier?

'He took a fever. Many others had it too. We thought he would recover, as they did. But, in his case, it got worse.'

'Were you with him?'

'Yes.'

'Did he ask for me?'

In his delirium the boy had asked for many things. 'Yes, he did, many times.'

'I would have liked to see his grave.'

'So you will, soon.'

'I don't think so.' She had been trying hard not to weep, but now she wept. 'They have shut up James in Edinburgh Castle.'

'Yes.' How like those canting cowards to persecute a child.

'Will you set him free, James? I would like to see him again.'

'You may be sure I shall, as soon as I can.'

Which might not be soon enough. In Edinburgh, he would not be able to afford the time to besiege and take the Castle. Destiny awaited him in the south.

He looked up at his portrait. 'Where is yours? Mine looks lonely by itself.'

'I sold it. You never liked it anyway, James, and I needed the money.'

He could say nothing to that. He had impoverished his family

303

to finance his war. It vexed him that she and his sons were being kept by her father. One day he would make it up to her: she would be the grandest lady in Scotland, after the Queen. But she would not want that and, in any case, she would be dead.

'I think Francis Gowrie bought it,' she said.

He felt then the same shock as when he had been told that Lord Gordon had been killed. It wasn't that he was jealous of Gowrie or distrustful of her. He just realised that he had not appreciated her as Gowrie had, and other men too, and it broke his heart. He could not buy the portrait back, for it would have been destroyed with all the other paintings at Mintlaw. There was no other portrait of her. He would have nothing to remember her by.

What he did then would have amazed his men laughing and jesting in the courtyard below, who had seen him walking, calm and dry-eyed, through scenes of carnage after a battle. He put his head down on the bed and shed tears.

For years now, he had been under tremendous strain, mental, physical, and moral too. He had had to decide for the King and against the Covenant, thus offending old comrades and earning the name of 'traitor-rebel'. He had had to work ceaselessly to keep part of his army, the Highlanders, from walking off, and another part, the Irish, from being too savage. Once, so as not to discourage them, the most effective of his troops, he had deliberately condoned their plundering of a city that, as a wedding gift, had made him a freeman. He had written appeals to the King for guns and men and received barren replies. All that time he had had no one to confide in, to share his doubts and anxieties with, and to receive reassurance from. He had been alone.

So, for a minute or so, by his wife's bedside, he gave way, not to despair, for it was not in his nature to lose hope, but to a wish for rest and peace. They were not to be had from anyone but this dying woman, his wife, came closest. Her hand on his head was giving him her sympathy and love but not her blessing.

At last, he stood up. 'Next time I hope to see you much better. We shall have a lot to talk about then.'

They both knew there would be no next time.

He bent down and kissed her, not on the lips but on the brow, as he would have done if she had been dead.

Half an hour later, not having waited to benefit from his father-in-law's frankness, he was on his way back to the army at Kilsyth. His companions, respecting his sombre mood, tried to fit in with it, but they were young, they had drunk a good deal of wine, it was a splendid summer's day, two days ago they had won a great victory, and they had before them a triumphal march to Edinburgh. They could not help being merry and showing it. They were sorry that the Marchioness, poor lady, was gravely ill and it was natural that the general should be sad about it but she didn't really matter, did she?

31

IN SEPTEMBER, WHEN the rowan berries were red, at Philiphaugh in the south of Scotland, Montrose's army was decimated by the Covenanters under General Leslie and, at Kinnaird, Lady Magdalen slipped closer to death. The servants tending her whispered that you could see that the angels were already holding her hands; these, though, were icy-cold. She lay still and silent, with her eyes shut most of the time. When she opened them, she seemed to recognise no one, not even her children.

Her father and her brother, James, in her room, thinking that she could not hear or, if she did hear, could not understand, discussed, with a little worry and much satisfaction, Montrose's rout at Philiphaugh. It delighted James that the great invincible general had galloped from the field like a coward, leaving his troops to be slaughtered. He would try to escape to France, but every port was being watched.

Her father was more restrained. He was concerned about the effect of Montrose's downfall on Magdalen and her children. She herself was safe, for she would soon be in God's keeping, but her children and the Graham properties and titles were in danger. Kincardine Castle had already been burned to the ground.

She heard and understood, though she gave no sign, neither tears nor sighs. She prayed that James did escape to France and she remembered the Bible he had given her all those years ago. How many? Only 13. It had angered Mr Henderson, that Bible. It was an insult to the Lord having His holy words put into the language of Papists.

She was sorry that at present Mr Henderson was ill but glad that he wasn't able to come and pray for her. She smiled, as she remembered Margaret's indignant tale of how the old minister had used prayer as an excuse to put his face close to her bosom. She and Margaret had often laughed at that.

Who, of all the people she had known, did she wish to see again before she died? James, her husband? She wasn't sure. It would be too painful for them both. She would not want to see him in disgrace and with so much more blood on his conscience. Besides, there were soldiers surrounding Kinnaird, in case he should venture there. Better just pray that he escaped to France. Would he spend all his time trying to raise another army or would he spare some to look for his sister Katherine?

She would have liked to see Katherine Graham again but she supposed that Katherine would have refused to come. It wouldn't matter to her that 'the pious little cunt' was dying. That probably was still her opinion of Magdalen. Her experiences could not have sweetened her nature. Was she dead herself, as all her family hoped? Or was she living somewhere in France, in poverty and misery? Lilias, now back at Luss, had never forgiven her. Sir John was expected to join his wife soon, with a pardon in his pocket.

The person she most wanted to see was her son James. Her father seemed to be confident that he would be released unharmed but it might take weeks or even months: it might have to wait until his father was dead. Moss would have grown on her tombstone by then. He would kneel by it and weep.

Mrs Witherspoon, by the bedside, was amazed to see tears in her friend's eyes.

Francis Gowrie? Yes, she would have liked to see Francis again. But he was dead. What kind of sin would Mr Henderson call it, a dead man coming to visit another man's wife on her own death-bed? He would have a name for it. Once, in the pulpit in Kinnaird kirk, he had yelled that the list of man's sins, he had meant women's too, stretched from earth to heaven, like a rainbow. It had puzzled her that he did not seem to realise that a rainbow was beautiful.

The dominie Mr Blair and his wife, Cissie? Yes, they would have been welcome, he so concerned and she so cheerful. Their house would ring with the laughter of children. It would be fragrant with the smell of new-baked bread. No home in the country would be happier.

Sometimes it was hard for her to tell which of her visitors were real and which imaginary.

Her sisters, Margaret and Agnes, were very real. As soon as they came in, they ordered Mrs Witherspoon to leave. Then they sat by the bedside and spoke sternly. This silence of Magdalen's was her last act of wilful perversity. She could speak if she wanted to, she was trying to put them all to shame as she had done most of her life. Let her remember that she would soon be answerable to God. *He* would have no patience with her childish huff.

But, in the end, they had to admit that she was not playing a game. They wept then, held her cold hands, and asked her to forgive them. If they had been stern, it was for her sake. Their father was the one to blame, he should never have married her to that abominable man, James Graham, who, thank God, would soon be hanged. They promised they would do all they could for her sons.

There were many things that she would have liked to know but was unable to ask. She had to depend on pieces of news let drop by visitors. It was thus that she learned that the younger of George Graham's nephews had been killed at Philiphaugh.

Her father came every day, even if only for a few minutes. Once he took Mrs Witherspoon aside. Their heads were close to Christ's in the tapestry. He had something to say to her. He spoke in a normal voice, she in an agitated whisper.

'I think, my lord, Lady Magdalen understands what we say, but is not able to show it.'

He looked at the corpse-like face in the bed. 'Why do you think so? Has she said anything?'

'No, my lord. It's just a feeling I have. I've seen tears in her eyes.'

'Merely a physical manifestation, I should think. Mrs Witherspoon, you will, no doubt, have been considering your future?'

'Yes, my lord.'

'What would you say to an advantageous marriage?'

'I would give it very serious consideration, my lord.'

Magdalen smiled inwardly. She knew that ironic tone of Margaret's so well.

'You are still a fairly young woman.'

'I'm thirty-two, my lord.'

Therefore a year older than Lady Magdalen. He paused to reflect on that.

'That is scarcely old. Let me be frank. Sir Thomas Hairmyres has expressed a strong interest in you.'

'Sir Thomas Hairmyres?'

'As you may know, he recently lost his wife. He is not the kind of man who can endure loneliness.'

Margaret had told Magdalen about Sir Thomas. It wasn't loneliness he couldn't endure, it was not having a woman in his bed. He was 53 and had seven children, the oldest only eleven. He was fat. He had a carbuncle on his chin. He seldom bathed, so that he stank. Everyone stank but he worse than most. As against all that he was well-off, with a large estate not far from Crail, her birthplace. She rather fancied, she'd confessed to Magdalen, the idea of driving through her native streets in her own carriage, with all the shopkeepers at their doorways touching their forelocks.

The Earl dropped his voice but Magdalen still heard. 'He will be one of those invited to the funeral. May I inform him that you would not be inclined to reject his overtures?'

'Thank you, my lord.'

Magdalen again smiled inwardly. No woman would be able to deal with those overtures more adroitly than Margaret.

When the Earl was gone, Margaret sat by the bedside. 'Well, did you hear that? What do you think I should do? Consult an astrologer? Or just get Annie to read my palm? I quite like the idea of being Lady Hairmyres, but just imagine waking up every morning and seeing that carbuncle!'

That very night, Mrs Witherspoon, who slept in the same room, suddenly awoke in alarm. The room had turned very cold. She got up and hurried over to her friend's bed. This time, there was no doubt. Lady Magdalen heard and understood nothing.

32

CROUCHED IN A corner, George Graham of Braco tried not to be noticed, for he had come without an invitation, and got ready to smile meekly at anyone who deigned to glance in his direction. Within, he was raging with anger and disgust. This was supposed to be a funeral but it was more like a celebration.

These were some of the most powerful men in Scotland, dignitaries of the Kirk, representatives of the Estates, and soldiers of high rank. On their self-important faces there appeared frequently expressions of satisfaction, seldom of sorrow. It did not concern them that, an hour or so ago in Kinnear kirkyard, they had attended the burial of a beautiful young woman. They were too intent on congratulating one another on the downfall and imminent execution of her husband, the traitor-rebel, as they called him, James Graham, Marquis of Montrose.

Present also were the lady's sisters in splendid black dresses. They had not wept much. Their eyes were not red. No doubt they had loved Magdalen in their own way but, as Montrose's wife, she had been a danger to her family. They could not help feeling relieved.

All over the big room there were gloating smiles and exclamations of delight as accounts were given of the rout of Montrose's forces at Philiphaugh recently; how the great general, the invincible hero, the self-styled King's Lieutenant, had fled like a coward from the field, leaving hundreds of his troops dead or dying. These, to be sure, had been mostly Irish, the savage brutes he had enlisted to kill his fellow countrymen. With their

Erse gibbers and hairy legs, they were hardly human. Mercy and pity would have been wasted on them or on their wives and children, slaughtered in cold blood or drowned in the Tweed.

Braco remembered the song of the woman mourning her man in the camp at Blair Atholl.

Suddenly he got ready to cringe. Southesk, the host, was coming towards him, venerable with white hair and beard, and wearing a plain black robe. His hands, clasped on his breast, were white too and as soft as a lady's. They had never done any manly work with axe or spade, or even sickle or sword. What they had done was sign death warrants, and they would do it again, one of them his son-in-law's.

'Well, George,' he said, smiling, 'it was good of you to come.'

'I have to apologise, my lord. I am here without invitation.'

And therefore had difficulty getting pas the soldiers surrounding the castle. It was thought or, rather, hoped, that the dead woman's husband might try to see her before she was buried.

'It's I who should apologise, George. You and Jean will always be welcome at Kinnaird. Do you know, I often point to you as the kind of landowner we need in Scotland. If our country is ever to become prosperous, it will have you and those like you to thank.'

It was true and yet, said by this man, sounded false.

'I wanted to come, my lord, for Lady Magdalen's sake.'

Southesk sighed. 'She had a fondness for you, George.'

'And I for her. She was a very kind lady.'

'She thought you frank and honest.'

Braco found tears coming into his eyes. He had something to say, which would not please her father but, if he did not say he would not deserve her praise.

His voice trembled. 'I thought, my lord, young James would be present.'

James was still a prisoner in Edinburgh Castle.

Southesk frowned. 'He is not well enough.'

No wonder, shut up in that grim place for months.

'I am very sorry to hear that, my lord. He was very close to his mother.'

'He is now his father's heir. I do not have to tell you, George, these are dangerous times. It is, of course, all James Graham's fault, as I am sure you agree.'

Southesk laid his hand on Braco's arm. 'You will have heard the sad news of your nephews, Tom and Gavin Ogilvy.' That was said with a kind of relish.

A few days ago, a friend of Braco's, fleeing from Philiphaugh, had called at his house with vague but terrible news. Tom, he thought, had been killed. Gavin had escaped, wounded.

Their mother was at Braco, weeping and wailing and putting ashes over her hair, as in the Bible.

Braco had come to Kinnaird, to honour the dead lady but also to find out the truth about his nephews. Southesk would know, he had spies everywhere and knew everything, but he might not be willing to tell.

Meg did not blame Montrose, or General Leslie, commander of the Covenanters' army, or the Estates: she blamed her brother. She held him responsible for her sons taking part in the war.

'We have heard rumours, my lord.'

Again Southesk laid his hand on Braco's arm. 'I would not lie to you, George. There is, it seems, an account taken after a battle. The victors feel obliged. It is, you might say, a Christian courtesy. A list is drawn up.'

With bloodstains on it.

'Have you seen the list, my lord?'

He didn't have to ask. This old fox made a point of seeing every document.

'Yes, George, I have seen it. Thank God it is not very long. The battle, mercifully, was over soon. Most of the slain were Irish, who, of course, were not counted.'

'My nephews' names were on the list, my lord?'

313

'Yes, George. It broke my heart, I assure you, to see them there. As boys, you know, they often visited Kinnaird and were very welcome.'

'Tom was killed then?'

'I'm afraid so. If it is any comfort to their mother, they had a Christian burial. Well, as Christian as could be, considering the circumstances.'

It was no comfort to Braco but it might be to poor Meg.

'His brother's name was among those who escaped with Montrose. He was wounded, though.'

'Seriously?'

'That is not known. My advice is that he should get out of the country as soon as he can. If he is taken, he will be hanged.'

'He is not yet twenty-one.'

'Old enough to take part in a bloody rebellion. Old enough therefore to be hanged.'

Braco could have said that Montrose had never hanged any young men; indeed, he had hanged no man.

What he did say was, hoarsely, 'Do you think, my lord, that the Marquis knows?'

'The Marquis?'

'The lady's husband, my lord.'

Southesk frowned. 'Knows what?'

'That she is dead.'

'How can I tell that? I have sent no messenger. As you see, he has not come himself to find out. But then, he never showed much concern for her while she was alive. He will be hanged, himself, you can be sure of that.'

'She would have wanted him to know.'

'I hope, George, you are not so foolish as to be thinking of sending an emissary or, worse still, of going yourself. You went once before, I believe, and were rebuffed. Indeed, your reward was to have your nephews snatched from you.'

'They were not snatched, my lord. They went willingly.'

314

Too late Braco realised that he had condemned Gavin. If there was a trial, the lad would not be able to plead that he had been coerced into joining the rebels. But there would not be a trial.

Southesk was pretending not to have noticed.

'Well, George,' he said, 'I must attend to my other guests. Go home, my friend. Comfort your sister, look after your bonny black cattle.'

Then off he went, at a stately pace and was soon conversing earnestly with a group of senior elders of the Kirk.

As he crossed the stone-floored hall towards the door, Braco was accosted by a woman dressed in black, who came hurrying out of the shadows. He was about to greet her curtly and then pass on, for she was Mrs Witherspoon, whom he had never liked or trusted, but something about her now caused him to pause. He had always thought her eyes too bold and coquettish for a minister's widow but today they were red and swollen with weeping. No doubt part of the reason for her obvious grief was that her ambitions would be thwarted now that her protectress was dead, but only part, the rest was sincere. Apart from himself, she was the only person in the castle mourning Lady Magdalen.

He remembered how Tom and Gavin had admired and made jokes about her rather brazen beauty.

'This is a sad time, Mistress Witherspoon,' he said.

'Very sad, sir.'

'What will you do now?'

James, Magdalen's brother, would get rid of her as quickly as he could. He thought her an upstart.

'My lord, the Marquis, wants me to marry Lard Hairmyres.'

'Lord Hairmyres!'

Braco had noticed that nobleman among the throng in the big room, one of the most self-important: a small, fat, unbraw man with a large estate; a widower with six children and at least three bastards; nonetheless a staunch Presbyterian, with influence among the leaders of the Kirk; a useful ally, therefore, for Southesk.

Braco saw her difficulty. She would like very much to become a lady with servants of her own but she might think the price too gruesome.

He was sorry but he could not help her. 'I wish you well, madam,' he muttered as he hurried away.

'But what am I to do?' she cried.

It wasn't Braco she was appealing to, it was her dead friend. The despairing words echoed in the vast hall.

They echoed in Braco's mind as he left the house and made for the stables. What was *he* to do? Should he risk his life trying to reach Montrose to tell him that his wife was dead and also to find out for certain what had happened to Tom and Gavin, or should he take Southesk's advice and stay at home, craven but safe?

Jean very much wanted him to stay at home but she did not say so. She did not have to, she kept silent and, therefore, said more than words could. That had always been her way. He had learned to respect and interpret her silences. He had long ago realised that she was wiser than he, with sounder judgment.

Meg, his sister, was very different. She had always said too much, in a shrill complaining voice. But then, she had had plenty to complain about, her husband dead before he was 30, leaving her with two small boys to bring up and with little money. Now her sons had been cruelly taken from her and her brother was to blame.

When Braco said that he was thinking of venturing into the north, she fell on her knees and clasped his legs, yelling that she would go with him.

When he managed to get away from her, and from silent Jean too, he went off, as he often did, to seek comfort from his bonny cattle, as Southesk had sarcastically called them. Their patient acceptance of their fate was more than a comfort, it was an

316

example. They would gaze at him meekly, as if they knew by instinct that, though he treated them with kindness and even with affection, he must one day have them and their calves slaughtered. That was the way things had been for many centuries between man and beast.

In their room, with Meg shut out, he told Jean he had made up his mind. He wouldn't send a messenger to Montrose, he would go himself. It was too important a mission to entrust to anyone else.

In what he called her spaewife's voice, Jean said simply, 'You ken you'll never come back.'

'What's to stop me coming back?' he asked crossly.

'Isn't the haill country hoatching with disbanded sojers, men with guns and swords that haven't been paid for months, that'll cut a throat for a couple of maiks? You're too auld for such a journey. At least take somebody with you, Dugald or one of the lads.'

Dugald, his grieve, was older than himself, and the lads were too young. Besides, he had no right to ask them to risk their lives.

'You would do this for James Graham's sake? He doesn't deserve it.'

'For Lady Magdalen's sake.'

He would say it to no one, not even to Jean, but he was looking forward, with a little unworthy gloating of his own, to seeing how the proud King's Lieutenant, the great commander, received the news of his wife's death. Even if Montrose had truly loved her, he must have seen her as a hindrance. Many had encouraged him and consoled him with lies, she would have told him the truth always, for that had been her nature. Braco had never forgotten the dominie's word for her: genuine. How true. In these confused times, there were so many false people, her own father being one, and he, Braco, God forgive him, another,

Though she did not want him to go, Jean helped him to pack. She thought he ought not to take the two pistols that had

317

belonged to his father, beautiful deadly things made in Italy. Would-be robbers seeing them would think he was carrying valuables. The pistols themselves would attract thievish glances. But she gave way and offered no objections to his taking his sword; it was part of a gentleman's dress and her husband, though he was laughed at by other gentlemen because he was so devoted to his beasts, was in her eyes the foremost gentleman in the land. In any case, he would hardly be able to use it, for his right arm was stiff and painful with rheumatism.

She baked bannocks and stowed them, with a lump of home-made cheese, among his luggage. They were gifts for the dominie and his wife, whom Braco intended to call on in Perth on his way north.

She stood at the door to see him off. She did not wave or weep, though Meg, by her side, was waving and weeping like a madwoman but then, as she had said earlier, she had never had a son killed.

Nell, the old white horse, with no speed but enough stamina to carry him to John o' Groats and back, plodded along, taking care not to trample on the hens that scurried about.

Some of his workers saw him and waved. They wished him well. They were his and yet they were not his. Nor were they Montrose's or the Estates' or the Kirk's or even the King's. They were their own men and women. That was his deep belief.

Similarly with the cattle, sheep, and pigs, and also the wild creatures on his estate, like otters and deer. They did not belong to him. He had been given the task of looking after them. It had been given him by God. He had once tried to explain this to a company of noblemen, James Graham among them, and he had been mocked. To be fair, Montrose's laughter had been good-natured. He had not approved but he had understood. He had that kind of understanding and compassion. Was it not said that his soldiers were free to leave whenever they wished without being accused of desertion and threatened with execution, as

318

happened in other armies? He would grieve for his wife, in his own private resoluteness. There would be no gloating on Braco's part.

It was a crisp sunny autumn morning, with more brown and yellow leaves on the ground than green ones on the trees. If its purpose had been happier, Braco might have enjoyed the journey.

At first, his way led through villages and townships where he was known, respected, and even liked, or, at least, so he had been before Montrose's disruptive war. As a kinsman of Montrose's, though an insignificant one, Braco was inevitably regarded with suspicion. If he had openly disowned Montrose and miscalled him, he might have been forgiven and absolved but he could not, it would have been a kind of treachery. So, that morning, he got grudged smiles and sullen looks. There were men missing limbs, women missing husbands, children missing fathers. How could he expect a friendly welcome? The poor, and most of these were very poor, did their best to keep out of wasteful wars, but often they were bullied and cowed into taking part. They worried more about a sick child or a cow gone dry than they did about the King's great woes.

In the chilly gloaming, when he had travelled almost 20 miles and Nellie was wabbit but still willing and he himself stiff and sore, he came to an inn where he was known and where he hoped to spend the night. It was not far from Mintlaw Castle, whose scorched towers could be glimpsed through trees. It had been burned to the ground by Montrose's drunken Irish. It was said he had just shrugged his shoulders. Gowrie, he had thought, should have spent his fortune, or rather his wife's fortune, on helping the King's cause, not on beautifying his castle. Many beautiful objects, the work of craftsmen and artists brought from France and Italy, those Papist lands, had been destroyed. It was said, though, that some had been rescued by villagers dashing into the flames, The Kirk had quickly sent agents who had

319

searched all the hovels round about, and there had been more bonfires.

Braco had sometimes wondered what had happened to the portrait of Lady Magdalen painted by Mr Jameson of Aberdeen. He had admired it when it hung in the great hall at Kincardine.

So far his journey had been safe enough, though he had encountered some desperate-looking fellows who looked like deserters from the war. There could be spies among them. Perhaps Montrose would be told of his coming before he arrived, if ever he did arrive.

Luckily, the inn was quiet. He was able to get a room to himself, a very small one but sufficient. The innkeeper sensibly kept his remarks to that season's harvest. There had, he said, been a fine crop of haws. The birds would be grateful for them when the snow came. They talked about birds. The innkeeper was know-ledgeable about them. He had a stuffed hawk in his parlour.

Next day, Braco's luck held. No robbers or would-be assassins were encountered. The sun shone again. Roads were dry and easily passable. Nellie kept going sturdily. He himself ached all over but a potion that Jean had prepared for him, made up of herbs, alleviated the pain a little. There were times, though, when he felt tempted to turn back.

It was dark when he crept cautiously into Perth and found it hoatching with swaggering loudmouthed Covenant soldiers. Evidently they were getting ready to venture northwards to destroy Montrose but they were in no hurry. It was known that he had got away from Philiphaugh with a strong force of cavalry. As always, he would prove a dangerous adversary. So it was safer to linger in Perth and crowd out the taverns and brothels.

Braco had a false name ready if challenged: Angus Campbell, of Inveraray. He had enough Gaelic to play the part and could imitate a Highland accent well enough. As a boy, he had used to do it for fun.

He lodged Nellie with stables not far from the dominie's

house. When he remarked, in his false voice, that he was visiting Mr Blair, he was attended to with smiles. The dominie was apparently well known and well liked; the dominie's wife more so.

As he chapped on the door of the house by the river, he felt misgivings. He had no right to put the dominie and his family in danger. They had had the good sense and good fortune to keep clear of the hostilities so far but, if it became known that a kinsman, however distant, of the traitor Montrose had visited them in secret, they would be immediately suspected. Blair would be flung into jail. He would lose his post.

Braco was about to hurry away when the door opened. It was the dominie, with a bawling baby in his arms. He himself was as always calm and patient.

He did not at first recognise Braco.

'I'm sorry to trouble you, Mr Blair,' said Braco. 'George Graham of Braco. I visited you once.'

'Yes, of course, Mr Braco. With your nephews, Tom and Gavin. Are they with you?'

'No.'

'Wha is it, John?' called a cheerful voice and Cissie appeared, wiping her hands with her apron. She was a bit stouter but as brisk as ever.

She recognised Braco at once.

'Come awa' in, Mr Braco,' she cried. 'Don't keep the gentleman on the doorstep, John.'

Braco was taken into the warm tidy kitchen. Two little girls peeped shyly at him from behind chairs. He remembered Tom and Gavin eating heartily at that table.

'Didn't your nephews come wi' you this time?' asked Cissie.

'No.' It had to be said some time but how to say it without breaking down? 'They couldn't.'

Blair was too well mannered to ask why but Cissie would always put human interest before good manners.

'Whit prevented them?'

'What have you done with your horse?' asked Blair.

'I left her at stables up the road a bit.'

'She'll be well looked after there.'

'Especially if you mentioned you were visiting us,' said Cissie. 'John's weel liked and respected in the toon. They're saying he micht be provost yin day. But whit aboot your nephews? John and I often talk aboot them, sich handsome and jolly young men.'

Blair had noticed Braco's uneasiness. 'Is there anything wrong?' he asked quietly.

'Last time they didn't go back with me. They joined Montrose.'

'As sojers?' cried Cissie, in horror. 'The daft young gowks.'

'They were at Philiphaugh. You will have heard of Philiphaugh.'

'Yes, we have heard,' said Blair.

'Tom was killed, it seems, and Gavin got a bad wound. I do not know how bad. That is what I am going north to find out.'

The baby in Blair's arms was now asleep.

'So you are on your way to Montrose?' said Blair.

'Aye. I have a message for him. His wife's dead.'

Cissie let out a cry of anguish and covered her face with her hands. 'Puir lady. We used to say in the servants' ha' that she wad never scart a grey heid.' Her voice sharpened. 'But why gie yoursel' a' this bother, Mr Braco? He'll no' care. He never did when she was alive. Why should he noo she's deid? We used to say it was a sin merrying her tae him.'

In the servants' hall, thought Braco, they had been a bit too free with their criticism of their betters.

Cissie took the baby from her husband's arms and cuddled him. 'His name's John, like his faither's. He'll never be killed in ony war if I can help it.'

But that, thought Braco, was what Meg thought, and every woman with a son.

'I'll lay him in his cot,' said Cissie, 'and then I'll get you something tae eat.'

She went out with the baby.

'This is a very dangerous journey to make by yourself, Mr Braco,' said Blair. 'They're saying Montrose is camped up by Glenfeshie. That's wild country. You would need a guide.'

'Where could I find a guide in this town?'

Braco felt a shiver of fear. Winter came quickly to the mountains, with snow, and he was too old and rheumaticky to camp out of doors.

'I think you should go no further, Mr Braco.'

'To tell you the truth, I think so too. But I have to tell the man his wife's dead.'

'I'm sure he already knows. It's been the talk of the town. It's been toasted in every tavern.'

Braco was shocked. 'Why would they do that? She harmed nobody.'

'She was his wife.'

The two little girls, bolder now, came out from hiding and smiled at Braco. One went forward and took his hand.

Though his bed was comfortable, Braco was unable to sleep. He spent hours trying to make up his mind whether sensibly to turn back or foolishly to go on.

He had asked to be wakened at dawn and Cissie knocked on his door then.

'We think, Mr Braco,' she said, through the door, 'John and me, that you should tak a guid long lie the day and gang straight hame the morrow.'

'Thank you, Cissie,' he said, and realised that was the first time he had used her Christian name.

He got up and dressed. His hands were shaking. Never had he felt less heroic.

'You're going on then?' she said in the kitchen.

'I promised Meg, my sister, I would find out about Gavin.'

'Maybe it wad be better no' tae find oot. I mean, whit if you find oot he's deid as weel, and you hae tae tell her that?'

'Then she could grieve for him.'

Blair came in then. He had been attending to the children. 'So you're determined to go on?'

'I feel I must. I'll go first to Atholl. I ken the way there.'

But last time he had Montrose's scouts to guide him and Tom and Gavin to give him support. This time he had no one.

'Mind, on your way back, ca' in and tell us how you got on,' said Cissie.

It was raining when Braco went to the stables for Nellie. She neighed, glad to see him. He felt heartened.

'She kens you,' said the stableman.

'She should do.'

'A strong auld nag. She'll carry you whaurever it is you're going.'

It was as good as asking Braco his destination. It was concern, not nosiness. This old man who loved horses was no spy. Still, Braco was careful not to say.

They listened to the rain.

'It'll clear up,' said the stableman. 'Be carefu' when crossing burns. Guid luck.'

Alas, the man's wish for better weather and good fortune was not to be granted.

Braco was still in the outskirts of the town when he was suddenly surrounded by a gang of filthy-looking creatures that hardly looked human. They grabbed his legs as if minded to drag him off his horse and murder him, though they seemed to have no weapons except their claw-like hands. He soon saw they were not murderers but starving beggars. They clamoured in a mixture of Gaelic and Scots. Luckily, he had foreseen such a situation. He had a handful of coins ready. These he tossed as if it was a wedding: a scramble it was called, and they certainly scrambled on hands and knees.

As he rode on hastily, it occurred to him that in the war, which, to be honest, Montrose had started and still pursued, a vast fortune was being wasted, which would have given these unfortunate people and many like them a decent life. What, he wondered, would James Graham, that compassionate man, say if that was put to him? Braco knew what he would say. That if every man did his duty to the King, the country would be peaceful and prosperous. Not a very honest answer, thought Braco.

He was proud of old Nellie. She hadn't panicked. She had always been patient with children and had recognised some of the ragamuffins as children.

His reward for his philanthropy was that the rain soon stopped and the sun came out, shyly at first.

He wasn't a religious or superstitious man but he liked to think that good deeds were rewarded and bad deeds punished, though who did the rewarding and the punishing he preferred not to consider.

He began to feel confident that he would indeed be lucky and meet up with Montrose. He even hoped that he would find Gavin alive and well.

In the late afternoon, he arrived at the inn where he and his nephews had fallen in with Montrose's scouts. It was now ruinous and deserted. A consequence of war, he thought.

He had to decide whether to turn back, having made a praiseworthy effort, or to press on into the mountains, as far as Atholl. He thought he would remember the way. If he didn't, Nell might. Three well-defined paths led into the hills. If he took the wrong one, God knew what wilderness he would end up in. There was a burn, in spate now. He thought he remembered crossing it. Tom and Gavin had held his horse's reins. So that was probably the way to Atholl. He had no hope of reaching the village that day. He would have to spend the night in the open. Well, he could survive that, he had been a soldier himself once.

325

There was always a chance that scouts or foragers from Montrose's army might find him. It was just as likely that a band of deserters, now outlaws, would. They would cut his throat and rob him. They would slaughter poor Nellie out of sheer wickedness.

In the gloaming, he came upon a small shed that still had a roof. Inside it smelled of oxen but there was a dry corner. It would do. In the morning he would be as stiff as a board but still alive. Thinking of Jean gave him courage and hope. Whatever happened, he must see her again. Otherwise there was no goodness in the world.

In a small hunting lodge grudgingly lent him by Huntlie, in the midst of a forest of pines 50 miles north of Blair Atholl, Montrose was writing a letter to the King and finding it difficult. He had to make very clear how desperate his present situation was and how absolutely necessary were the reinforcements so often promised but never sent but, at the same time, he must not appear to be blaming the King though, in his inmost heart, he knew that the King was at least partly to blame. Making it still more difficult, he had recently learned that the King, behind Montrose's back, was negotiating with the Estates, their enemy. Not only that brusque simpleton, George Graham, had hinted that the King was not to be trusted.

With a sigh, Montrose raised his head and gazed out of the window. It was a beautiful tranquil scene now that the sun was shining. Squirrels were busy in the tree-tops. The tall pines reminded him of the pillars in a cathedral in France long ago. There had been a tryst among those pillars. He remembered raven-black hair, lively blue eyes, and a merry reckless laugh.

He closed his eyes and then opened them again, erasing that heart-breaking part of his past.

His soldiers were going about their camp duties with the devotion of priests. He felt severe qualms of conscience. These honest faithful men were prepared to give their lives for him and

326

the King. Surely they must one day get their reward in a Scotland where honour and justice prevailed, under the rule of a beneficent King appointed by God?

But did Montrose himself believe that that would ever happen? It could turn out so differently. There could be another disastrous rout like Philiphaugh. He himself could be captured and dragged off to Edinburgh to be hanged. The King would not be able to save him, indeed might not want to save him, for Montrose could have become a hindrance. But then the King was entitled to sacrifice as many of his subjects as was necessary to achieve his ultimate triumph. God had given him that right.

Was that true? When he was younger and more idealistic, Montrose had written a treatise defending the King's rights derived from God. He had meant it then but did he still mean it, absolutely, without doubts? He did not want to think of Magdalen, he had vowed to put all memories of her aside until later but he could not help remembering how, in her naïve way, she had urged him always to be true to himself. She had not understood how circumstances could make that impossible.

Poor Magdalen. He knew that she was dead. He had had a spy at the funeral in Kinnaird Castle, who had reported that it hadn't been a funeral at all but an occasion for his enemies to gloat. They had thought that her death would be as heavy a blow to him as the defeat at Philiphaugh.

They were much mistaken. He had never loved her as he could have loved another woman and she had not loved him as she could have loved, say, Francis Gowrie. They had been forced into marriage, she by her father, he by his mentors. Perhaps if he had stayed at home and looked after his family, they might have come to love each other truly like a man and his wife but he did not think it likely. In a way that he had never tried to examine, she had been a little repulsive to him. Was that not why, at the beginning of their marriage, he had gone off to tour the Continent and stayed away for three years?

The cruel truth was that, except as the mother of his children, she had never been of much importance to him and, now that she was dead, even less so.

He was aware how despicable that confession was and he felt the same depth of shame as when he had galloped off the field at Philiphaugh, leaving his Irish to be butchered in cold blood.

He became aware of a commotion among some of the soldiers. They were gathered round a big white horse. He thought he recognised its rider but surely he was wrong. He picked up his field glass. Yes, it *was* George Graham of Braco, that well-meaning bucolic fool. No, that was unfair, but what in God's name was the cattle-breeder doing so far from home?

Captain McLay, Montrose's aide, came in. 'There's a fellow saying he's a kinsman of yours, my lord. He was found wandering about. He's armed. The men thought he might be a madman sent to assassinate you, my lord, though I have to say he doesn't much look like an assassin. More like a farmer.'

'Which is what he is, Angus. He is a kinsman of mine, distantly. We're all Grahams in that part of the world. But what the devil does he want?'

Montrose, though, could easily guess why Braco had made such a long perilous journey. He had come to enquire about his nephews. Good God, if the relatives of all the men killed or wounded visited the camp to make enquiries, they would amount to an army themselves.

'Shall I have him sent away, my lord?'

'No. I might as well hear what he has to say.'

The captain went out, shaking his head. He had never seen the general so much on edge. It was, of course, little wonder. A few days ago, another man had come to the camp, to tell Montrose that his wife, Lady Magdalen, was dead.

There had been no mourning. After all, Montrose had remarked in that resolute way he had, every man in the army

328

must have a sweetheart or wife or sister or mother sick and maybe dying.

McLay came in, followed by George Graham, who was limping.

Montrose rose and held out his hand. 'Well, George, this is a surprise. Please sit down. What's the matter with your foot?'

More than a sore foot ailed Braco. He had a big bruise on his face and he could scarcely move his right arm. His clothes were wet and dirty. He certainly looked more like a farmer than a gentleman.

He spoke resentfully. 'I took a tumble crossing a burn. I'm sorry to bother you, James, especially as it seems you already know what I have come to tell you: that Lady Magdalen is dead.'

'Yes, George, I know. Sad news. I hope your own wife, Jean, is well.'

'She was when I left. Lady Magdalen died in her sleep, peacefully.'

'Thank God for that small mercy. She had more than her share of pain.'

'Nobody ever heard her complain.'

'That was never her way.'

'She hoped she would see Lord James before she died.'

Lord James, now Montrose's heir, was still a prisoner of the Estates. It was rumoured that they had persuaded him to go over to them.

'There's something else,' said Braco. 'When my sister, Meg, heard I was coming here, she asked me to find out what had happened to her sons, Tom and Gavin.'

'I thought she had been informed, George.'

'That Tom had been killed at Philiphaugh, yes, she had been told that, and that Gavin had been wounded.'

'I am sorry to have to tell you, George, that Gavin died four days ago. He is buried in Bellie graveyard, beside my own son, Lord John. That was his wish. I am terribly sorry, George. I have written a letter to Meg. I would be obliged if you would deliver it to her.'

For a few seconds, Braco was minded to ask angrily if Montrose thought that a letter written by the great general, the King's Lieutenant, was compensation for the loss of two sons but it occurred to him in time that poor Meg might indeed find it some consolation, especially if Montrose was triumphant in the end.

Braco got to his feet unsteadily. Captain McLay stepped forward to help him.

'I'll waste no more of your time, James,' said Braco. 'I would be obliged if I could have a guide as far as Blair Atholl.'

'Certainly, George. All the way to Perth if you like. Captain McLay, would you please see that George is supplied with refreshments before he leaves?'

'There's no need,' said Braco dourly. 'I've still got some of Jean's bannocks left.'

With shoulders back, Braco limped out of the room.

'George used to be a soldier,' murmured Montrose, 'before he decided that he would rather be a farmer. It seems he's a very successful one. His black cattle are the envy of his neighbours.'

'He has forgotten the letter, my lord.'

'No. He's just reluctant to deliver it. Would you give it to him, Angus?'

Montrose took the letter out of a drawer. There were other letters to other parents in it.

McLay hurried out with it.

With a sigh, Montrose sat down and finished the letter to the King.